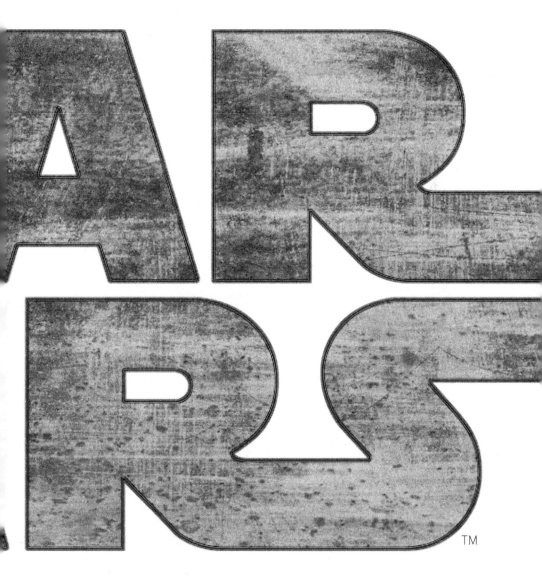

BY LAMAR GILES

Ruin Road
The Getaway
Not So Pure and Simple
Spin
Overturned
Endangered
Fake ID
Static: Up All Night
Epic Ellisons: Cosmos Camp

LEGENDARY ALSTON BOYS OF LOGAN COUNTY

The Last Last-Day-of-Summer
The Last Mirror on the Left
The Last Chance for Logan County

SANCTUARY

A **BAD BATCH** NOVEL

STAR WARS

SANCTUARY

A BAD BATCH NOVEL

LAMAR GILES

RANDOM HOUSE
WORLDS

NEW YORK

Random House Worlds
An imprint of Random House
A division of Penguin Random House LLC
1745 Broadway, New York, NY 10019
randomhousebooks.com
penguinrandomhouse.com

Library of Congress Cataloging-in-Publication Data
Names: Giles, Lamar, 1979– author.
Title: Star wars : sanctuary / Lamar Giles.
Other titles: Sanctuary
Description: First edition. | New York : Random House Worlds, 2025. | "A Bad Batch novel"
Identifiers: LCCN 2025008126 (print) | LCCN 2025008127 (ebook) |
ISBN 9780593874462 (hardcover) | ISBN 9780593874479 (ebook)
Subjects: LCSH: Star Wars fiction. | LCGFT: Space operas (Fiction)
Classification: LCC PS3607.I433 S73 2025 (print) |
LCC PS3607.I433 (ebook) | DDC 813/.6—dc23/eng/20250307
LC record available at https://lccn.loc.gov/2025008126
LC ebook record available at https://lccn.loc.gov/2025008127

Printed in the United States of America on acid-free paper

2 4 6 8 9 7 5 3 1

First Edition

BOOK TEAM: Production editor: Abby Duval • Managing editor: Susan Seeman •
Production manager: Ali Wagner • Copy editor: Jacob Reynold Jones •
Proofreaders: Rachael Clements, J. J. Evans, Laura Petrella

Book design by Elizabeth A. D. Eno

Texture art used in Star Wars splash page art and in
chapter elements throughout: Adobe Stock/ivanvbtv

The authorized representative in the EU for product safety and compliance is
Penguin Random House Ireland, Morrison Chambers, 32 Nassau Street, Dublin
D02 YH68, Ireland. https://eu-contact.penguin.ie

For Adrienne and Melanie, the queen and princess of my galaxy

THE STAR WARS NOVELS TIMELINE

THE HIGH REPUBLIC

Convergence
The Battle of Jedha
Cataclysm

Light of the Jedi
The Rising Storm
Tempest Runner
The Fallen Star
The Eye of Darkness
Temptation of the Force
Tempest Breaker
Trials of the Jedi

Wayseeker: An Acolyte Novel

Dooku: Jedi Lost
Master and Apprentice
The Living Force

I THE PHANTOM MENACE

Mace Windu: The Glass Abyss

II ATTACK OF THE CLONES

Inquisitor: Rise of the Red Blade
Brotherhood
The Thrawn Ascendancy Trilogy
Dark Disciple: A Clone Wars Novel

III REVENGE OF THE SITH

Reign of the Empire: The Mask of Fear
Master of Evil
Sanctuary: A Bad Batch Novel
Catalyst: A Rogue One Novel
Lords of the Sith
Tarkin
Jedi: Battle Scars

SOLO

Thrawn
A New Dawn: A Rebels Novel
Thrawn: Alliances
Thrawn: Treason

ROGUE ONE

IV A NEW HOPE

Battlefront II: Inferno Squad
Heir to the Jedi
Doctor Aphra
Battlefront: Twilight Company

V THE EMPIRE STRIKES BACK

VI RETURN OF THE JEDI

The Princess and the Scoundrel
The Alphabet Squadron Trilogy
The Aftermath Trilogy
Last Shot

Shadow of the Sith
Bloodline
Phasma
Canto Bight

VII THE FORCE AWAKENS

VIII THE LAST JEDI

Resistance Reborn
Galaxy's Edge: Black Spire

IX THE RISE OF SKYWALKER

A long time ago in a galaxy far, far away. . . .

SANCTUARY

A **BAD BATCH** NOVEL

It's been over a year since Emperor Palpatine declared the Jedi traitors and turned the clones, the very ones they fought beside, against them. In the aftermath, the Empire, with the aid of its iron-fisted Imperial Security Bureau quashing any threats to Palpatine's rule at the root, has proclaimed a time of "peace and tranquility" for all who yield to the Emperor's will.

Clone Force 99 (aka the Bad Batch) did not obey Order 66 and has been on the run ever since. In an increasingly chaotic galaxy, the team survives as soldiers of fortune. Without work ever since a less-than-amicable separation from the duplicitous mercenary Cid Scaleback, Hunter, Tech, Wrecker, and Omega have sought refuge on Pabu, in a small island village, where a once-in-a-generation sea surge recently left the city in disrepair.

With the aid of contacts in the galactic underworld, ally and pirate Phee Genoa has concocted a pair of schemes to assist the island in its extensive repair efforts. She enlists the Bad Batch to help, but all is not as it seems . . .

CHAPTER ONE

PIPROO AUCTION HOUSE, HOSNIAN PRIME

Clone Force 99 knew all about challenging missions. Tackling and overcoming arduous tasks was what they were made for. However, even after all these years of fighting through muck and mire and beating unbeatable odds, Hunter could not recall a set of parameters he loathed more than what lay before him now. The mission was the mission, though. Each of them had a role to play. Failure was not an option.

"These jogan fruit are not peeled properly," a looming multilimbed culinary droid said.

Hunter faced his "superior" and used a poorly maintained paring knife to strip the last bit of rind off a seeping orb that stained his hands purple. He dropped the fruit into the bin with the dozen others he'd worked on since slipping into his cover as a lowly caterer. "You wanted them not to have peels. They don't. What's improper about it?"

The droid's posture went rigid in the face of mild insubordination. Hunter felt that his defiance followed Phee Genoa's advice on this kind of laborious subterfuge—"Put a little bit of yourself into the ruse to make it more believable!"—as much as he cared to.

He never took a dressing-down well, even when deserved. And this was not deserved. *He'd peeled the blasted jogan fruit!* The task assigned to him—or rather assigned to the laborer he had subdued and now impersonated—was one of many in the sweltering, bustling auction house kitchen.

While the droid took issue with Hunter's blade work—something no one else had ever questioned and lived to tell—it somehow missed more serious offenses throughout the evening that should've drawn its ire. Like the Volpai dishwasher who seemed incapable of keeping the stubby digits of his lower left hand out of his ear—disgusting. Or the Ikkrukkian pastry chef who'd snuck nibbles from several sweet tarts and covered the trespass with fresh frosting.

Yet this droid, a COO cook model with multiple arms and as many annoyances, had the nerve to treat Hunter as if he were the problem.

"A correct peeling," the droid said, "would not exceed a width of 4.5 millimeters and is ideally done in a single coiled strip to preserve the rind as an aesthetically pleasing garnish . . ."

The tedious spiel continued, but Hunter's attention shifted to the crackling audio from the microcomlink in his ear.

Through the device, Tech said, "Do not dismantle him. He is correct about the proper technique for crafting a jogan garnish."

A second voice crackled through the comlink, instantly dulling the sharp edge of Hunter's temper. Omega said, "I think it's a fine-looking peel, Hunter."

Hunter glanced over the culinary droid's shoulder and spotted Omega with a freshly refilled tray, crossing the threshold from the kitchen to the ballroom, where the galaxy's elite (criminals) milled about. She was dressed in black pleated trousers and a matching waitstaff shirt. She wore a dark wig to disguise her blond locks, just as a sheen of makeup concealed Hunter's face tattoo for the day. Omega, the shortest waiter on staff, was easily identifiable among the sashaying robes and polished dress armor of the auction's wealthy attendees.

She balanced a tray of Daruvvian champagne while holding Hunter's gaze. He gave a curt nod, signaling he was fine and would not be tearing this droid limb from limb, so she could go about her duties and not blow her cover. She offered a drink to the nearest attendee, who accepted it greedily as the kitchen door slid shut. These beings accepted everything greedily, even what they had no rightful claim to. Thus, the mission.

The culinary droid droned on and on about proper slicing, hand position, leverage, and so on, and Hunter tuned it out, secure in his knowledge of what he could do with any blade, dull or otherwise. The droid stopped abruptly, perhaps sensing its tutelage was not getting through.

"Upon further consideration," it said, "I think a tool more suited to your skill level is appropriate."

The droid plucked the paring knife from Hunter's hand, then presented his new instrument: a safety peeler, suitable for a child who'd been allowed in a kitchen for the very first time.

Droid, be thankful I'm letting you believe you're the expert, Hunter thought, taking the peeler. *This is the last time I let Phee plan anything! Ever!*

HALL OF TREASURES, PABU
Four Days Ago . . .

Phee Genoa's umber skin took on a violet sheen in the hazy glow of the holographic floor plans she orbited while attempting to get the team on board. She was animated as she spoke, hands passionately chopping the air. ". . . and then we stroll right out. No muss, no fuss."

Hunter stood, his arms crossed, his scowl fixed. "Why am I in the kitchen?"

Instead of stating the obvious—that Hunter's natural disposition was not well suited for the social aspects of an undercover con job—Phee took a more diplomatic approach and reminded him of the other option. "You could wait on the ship with Mel."

MEL-222, Phee's cylindrical and eager power droid, had been freshly refurbished with junk parts and a memory backup after a rough outing on Skara Nal got her old body smashed to bits. She zipped to Hunter's side on mismatched treads, chirring enthusiastically about a possible collaboration.

"Everyone else is going in, so I'm going in," Hunter said, dismissing the suggestion and triggering a series of disappointed beeps from MEL-222.

Everyone else *wasn't* going in, though. Wrecker, for example, would be outside playing the role of a valet, keeping an eye on the auction house's exterior while ensuring they had transport and a clear escape route should things go awry. But Hunter didn't really mean *everyone*. He meant Omega.

The young clone was sharp-eyed, taking in every detail, her enthusiasm radiating to the point she seemed to vibrate. "I'll maneuver through the crowd," Omega said, confirming her understanding of her role, "with the auto-slicer strapped to my ankle. For every bidder I get close to—"

"Mel-Tootootoo's crude code will upload to their assigned bidder datapads and initiate a moderate credit siphon from their auction house accounts into ours," Tech finished, sounding miffed.

MEL-222 chirped, also miffed.

"Easy, you two!" said Phee.

Tech said, "*I* would've written a much more elegant program. And foolproof."

The droid had a few more choice beeps and burrs for Tech.

"Hush. He didn't mean anything by it," Phee told the droid, clearly a lie. Then she said to Tech, "You might have done it differently, but you have to admit it will work."

"Given the available intel, with no deviations, it will *probably* work. Still—"

"Still nothing," Phee said. "We all play our parts. And you have yours. Care to recap?"

Tech sighed deeply. "You and I will portray a married couple that has built a sizable fortune through beverage distribution—and an ancillary business smuggling blasters. I am to appear friendly."

"Easy work for you, Brown Eyes," Phee said.

Wrecker, with his brow creased from deep concentration, spoke up for the first time in an hour. "Maybe *I* should be in the kitchen. Because the food's there."

"Valet!" Phee said, refusing to go down this path again.

Wrecker's shoulders slumped, but he did not argue.

"Look, I know this isn't your usual kind of gig," Phee said, attempting to ease the resistance in the room. "Way less *pew-pew*"—she mimicked firing rifles—"and *boom-boom*"—she spread her arms in a wide arc over her head for a pantomimed explosion that tugged a big grin from Wrecker—"but Pabu needs this."

As if on cue, a slight tremor rumbled through the floor and their bones, an aftershock from the once-in-a-lifetime groundquake that sent a sea wave smashing into the island last month. A drizzle of dust shook loose from the rafters overhead. Though the aftershocks were less severe than in the first days after the sea wave, the island's recovery had been slow and uncertain. Immense progress had been made on repairs through the combined efforts of every single resident chipping in and applying whatever skills they possessed—from engineering to carpentry—but the reality of such a damaging natural disaster still held true: Pabu might never be exactly what it was.

Especially if they couldn't secure the resources and credits for deep structural repairs and levees to prevent catastrophic damage from future surges.

Another tremor shook the Hall of Treasures, knocking Phee's holoprojector disk off the table, which tipped the floor plans sideways as it fell. Omega leaped forward nimbly, catching the disk before it hit the ground, deactivating it. The hologram winked out of existence.

The tremor persisted for another few moments. When it finally ended, Phee said, "Maybe it's time for a break."

Wrecker raised his hand.

Phee did not need to hear the question. "Yes, you can go eat."

He left the conference room at a run.

Hunter watched his brother go, then eyed Phee warily. "I suppose we could all use a little fresh air. Let's walk, you and me."

Omega sprang between them. "Can I come?"

Sensing Hunter wanted a private conversation, Phee said, "Can you help Tech and Mel go over escape routes? Later, I'll tell you about the time I infiltrated a gang on Jedha and became their leader for nine days."

"All right!" Omega said and sidled up beside Tech, who was arguing programming languages with MEL-222.

Phee and Hunter left the Hall of Treasures for the salt-sea breeze of Pabu's exterior slopes. A few steps outside the hall, a group of island youths tossed a ball in a game of keep-away with Gonky, Clone Force 99's sometimes—not often—useful power droid. The boxy, bumbling droid had become an unofficial mascot to the kids, and boosting their morale might be his true calling. One child's throw was off, and the ball caught Gonky in the side. The droid squawked and fell over, his bipedal treads kicking the air. The children cackled. Yes, definitely Gonky's calling.

Phee and Hunter moved on. The mix of foliage and architecture, of the natural and the constructed, felt like harmony made solid. This was easily one of the most beautiful places Hunter had ever seen. However, he wondered if the assessment was relative. He'd seen horrors during the countless battles fought beside his brothers and now Omega. What doesn't look beautiful compared with war?

Skewed perspective or not, Pabu was a good place. Worth saving. Thus the jobs—*plural*—that had fallen into Phee's lap by way of her various contacts throughout the galaxy.

The auction house con was just one-half of an equation that should solve Pabu's problems, according to Phee. The items for sale at this pricey (and illegal) gathering included all sorts of plundered relics acquired by ill means during the Clone Wars. The invite-only bidders were among the more insidious criminals in the galaxy, the kind who *funded* brutality from a distance, who were silent partners in the unsavory, who hid their true nature behind seemingly legitimate business (like beverage distribution) to not get their hands dirty. What those beings really traded was pain and misery.

Despite his discomfort with the playacting involved, even Hunter had to admit the satisfaction in making that kind of glossy, snobbish scum go home with their pockets a bit lighter. However, he still had reservations.

He said, "Tell me about your source and the intel again."

If Phee was irritated by him asking the same questions repeatedly, she didn't let it show, though she did push back. "Don't you want to wait until we reconvene with the others? That way—"

"No. Here. Like this." He never did his best thinking in briefings. He preferred being on the move, in the elements, where his senses could stretch.

"Fine. A colleague by the name of Ven Alman—"

"The Balosar pirate."

"Yes. He did a job for the entrepreneur sponsoring our gig."

"A devoutly religious Caridan with the construction company."

Hunter closed his eyes while he walked and listened, effortlessly avoiding flowerpots, running children, and fresh cracks in the pavement that threatened to roll an ankle. Recognizing the immediate obstacles in his path required no effort and, in fact, felt more like a thin scrim over what he sensed beneath the obvious. The energy generated from Pabu's power plant traveled by cables to every structure throughout the island, registering like a root system made of lightning. The day's catch from the docks hundreds of meters away scented the air in a language recognized by only Hunter's nose, his sense of smell so keen he'd be able to identify each fish by its species once he learned their names. His ears were tuned to Phee's voice, but a shift in focus could've plucked details from several nearby conversations. His enhanced senses were part of his so-called "defect," which made him a CT-99, the designation granted to him and his brothers because of how they varied from the Regs—regular clone troopers.

Hunter and Phee walked a coiling cobblestone path on a downward trajectory, strolling beneath scaffolding erected as part of the island repairs—repairs that would soon be impossible to complete as materials and credits dwindled. Still, workers hammered, sawed, and welded with the optimism that all would work out for the best. That was the Pabu way.

Hunter and his family were somewhat adrift when Phee brought them to this island city. There were hardly any good days in war, but Hunter wondered if the worst he'd seen was that still-surreal day then Supreme Chancellor Palpatine ordered the clones to summarily execute every Jedi they'd fought side by side with for years.

Losing fellow clones to blasterfire or thermal detonators or proton torpedoes was expected. Losing brothers to an irresistible compulsion to betray comrade warriors was nothing he could've prepared for. Even that wasn't as devastating as his brother Crosshair betraying them of his own free will in pursuit of being an exemplary soldier.

The others didn't know this, but when Hunter dreamed, it was too often Crosshair and fallen Jedi that he saw.

For a while, they'd made their way taking high-risk, low-reward jobs brokered by the unscrupulous Trandoshan Cid Scaleback through the galactic underground. It was a living, but their relationship eventually soured as Cid's jobs became increasingly ill conceived and dangerous, forcing Hunter and the rest to cut ties.

The benefit of all their narrow escapes from Cid's sketchy assignments was that Hunter had become much more discerning than he used to be. Being a mercenary allowed him more freedom to question dodgy parameters than back in the "good soldiers follow orders" days of Republic fighting—not that he'd been so great at following orders then, either. Still . . .

"Awfully convenient," Hunter told Phee, opening his eyes and breaking the extended silence between them. "A follower of this Holy Husk and Stone faith whose devotion is so great that he's willing to trade an unseemly amount of building materials for a single relic during our time of greatest need."

"He might tell you it's not convenient at all but divine!"

"I suppose he might," Hunter said, though he didn't say he wouldn't have believed that. "Why is this thing—"

"A mortar," Phee clarified.

"Why is this *mortar* so important anyway?" Hunter had investigated it after Phee first mentioned the plan. It seemed like nothing more than a simple stone bowl to him.

"All I know is it's ancient and sacred. High priests used it in ceremonies to mix potions that followers ingested as a path to high consciousness. Do I understand it? No. I never bought much into the 'higher power' thing. I don't need to understand it to respect it."

Hunter nodded. That was fair. The galaxy was vast, and he'd never grasp every wonder and belief it held. Questioning the logistics of all they were about to do was also fair.

He said, "Once we *liberate* the artifact from the auction, we're on to the second job?"

"Yes. That one's so easy it's barely worth discussing again."

"I've never seen a big payday come easy."

"Did the Republic pay you guys?"

Hunter glared.

"As I thought. So you're talking about the occupational hazard of working for Cid. Freelancing's a different animal altogether. You'll see."

That was what Hunter was afraid of. Different didn't necessarily mean better. While the soldier's life left much to be desired, he never underestimated the possibility of best-laid plans going to druk.

Hunter caught Phee staring. "What?"

"You're catastrophizing, aren't you?"

"I'm . . . no."

"Everything's going to be fine, Hunter. Let's get through the auction, and you'll thank me later."

"For what?"

"You said this is all coming together in *our* greatest time of need. You're warming up to Pabu. Soon you'll be all-in on the place, as I knew you would be."

Hunter scowled, annoyed by her presumptions. He wasn't all-in on anything. Not her schemes, not even Pabu. But he'd do his part.

Phee noticed the look on his face and said, "You know what, why wait? You're welcome."

CHAPTER TWO

Tech's endurance was being tested by the confines of his formal—and uncomfortable—disguise. His trousers were royal blue and fitted. The suit coat was dark crimson with a collar high enough that he had to resist tugging at it. He was supposed to be a criminal patron comfortable in these clothes and environment. But he would not agree to any future role-play unless his disguise was tailored to his exact specifications based on an increasingly long list of improvements. He leaned in to Phee and voiced his primary complaint. "I am itchy."

"No, you're not," she countered with a certainty he'd come to think of as her trademark. "You feel exposed because it's not your armor. But I must tell you, this is a much better look."

The ensemble complemented Phee's gown, which shimmered with tiny electrodes that shifted into gradients of Tech's color palette.

She said, "We fit in and, more importantly, we look fabulous. Roll with it, Brown Eyes."

Tech did not "roll with" things. For his entire life he'd utilized a shifting hierarchy of algorithmic calculations to determine optimal decisions. Data produced options. Probability presented choices. Choice determined action. Simple.

"*Roll with it.*" A declaration so casual it would've been offensive coming from anyone else. Proximity to Phee demanded looser parameters if for no other reason than to preserve his own sanity. Plus, there was the X factor of it all. He *liked* being in close proximity to Phee. The why and how of that was somewhat of a mystery to him, which was unnerving. He couldn't crack the calculus of him and her. But he'd keep trying.

They milled about the cavernous ballroom arm in arm, strolling past uniformed security guards of varying species, from one tastefully arranged pedestal to another. On each platform—save one—was an item that would be auctioned off later in the evening. There was heirloom jewelry from some dismantled dynasty, a lightsaber with a polished wooden hilt crusted with what Tech assessed as dried blood, and the Caridan mortar that had drawn their team here. It was an unremarkable bowl of grayish-black stone with golden etchings embedded in its rim, lit and displayed alluringly for potential buyers. It sat behind laser shielding that crackled an ominous warning: *Look but don't touch.*

When they stood before the mortar, Tech said, "The majority of modern Caridan religions are segregated into three denominations, none of which engage in practices that would utilize a mortar such as this. The Holy Husk and Stone sects are considered dormant, if not extinct."

"You've been doing homework," Phee said.

"The information is easy enough to gather. This item would be desirable to museum curators. Rare, but not priceless."

"Since we have an agreed-upon price for acquiring it, that's good news."

"A Caridan practicing this religion would also be rare."

Phee's jaw clenched. "Have you been talking to Hunter?"

"I know he's wary of the client, but that's not why I'm bringing this up. I wanted to demonstrate that to support your plan and back our cover to the best of my abilities, I have compiled a knowledge base suitable for hours of small talk."

Phee grinned. "You hate small talk."

"Thorough mission prep, though often unpleasant, is standard." He cleared his throat. "It's easier when I respect the mind behind the mission."

"Now you're just teasing me," she said, pleased. "Let's keep making the rounds."

Eleven items in all were arranged on pedestals, and only one required no shielding. It was simply a flickering hologram of a solid black cube, the display screen beneath it declaring, MYSTERY ITEM.

The patrons who'd come to flaunt wealth and pat one another on the back over the prestige of being in the same room together expressed mild *ooohs* and *aaahs* over whatever item suited their larcenous tastes, since most had been pillaged from some war-struck world.

A tall handsome Falleen couple sauntered by. Their species was reptilian and regal. This particular pair leaned into a monotone palette, both garbed in lengthy emerald robes a tone lighter than their green skin, with their facial ridges and spines accentuated by dazzling gems. One of them made a show of admiring Phee's garment, saying, "Gorgeous, a classic look."

Phee accepted the compliment with a gracious nod. Surely she'd pass it on to the Pabu seamstress from the island's playhouse wardrobe department who'd tailored the team's clothing.

The other Falleen was not as taken with Tech's look, at least not the eyewear. "Have you seen the visor line coming out of A/KT Fashions this season?" the Falleen asked in a dig poorly disguised as an unsolicited inquiry. "Their new ones are showstoppers. Suitable for any occasion."

"I'm afraid I haven't had the opportunity." Tech eyed the slyly insulting Falleen through his scratched and scarred spectacles he'd relied upon for years, passively reading the scrolling data on the lenses' interior display, visible only to him.

NAME: Kime and Trast Trod
HOMEWORLD: Falleen
LEGAL TRADE: Textiles
ILLICIT TRADE: Glitterstim Trafficking
ESTIMATED NET WORTH: 200 Million Credits

The information came from a data disk loaded with details on each attendee, sent via encrypted channels by Phee's colleague Ven Alman. The forearm-mounted computer he wore beneath his jacket sleeve fed the information to Tech's display. Similar information appeared for any being he focused on—except for one.

A single Muun transferred meaty appetizers from the buffet table to his tiny plate, an unsteady mound of food close to toppling off. He was shorter than other Muuns whom Tech had encountered, with a fashionable golden chain encircling his bulbous head and the dull gray skin around his mouth flushing pink as he chewed. When Tech settled his gaze on him, what appeared in the HUD was mildly disconcerting.

NAME: ?
HOMEWORLD: ?
LEGAL TRADE: ?
ILLICIT TRADE: ?
ESTIMATED NET WORTH: ?

"Excuse me, darling," Tech said, interrupting Phee's conversation with the two Falleen. "A word?"

Phee made the socially acceptable gesture, indicating an unlikely continuation. Then they drifted toward the closest corner, allowing the murmuring crowd to form a natural separation between them and anyone who might care to eavesdrop.

"We got trouble?" Phee said, tapping a spot behind her ear that switched her comm to a wide broadcast so the entire team could hear.

"Not necessarily," Tech indicated, though his furrowed brow signaled otherwise. "You were provided a comprehensive dossier on all attendees, but there's a Muun who is not accounted for on the data disk. He is currently gorging himself on tip-yip skewers."

Phee glanced over Tech's shoulder, spotting the being that worried him. "So what?"

"The siphon code," Tech said with no inflection whatsoever, which in itself was a kind of inflection.

MEL-222 chortled her annoyance through the comm.

Phee let loose a mighty eye roll. "This again? It shouldn't matter."

Tech persisted. "The code's written assuming we know all bidders, what they'll likely bid on, and their estimated net worth. Every one of those factors affects the calculations for how much we can covertly siphon from each attendee's buy-in. If a big enough deviation were to be captured by Mel's code—"

MEL-222 screeched.

Phee, attempting to comfort the droid, said, "We know a problem is unlikely."

"But not impossible," Tech said.

A high *ting-ting-ting* sounded from the room's far end as the auctioneer, a blue-skinned and portly Pantoran, tapped his champagne flute with a fashionably long fingernail. "Hear ye, all! I hate to interrupt the festivities, but our first item will be brought to the dais shortly. Please finalize any deposits into your bidder accounts and make your way to your assigned pods in the auction parlor. You won't want to miss out on these rare antiquities. And I'm sure some of you have noted a mystery item teased. While I won't reveal details, I will say that one is for you collectors of exotic and unique beasts—I know there are several of you in attendance!"

There were chuckles and champagne glasses thrust high from what Tech assumed were the animal collectors the auctioneer referenced. Through the comm, the clanking of kitchen noise muffled Hunter's whispered inquiry. "What's this do to our chances of success?"

"Eighty-two percent chance we're still good to go," Tech said.

Hunter said, "Omega, check in."

"I've uploaded the code to all the personal datapads."

"Good," Hunter said. "Wrecker, you've been quiet. Report."

Wrecker's voice crackled in from his valet post. "Expensive speeders are tiny!"

"Report your *mission status*!" Hunter clarified.

"All clear. Should be easy getting out."

"Don't speak so soon," Hunter said.

Attendees milled from the ballroom to their bidder pods in the adjacent parlor, ushered along by the bored-looking guards. Tech worked his forearm computer through his sleeve, so familiar with the device that seeing it wasn't required. "I'm slicing into the auction house data-banks for intel on the Muun. He's probably inconsequential to our purposes, but I still want to know."

Phee, not unkindly, said, "You are thorough, aren't you, Brown Eyes?"

"I try."

"Keep us posted, Tech." Hunter's voice crackled. "Let's get it done, squad."

The worrisome culinary droid's voice could be heard in the background. "Are you cutting wedges or slivers, hmm?"

Hunter groaned and his comlink went mute.

"I bet he loves me right now," Phee said.

"He'll survive," Tech said, then grimaced. "Though I anticipate we'll be hearing about it for quite some time."

With the auction about to get underway, Omega's co-workers resigned themselves to a short break before commencing the cleanup and break-down of the buffet left in the ballroom. While most drifted outside to make holocalls or spark a cigarra, Omega observed that the disgrace-fully inattentive security guards were chatting among themselves, dis-tracted, giving her an opening to follow the short anvil-headed labor droids moving auction items from their pedestals to where they'd be sold. While the droids took a direct path, Omega slipped into the shad-ows, following the creases of the auction house, navigating the back halls with uncanny certainty. Hunter once said she had a compass in her head that pointed to mischief.

Eventually, she found herself in a staging area beneath the central dais, with items arranged on a conveyor belt that would carry them to a column meant to rise through the floor as each item came up for auc-tion. The droids deactivated the protective laser shielding—which had clearly been for show since there appeared to be no security precautions of note backstage—and arranged the goods for purchase, tagging them with scannable lot numbers until the belt was crammed twelve items deep. Statues, paintings, vases, and gems were accentuated with tiny ambient lights, cradled on cerulean pillows. The Caridan ceremonial mortar they'd come for was seventh in line.

The oddest of the bunch was a nondescript crate, last in the order of sale—the mystery item. It had been represented by a hologram in the ballroom but was here, real, and ready for closer examination. It seemed to be made of opaque glass, unremarkable in every way. When Omega leaned out of her shadowy hiding spot just a smidge, she thought she heard it whimper.

"Hello, fellow procurers of the sublime!" The auctioneer's voice boomed throughout the facility. "I am Shimrin Rugard, your host for the evening, and we have a lovely assortment for your burgeoning collections."

Omega scooted forward, easily avoiding the preoccupied droids, to a position just left of the dais where she had a better view of everything. The floor of the auction parlor was something like the bowl of an arena, resembling another impressive facility she'd recently visited— the Galactic Senate chambers on Coruscant. This, of course, was a fraction of the Senate's scale, with individual pods for a few dozen bidders compared to the thousands who could comfortably fill a political hearing. Still, it was much more opulent, with plush seating and lush draperies that hung from the high ceiling all the way to the floor. Omega squinted, attempting to spot Tech and Phee's pod, but the show lighting turned everyone beyond the stage into indistinguishable silhouettes.

"Omega," Hunter said through her link, "where are you?"

She whispered, "Backstage. The auction's starting."

"You're out of position. You should be with the waitstaff, close to your exfiltration point."

"I will be when we're done."

"You know that's not how missions work."

She nearly said, *When do our missions actually work?* but recognized that would be speaking foul luck on the current proceedings, and so far, so good. Hunter seemed to forget there almost always came a point when they needed to improvise. Maybe she was getting a head start!

"First to the floor," the auctioneer said, "is a relic of unknown origin, acquired in the Quarzite system. Our staff historians believe it to be a fertility idol of some sort."

The conveyor belt lurched forward, positioning the item on the column, which pistoned up slowly until it became visible to the bidders, some of whom gasped with adoration. It was a golden totem with exaggerated humanoid features. Its body was crouched, the overly large head was angled skyward, and the mouth stretched in an eternal, silent scream.

The auctioneer said, "We'll start the bidding at one hundred thousand credits!"

A green light flashed in one of the higher pods.

"Can I get one twenty-five?"

Another green light flashed in the dark.

Omega watched the bids creep up incrementally and decided auctions were dull. She sank backstage, once again intrigued by the black crate. The labor droids had retreated completely, their jobs done, so she approached the odd lot without concern. Sure enough, the closer she got, the louder the box's internal whining. A control panel was built into the crate's frame, and she punched a button marked "transparent." The black glass blinked clear, and Omega's eyes went wide at the sight of what was inside.

"Well, hello there!" she said.

The crate's occupant growled back and pounded its fists against the wall.

It was a teacup-sized gundark.

The creature was maybe twenty-five centimeters tall with four arms—two long and two short—and sixteen claws. It had red leathery skin, a wide jaw crowded with glistening fangs, and pointy ears capable of extremely keen hearing. It raked its longest claws across the interior of its cage in an aggressive display suggesting it didn't comprehend how tiny it was.

A mix of wonder and barely restrained rage washed over Omega. During her time on Kamino, where there were no shortages of fringe biological experiments, she'd witnessed small-scale trials that produced miniaturized versions of the galaxy's fiercest creatures. Teacup-sized rancors, krayt dragons, and so on. All meant as domesticated trophies for wealthy, heedless patrons. It was a niche business, considered more of a hobby than an economic engine for the planet the way cloning was. Also, it was cruel because most of the miniaturized animals were not suited for survival outside of a lab, their diminished size often transforming them from predator to prey.

The gundark seemed heartier than other miniaturized creatures she'd seen. Full-sized gundarks were highly adaptable creatures. Omega hoped that trait hadn't been edited out of this little guy's genetic code.

The gundark gave the glass another mighty swipe, then seemed to tire of attempting to dominate Omega through the barrier. It flopped into a seated—and defeated—position.

Omega could not tolerate the hopelessness she sensed in the creature. She retrieved a wrapped pastry she'd snuck from the kitchen, intending to share it with Wrecker post-mission, and held it before the crate. The gundark perked, attentive.

Omega said, "Is it all right if I call you Teacup?"

The gundark grunted indifferently.

"You're hungry, aren't you?" She identified the button that would unlock the cage. "If you promise to keep quiet, you can have this."

Of course it didn't understand what she was saying, but in her experience there was no creature that didn't understand kindness. She opened the cage.

The gundark hopped onto its hind legs, skittish and defensive. Omega poked the pastry into the cage. "It's all yours."

It hesitated, then leaped forward, snatching the pastry and retreating to the cage's far corner, where it devoured the sweet treat greedily.

"Tasty, huh?"

The gundark growled in the affirmative.

Omega heard the bidding conclude on the first item. "We better get out of here. You want to come with me?"

It leaped from the cage to the floor, where it lowered its head in what Omega interpreted as a grateful salute. But then it ran for the shadows, choosing to find its own way. Another thing about gundarks—fiercely independent. That comforted Omega.

"You're going to do just fine."

Phee leaned forward in the pod, both hands on the outer edge, as eager as a shockboxing fan at a title bout. She mumbled unintelligible things Tech couldn't make out.

"What are you doing?" he asked.

"Just taking mental notes. That slick-talking Falleen couple just won that fertility idol," Phee said, thoughtful. "Gonna add them to my list of future liberations."

The pods were relatively private, well out of earshot of the bidders on either side of them, so Tech wasn't concerned about Phee's openly vocal pirate plans. He was, however, concerned about the Muun whom he still hadn't been able to find on the auction house's most recent guest list. With an enhanced scan of the darkened chamber, he knew where the being was—two pods over and three down. The mystery being made a 250,000-credit bid on the idol Phee would steal from its buyers sometime in the near future, but otherwise . . . he was an enigma.

"Next to the dais . . ." the auctioneer announced, presenting the second lot and its starting bid. This item led to a heated four-way battle that ended at a whopping 725,000 credits. Again, the Muun made a single early bid, 400,000 credits, but backed off when the price climbed.

The excitement and competition grew through the third and fourth lots, some dynastic jewelry and the blood-crusted lightsaber, respectively, with the Muun submitting an enticing bid whenever the fervor cooled. Tech's intuition angled toward concern.

The fifth lot, an abstract sculpture, had its bidding get off to a sluggish start, but it eventually sold for 500,000 credits, again with some nudging from the Muun.

Five items so far. Little similarity between them. Each one attracted different sets of bidders with only a single constant in the mix. The improbability was like a flare in Tech's mind.

With a few taps on his keyboard, he stopped searching the auction house's guest list and turned to its personnel files.

The auctioneer called the sixth lot to the dais, but Tech didn't pay attention to the proceedings, because he knew the pattern. Once that lot sold, the item they came for rose on the column. At that moment, Tech discovered who the Muun was.

"This item stems from Carida and was used in religious ceremonies for centuries before its acquisition. This would be a handsome piece for the pious"—the auctioneer chuckled at that—"among you."

Tech squeezed Phee's shoulder and broadcast across their comms. "The Muun isn't a guest. He's an auction house employee identified as an assurance contractor."

"A what?" Phee and Hunter asked at the same time.

"He's a spiker," Tech explained. "Here to artificially drive up bids to the auction house's satisfaction. The bigger the bid, the bigger their commission."

The auctioneer continued heaping accolades on the Caridan mortar like the salesman he was. Hunter pressed Tech for more information. "What's that mean for us?"

The sullen look on Phee's face told Tech she already knew, but he clarified for the others.

"There will be competition for our item. The Muun will see to it. The credits we've siphoned from the other attendees may not be enough to win."

"All right," Hunter said, sounding somewhat relieved. "If we can't win it, we exfil and acquire the item from whoever does win. That was always our best option."

"It was always a *contingency*," Phee said, defensive, "but fine. We'll see if we can salvage Plan A. If not, everyone begin exfiltration while me and Tech stay until the end so we won't arouse suspicions."

It was settled, then. Tech prepared to endure the sheer boredom of the auction as the auctioneer announced the opening bid for the item they'd probably have to steal later.

"We will start the Caridan ceremonial mortar at one hundred twenty-five thousand credits."

It was the opening bid they'd anticipated. And someone went for it immediately: Phee.

Or rather, her datapad bid on her behalf. She never touched it.

Tech and Phee stiffened in their seats as the pad flashed green in time with the display on the front of their pod, signaling the auctioneer that they were in the competition.

"I have one twenty-five. Can I get one fifty?"

The Muun did his job and raised the bid to 150. Almost instantly, Phee's datapad flashed green and raised the bid to 175. Still, neither she nor Tech had touched it.

Tech massaged his temple as if staving off a headache. "Mel, you added an automation routine to the code sometime after I reviewed it." It was not a question.

MEL-222 booped. A drawn out, shameful sound.

Phee pinched her lips into a thin line, perhaps feeling secondhand embarrassment on behalf of her droid.

"Ohhhh, we have a battle here!" the auctioneer taunted. "Can I get two hundred?"

A third bidder leaped in, likely caught in the moment, but instantly Phee's datapad catapulted the bid up to 250.

"Well, that was quick," the auctioneer noted with a raised eyebrow.

Sure was. As quick as that faulty code MEL-222 put together.

Phee touched her comlink. "Mel, shut it down."

The droid chortled sheepishly.

"What do you mean you can't?" Phee said.

Tech exposed his forearm computer, snatched the datapad, and sliced into it.

"What's happening?" Hunter asked.

Wrecker said, "Convor just shabbed on an AV-15. The owner's going to be mad."

"Not you! Tech?"

Tech swiped through screens and typed commands while detailing the suddenly perilous circumstance. "Mel's code contained several subroutines geared to siphon credits from our unsuspecting benefactors and help us defeat them in the case of a few competing bids from *known attendees*. It seems the spiker's absence from our initial intel has exposed a bug in the code."

"What kind of bug?"

"I'm hesitant to guess," Tech said, not being truthful. There was no need to rile Hunter over what was inevitable. Tech knew full well where this was going, and despite his best efforts to purge the droid's shoddy code from the auction house's system, he knew there was only a 4 percent chance of abating what came next.

The Muun raised the bid to 300. Just 50,000 credits shy of their predetermined limit.

Tech said, "High alert, everyone. Things are about to get frenetic."

Hunter cursed.

A 325,000-credit bid came from the dark, and then MEL-222's code—completely bugged out now—shot the bid up to 450,000 credits. That was well over their old limit of 400,000, though well in line with their new limit since the code just siphoned an additional 350,000 credits from various attendee accounts.

Several bidder pods flashed undulating red lights, a sign that they were ineligible to participate as the current bid was higher than their auction account balances. There were audible gasps and outcries over what had to be a mistake on the part of the auction house because they'd certainly deposited more credits than what was showing on their datapads.

The Muun continued his function and raised the bid to 500,000 credits. To which MEL-222's completely fried code triggered a bid of one million credits—after it deducted even more money from the other attendees, causing more undulating red lights as additional account balances went to zero inexplicably.

The Muun and the auctioneer recognized some sort of grift at work as many attendees loudly protested the disappearance of their funds. There were no competing bids to top the last one from Phee's datapad. Yet . . . the code upped the price again, to five million credits, emptying the last of the attendee accounts so that every single pod flashed red in the darkened theater, except for Phee and Tech's, where a solid healthy and wealthy green light glowed.

Every single eye turned their way.

Tech could not resist. "I told you I should have written the code."

MEL-222 remained conspicuously silent.

Phee sighed and said, "Omega, are you still backstage?"

"Sure am!"

"Good. Grab anything you can carry while we get the mortar. Thanks!"

An upbeat Omega could not contain her excitement. "Plan C it is!"

CHAPTER THREE

PIPROO AUCTION HOUSE, HOSNIAN PRIME

Outside the auction house, twilight dwindled. The city lights switched on, creating the illusion of minor constellations flaring to life along the faces of structures, both squat and looming, all the way to the horizon. As the sky dimmed, Wrecker issued a late-arriving couple a retrieval code before wedging himself into their sleek C-B7 Interceptor and zipping toward a designated compact lot behind the auction house.

Wrecker took in the Hosnian skyline from the undersized sports-speeder's pilot seat. His admiration shrank to a narrow, purposeful focus as an agitated conversation over his comm concluded with Omega's voice in his ear. "Plan C it is!"

He hopped from the speeder, its repulsorlift raising the vehicle several centimeters now that it was unburdened by his bulk. The V-Runner, a bulky, fuel-guzzling consumer model of the military-grade V-Wheel that Tech and Phee arrived in, was three rows over, looking as conspicuous as a sandcrawler among the lot's sleek luxury transports. Its unsightly bulge was why this job required someone in a valet role—to park it without asking questions and have it ready to go if things got hot.

He bounded toward the V-Runner using the parked speeders like leap pads. The fortunate vehicles got one of his gigantic boots on a cushioned seat, no worse for wear. The unlucky speeders took a heel to the hood, leaving an expensive dent that the true valets would have difficulty explaining later. So it goes.

At the V-Runner, he climbed into the pilot's seat, preparing to hit the rendezvous at the auction house's back exit, when another valet— a slim, brash humanoid with dirt-brown hair and skin leathered from too much dual sun exposure—zipped into Wrecker's lane ahead of the V-Runner and parked too close to Wrecker's front bumper, blocking the way. The valet hopped from his speeder, whistling, not a care in the galaxy.

Wrecker leaned from the pilot's port. "Hey, gimme some space to get out."

"For what?" the valet said, examining his datapad. "I don't see a retrieval code for that one."

"I need to rearrange the stack. Make some room."

"No, you don't! We don't move speeders once they're parked unless we get a retrieval code from an owner. This your first day?"

Wrecker sneered. "You could say that."

"Well, allow me to alleviate your jitters. That one's fine where it is." The valet went on his way. As Wrecker needed to be.

He alerted the team. "Let me know when you're coming to the exit. Twenty-second countdown."

"Roger that," Hunter said between grunts of exertion and what sounded like terrified screams in the background.

"Plan C it is!"

Hunter snatched off his apron, grateful to be done with playacting, and when the culinary droid attempted to chastise him, he threw the jogan-stained cloth over its head, covering its optics. Its multiple arms convulsed and twirled, attempting to free itself while advancing toward Hunter. Usually, it wouldn't be a problem, except some of those twirling limbs held sharp utensils.

Hunter pivoted away from a hatchet's downward swipe, then ducked the horizontal swing from a slicing blade. Crouched, he wedged his fingers beneath the droid's treads and hoisted it into the barrel of jogan fruit rinds, where it thrashed and mewled. Hunter quickly exited to applause from the Volpai dishwasher, the Ikkrukkian pastry chef, and every other kitchen worker who'd grown tired of the droid's nagging.

On the move through the banquet hall and then the back hallways of the auction house, Hunter hopped on the comm. "Omega, where are you?"

"Leaving the backstage area now." Her voice was strained from exertion. Knowing Omega, she was likely taking to heart Phee's request that she grab anything she could carry.

"I'll find you."

The corridors making up the innards of the auction house were not complex, especially for someone with Hunter's gifts. He located Omega backing out of a wide doorway, dragging a heavy transparisteel crate filled with myriad trinkets. Her black wig was crooked, forcing her to blow air poofs to keep fake hair out of her eyes. When she spotted Hunter, she snatched the wig off and tossed it back the way she came. "Help me with this, will ya?"

He skidded to a stop, evaluating the goods she'd collected: a medallion, what looked like an ancient scroll, a metallic and stone sculpture that seemed the heaviest thing in the box. It was a lot for Omega to lug, but Hunter easily handled the weight, hoisting the crate onto his shoulder. Then he spotted a series of laser-drilled air holes in the side and said, "Is this a cage?"

"Yep."

"Do I want to know?"

Omega gave a half shrug before a pair of felinoid Cathar guards rounded the corner ahead of them, their postures tense with malice. They were dressed in burgundy and black, snarling through their teeth, wielding stun batons in their clawed hands, and, judging by the odd imprints beneath their coats, concealing hand blasters.

"Stop right there!" one shouted.

Not good. Tight quarters, no armor. Cathars were fierce fighters. Fast and strong. He was confident he could take them, but it wasn't going to be fun—or quick. Time was of the essence now. Same druk, different day.

Hunter prepared to rush the guards with the artifact-stuffed crate as a makeshift battering ram, but a tiny, vicious growl sounded from somewhere around his ankles. He glanced down and caught a streak of red flesh.

"Teacup!" Omega yelled. "Be careful."

The minuscule creature rushed the closest Cathar, made a mighty leap, and wrapped its four small but muscular arms around the guard's kneecap in what looked, at first, like a gentle hug.

Hunter heard the bones shatter before anyone, except maybe the screeching Cathar, who'd just become intimately acquainted with a . . . tiny gundark?

Well, that ain't something you see every day, thought Hunter, who'd seen quite a lot.

The second guard swiped at the gundark with his stun baton, but the creature dodged, and the baton emitted its full voltage into the injured guard, knocking him unconscious—a mercy.

The gundark took another leap onto the standing guard's face, and Hunter spun, forcing Omega to do the same because he didn't want her to see this part. "Come on, we're going this way!"

So they ran, taking an alternate route to the exfil point, and Hunter, for one, was glad they and that little gundark shared a common enemy—at least for today.

"Plan C it is!"

Tech shed his confining suit coat while Phee produced a small blade from beneath the hem of her gown. She sliced through the front and back of the garment, from thigh to ankle, exposing the leggings she wore beneath and expanding her range of motion. She clamped her teeth on the blade while twisting her locks into a more manageable high bun.

"Are we going?" Tech asked.

"We're going," Phee confirmed.

They leaped from their pod into the one beneath. The repulsorlift bounced with the sudden weight adjustment but reacclimated as they jumped onto a lower pod again.

Another few leaps and they were on the dais, awash in the glow of a small galaxy's worth of red lights—and backed by the angry murmurs of beings suddenly aware they'd been robbed.

The auctioneer was appalled. "What do you think you're—?"

"I'm going to stop you right there," Phee said, voice amplified by the microphone on his lapel. "None of you have claim to any relics on this auction block. Therefore, I am here to unburden your undoubtedly heavy conscience before you have to feel the guilt of pillaging another culture's treasures. You're welcome."

Tech marveled at her audacity, nodded his approval, and then snatched the mortar off its display.

"Security!" the auctioneer shouted, though he did not have to since several guards were already weaving between the lowest pods, their stun batons sizzling in the dark.

Tech eyed a gap between the curtains concealing the backstage storage area. "This way, then."

He slipped his free hand into Phee's—they still looked like quite the handsome couple—and they ducked into the shadows as security pursued.

They rushed toward the first door they saw. It retracted in a *whoosh* as they drew near, putting them in a narrow corridor with a second power door ahead and to the right. That one retracted before they got close, prompting Tech and Phee to skid to a stop, prepared to defend themselves against more guards.

No need. Omega and Hunter appeared, him balancing a crateful of trinkets on his shoulder. Hunter and Tech locked eyes, and then Hunter's gaze slipped past Tech and Phee to a trio of guards spilling into the corridor.

Instinctually, Tech tensed to fight, but a low motion by Hunter's ankles caught his attention. What appeared to be a baby version of the fearsome and terrible gundarks native to the planet Vanqor skirted between Omega and Hunter, growling and pounding its chest.

Those creatures were usually upward of two meters in height, a hulking one hundred kilos. This one was a quarter meter, approximately ten kilos. Somewhat adorable?

Phee asked Omega, "You know that little guy?"

"He's a friend."

"Will he get mad if I throw him?"

Omega considered quickly, then retrieved her last stolen pastry from her pocket. "Maybe safer to throw this."

Phee nodded and took the pastry. "Hey, tiny guy."

The gundark sniffed, then saw the pastry in Phee's hand. She pointed with it, then hurled the pastry at the closing guards. It splattered on one of their chests, and the gundark loped to retrieve it, growling greedily.

The creature collided with the lead guard's chest, a clawed hand snagging on the fabric of her suit coat, then punched her sternum with lung-flattening force, while scarfing up dough and cream.

The guard said, "*Oof,*" and collapsed. The gundark sprang off her as she fell and affixed itself to the next closest guard's biceps, where additional whipped topping had splattered. The third guard did his best to pry the creature off, and in the chaos, Tech, Phee, Omega, and Hunter slipped toward the exfiltration point.

Omega yelled over her shoulder, "Teacup, come on!"

The gundark heard and separated from the mewling, injured security guard, chasing his rescuer to the exit.

Hunter shouted through the comm, "Wrecker! Twenty seconds!"

Wrecker leaned on the V-Runner leisurely, waiting. When Hunter's voice crackled, starting the countdown, he sprang upright and positioned himself at the back fender of the Corona Limited speeder that boxed their transport in. He pressed his fingers into the sides of the speeder's body, leaving digit-sized dents, and strained against the tiny but heavy vehicle. With some assistance from the repulsorlift, he raised the vehicle to throwing height and hurled it one row over. It landed sideways across the bodies of two other luxury speeders, destroying them in a satisfying, crunchy crash.

He returned to the pilot's seat of the V-Runner. Throwing the speeder took more time than expected. To make up for it, Wrecker used the vehicle's slightly cone-shaped nose like a wedge and nudged several speeders aside as he bypassed the narrow lot lanes and took a rough, screeching, metal-on-metal path straight to the auction house exit.

The valet who'd blocked him earlier rounded the building with his arms raised, his face an image of wide-eyed horror. Yes, there would be a lot of disgruntled drivers to answer to.

"Sorry, friend!" Wrecker shouted, passing the man with at least six speeders crumpled against the V-Runner's front fender.

Hunter, Omega, Tech, Phee, and a little lizard fellow emerged from the auction house as Wrecker halted. Hunter flung the side door open while the rest piled in. He then leaped inside as Wrecker gave up the driver's seat to Tech, and they hopped a curb to drop into the nearest skylane. The tiny, frightening creature who'd hitched a ride hopped onto the dashboard and flattened its claws on the viewport transparisteel, howling triumphantly.

They were lost in the heavy traffic almost immediately. The clones all sat stoic, focused until the mission was done, though the rush of it all faded slowly.

Hunter stared at Phee. "For all that trouble, we could've blown a hole in the place last night and walked this stuff out before anyone was the wiser."

"I guess," Phee said. "But then I wouldn't have been able to prove my theory."

"What theory?" Tech asked.

Phee said, "That you would look so good in a suit."

Hunter banged his head against the transport wall.

Omega said, "You did look very nice, Tech."

The gundark left the dashboard to climb into Omega's lap and pump a claw in the air.

Tech pressed his lips into a thin line before responding. "Your compliment does not ease my displeasure over the outcome of today's events." To Phee, he said, "I do hope this is not indicative of how all of our outings will be."

One corner of Phee's mouth curled up. "Are you referring to future jobs or something more . . . *personal?*"

"All of the above."

Tech exited the skylane into a less populated part of Hosnian Prime. Soon, they'd reach the warehouse where they'd parked a switch vehicle, as the authorities were undoubtedly aware of the V-Runner by now. Then, onto the *Marauder,* where MEL-222 awaited their return for whatever came next, though Tech was hoping for less excitement.

CHAPTER FOUR

HYPERSPACE, NEARING THE MYGEETO SYSTEM

The *Marauder*, a modified *Omicron*-class attack shuttle, hummed inside the hazy blue tunnel of a hyperspace lane. The ship, ofttime Clone Force 99's home, sometimes felt to Omega like an unofficial member of their family—a member Tech insisted she learn inside and out if she were ever to pilot it solo one day.

She stared through the *Marauder*'s viewport, missing Teacup already. She'd invited the gundark along, but at the warehouse where they'd switched vehicles, he'd defeated an alpha scrap rat in combat and seemed content to rule over the scrap rat colony. Probably for the best, because Hunter was already irritable, and another passenger wasn't going to help his mood.

"This is not operationally sound," Hunter told Phee, not hiding his frustration over the mess on Hosnian Prime.

"We're not the military," Phee countered. "It doesn't have to be."

Omega sat in the copilot's seat while Hunter and Phee occupied the navigator's and passenger's seats, respectively. They were too busy bickering to notice Omega cast an exasperated glance to Tech in the pilot's seat, who simply tipped his chin in a *We must embrace the inevitable* gesture.

"We should focus on a *single* objective," Hunter argued. "Get that mortar to your contact and arrange for the building materials to aid Pabu. Considering how badly acquiring that blasted relic went, we should secure the payment before something else goes wrong."

Omega understood why Hunter was so insistent. His thinking was sound. However, Hunter's thinking could also be unyielding, as if there were only one way—*his* way—to tackle any given problem.

"Look at the star map." Phee motioned that way. "To drop the mortar off we'd have to pass the Mygeeto system, where our clients are. Doing it your way means we'd have to double back. We'd lose a day—and possibly the credits we stand to earn—if the client decides to grab another ride."

Hunter scoffed. "We're not a taxi service, so maybe that's for the best."

"Best for who? Pabu needs funds."

"What do we even know about these clients aside from their need for our assistance, coming from your questionable contacts?"

"First, I'm the only one who can call my contacts questionable. Second, there's no mystery. I know plenty. There are two of them. A Keshiri woman and her longtime servant, who wears a mask."

"Are you serious?"

"Yes."

"Why does the servant wear a mask, Phee?"

"I'm told they're too attractive."

Hunter raised an eyebrow.

This was going to be a long ride. Omega hopped from her seat and escaped the war of words for a quieter compartment. The cockpit door sealed behind her as she made her way to midship, where MEL-222 zipped back and forth anxiously. The droid noticed Omega and sounded a series of despondent beeps.

"I've messed up on missions before," Omega said in solidarity. "We all have. You can't beat yourself up."

MEL-222 booped, a grateful sound.

Omega kept moving. Wrecker was asleep on a bench and snoring louder than the hyperdrive could ever hope to be.

She hated to disturb him but felt guilty about leaving Tech alone with Hunter and Phee. While she had no intention of getting between them, arranging some backup for Tech was the least she could do. She nudged Wrecker awake.

"Are we there yet?" he said without opening his eyes.

"No. We might never get there if Hunter and Phee keep at it."

Wrecker sat up, scratching his head. "I don't know what to do about them."

"Them or *him*?" Omega finally said the part they'd all been dancing around.

Ever since Echo left and things went sour with Cid, Hunter had been wound tighter than usual. Omega considered asking him directly what was wrong, but she knew part of it was the same shadow that had been cast over her since their family shrunk on Coruscant. She missed Echo, too. While she'd gladly admit that to anyone, getting Hunter to speak plainly about his feelings seemed as likely as him enthusiastically agreeing to Phee's spotty plan. So everyone tiptoed, secretly hoping his bad mood would subside like the Pabu sea surge eventually had. The sea surge was proving less stubborn.

Wrecker stood, stretched his creaky back, and clapped a hand on Omega's shoulder. "Let's go referee."

They opened the cockpit to see Hunter punching his own hand for emphasis.

"Since we don't have thorough intel and won't have time for proper reconnaissance, I hope you can see the wisdom in a baseline mandate of *no delays*," Hunter said, his tone compromising, almost pleading. "If the clients aren't ready when we reach Mygeeto, then we dust off. When we drop that mortar with the Caridan, we don't linger. Everything goes quick, smooth, and by the numbers for the rest of the trip. Agreed?"

Phee threw up her hands in a gesture of peaceful resolution. "Fair enough. We pick up two passengers. Drop off a mortar. Keep it moving. Quick and smooth."

Tech inserted himself into the conversation, dodging the thorny bits as lithely as the *Marauder* through an asteroid belt. "Dropping out of hyperspace for Mygeeto."

The hyperspace tunnel unspooled from luminescent mist to elongated streaking stars before snapping into the false stillness of planetary approach. Mygeeto, with its icy coral-pink continents and expansive oceans, seemed to wink into existence. Tech made orbit, and the flight computer calculated an entry trajectory.

"Brown Eyes, you refuel," Phee said. "I'll go meet the clients, then—"

"We," Hunter said.

Phee's eyes narrowed.

Hunter said, "Since you agreed we don't know all we should know, some backup's better than none."

"Yes, *we!*" Omega said, also insistent, knowing it'd be trouble for Phee and Hunter to go unchaperoned.

Phee seemed fed up with all of them. "Fine. *We'll* be on our way."

The ship bounced as they broke through the atmosphere. Omega strapped into the copilot's seat for landing, studying every button push, switch flip, and steering adjustment Tech made. She was already capable of touching the ship down gently, but she never wanted to stop learning.

The rest of them followed her lead, securing their harnesses. Mygeeto's frigid, crystalline terrain began a quick transformation from tundra to city shore as dark-gray industrial complexes sprawled toward a vast metropolis, though some buildings were missing notable chunks. Battles had been fought here. It was as if the Clone Wars were some titanic beast that had stumbled through, taking bites out of this world. Out of every world.

The remnants of heavy artillery strikes necessitated the repair of some structures, while others were little more than scorched husks that would eventually be demolished. As far as Omega knew, Clone Force 99 had never been involved in any conflicts here, but they'd all heard tales.

Ascending and descending ships were visible ahead. This spaceport was a busy one. Tech broadcast a false identification that concealed the *Marauder*'s fugitive status, and they drifted to a designated pad where the landing gear touched down with a small thump.

"Let's go," Hunter said, already out of his harness and all about business. He had bypassed his armor for dark trousers, a simple tan tunic, and a long thermal duster for protection from the Mygeeto cold. However, he cut at least half of the duster's efficacy by leaving it unfastened, giving him quick access to his concealed blaster and vibroknife.

"Gear up," he told Omega, who'd already donned a similar but appropriately sized duster.

Phee also packed on layers, and Hunter told Tech and Wrecker, "Stay sharp while we're gone."

"Always," they said together.

Phee, not to be outdone, told MEL-222, "You stay sharp, too."

The droid beeped, noncommittal.

As with any bustling spaceport, diverse crowds of galactic citizens were milling about, focused on tasks both simple and urgent. An orange-skinned Gran couple attempted to wrangle a quartet of three-eyed children bopping about in awe of their surroundings. An elderly, grumpy Rodian with flaky scales and milky, bugged-out pupils shoved his way through the masses with a swaying cane that might have doubled as a club if anyone was too slow making way. Whether grabbing a quick meal or a slow drink between flights, the beings churned, and several establishments maintained open doors that welcomed customers and credits. The bar Hunter, Phee, and Omega sought was called Fair Flight, a cutesy play on words referencing the constant overhead space traffic and the varietal drinks inside.

They nudged between patrons, Hunter's gaze hopping to one face before quickly moving on to the next. Hunter spotted them almost instantly. The pair had secured a table in the back corner of the place. The masked man had his back to them, and the blue-skinned Keshiri was checking everyone that came through the entrance. The moment Hunter saw her, she locked her eyes on him. There was no way she could have known his face—contact had come through Phee, and she wouldn't have mentioned anything about Hunter and the rest—yet the Keshiri could obviously tell that he'd spotted her. It gave Hunter pause. Had he been sloppy in his reconnaissance, or was she that attuned to her environment? In his experience, that kind of situational awareness wasn't commonplace among civilians.

The Keshiri raised one hand in greeting, then waved them over, her charming smile lifting her plump cheeks. Her servant twisted in his chair and stood to greet them. The mask covered his entire face while a hood concealed his hair.

His mask itself was nothing more than a polarized visor over a mouth guard pocked with breathing holes. It bore no markings and was plain and unintimidating. It could've been homemade and did not appear to serve any tactical purpose, which gave credence to the intel about it being an aesthetic choice.

The masked man rose quickly but distributed his weight in a noticeable manner, favoring his right side. Hunter understood immediately. Though his trousers covered both legs, the fabric on the left clung to a limb that was too slim and spindly to be flesh—a cybernetic prosthetic.

Hunter directed Omega and Phee to the pair, still wary for reasons he couldn't quite pin down. So far this was all going according to plan.

"Phee Genoa?" the Keshiri asked, still seated.

"The one and only."

The Keshiri zeroed in on Hunter. "And you are?"

"Phee Genoa's friend."

Phee stared daggers at him.

The corner of the Keshiri's mouth curled. Put off or amused by his evasiveness? Hunter didn't know or care. His unease grew. Something small—minuscule—was off. He craned his neck, genuinely unsettled. What was wrong here? What was he missing?

The Keshiri turned her focus to Omega. "Hello."

"Hello! I'm Omega and it's a pleasure to make your acquaintance." Omega flicked a glance Hunter's way as if to indicate *that* was a proper way to greet people and not seem like a grump.

Hunter cocked his head toward Phee. *Get on with it.*

Phee said, "I'm told you're—"

The Keshiri introduced herself. "Sohi. And my companion is Kuuto."

"He doesn't speak?" Hunter's brow furrowed.

"Unfortunately, no," Sohi said. "Injuries sustained in his youth mean he communicates in other ways."

"The same injuries that require a mask?" Hunter nearly asked about the leg but understood that was inconsequential. He'd offended their clients enough already.

Sohi was no longer smiling. "That is correct. Do we have a problem here?"

Yes, Hunter thought. There were the unanswered questions he'd walked in with: Why were these two traveling the galaxy using back channels and underground contacts? How did they have so much money? But now his gut told him some glaringly obvious gap in Phee's intel was right in front of him. He still didn't know what it was, and it was putting him more on edge by the second.

Then, a drunk, staggering, long-limbed Gungan carrying two swishing mugs of ale tripped on something—a traveler's luggage or her own feet—spilling her drinks across the Keshiri's table. Sohi moved quickly, avoiding the wave of brew splashing her vacated chair, exposing a key detail about their passengers Phee certainly didn't have, something he hadn't consciously picked up on when she was seated.

Sohi was pregnant. And from the looks of it, quite far along.

So Phee's plan already wasn't right by the numbers. They were supposed to be picking up a *pair* of passengers.

And now there were three.

CHAPTER FIVE

SPACEPORT, MYGEETO

"Aword," Hunter said, motioning for a quiet huddle.

Phee and Omega exchanged wary glances, both knowing this wasn't going to be a fun conversation.

They stepped away from Sohi's table while a server droid attempted to wipe up the spill. The clumsy Gungan slurred an apology.

With the three of them crowded together, Phee started speaking before Hunter could. "It's a tiny surprise, but not bad."

"Your contact mentioned nothing about a passenger being with child," Hunter said. "There are all sorts of things to consider. Contingencies we aren't prepared for."

"If we get them to their destination quickly, I don't see any additional risk."

"How many times do I have to say it? Our ignorance is the risk. If those two didn't pass on information about a baby, what else are they hiding? We cannot be so desperate for credits that we hurl common sense out the air lock."

Omega said, "We can't leave them."

Hunter looked to her. "I haven't said we should, but given how sideways everything is going, do you really think this is a good option for us—or them?"

"But it's . . ." Omega struggled for a response Hunter couldn't counter. "It's rude!"

He could definitely counter that one, but a glance revealed Sohi observing their animated conversation, calmly, keenly. Hunter said, "Let's talk outside."

He made his way to the door with Omega and Phee trailing. He didn't have to look back to know Sohi and her companion were following, too.

Outside the bar now, Hunter spoke over his shoulder. "Our crew needs a moment to confer."

The Keshiri caught up to them, her hands resting on her protruding midsection. They walked into the crowd, passersby giving them a wide berth either due to Hunter's intimidating disposition or out of politeness for the pregnant woman.

"I was under the impression we had a deal," Sohi said. "We have the agreed-upon credits."

"You also have a tiny being living inside you. Our ship is not suitable for babies."

"The baby's going to ride in her belly, Hunter!" Omega offered.

"We hope!" Hunter looked at Sohi. "How are we supposed to know the stress of space travel won't . . . *activate* it?"

"That is a strange way of phrasing it," Sohi said. "It's not a concern. We will be fine."

"When are you due?" Phee asked.

Sohi hesitated, then said, "Seven days."

Hunter stopped walking and stared in disbelief. "Seven—?"

He didn't bother to finish his thought. He started walking again.

Sohi kept pace. "A trip to Felucia won't take more than two days if I'm to understand your ship's capabilities."

Hunter cut his eyes to Phee. "Two days if we went directly, but we take scenic routes now."

"Dropping off the mortar adds a day," Phee said. "It's still the most direct route that gets us home with everything we need."

Hunter turned sharply into a nearby alley. What he had to say next was not a conversation for an open street. "Why us? You could've bought passage on a commercial transport for a fraction of the cost. It might've added a day or so, with stops, but according to you, that time wouldn't have been an issue. What are you two not telling us?"

Omega stood beside him, and Phee joined them. Sohi's masked friend stood with her in an elongated silence.

Finally, Sohi said, "We're going to Felucia because that's where my life partner is. And we can't take commercial transport, because I'm wanted by the Empire. If they catch me, they might never let me or my baby go."

Hunter leaned in. Sohi had his undivided attention. "Go on."

She sighed deeply and massaged her stomach. "I lived and worked on Coruscant as an aide to Senator Tanner Cadaman in the Feenix office. The senator was part of the Delegation of Two Thousand, the group of politicians who openly opposed the unfettered power granted to then-Chancellor Palpatine during the Clone Wars and petitioned him to voluntarily relinquish such might."

Hunter let it sink in. He knew firsthand how the Emperor's opponents were treated once he took power. The luckiest still drew breath. Not many were that lucky. Ask the Jedi . . . if there were any left.

Sohi went on, "When the war ended, rumor had it that *Emperor* Palpatine was having his political opponents rounded up and arrested. And not just his opponents, but their staff. Kesh may be in Wild Space and far from the general trajectory of political upheaval, but we were not without our homegrown autocrats. Such a ruler was responsible for Kuuto's scars and . . . and my parents' deaths."

Her silent companion grunted and placed a gentle hand on Sohi's shoulder.

Phee said, "I'm sorry about your folks."

Omega stepped forward and wrapped her fingers around Sohi's.

"It's fine," Sohi said. "It happened a long time ago, and I built a good life with Kuuto's guidance. But we fled Kesh in the shadow of an ambitious man with a fraction of the Emperor's power. We knew better than to wait and see if the rumors of mass arrests would come true. The day after we left Coruscant, I heard Senator Cadaman's entire office had been taken in. And worse, my absence was noted. We've been in hiding ever since."

Hunter filled in the blanks on his own. "Since you're on an Imperial watch list, it's underground channels and pleas to pirates for you, eh?"

Sohi nodded.

"What you're paying us," Hunter said, "seems a bit much for a senatorial aide."

"Maybe one who didn't flee Kesh with the bulk of her wealthy family's fortune. A fortune that was invested and compounded between adolescence and adulthood."

"Kuuto helped with that, too?" Hunter asked.

The masked being's posture stiffened with pride. He reached beneath the folds of his cloak and produced a pouch heavy with clinking contents. Credits, presumably.

"Small bag," Hunter said.

"Large denominations," Sohi countered. "Our belongings are stowed in a locker at the spaceport. There's more where this came from. I understand your trepidation, so I'm willing to pay a ten percent surcharge on the previously agreed-upon fee for your trouble. Doesn't that sound like a good deal to you?"

Phee said, "Does to me."

Hunter's irritation hadn't cooled completely, but something still felt off. Perhaps it was simply the desperation radiating off Sohi, which was understandable with a child on the way. He felt Omega's big sappy eyes pinning him.

"You still like this arrangement?" he asked her, knowing the answer.

"Even more. Before it was about credits to help Pabu. Now it's the right thing to do."

What was he supposed to say to that?

He settled on, "Promise not to birth your child on our ship, and we're golden."

"Oh, thank you!" Sohi gripped both his hands in hers. "Thank you so much!"

Sohi led the contracted pilots to the spaceport lockers, where they retrieved two trunks containing a mass of credits and some tools. The pirate and the child had been easy enough to convince, but the clone pressed harder than she liked. He might be a problem.

Or not. She could tell her tale got to him, as intended. She'd played on every sympathy she could, using every social engineering tactic she knew. It might be enough to conceal her lies for the duration of the trip.

And if not, there were more drastic measures.

Time would tell.

CHAPTER SIX

RONIK CASINO, CANTO BIGHT, CANTONICA

"Have a good evening, Mr. Nandt."

Chimlor Nandt, the well-dressed but careworn manager of the Ronik, tipped his driver while debating having the transit droid replaced. It would not be a good evening. The suggestion of such irked the already-exhausted Devaronian. In his younger days, he might've speared the disgustingly chipper rust bucket with his horns.

Instead, he lugged himself through the casino's private entrance to his private lift, already forgetting the droid's minor trespass of positivity. The night's inevitable unpleasantness superseded all prior annoyances. After fifteen years of maintaining the exacting standards at one of Canto Bight's most highly regarded resorts for the ultra-rich, he knew that even a good night would include making fights appear as if they never happened, punishing a cheater or two, ignoring or covering up scandals and copious illegal substances changing hands, either enriching or enraging his employers, and on and on . . .

The lauded safety and security of Canto Bight was nothing without those like Chimlor who oversaw the illusion.

On his floor, at his office, he placed his palm on the jamb scanner, and the door swished aside. Chimlor took three steps beyond the threshold before registering the stranger seated behind his desk.

The door swished shut, and the mystery being said, "Chimlor, have a seat, please."

Who? How? Why?

The being was humanoid, pale-skinned, with dark hair and gray streaks threaded throughout. The creases in his forehead and the deep pockets beneath his sunken brown eyes suggested a hard life. None of that told as much as what he wore. His white tunic and the red and black bars indicating his rank answered at least two of Chimlor's most pressing queries.

The uniform was that of the Imperial Security Bureau. How he got into Chimlor's office . . . same answer. ISB went where they wanted.

Why here, though? Whatever that answer might be made Chimlor extremely nervous. He tried not to let it show.

Chimlor and the stranger eyed each other through a hazy blue hologram of seemingly random foot traffic on the casino floor. The image was frozen mid-review. Beyond the intruder, grand floor-to-ceiling windows gave view of Canto Bight's other luxurious gambling dens. When Chimlor stared out, he often wondered if the polish of each casino existed in enmity to the toll maintaining the city's glamorous myths took on managers like him. He felt seconds, if not hours, of his lifespan sloughing away from the stress of a conversation he technically hadn't even started yet. All part of the job. Chimlor's naturally deep voice felt weak when he said, "You're in my chair."

"I'm accessing security records of the robbery you reported to local authorities three days ago. They are not very good."

"The authorities or the recordings?"

"Both. Sit."

Chimlor sat in the spot typically reserved for employees, cheats, or enemies who required a harsh reprimand, up to and including termination—in every sense of the word. Such nasty trivialities were a professional hazard when you ran a casino, even in a place like Canto Bight, where the wealth flowing through the coffers was so gargantuan that the *concept of danger* couldn't afford a buy-in. Or so most were led to believe.

Why was the ISB interested in a robbery? At *his* casino?

Undoubtedly, questions were coming, and Chimlor tried to regain some dominance by starting the interrogation himself. "What's your name and what's your drink, friend? I'll have it brought up. No charge."

"I am Agent Sendril Crane, and intoxication while on duty is prohibited."

One of those by-the-rules guys, then? Chimlor thought. Maybe. Drink might not be the vice to turn him from the ISB's regulations, but there were other options. They'd get to that. Chimlor said, "How can I help you, Crane?"

Instead of answering, Crane played a holo segment Chimlor was intimately familiar with. Two inept security guards—a couple of young, tanned Onderonian cousins—loaded up a transport with bags of credits meant for deposit at the central bank. The guards, Chimlor knew, were now unemployed and nursing broken arms for what was about to transpire.

The pair was suddenly interrupted by a rifle nudging into the proceedings. Two quick stun blasts incapacitated them. The masked gunman began snatching the heavy sacks, tossing them into a levitating cart that he then pushed to a getaway vehicle waiting outside.

All of this was caught on discreet backup cams—the assailants had managed to deactivate the older, less reliable models. Thankfully, a persnickety technician had insisted on redundant systems despite ever-looming budget cuts. (All the profit the bosses made, and they still looked for cutbacks in exactly the wrong places. What else was new?) Anyhow, one of those discreet cams got an angle on the getaway driver—though not a great one.

Crane typed commands into the console, sharpening the image as much as possible, which wasn't much at all. The casino lights glaring off the vehicle's viewport allowed only a ghost of the driver's face: a woman—beige-skinned with round cheeks, a soft jawline, and long, scraggly brown hair.

Crane's fingers flew over the console, executing another command that cropped and enlarged that hazy visual. He moved the cropped driver's image aside and returned to the casino floor recording.

Crane said, "I'd like to see feeds from three days before the robbery, but I need to filter on specific criteria. Your system is rudimentary, so I hope that's possible."

Chimlor felt insulted, like he'd programmed the system himself. He left his seat and rounded the desk. "We're not some backwater outfit. We can filter on whatever you want. May I?"

Crane rose, giving up the seat, and Chimlor made a point to bump the agent aside as he took command of the console. "Tell me what you're looking for."

"A woman. Skin tones other than blue. Oversized, flowing robes. Avoiding the alcohol at the bar. Frequent trips to the restroom."

Chimlor typed as Crane spoke, though the last of the criteria gave him pause before he recovered and continued. Soon, they had six recordings running simultaneously, all women fitting Crane's description.

"There," Crane said, pointing to the bottom left portion of the grid, an image from the day before the robbery. Chimlor froze it.

This woman had short, neatly styled platinum hair and bright-pink skin. Her robes looked like sacks draped over her, and the only thing in her cup was blue milk. Chimlor could not understand what was special about this guest until Crane punched in a command that put the image of the getaway driver and this woman side by side.

Two different skin tones—makeup? Two different hairstyles—easily accomplished with wigs. Same cheeks. Same jawline. So the driver and the masked man had been casing the Ronik for days. This was a great discovery that Chimlor would take credit for with the bosses whenever the agent took a hike.

Since Chimlor had successfully provided the agent with information he'd been looking for, perhaps some reciprocity was in order. "What interest does the ISB have in our unfortunate security breach? I thought you all chased terrorists."

"The ISB addresses threats to the Empire, in whatever form they take," Crane said. He had been staring at the frozen image of the disguised woman.

Something was there. Something personal. Leverage, perhaps? Chimlor fished for more. "What kind of threat are my robbers, then?"

"The woman stole state secrets that must not fall into the wrong hands. It is imperative that I acquire her."

Chimlor, who had become an advanced study in inflection and body language—a necessity to stay ahead of those who'd take advantage of a casino boss on any given night—detected more snap in the agent's voice. Definitely something personal there. In this place, anything personal could be exploited. The agent had singled out the woman, despite the robbery being a team effort. Interesting.

"You been chasing those two for a while?" Chimlor asked.

Crane's jaw flexed, his eyes on the getaway driver's frozen image.

Chimlor pushed. "Or just her?"

Crane pinned him with durasteel eyes. "Show me the illegal credit-tracking system your casino uses."

Chimlor's body temperature dropped, and he willed away a shudder from the abrupt shift in conversation. "I'm not sure what you're—"

Crane cut him off with a dismissive wave. "You have a system that encodes all credits passing through your establishment with an algorithm telling you where they're spent next. It's meant to provide data on the patrons and gamblers who frequent your casino—without their knowledge or consent—so you might create more bespoke experiences on their next visit, motivating them to spend and lose more credits. Your bank is aware of the technology and purges the code from any credits you are mandated by law to deposit to your various accounts. The credits stolen in the robbery, having never reached the bank, would still be encoded. This is likely why you and your employers have only been mildly cooperative with the Canto Bight Police Department. You're waiting for a ping from your system, after which you'll administer some form of illegal and final underworld justice to the thieves."

Chimlor felt breathless, as if he were the one who'd delivered a shockingly accurate monologue about Ronik's proprietary secret. He struggled for a deflection that wouldn't incriminate him.

Crane said, "You don't have to respond. Instead, bask in the relief that you no longer have to worry about being found out. The worst has happened in that regard, and it's not so bad, is it? Now, show me how it works, and you may gain some favor from me. Which, you must understand, is favor from the Empire."

Chimlor exited the security recordings and punched up the credit-tracking system.

Crane said, "I'll be taking a copy of this program with me."

Chimlor tried not to let his indignation show. "If you say so."

Crane motioned for Chimlor to surrender the seat again, and the ISB agent explored the various menus within the program, absorbing the complex data as if he'd been using the program for years.

"All you ISB guys so tech savvy?" Chimlor asked.

"No. I have an expanded skill set due to the nature of my previous work."

"What'd you used to do?"

"I was a spy. And spymaster, for a time."

"I guess you like the easy gigs," Chimlor said, sarcastic, wanting the agent gone as soon as possible. "I'll get a droid to copy the program for you—"

"Don't bother. I've already had one of your droids create a datacard for me, so there's just the final matter to attend to."

"What's that?" Chimlor asked, somewhat furious now. He'd had enough of being bossed around in his own establishment.

Crane's fingers danced along the console, bringing up several security feeds. Real time. "The various violations of Imperial law I've informed your local law enforcement about. They will, of course, require the arrest and detainment of you and many of your guests."

"Excuse me?" Chimlor's hot fury became a cold chill. He backed up several steps, putting the desk between them again. He turned his body slightly, hiding his hand as it reached for a blaster at the small of his back. "I must've misheard you."

Crane's focus remained on the feeds. "There's a pazaak dealer in league with a cheater at table seven. They've used a sloppy hand signal twice now. Since your pit bosses didn't catch it, we must assume they're in on it, too. Gaming fraud violates Imperial statute number . . ."

While Crane rattled off a ridiculously long statute designation, several uniformed Canto Bight law enforcement officers swarmed the table in question, subduing the alleged cheaters with restraints—and sharp blows to their jaws.

Crane closed that feed and focused on another, one of the Ronik's pubs. He pointed. "There's a spice deal happening in that back booth. The sale and distribution of narcotics violate statutes, of course. Though

I'm happy to overlook the vial of sulfur dust in your desk drawer given how helpful you've been."

More officers swarmed the pub, taking down the dealers and several servers.

Crane moved to another feed, another accusation, at which point Chimlor had enough. "What happened to all that favor from you and the Empire?"

"I promise I will not personally pursue any data theft charges. However"—Crane brought up a feed from the night before, when Chimlor and a few of his most trusted lieutenants roughed up the guards who'd been incapacitated in the robbery—"assault, wrongful termination. Perhaps some violations of worker compensation laws, though I'll leave that for the local litigation droids."

Chimlor drew his blaster, a mental checklist of whom he'd have to call for body disposal, bribes, and so on hovering at the back of his mind. "You should've had a drink and moved along, Crane. Now I've got another mess to clean up."

Crane stared down the blaster's barrel, unreadable.

That's fine, Chimlor thought. *I don't care how he feels. I hope his blood doesn't smear my window too badly.*

Chimlor pulled the trigger.

His arm spasmed as blue lightning crackled from a small disk magnetically affixed to his weapon, sending a jolt of electric agony to his shoulder, forcing him to drop the blaster to the floor, where it continued to bounce and sizzle from the disk's arcing energy. Chimlor, frightened and hurting, backed away from his malfunctioning blaster, not even noticing the other half-dozen tiny disks affixed to the wall, floor, and ceiling. When he was within their effective range, the disks activated, ensnaring him in a netlike pattern of electric-blue agony.

Chimlor collapsed, writhing as electricity arced through every nerve in his body.

As quickly as the shock treatment began, it ceased, all of the disks deactivating at once. None of Chimlor's muscles were capable of compliance. He lay in a quivering heap.

Crane stood over him. "Your posture upon arrival suggested a hidden weapon, which was of some concern, but when you attempted physical intimidation by colliding with me, I slipped a jolt disk onto your blaster. I was unsure if I'd need my larger trap, but you've proven that chance favors the prepared yet again. Thank you for that confirmation."

The door swished open, and officers spilled in with shackles—and a muzzle, of all things.

"Brandishing a weapon," Crane said, "attempted murder of an ISB agent, resisting arrest. Again, the litigation droids will sort it out. In the meantime, it's off to the nearest detention center, where you and your fellow violators can be reminded of the importance of abiding by Imperial law."

Every muscle cramped as Chimlor was dragged to his feet, whimpering. The jolt disks' shock lingered while fear sank in.

Crane returned to the desk Chimlor would never see again, pulling up the image of the woman, a target that surely meant more than some ISB case he'd been assigned. "We know what's best for you all."

CHAPTER SEVEN

HYPERSPACE, EN ROUTE TO THE DALLOW SYSTEM

Hunter brooded while everyone else acted like this was a party ship. MEL-222 had brought a crate for Sohi to elevate her swollen feet while Omega peppered her with questions about the baby. *Can you feel it move? Does it make you extra hungry? What will you name it?*

Sohi chatted gleefully, enlightening Omega with all sorts of mother-to-be facts. Omega had a way of making fast friends wherever they went, and Hunter often thought he'd never seen someone quite as congenial . . . until Sohi.

The woman was charming, excessively so. She complimented Tech's forearm computer—a model she'd seen the specs for while handling technology briefings in her senatorial role—and somehow guessed that Wrecker was a dejarik enthusiast and suggested he play a few rounds with Kuuto.

She thanked Phee profusely, and they had a brief but intense conversation about the long-term harm caused by pillaging cultures for profit. Sohi capped the discussion with, "'Pirate' is the wrong term for what you do to reclaim artifacts, Phee. They should call you a . . . a . . . '*champion of cultural retrieval.*'"

Phee basked in the flattery. "I prefer 'liberator of ancient wonders,' but that's a good one, too."

Hunter interrupted Phee's ego stroking. "Have you contacted your Balosar friend about the mortar to ensure we're still good to go?"

Phee said, "I have not been able to reach Ven directly. But he left drop-off instructions by way of a coded comms channel. When we land, we'll need to meet the Caridan at their home to deliver the artifact and settle up."

Sohi's head tilted. "And where did you say we're stopping?"

"We didn't," Hunter said, triggering mean stares from everyone. He glowered back, then added, "The Dallow system."

"It's just a short stop," Phee said as if she were the over-accommodating director of a galactic cruise ship. "You'll be very comfortable while we attend to our business matter."

Sohi nodded, seemingly familiar with the area. "It's a fairly well-to-do world. I had friends who worked for one of their senators. I wasn't aware that any Caridans had settled there."

"That would be some feat if you were aware of every inhabitant of every planet you'd ever heard of during your time in the Senate," Hunter said.

Sohi shook her head. "No. You're right. Of course. Forgive me for intruding into your personal matters."

While the apology seemed genuine, with no bite, Kuuto's helmet tilted Hunter's way, projecting menace. Hunter imagined a scowl beneath. Could that mask be hiding more than annoyance and scars?

Under different circumstances, Hunter might've wondered if he was being unfairly terse with the passengers, but his reservations about them had not subsided. As much as he wanted to dismiss what might be minor misgivings, his gut had saved his life too many times, and he respected it.

Since Sohi was such an eager conversationalist, Hunter decided on direct engagement. "Your life partner is on Felucia. Doing what?"

"He is an aid worker. Assisting in areas hard hit by the war."

"Will that be a final stop for you and your growing family?"

"No. The Imperial presence in that system isn't slight by any means, but the planet is recovering from the many battles fought there. The military has abandoned several cities, allowing small-scale reconstruction efforts to flourish. My partner is waiting near a discreet medical facility that was known to members of the Senate in the event care was needed during diplomatic visits. There we plan to safely welcome our child into the galaxy." She motioned to her stomach. "After, we'll move on."

"To a glamorous life befitting a former Coruscant senatorial aide."

"If you think it's anything close to glamorous, you don't know much about working in the Senate."

The story is plausible, Hunter thought. *But still . . .*

Hunter nodded, conceding the point. "Seems you've been on the run for some time. Why haven't your assets been frozen?"

The abrupt swerve in conversation charged the cabin.

Phee said, "Hunter! What are you—?"

Sohi raised a hand, indicating she could handle this. "The Empire can only seize what it knows about. My family's fortune is well diversified."

"A Keshiri heiress. Gotta say it's the first time I've heard of such."

Steely-eyed, Sohi said, "It would be some feat if you were aware of every wealthy family from every planet, wouldn't it?"

Omega laughed, and Hunter forgave her for it immediately. She and the others might find this amusing, but he felt like he was chasing something important. He told Sohi, "I'm impressed. It's almost like you're prepared for anything."

"I'd consider it foolish not to be."

"An answer for everything, too."

"Hunter . . ." Tech said, his mild way of asking Hunter to back off.

Too late for that. Hunter said, "The Senate must be a tough place. How long did you work there?"

"Two years."

"Someone as sharp as you appear to be, and you were a lowly aide? Seems your skill set would've shot you up the ranks fast. Unless there's something else you're not telling us."

"Enough," Phee said.

Sohi kept talking, though. "Again, you don't know much about the Senate. Is there a point to all this hostility, or can I pay more to keep you silent the rest of the voyage?"

Kuuto's hand fell on Sohi's knee. As comfort or admonishment, Hunter couldn't tell.

Sohi said, "If you'll excuse me, your interrogation is exhausting. I *will* rest now."

Phee said, "Wrecker's offered his bunk. It should be comfortable enough."

"The smell from the channelfish soup I spilled on my pillow should be almost gone," Wrecker said.

Phee grimaced. "I'm going to get you a new pillow."

"Um, thank you," Sohi said.

Omega led Sohi to her accommodations while Phee and Kuuto stared Hunter down. Finally, Hunter said, "I'm tired, too. I'll see you all after some shut-eye."

Then he retreated to his quarters, where he didn't sleep a wink, because Sohi and Kuuto—if those were even their real names—were hiding something.

Phee settled into the copilot chair next to Tech and leaned close in a way most copilots didn't. "Me joining you won't make it hard for you to concentrate, will it, Brown Eyes?"

"I'm used to piloting in all sorts of conditions. Through asteroid belts, evading missile attacks, slimy monsters clinging to the hull. So, your presence, while welcome, won't distract me."

"You always know the sweet things a girl wants to hear."

He cleared his throat and checked his consoles. All ship systems normal. His systems, though . . . he estimated his body temperature might have raised by at least a degree, and his pulse felt slightly elevated . . . as was often the case when Phee was in such close proximity.

"What's Hunter's deal?" Phee said. "He's been grilling our well-paying passengers for reasons unknown."

"Unknown to *us*."

"Does he get like this often? He's been acting like a dunghead for days."

Tech understood her frustration and shared some of it. Hunter's animosity toward the clients wasn't making the mission *easier*. In fact, he wondered if the antagonism was a manifestation of a larger pattern Tech had been tracking within their family.

Phee hadn't known them long and wouldn't be privy to the dynamic, so Tech still felt a need to defend his brother. "He's *particular*. Not without cause. On the battlefield, surprises usually mean someone you expect to come home doesn't."

"Fine. Yes. The baby was a surprise. But I don't know. I thought he'd get over it faster. Another kid means another potential student at Hunter's School for Wayward Children, right?"

"You know he doesn't like that joke. Also, technically, Omega's older than us, so . . ." Tech pivoted. "I doubt Hunter's consternation is as much about Sohi's baby as it is that we've allowed two additional fugitives from the Empire on board. The unseen variables in our current missions have not forced us to deviate dangerously, unlike when we were in Cid's employ. Still, it does make me revisit a loose theory I've been postulating for a while. I wonder if there's some inherent quirk in our team dynamics that draws us toward chaos no matter how carefully we plan for calm. It feels like we're in over our heads every week." He stroked his chin, considering.

"Check it out, Brown Eyes . . . the galaxy is chaotic, and that's not on you. Here's what you ought to know: You got surprised sometimes, you had to improvise sometimes, but you've never truly been in over your head."

"How did you reach that conclusion?"

"Because when you're really in over your head, you drown. I'm still here, and you are, too. Until that changes, we're doing exactly what we're supposed to."

It was a whimsical notion, but Tech liked it. He liked a lot of what Phee said. And did. He should tell her. Soon.

She leaned over the comms station, cycling through screens, frowning.

Tech said, "Something's troubling you."

"It's just—I still can't raise Ven directly. Those drop-off instructions are the last I've heard from him."

"Is that odd? From how you described him, I thought he could be erratic."

"Not so erratic he'd miss out on a finder's fee. The dossier on the auction guests came from him."

"Also, through your encrypted text channel," Tech said, unsure if that fact was significant to a larger truth. Or problem. "If you fear something is amiss, we should tell—"

Phee shot to her feet. "No! Absolutely not. Hunter is looking for a reason to turn this ship around, throw our passengers out the air lock, or whatever. We have to finish this—for Pabu."

"Very well. We'll handle the drop-off and let Hunter process his concerns in his own way."

"Great. We'll get through these jobs, and he'll see all this stress was for nothing."

CHAPTER EIGHT

DALLOW, DALLOW SYSTEM

Nocturnal fauna croaked and growled and scurried under a red moon. A contingent of four guards, droid and humanoid, dragged a thrashing hooded figure over lush grass into a thicket of sapling veshok trees, where they dropped the unfortunate soul next to a grave they'd dug for him earlier.

His wrists were still bound behind his back, but free of his captors' grasps, he thrust a low kick into one droid's ankle, dropping the mechanized bastard, and attempted to take down one of the humanoids when a rifle butt caught him across the jaw. The sack over his head offered little cushion. After a week of torture that saw him beaten and drugged, rambling all sorts of secrets that should follow him into the grave, the blow knocked away his last bit of fight. He lay on his side gasping, yielding but no less angry about this ignoble end—and the scheme that had brought him here.

"Are you there, Cellia?" Ven Alman shouted. "Do you have the spine to see this through yourself, or is this work just for your goon squad?"

The woman answered from the night's shade of a full-grown, silver-leaved galek tree a few dozen paces away. "Remove his hood."

The toppled droid righted itself in jerky fits and exchanged glances with the other guards. The leader of the bunch, a bronze-skinned Kiffar named Parlin with his clan's symbols tatted cheek to cheek, said, "Mistress Moten, that's not necessary."

"No. It is desired. Remove the hood."

Parlin snatched the hood and dropped it in the hole. Ven got to his knees, and his eyes and antennae adjusted to the balmy night. His blood remained chilled. He was not going to see the sunrise. He knew.

Cellia Moten, a humanoid whose pale skin and sandy hair revealed no details about her heritage, emerged from the shadows in a crimson cloak. Her arms were hidden in huge sleeves folded across her chest, and golden tassels dangled from her shoulders.

"I see you've worn your murderer's best." Ven spat blood on the ground. "I'm honored."

She came closer but remained at a distance. Her thugs maintained a safe zone between her and any desperate last-second move Ven might make. They didn't realize he was all out of those.

During his long pirating career, a swath of time where he'd lightened loads of Republic supply ships, acquired small fortunes from poorly guarded mineral mines, and so on, there'd never been a job without risks. He'd come to terms with the high chance of a messy end long ago. But he hadn't seen this coming.

This was supposed to be an easy payday. Filch some ridiculous religious artifact from some rich dolt with too many junk possessions as it was. He'd pulled it off. Simple. A death sentence for a job well done had come as a surprise.

Though not for the two-faced double-crosser Cellia Moten. This had been her plan all along.

He sneered. "You ruthless, gloating hag! Are you going to think of me every time you look at that chalice I brought you?"

"No," Cellia said. "I doubt I'll ever think of you again."

"Not quite the impression I was hoping to leave." Ven let loose a humorless chuckle. "Get on with it."

"Certainly, but before I do, I came out here for a reason. I want you to understand that even though I'll move on to a grander destiny than what you could accomplish on Dallow, you should find solace in your contribution to this beautiful world."

"Grand destiny? You mean that ridiculous holo you made. Are you daft, woman? It's the most absurd thing I've ever seen!"

Cellia scowled.

Ven laughed, a hollow guffaw aimed at the sky. "You're the one who dosed me with truth-telling drugs. You got your wish."

Cellia tilted her neck from one side to the other, releasing unnerving cracking sounds. She managed to compose herself and play the magnanimous role she'd scripted. "Despite your insolence, you will have a legacy here."

"What are you on about now?"

"Look around. See what you will become."

Ven didn't want to play her game, but he couldn't help what he saw. The trees in this section of the grove were all young, some very new. Each was planted upon a conspicuous bulging mound of soil, roots tapering down and away.

"Ah, no," Ven said, flinching away from the nearest tree, horrified.

There were dozens of saplings here, each a marker for a grave. The woman was a monster!

"You shouldn't fret," Cellia said. "I wouldn't abandon you to this fate alone."

That was when he noticed the second hole. For Phee. Because where Cellia's goons couldn't knock the encrypted pirate protocols from him, the drugs could. Cellia had been interested in Phee even before Ven had completed the chalice job. Foolishly, Ven made initial contact with Phee, informing her of a promising opportunity—and his finder's fee. Had Cellia already lured Phee into her web off Ven's history with her? Was Phee walking into the same blasted trap he had?

A new fight sparked in Ven. He wouldn't call Phee Genoa a friend, proper, but she was a fellow pirate, and that was close enough. Cellia had to be stopped!

Ven summoned his final vestiges of strength, one last-ditch plan forming. He just needed a distraction. So he got loud.

"If you think you're going to use me for fertilizer"—he shifted his weight toward the same droid he'd toppled earlier, planning to spring to his feet and use it as a shield—"I've got news for—"

Parlin shot Ven through the heart.

The pirate's eyes glazed, and he toppled into his final resting place.

Two guards grabbed shovels they had stowed in the empty grave earlier, ready to finish the night's work, while a third produced a new ve-shok sapling from a sack strung across his back.

The two diggers climbed into Ven's hole, set their shovels aside, and as was their routine, did a final rough frisk for missed valuables. Parlin whistled a jaunty tune while they had at it. As they jostled the body about, Ven's tunic sleeve scrunched up, revealing a glimmer that caught Cellia's eye.

She said, "Wait. What's that on his wrist?"

A digger lifted Ven's limp hand into the moonlight for a better look at the bracelet. "Beadwork and common metal, miss. Worthless."

Cellia disagreed. "Retrieve that for me, Parlin."

Ever obedient, the Kiffar gently unclasped the bracelet, then passed the trinket to his mistress, who held it high for a better look. The largest charm among the beads featured a one-eyed face framed with a few thick dreadlocks, but the image was an optical illusion. To view it from a different angle, the dreadlocks looked like grasping fingers, and the eye a gem just in reach.

Cellia rotated the trinket in the light. "I've read of this. Did you know some pirates worship a deity of reclamation?"

"A thief god?" Parlin said.

"That's one way to look at it, I suppose. I wouldn't have thought Ven a person of faith. Perhaps his god welcomed him into its warm embrace." The bracelet vanished within the folds of Cellia's cloak. "But I doubt it."

She turned back toward the towering spires of her estate, the thick hem of her cloak sweeping loose dirt on Ven's face like a final insult. "Hurry here and leave the shovels. We'll be planting another tree tomorrow."

CHAPTER NINE

DALLOW, DALLOW SYSTEM

The *Marauder* broke through the high cloud cover into a world so vividly blue and green that Omega winced at the sight, overwhelmed by the lushness of Dallow. The pale sky tapered lighter and lighter before colliding with a deep-blue ocean. Before Omega could confirm it visually, the cockpit instruments detected the landmass of a continent ahead, the land shelf appearing inconsequential at a distance, then swelling to fill the viewport as they approached at speed.

Tech worked the controls quickly, descending and guiding them through turbulent air pockets instinctively. They were over land, the forest canopy breaking periodically to reveal gulleys, rivers, and the roofs of village huts before returning to ancient and undisturbed foliage for a time. Soon, the wide-open expanse of a bustling city overtook the trees as they drew closer to their destination.

Comms crackled as the spaceport agents detected their approach. Tech provided the appropriate—fake—landing codes and was informed of the docking fees. Omega went bug-eyed at the number, and Tech whistled through his teeth. The fees were triple what they had paid on Mygeeto the day before.

Phee's hand fell on Tech's shoulder, comforting him. "Don't worry. We've got it."

Hunter emerged from his quarters to find Phee crouched before the bag of credits Sohi forked over yesterday. She'd counted out a neat—and outrageous—stack of currency.

"Buying a new ship?" Hunter asked.

"As our guest said, Dallow's fairly well-to-do, especially based on the docking fees."

"At that price, maybe they'll sandblast some carbon scoring off the hull while we're here."

"I'll ask if they offer massages, too."

The tone of their conversation lacked the sharpness of their prior verbal jousts, so Hunter knew they'd moved beyond some of their mutual aggravation. A good night's sleep tended to diminish the intensity of such things, but that didn't mean all the tension was gone. Hunter hadn't slept as well as he'd wished. He'd tossed himself awake more than once with Sohi on his mind.

"You know, I do want these jobs to work out," he said, trying to open today's interactions with Phee more productively while not swallowing the bile of his discomfort. "It's just my job to ensure the safety of our team."

Phee gave him a sincere look. "Says who, Hunter?"

"I . . ." He meant to say more but realized maybe that was the answer.

"This isn't the Republic Army," Phee said, "and it's certainly not the Empire. Who outranks who doesn't matter so much anymore, right?"

"What's that supposed to mean?"

"You were *once* the appointed leader and protector of some pretty capable individuals."

"We watched *each other's* backs. Always will."

"Excellent. As you should. But if that made you the boss of Clone Force Ninety-Nine, I don't know if the same dynamic applies these days. Haven't you noticed?"

Phee gathered the credits and left him to ponder, which made him irritated with her again. Perhaps unfairly. Had she said anything untrue?

Was Clone Force 99 still a unit if they weren't even whole? Cross-

hair was close to being a nemesis now. Echo, who'd become a trusted
brother-in-arms, left to follow his heart and search the galaxy with
Captain Rex, freeing clones held captive and experimented on as he
once was. If Hunter was being honest, last night wasn't the first he'd
spent in restless sleep. For so many he worried about who his family
used to be versus who they were becoming. Not to mention in the
waking hours, too.

He shook off the encroaching malaise, focusing on the day's task.
Making his way to the forward cabin, he found Wrecker snoring on a
bench. Hunter let him be and kept on to the cockpit, crowding it along
with Tech, Phee, and an excited Omega, who were having a discussion
in hushed tones. At this point, the wide-eyed grin of excitement from
Omega automatically made him nervous. Everyone got quiet when he
entered, which did *not* help his nerves.

Hunter crossed his arms. "What'd I miss?"

Tech, his voice ominously neutral, said, "Omega was making a proposition."

"About?" Hunter eyed her warily.

"I was thinking," she said in that direct and charming way of hers
that would likely take her very far in life or eventually get them all killed,
"that we should ask Sohi and Kuuto to return to Pabu with us."

Hunter felt a vein pulse in his temple and forced himself to at least
sound calm. "I don't think so."

Surprisingly, Phee responded with something that didn't make him
more furious, saying, "I agree."

"She's going to have a baby," Omega said, making her case. "She
shouldn't have to do it on a planet rebuilding from war."

"Her partner's there," Hunter reminded Omega, even though he
didn't know if he quite believed that—or any—part of Sohi's story. But
it was useful, so Hunter hoped it was true. "She'll be fine."

"But what about *the baby*?" Omega said, emphasizing her authentic
and admirable concern.

Wanting, for once, not to be the nagging voice of reason, Hunter
glanced to Phee, who said, "Pabu is a wonderful place, for sure. But it's
not up to us to offer it to every being we meet without some say from
the community that's already there."

"Isn't that what you did for us?" Omega said.

Phee's head bounced as she considered her words carefully. "I did. Only after I spoke to members of the Pabu council."

"So we can speak to them again. Right, Tech?"

Hunter held in a chuckle. The kid knew who to lean on for backup.

Tech stroked his chin. "It's not an unreasonable suggestion. If the council granted refuge once, they very well might again."

Hunter's counter was one he'd hoped to avoid. "Phee, when you told the council about us, did you tell them the truth? All of it?"

Phee caught his meaning, but her brow creased in annoyance. Her reluctance radiated. "I did."

"Would you feel comfortable sharing Sohi's story, then vouching for her and Kuuto like you did for us?"

Hunter waited. They all did.

Phee, always clever, said, "I would not feel comfortable without Sohi's permission. Perhaps it's a conversation to be had *after* we finish up here. I'm going to pay our docking fees."

She left for the exit ramp, and that was when Hunter knew for sure.

Phee didn't believe Sohi's story, either.

Urdo Meldad sat at his spaceport welcome desk, his chin propped on the heel of his hand. He had dozed off immediately after receiving notice from Space Traffic Control that an *Omicron*-class ship was cleared for landing.

A year ago, he'd have thought it odd for this spaceport, which typically serviced luxury vessels, to get an incoming military shuttle. Since the end of the war, though, there was no limit to the nonsense the wealthy brought planetside just because they could. This ship could very well be the latest acquisition of a notorious collector who kept a hangar full of vessels at his North Peak home.

Or it could be another diplomatic visitor for Lady Moten up on East Ridge. She'd had her fair share lately.

Then Urdo's head throbbed, and he lost all concern for the circumstances that brought such a rough-and-tumble ship to his part of the world. He'd spent a harrowing night partying with some village girls in a downtown pub and thought the spaceport should be grateful he made it to work today.

The lounge door whooshed open, and a gorgeous brown-skinned, thick-haired woman walked in. Urdo became instantly alert. Those village girls had nothing on *her*.

"Well, hello," he said, despite his pounding headache. His voice may have been slightly slurred, but so be it. What was done could not be undone—a personal motto.

"I'd like to pay my docking fees," the woman said, then produced neat stacks of physical credits from her satchel.

Urdo counted the currency absently, wholly taken by her beauty. While many wealthy elites resided on Dallow, he was not rich. The amount of credits passing through the spaceport on any given day was enough to leave a less confident individual with a complex. Urdo spent his entire adult life cultivating charm in lieu of currency, accepting that if the Dallow deities had blessed him with good looks *and* money, they would've made him too powerful.

"What brings such a gorgeous creature like you to town?" he said.

"My husbands," the woman replied.

Urdo repeated the word to make sure he hadn't misheard. "Husbands? Plural?"

"Yes, there are three of them."

Urdo considered himself a man of the galaxy. He'd been all over and seen all kinds of things. A four-person marriage fazed him not a bit beyond the question he was about to ask. "Any room for one more, beautiful?"

"Always," she said, "but you should know that in our culture, my husbands must fight for supremacy every three years. There used to be four of them. You still want in?"

Urdo chuckled and sought a graceful way to reverse his flirting. "Let's scan your credits into our system so you can take your receipt and go."

He passed the first stack of currency beneath his terminal's scanner, and the machine glitched immediately. Urdo smacked the side of the box. His screen did one flickering roll, then reset to normal, finally showing the expected tally of the first credits stack.

"There we go," Urdo said, ready for the thrice-married woman to leave so he might resume his nap. "Let's get you and your husbands on your way."

On the deck of the *Jurat*, his ISB-assigned *Gozanti*-class cruiser, a monitor pinged with coordinates fed from the Canto Bight credit-tracking system. Crane leaned over the console, his face as still as always.

He said, "Dallow, then. Set a course."

CHAPTER TEN

DALLOW, DALLOW SYSTEM

"Rise and shine." Hunter's boot nudged Wrecker's thigh, rousing him. He rose, grunting and groaning with each incremental movement. Standing, he ground both fists into his lower back to defeat an ache that came from sleeping on a bench midship.

"You regret giving up your bunk?" Hunter asked.

"I don't. But my neck and back might start a rebellion."

Hunter laughed, then said, "Gear up."

"For what?"

Hunter snapped his vibroblade into its sheath, then checked the sights on a rifle he'd grabbed from the armory. "Overwatch."

Wrecker took a moment to clear the fog of slumber, considering he might have misheard. As far as Wrecker knew, there wasn't any kind of operational support needed for the rest of the trip. The auction house—the hardest part—was behind them. "Did something happen?"

"No. I plan to keep it that way."

Sarcasm almost got the best of Wrecker. He nearly said, "Like last night?" but decided the pain in his back was enough. He wasn't interested in the headache of telling Hunter he'd gone too far with their passengers. In this regard, Wrecker's thinking aligned with Phee's. The particulars of the client weren't important as long as they paid and got off where they were supposed to.

Besides, Hunter's aggression messed up Wrecker's best dejarik game. Kuuto had beaten him in three back-to-back matches. He was probably going to beat Wrecker again before the argument made him abandon the last match, but it was still Wrecker's best game all night.

Wrecker decided against pushing back. As much as he loved a fight, he didn't love *this* fight. Hunter's mind was made up, and Wrecker wasn't letting him go alone.

Wrecker began down the corridor to the armory with Hunter trailing. They encountered Phee gingerly placing the Caridan mortar in a large satchel, her expression concerned. "Where are you two going?"

Incredible, Wrecker thought. *"Overwatch" is going to be news to Phee, too. This ain't going to go over well.*

Hunter said, "Tech shared the coordinates for the client's residence. I couldn't find any schematics on the dwelling, though. I don't like that."

"I'm told it's a modest home. The client is sending transport for me and Brown Eyes—"

"And me!" Omega shouted from the cockpit.

"And Omega," Phee agreed, clearly believing Omega to be the most civilized and presentable of the entire bunch. "We're going to the residence to close the deal. No rifles needed."

"Agreed," Hunter said, "for your part."

"There are no other parts, Hunter."

"Overwatch," he said, like the conversation was done.

Wrecker felt that headache coming on.

Phee opened her mouth to say more, but Sohi spoke first. "It's not a bad idea."

No one noticed she'd joined them from where she was resting, freshfaced and in a flowy cerulean gown. Kuuto emerged, too, his clothes and mask unchanged.

Hunter raised an eyebrow. "You approve of our strategy?"

"I do," Sohi said without flinching. "A lot of after-action reports came through the senator's office during the war, and from what I read, the most cautious squads suffered the fewest losses. Better to have backup and not need it than to need it and not have it."

Phee said, "That would mean leaving you and Kuuto alone in the *Marauder*. I'm sure Hunter's *hospitable nature* is already bucking against the notion."

Wrecker smirked, seeing the mental holochess match playing out between Phee and Hunter. She knew that he was suspicious of Sohi and Kuuto and that leaving them unattended in the *Marauder* would be a nonstarter. *Nice move, Phee.*

Hunter countered. "That's why Mel-Tootootoo will keep them company. Isn't that right, Mel?"

The droid came zipping from the back of the ship, chirping confirmation.

"Me and Mel had a chat earlier. She'll ensure our guests are fed, watered, and far away from anything that's not a common area." Hunter gave a pointed look to Sofi. "The cockpit will be locked, as will the armory and the engine room. You and Kuuto are free to nap and play dejarik to your heart's content until we return."

Sohi tipped her chin to the droid, her expression unreadable. "We are grateful for your attention, Mel. I assure you I'll be resting in our quarters most of the time. There's no need to worry about us."

Hunter turned back to Phee. "Topographical maps show some promising cover in the hilltops just west of your destination, roughly three klicks from here. Wrecker and I will double-time it on foot so we're in position before you reach the residence. Keep comms open. We'll stay silent unless there's a reason—"

Omega came from the cockpit and stood next to Phee. "We know the drill, Hunter. Everything will be fine."

"Remind me of that after." Hunter tipped his chin to Wrecker. "Hurry up. We're on the move in five!"

Wrecker obliged and looked at the bright side—it was a beautiful day for a long, hopefully unnecessary, hike.

When the big-body 8880 limousine arrived, the Kiffar driver's eyes narrowed at the sight of Phee's entourage. "I wasn't aware I was transporting three today."

"They're my lawyers," Phee said, straight-faced.

The Kiffar left the driver's seat and opened the back door. "The more the merrier, then."

Inside, they raised the partition for "privacy," everyone knowing better than to say anything too confidential while in the client's vehicle but also wanting to keep Hunter and Wrecker abreast of the situation.

Tech and Omega, being more familiar with Clone Force 99 schemes, did most of the talking.

"This road is lovely," Omega said. "I wonder how far north it runs. Do you think such beautiful trees border the entire thing?"

"I am unsure," Tech said. "I don't suppose we'll see much of it on such a short ride. We'll be at our destination before you know it."

". . . We'll be at our destination before you know it."

Tech's and Omega's voices came through Hunter's earpiece loud and clear. He glanced back to Wrecker, who gave a thumbs-up, indicating he heard the same.

They worked their way to the top of a steep hill, thick with foliage, a mere half klick from the perch they'd occupy for the duration of Phee's delivery. The day was warm, which made their armor sweltering, but it was discomfort they'd grown used to long ago. Everyone who served heard the saying "Get comfortable with being uncomfortable" innumerable times. A disciplined mind could overcome physical irritation.

Other irritants required more discipline to master, and Hunter hadn't quite conquered all of them. He said, "Hey, Wrecker, do you ever get tired of this?"

"This what?"

"Planet-hopping. Scraping by job after job. Soldiering when we maybe aren't soldiers anymore."

"We'll always be soldiers," Wrecker said, with not one bit of irony in his tone.

Hunter grabbed a slim tree for leverage and hoisted himself over a tricky rock outcropping. With his feet on steady ground again, he still treaded carefully with the next bit of conversation. "Even on Pabu, you think?"

Wrecker worked his way over the same outcropping, accidentally tearing off a chunk with an overzealous grip. He tossed the loose stone away and stood upright. "Yeah," he said finally, "stopping at nice planets don't change what we are."

"Even if it's more than a stop?"

Wrecker's helmet bobbed. Depending on one's perspective, the sharp-toothed mouth stenciled along the front could've been laughing or crying. "You want to stay there, don't you? I mean, forever."

Pabu was the first place where forever was a possibility. Kamino was more of a staging ground. Missions never led to potential homes, and missions were all they knew. Before.

"I don't know," Hunter said. Which was the truth. Sure, he was the one who suggested an extended stay. And it'd be a lie to say he hadn't considered making Pabu permanent. How much he *wanted* that was debatable. Perhaps he wanted it a little. Perhaps he wanted it a lot. Perhaps he wanted it too much.

Wrecker said, "Pabu's a good place. Not everyone might want their forever there. You know that, right?"

Hunter detected the hesitance in Wrecker's voice and felt a pang of defensiveness. "Have Tech and Omega said something?"

"No. I'm only speaking for me. I like the place—especially the food—but there's not much to blow up there. I guess I could toss detonators in the water if I got bored, but the fish probably wouldn't appreciate it."

"Probably not."

There was more to discuss here, but Wrecker pointed to a ring of vultures circling the sky about a klick east of their current position. "Something had a bad day."

Two of the carrion birds broke formation and dived, presumably toward some rotting meal, triggering a grim thought from Hunter: *Let's make sure that's the only meal they get.*

He continued their trek in silence, focused until they crested the hill and caught sight of the residence.

They stood stunned for a moment. Hunter removed his helmet as if that would somehow change the view. "That look like a *modest* home to you?"

The home their hilltop overlooked didn't seem residential at all . . . at least not for a single, devoutly religious Caridan. Or an entire Caridan family. Or ten families. The place was a palace. Perhaps the most luxurious Hunter had ever seen, and he'd been to the late Count Dooku's former home during one of Cid's disastrous jobs.

The structure itself had to be a kilometer's length on one side. It was hard to judge its total footprint without schematics or a view from an alternate angle. But several dozen spires rose in heights varying from fifty to one hundred meters, Hunter estimated. Each spire had to offer a stunning view of the ocean beyond the property's eastern edge. The entire structure was done up in varying hues of gold, silver, and umber, giving the illusion of warmth. Though nothing that big could stay warm for long.

Hunter unclipped his macrobinoculars from his belt and scanned the palace as the transport carrying Phee, Tech, and Omega cruised into view near the main entrance.

"Oh wow! What is that?" Omega exclaimed through the earpieces, clearly seeing the place for the first time, too.

"Well-to-do, indeed," Phee said.

Tech said, "This structure is relatively new. I'd estimate it was built in the last—"

A blast of static made Hunter and Wrecker wince, then all audio was lost.

"Comms are down," Wrecker said.

"Or jammed," Hunter said. "Try to work an alternate channel. Any local comms will do. If we can't hear how that meeting's going, I want to know what anyone around us is chatting about."

"On it." Wrecker knelt, unpacked a small mobile communications array, and went to work.

The spires had armed guards. Every. Single. One. They all focused on the transport parked at the grand entrance.

Hunter zoomed in on the vehicle, where a black-hued battle droid opened the passenger cabin and welcomed Phee, Omega, and Tech as they exited the speeder. This was very out of character for that model of droid. Phee flashed an exaggerated smile, as did Omega. The Kiffar driver joined them, and a conversation began, though Hunter had no hope of reading lips at this distance.

"How are those comms coming?" Hunter asked.

Wrecker worked dials and levers. "They're not."

Then Phee and company were guided to the massive double-doored entrance, and Hunter's anxiety ratcheted up. No eyes or ears once they crossed the threshold.

They disappeared into the shadows of the palace one by one. Tech trailed, and just before the doors sealed them in, he twisted his body slightly, placed a hand behind his back, and discreetly flashed a thumbs-up.

"Thank you," Hunter mumbled, though the indication that all was well offered little comfort once those doors closed.

Hunter had a bad feeling about this.

CHAPTER ELEVEN

MOTEN ESTATE, DALLOW

Stepping into the palace didn't feel vastly different from being on the outside—at least not at first—because of how grand and brightly lit the entrance hall was. The ceiling had to be thirty meters high, with renderings of clouds and sky decorating it. At first glance, Tech thought it was a skillfully done painting, but when he noticed the clouds drifting and the sun peeking through in approximately the same position as this system's actual sun, he understood this was technology at work. High-resolution displays as ceiling tiles. Wealth shown off unnecessarily.

The theme of nature on the inside didn't continue through the rest of the structure exactly. The wall panels were the color of glistening rubies. The floor was white Craitian marble with red veins and swirls. Striking. But also something like the aftermath of a massacre. Tech imagined that the innards of a slaughtered beast left to rot in the sun wouldn't look much different from this foyer's motif. The possibility that imposing such a horrifying sensation on guests upon entry might be intentional did not bode well for a quick and easy transaction, Tech thought.

Aside from the grisly framing, the vast foyer was decorated with various art pieces—sculptures, vases, and such. In the center of the floor, like a not-so-tiny island, was a table supporting a model of a building

Tech recognized immediately—anyone would: 500 Republica, one of the most famous and exclusive dwellings on Coruscant, known the galaxy over. The elaborate model still doubled his height at what Tech estimated to be a one-to-one-thousand scale.

Omega was immediately drawn to it. "This is amazing!"

She got close, inspecting the model's features, then tensed with mild horror. "There are people inside."

Tech and Phee sidled up for a better look. Sure enough, the model residence also featured model *residents*. Not many. Someone without Omega's keen sense for detail might easily overlook the sparse population, but her pointing finger directed Tech's gaze.

A tiny humanoid figure had its hands pressed to the window, fingers splayed, eyes bulging, and mouth stretched in what might be interpreted as an eternal scream.

Tech said, "The Holy Husk and Stone faith is rooted in its expressions of kindness while emphasizing its followers shun vanity and idols."

"Are you trying to tell me every single thing we've seen so far is at odds with what we've been told about our client?" Phee looked around, her eyes narrowing. "If so, I already noticed."

The clanking steps of the battle droid echoed in the foyer, and while the Kiffar's lithe movements were near silent, their combined presence, looming over Tech, Phee, and Omega, was as loud as it needed to be.

"If you have weapons, we need to check them," said the Kiffar.

Before anyone could object, the droid began a rough frisk of Tech.

At Phee's advice, he hadn't worn his armor, opting for casual trousers and a loose tunic he'd hoped would conceal his gear. The droid found his blaster and other tools immediately, plucking them from Tech's person and dropping them into a sack that a third guard—a bulky, reptilian Nikto with orange scales and polished gray horns—held ready. The Nikto flashed his fangs at them, but out of greeting or intimidation—who could tell? He left Tech's forearm computer in place, seeing no threat in the device. Good.

The droid moved on, collecting Phee's blaster and blade. Then, a quick search of Omega revealed her energy bow before it was added to the Nikto's collection.

All three guards kept their armaments visible and in easy reach.

"Come," said the Kiffar, who strolled deeper into the estate. "Mistress Moten will be with you shortly."

"Mistress?" Phee said.

Tech picked up on Phee's skepticism. The honorific was yet another thing that didn't match the client's description as Tech had interpreted it, but there hadn't been much to go on after Ven Alman's initial referral.

They all followed the Kiffar, with his two armed friends tailing them.

The next room was even more spacious than the first, big enough to muster an entire clone platoon. Larger tables occupied the room's center, displaying more impressive scale models of buildings they didn't recognize. Illuminated placards on the edge of the tables identified the worlds on which these structures could presumably be found. Kuat. Berchest. Naboo.

As spectacular as the structures were, they were not what drew the eye or ear.

A short holovid broadcast from hidden projectors high up on both sides of the room, its display running on a loop. They entered in the middle of the recording, catching what seemed like a concluding slogan before the loop restarted.

A pale woman's visage, her red hair pulled away from a tastefully painted face and a top-credit smile, synced with a bold announcer's voice that claimed, "Moten Industries. Good. For the galaxy!"

The holo restarted with swooping bird's-eye views of sprawling structures. Factories. Cityscapes. Medcenters and more. The announcer's spiel ran the whole time.

"Moten Industries has built a track record of trust . . ." The holo cut to faces of diverse species, each flashing a smile at the lens as if greeting a long-lost friend. "Homes. Jobs. Legacies. In trying times, we've been a steady foundation for you . . ."

Phee leaned in to Tech and whispered, "What is this?"

"Your client, I presume."

Tech looked to the lead Kiffar guard. He seemed slightly embarrassed by the odd propaganda. He cleared his throat and motioned them along.

They left the holos behind and entered yet another lengthy room that made the place feel more like a museum than a home. The models in here were grand but less luxurious. They were industrial facilities, weapons factories—some of that foundational hope the holo had boasted about.

While much of the story Phee had been fed about their Caridan host was likely false, the truth of her stature as a developer tracked. What a power broker to be this tapped into the wealth *and* weapons of the galaxy.

While Phee and Tech were taken by the model displays, Omega's attention drifted east. This room differed from the others they'd traversed in that it offered floor-to-ceiling views, showcasing the estate's exterior and beyond, where the ocean met the horizon.

Adjacent to the exterior patio was a stable, its doors open wide, with busy handlers feeding, washing, and brushing the coats of majestic-looking fathiers inside.

"They're gorgeous," Omega said.

She wasn't wrong.

The quadrupeds' casual movements revealed ropy, healthy muscle even at a distance. The shine of their fur suggested pristine grooming. Whoever lived here cared as much for those animals as they did for their construction accomplishments across many worlds. Tech factored this deduction in as he calculated today's probable outcome.

They left that final grand room, turned a corner, traversed yet another lengthy corridor, and eventually arrived at a small door that whooshed aside, revealing the first modest space they'd encountered since arriving. It was an office with seating for three before a large desk. On the other side, a high-backed polyethylene chair.

"Sit." The Kiffar insisted. "She'll be along shortly."

The other two guards stood with their arms loose and fingers flexed. Their weapons remained holstered, but their posture suggested those circumstances could change at a moment's notice.

Tech sat down first. Omega, then Phee, followed suit.

The Kiffar nodded, satisfied, and backed from the room. Sealing them in.

Phee said, "Should we watch our words in here?"

"I don't know that it much matters now," said Tech. "I assume Mistress Moten is listening and likely knows we recognize the deception here. She is more than a modest builder and likely *not* Caridan. Escorting us so casually through the premises suggests maintaining the ruse that brought us here is no longer a priority."

Phee's neck craned, scanning the room for potential dangers and advantages. "Incredible. Hunter's never going to let me hear the end of this."

Tech asked, "Have you ever mentioned to your contact where the supplies we're trading for were meant to go?"

"No," Phee said.

"Good," said Tech. "It may be best to keep *that* to ourselves."

Omega, sharp as always, said, "Is this a trap?"

"Based on confiscating our weapons, the heavy presence of nervous guards, and the client's lies about their wealth and identity, I'd calculate the likelihood of this being a trap at ninety-two percent. I want to deduce more, though. So play along for now."

Hunter lay prone in the grass, panning over the estate with his macrobinoculars. No changes on the exterior. All the guards maintained their previous relaxed postures. A good sign. Still . . .

"You got anything?" he asked.

Wrecker continued working the receiver array. "Only chatter from the city. I'm on the local law enforcement channels, and all seems—"

Hunter lowered the macrobinoculars and twisted toward Wrecker. "Seems what?"

Wrecker double-tapped the side of his helmet, signaling Hunter to patch in.

Touching the control on his earpiece, Hunter patched into the back-and-forth of the local law's dispatch.

". . . repeat description of fugitives. I say, repeat description of fugitives. Over."

Hunter's stomach plummeted. He should've known the auction heist would catch up with them. He waited for particulars on the entire team to be broadcast but got a different story.

"This is directly from the *Jurat,* an incoming ISB ship. We're broadcasting to your counterparts throughout the city. The pair is wanted for the robbery of the Ronik Casino on Canto Bight. One male, approximately 1.8 meters tall, masked, so no further details there. One female, Keshiri, approximately 1.5 meters tall, with child. Over."

Hunter cursed. This was worse than having the auction heist catch up with them, because at least that's something that made sense. Sohi and Kuuto *robbed a blasted casino*? And they were wanted by the ISB?

"Roger that. We're receiving the official transmission now. We'll put together a team to canvass—"

"Negative. Agent Crane will arrive shortly and instruct your officers on next steps. Please have a few of your best meet him at the spaceport north of your current location. Over."

Hunter cursed again.

He was on his feet, working the problem. The ISB hadn't broken the atmosphere yet. There was still time.

"The deal's done, or it isn't." Hunter pointed at the estate. "Go. Get them."

Wrecker did not have to be told twice. He gathered their equipment while Hunter was already moving down the hill.

"I'm going to get the *Marauder,*" Hunter said, already working through how he'd eject the robbers if they hadn't made a run for it already. "I'll come to you. Hurry."

Wrecker was ready to move but had a question. "Do I have to be quiet?"

Despite how precious time was, that forced Hunter to still. He faced his brother. "Please try."

Hunter was on the move again, already questioning if he should've been more insistent with Wrecker.

Probably.

CHAPTER TWELVE

MOTEN ESTATE, DALLOW

Phee took in the office decor. More precisely, she took inventory of every single cultural item she recognized. Three shelves behind the desk displayed ancient weapons of varying origin. A Gorsh war hatchet. A Lybeyan stippled club. Rodian chain mail. A display in the corner was reserved for jewelry. A Helskan duchess's tiara. A Dorvallan necklace chunky with rough-cut stones. Behind them, more artifacts were mounted on the wall, including the most gruesome item so far—the bejeweled horn of a reek.

But the shelving on the far wall, just beyond Tech, troubled Phee most. It contained religious artifacts from, yet again, a multitude of systems and cultures: totems, icons, and precious stone tableaus. The display was nearly full except for one conspicuously bare spot on the center shelf—a spot just large enough for a newly acquired Holy Husk and Stone mortar.

It was in Phee's satchel, resting between her feet, and she'd already decided that unless the client had an excellent explanation for all the stolen items in her possession, the mortar would remain with Phee. Her gut told her the deal she'd made would not be honored.

The remaining question: What was all this about in the first place?

The office door opened, and a demure woman entered, wearing a scarlet gown with richly embroidered golden stitching. She beamed the same smile from the odd holorecording as if reunited with old friends.

"I'm terribly sorry to keep you waiting," she said, her gaze bouncing from Omega to Tech. Then finally, "You must be Phee Genoa."

"I must," Phee said.

The woman rounded her desk, appearing to glide the way the hem of her gown swept the floor with little sway. She took the high-backed chair, then activated a terminal that washed her face in its light. They couldn't see the display, but it seemed to please her.

She said, "I'm looking over the materials list we agreed upon. I was able to pull together everything you requested. Interesting specifications. Are you building waterfront property?"

Phee wasn't going to answer that question. Thankfully, Tech deflected with one of his own: "Who, exactly, are you?"

The woman's grin curled in one corner, flirting with malice. She fixed her face and feigned shame. "I'm so sorry. I haven't introduced myself. This old mind gets away from me sometimes."

Phee didn't believe that one bit.

"I'm Cellia Moten," the woman finally said. Despite the deceptions that brought them here, this much felt true.

Tech said, "I don't suppose you grew up on Carida?"

Cellia laughed. Fake and forced. "Oh no, I can imagine your confusion. I told your friend Ven Alman what a hoot this would be when we all sat down and clarified things."

"Ven's here, then?" Phee asked.

"He's on the grounds."

This . . . also felt true. Yet it chilled Phee for reasons she couldn't explain. The answer was right in front of her eyes.

Cellia flicked her hand dismissively, the charms on her bracelets tinkling like wind chimes. "No worries, we'll go meet him soon. First, the business at hand. Do you have the mortar?"

Phee said, "We do."

Cellia's eyes twinkled. "I heard you had some trouble at the auction. Surprising because I was assured a stealthy acquisition was possible."

"It was possible until it wasn't. Why do you want it? Being that you're not Caridan."

"I guess you can tell I'm a collector of ... precious things. Some might say I collect gods. Or, at least, their iconography." She gestured to some of the artifacts displayed throughout the room. "I don't believe any of the religious nonsense myself, but I've found over the years that imaginary deities can grant control over very real beings. It's admirable, useful, and, sometimes"—she chuckled, and it sounded like tiny blades chopping wood—"amusing."

Phee was far from amused. She glanced to Tech, certain he wasn't, either.

Tech remained quiet. The data scrolling on his lenses moved quickly. There were extensive public files on this Cellia Moten. A wealthy developer from a long line of rich developers. Her family's name was stamped on ancient and contemporary structures throughout the galaxy. Her wealth was in the billions. And her capacity for cruelty in her business dealings rated on a comparable scale.

Many files keyed on her rumored duplicity. She was known for shorting business partners on agreed-upon fees for completed jobs. Firing loyal workers for minor mistakes. Even rumors of kidnapping and murder. None of the offenses made it beyond allegations, though.

Any effort to hold Cellia accountable under the laws of the accusatory planetary systems met a swift and quiet end. The partners that she never shorted were her legal advocates in the galaxy's various courts. There was no defense like an expensive one, paid in full. All the data implied Cellia Moten had friends in high places.

Omega interrupted the long-winded woman. "Why pretend to be someone you aren't?"

"Child, the truth is I despise lying. There's nothing more pitiful than having to hide one's truest self. However, I have grand aims that require discretion, often putting me at odds with my most private desires. In the case of this mortar, I've been watching it change hands for some time. I could've attended the auction and gone about acquiring it personally, but I cannot be seen with attendees of such disrepute these days. They're notorious!"

As are you, Tech thought.

If Hunter were here, his brother would be pointing out the clear danger they were in. Hunter would have made them all aware that no one ever revealed this much of their hand if they intended to leave . . . witnesses.

Cellia Moten planned to kill them.

Operating on that assumption, Tech might as well get as much information as possible while this predator toyed with them. "Why would you not want to be seen with those who share a similar station in life as yourself? Were the auction attendees not your colleagues and peers?"

Cellia huffed. "Colleagues and peers? Hardly. We've done business together. We vacation in the same systems. Their ambitions are paltry compared to mine. I'm going to save the galaxy."

"Is that so?" Tech leaned in, overtly curious. He discreetly unspooled a thin auxiliary cable from his computer and plugged it into a spare interface socket beneath the desktop. Cellia was so busy hearing herself speak that she didn't notice.

"What part of the galaxy do you call home?" Cellia asked, impatiently fishing for information again. She steepled her fingers and grinned slightly as if enjoying a private joke. Her bracelets bunched on her wrist.

Phee stared at the jewelry, her eyes narrowed, recognition dawning. "I never much bought into the idea of invisible gods watching us and guiding us, but there are times when I wish I found that sort of thing comforting. I sometimes talk to Ven about that. He is a scoundrel's scoundrel in many ways, but he has a spiritual side he'll rattle on about for hours if you let him." Phee twisted in her chair, eyeing the door. "Bring him in here and see if he doesn't try to convince you of a higher power."

Cellia's eyes twinkled. "I'm afraid I can't. But you already know that, don't you?"

"Was he alive when you took that bracelet from him?" Phee asked.

Tech understood what had caught Phee's attention, and Omega tensed.

Cellia didn't hesitate. "No."

"Did he suffer?" Phee asked.

"Not in the extreme," Cellia said. "We had to get his encryption protocols out of him, or else you and I wouldn't have become acquainted. After, it was quick. I take no pleasure in prolonging the end."

"Just the deception. It's a game to you."

"Who doesn't like a good tease?" Cellia stood, relaxed, matter-of-fact. "To that point, I suppose our game is over now. As usual, I have won. My prize will be the coordinates, system, planet, and province you acted on behalf of. The builder in me loves new prospects, so the quicker you provide that information, the more merciful I'll be. Whenever you're ready."

The office door slid open. The guards from earlier crowded the threshold, weapons drawn.

Whatever mysteries surrounded gods and the afterlife, Cellia Moten seemed intent on solving them for Tech, Phee, and Omega sooner than later.

CHAPTER THIRTEEN

EN ROUTE TO SPACEPORT, DALLOW

Hunter darted through the tree line as quickly as he dared. The forest floor was dense with a century's worth of foliage and fallen debris, and a careless step at this speed could break an ankle. So he maneuvered fast but carefully, a little under one klick from the spaceport now.

Above, Imperial engines hummed in the distance. The hum would soon be a drone, then a roar as those ships passed overhead, threatening to beat him to his destination. Hunter sped up, knowing that a broken bone would be the least of his troubles if he didn't reach the *Marauder* fast.

A road was ahead. The quickest route meant following it straight to the spaceport, but more engines sounded. Speeders.

Crik! Hunter thought, ducking into the brush.

They bore the markings of local law enforcement and passed while he watched from cover.

Well, this is all going from decs to dung.

When the speeders vanished around the bend, he crossed the road and dipped into the dense forest, activating his comms device on the run.

"Mel, prep the *Marauder* for a quick dust-off. We've got company incoming. Over."

He awaited confirmation.

It didn't come.

"Mel! Answer me!"

Still no reply.

Ducking a low-hanging branch, then vaulting a downed tree trunk, he switched channels to broadcast throughout the *Marauder*.

"Sohi, Kuuto, or whatever your names are! Since Mel isn't answering, I guess you know trouble's coming. Maybe you've already abandoned us. Just know that if you have harmed Mel or damaged our ship in any way, it won't just be the ISB after you."

He left the channel open, not expecting a response.

"The ship is prepped and ready." Sohi's voice crackled. "You need to hurry. We won't wait for long."

The channel went dead.

Hunter didn't know who or what he was rushing toward, but hurry he did.

Cellia Moten's henchmen ordered Tech, Phee, and Omega to their feet with insistent gestures of their rifle barrels. The trio complied. Phee lifted her satchel in a two-hand grip, the heavy mortar sagging the material. Her rage was evident, painting her as the biggest threat in the room, drawing the most attention. Tech stood with his hands low behind his back, still plugged into Cellia's terminal, slicing. Omega kept her hands raised and fingers splayed while making a discreet sidestep closer to Cellia's weapons collection.

"Retrieve my artifact, Parlin," Cellia said.

The Kiffar extended a hand while angling his heavy rifle toward the ceiling. "To me. Now."

"I don't think so, big guy."

The Kiffar's posture stiffened, and his partners keyed on Phee's defiance, drawing closer to match her aggression. With the guards' attention elsewhere, Tech explored a virtual playground of exploits in the estate's various systems, all scrolling along his display. Omega noticed him working and slid even closer to Cellia's deadly artifacts.

Parlin leveled his rifle at Phee. "I'm going to shoot you—"

"In the leg," Cellia said, insisting. "I still want those coordinates."

Parlin angled the rifle lower. "I'm going to shoot you *in the leg* if you don't hand over that bag right now."

Phee flicked a glance Tech's way. He uploaded code that might prove useful if they survived the next few moments. However, no systems offered any promising solutions to the current state of affairs, either in the form of intervention or distraction. Suddenly cutting the lights would do nothing . . . there were windows and it was daytime. Making the office door open unexpectedly might draw some attention, but it was just as likely to startle Parlin into firing on Phee.

Tech unplugged, abandoning the technology route, and considered disarming the Nikto guard, but he'd be open to a counterattack from the droid. If he opted to attack the droid . . . the Nikto would have him sighted instantly.

Parlin's finger slipped onto his trigger, negotiations done. "It didn't have to be this way."

There was a whisper of something quickly parting the air, then a harsh *thunk!* The droid stumbled and dropped its weapon. Sparks erupted from its split skull, where an antique war hatchet was now embedded.

It lurched one step, collapsed to one knee, then toppled sideways. All eyes fell upon the defeated droid, then swept in the direction where the hurled hatchet originated.

Omega panted, hunched, her arms dangling low in the follow-through of her spot-on hatchet throw. She looked to Tech, somewhat annoyed. "You were taking too long."

Oh, Omega, Tech thought as he launched himself at the Nikto. Ducking beneath the barrel of its rifle, he grabbed its wrist and launched a devastating elbow into the nerve cluster in its armpit. The Nikto said, "*Oof,*" and its arm hung numbly. Tech confiscated the rifle and stepped back to fire two rounds into its chest.

With its body on the ground, still and smoldering, Tech turned the weapon in Parlin's general direction, but . . . there was no clear shot because Parlin held Phee by the throat, her body shielding his.

Though not for long.

She still had a two-hand grip on her satchel's strap, and she swung it up and over her shoulder, crunching the Kiffar's nose. Blood spurted as he released her and stumbled away.

"Are you mad?" Cellia bellowed. "That mortar is one of a kind!"

"It's survived centuries," Phee said. "I figure it's pretty sturdy."

Parlin pressed his hand to his bleeding nose while Tech sighted him with the rifle. The Kiffar kept his wits and launched himself behind Cellia's desk. Two smoking holes appeared in the wall behind where he'd been standing.

He scrambled, wrapped up Cellia in his arms, putting himself between her and Tech's line of fire. He pressed a button on her desk that made many things happen at once.

A secret door opened in the shelves behind Cellia, through which Parlin propelled them both before the escape passage sealed again. Alarms blared.

A flawlessly executed double cross and quiet triple murder wouldn't have required any backup. Now all of the dozen armed guards Tech had counted—and those were just the ones he saw—were on the way to finish what Cellia Moten started.

Tech met Omega's gaze, and even she looked worried—a bad sign.

Then his eyes locked with Phee's. While what had happened over the last couple of days hadn't diminished his growing affection for her, he was coming around to Hunter's way of thinking when it came to their working relationship.

No more jobs from Phee.

CHAPTER FOURTEEN

SPACEPORT, DALLOW

Plastoid and durasteel fencing rimmed the spaceport perimeter. Easily scalable. Hunter made the climb quickly, dropped silently into a cloud of baradium nitrate fumes wafting from a nearby fuel pump, and worked his way toward the *Marauder*, utilizing shipping containers, maintenance equipment, and other vehicles for concealment.

The *Marauder* was parked at a central landing pad surrounded by dozens of other high-end vessels, likely belonging to the facility's long-term local patrons. When he was within three rows of the *Marauder*, Hunter's awareness and anxiety ratcheted up. A convenient gap between the vessels and containers provided a clear view of the welcome lounge. The local authorities had beaten him there, as he knew they would.

A small contingent of five officers loafed near the entrance, where a superior casually conversed with a spaceport employee. Their postures suggested confusion and impatience. Good. The Imperial drop ships were still en route and apparently taking their sweet time. That meant no ISB enforcers had stormed in to take charge and lock down the facility yet.

Hunter kept moving into the next row, and from this angle, the twin points of the *Marauder*'s raised wingtips were visible. Whatever so-called Sohi and Kuuto had done on board, at least this part of her ominous response had held. They'd waited.

Hunter slinked into the row adjacent to his ship. Almost home.

Several rows over, an incoming luxury transport made its landing guided by ground crew droids. Hunter assessed a small window to get the *Marauder* airborne.

He moved through the deep shadows beneath a neighboring vessel, nearly invisible. The current unrestricted air traffic would mask the noise from firing the engines, and he'd be in the clouds before the local cops could scramble anything that stood a chance of taking the ship down. Then it'd be a matter of getting to that estate and picking up—

He felt *something*.

It was small—at first—a sharp tickle at the base of his skull, a brief premonition of charged air not dissimilar to the electric roots he sensed forking through the various layers of Pabu whenever he was on the island. Those he'd learned to ignore. This . . . he was glad he hadn't.

The sensation multiplied. Not *one* sharp, bordering-painful tickle, but several. Pinpricks of energy charging, overloading, all around him.

Instinct hurled Hunter backward as the tiny, barely visible jolt disks activated, sparking an electric net he'd barely avoided, making his shadowy path as bright as day for an instant. The trap snapped out of existence as quickly as it'd come, but the same could not be said about the peril that had revealed itself.

The ISB *was* here.

One of them, anyway.

On the other side of the trap, from behind the cover of a tall cargo stack, emerged a being that Hunter discerned in sections as he did when trying to identify weak points. Polished black boots. Pleated black pants. Pristine white tunic. The signature mix of red and blue bars on the chest.

The ISB agent was human and pale, though his eyes seemed to glow the same electric blue as his failed trap. The being faced Hunter, squinting for a better look at him in the gloom, and said, "Unlawful breach of an Imperial transit hub. Trespassing in unauthorized areas. Unlawful possession of a weapon in a secure area. My, how these violations multiply. Judging from the condition of the armor you're wearing, you've either stolen Imperial property, or you're a longtime deserter still prosecutable under the Imperial Formation Post-War Articles."

While segments of his scuffed armor were visible, Hunter's face remained shadowed. Something in him itched to retrieve his helmet from the clip on his belt, but caution superseded any careless movements. After all, he and the officer were sizing each other up.

The officer's movements were slow but measured and fearless . . . concerning since his trap confirmed he anticipated hostility. In the face of potential danger, that kind of calm suggested someone unshaken by probable violence, either as initiator or target. Hunter recognized a fellow warrior, even if the uniform differed.

The ISB agent said, "Your legal situation is dire. I may be of some help to you if you are a help to me. Please consider your options carefully as I broach my next question."

A warrior, yes, but he spoke with an oddly mechanical grasp of Basic that was characteristic of some protocol droids. Overly polite. Somewhat mocking.

"Is she on your ship?" the officer asked.

Hunter glanced over the agent's shoulder at the *Marauder* and guessed Sohi would've tried initiating a jump to hyperspace directly from the launchpad if she'd heard this being asking about her in this manner. Given the quiet menace radiating from the agent and his undertone that suggested a reward for confirmation or a punishment for a lie, Hunter might've understood if she had.

What is happening here? was one of many questions Hunter promised himself he'd pose to Sohi, either calmly or violently, depending on how the rest of the day went. The jolt trap was no longer a threat—now that Hunter had ascertained the nature of the small emitters, he knew they were a one-time deal. Yet somehow, this agent standing between him and his ship was the more considerable danger.

Hunter knew they were alone, but why? Why wasn't he surrounded by the local police, other bureau agents, or troopers commandeered into an impromptu quick-response team—a tactic the ISB was known to employ?

"Where's your backup?" Hunter asked.

"If you're cooperating, there's no need for all that. Will you cooperate?"

Hunter said nothing.

"You're observant," the agent said, breaking the silence. "I've ordered my team to maintain a low orbit. I wanted to assess the situation without bureaucratic oversight. I want discretion for the moment. There's no crime against that."

Hunter pressed. "You're looking for Sohi."

"Is that what she's calling herself now?"

The agent hadn't mentioned anyone else. Was he unaware of Kuuto?

The agent drew closer as if to join Hunter in the shadows, an intent that had Hunter's fingers grazing the hilt of the vibroknife behind his back. The truth was Hunter could end this right now if he wanted to, but he still didn't know what he'd be walking into if Sohi and Kuuto were indeed still on the ship. This agent was his only source of potentially actionable intel.

Hunter said, "If you want discretion, then this is personal. Who is she to you?"

The agent got closer to Hunter, his face still, contemplative. "I didn't think I'd ever say this to anyone but her, but since you were kind enough to ask—she's family."

The agent's hand twitched oddly.

Hunter's conscious mind didn't process the attack, but his soldier's reflexes allowed him to shift his weight in time to avoid having his throat slit. The micron-thick edge of the agent's blade sliced the air millimeters from Hunter's neck. He regretted not going for the helmet earlier.

No time to dwell.

Hunter's humming vibroknife was free of its sheath and on guard. As the agent went for a diagonal slice across Hunter's chest, their blades met. The agent's knife was longer than Hunter's by a third. Forged from strong metal meant for fighting. The same might be said of the agent himself.

Hunter grabbed his wrist, redirecting the blade and attempting to disarm him, but the agent moved with Hunter, freeing himself with a cart-wheel that spun him just out of Hunter's reach. As the agent cycloned away to create more distance, his hands slipped into his tunic, quickly sheathing his original blade and returning with a couple of throwing spikes he launched at Hunter.

Hunter deflected one projectile, but the other struck true, wedging in his armor's thigh guard. It didn't penetrate fully, but the tip touched flesh, a minor puncture that stung.

Darting sideways, making himself a moving target, Hunter snatched the throwing knife from his armor and returned it to its sender. The agent dodged, reaching into his tunic again.

His hands emerged with a fresh pair of throwing spikes, but he didn't launch them. Hunter, in evading the attacks, had moved into the light, fully visible. Recognition sparked on the agent's face.

"Face tattoo. Wiry build. Skilled with a bladed weapon. You're CT-9901. The one they call Hunter. Part of Clone Force Ninety-Nine. I thought your lot died on Kamino." He straightened and beamed. "Oh, Gayla, what have you gotten yourself into this time?"

Gayla? Sohi's real name? Perhaps.

Hunter's jaw clenched—enough of this.

He snatched his rifle off his back and fired three times. The agent dived behind a shipping container, still whole. He called out from behind the obstruction. "So much for keeping this between us."

Through the gaps between ships and cargo, Hunter spotted the local law on the run, alerted by rifle fire, set to block his path to the *Marauder*. He ran for cover, dived behind more crates, and prepared for a fight he might have no hope of winning. Thus proving his intuition accurate again.

The agent palmed a comlink and shouted, "Converge on my position. I have an assailant cornered."

No easy days, Hunter thought, ducking behind cargo and tugging on his helmet as his cover got perforated by blaster bolts. *Not ever.*

CHAPTER FIFTEEN

MOTEN ESTATE, DALLOW

"How long we got?" Phee said, cinching her satchel strap over her shoulder. The alarms continued blaring. Surely, every one of Celia's armed loyalists would converge on them in seconds.

"Not long enough." Tech hunched over the droid that Omega had defeated, flipping its body so he could reach the sack it carried. He undid the rope tying the bag's opening and was pleased to deliver some good news. "Our weapons."

He tossed Omega her bow, returned Phee's blasters, and claimed his gear, the whole time thinking, thinking, thinking . . .

"Hunter and Wrecker would've seen the exterior guards scrambling, so backup is on the way. We need to survive until—"

Omega fired an energy bolt at—no, *through*—Cellia's office door. A droid squawked incoherent static on the other side, then thudded to the floor.

"I heard his footsteps," Omega said. "He was eavesdropping. That's impolite."

"Indeed it is, kid," Phee said, firing two more shots through the door. No droids shrieked in response, so she shrugged. "Just following your lead."

Omega beamed.

Tech moved to the door, his blaster ready. "Now follow mine. It's going to be a fight."

"When has it been anything different?" Omega asked.

Tech opened the door. They each fanned through the threshold in different directions as a squad of Cellia's guards fired and missed.

So far, so good.

They pushed forward through a hail of blasterfire.

The spaceport police stacked up in precise, tactical formations—four pairs of two. None of the oafish, casual demeanor that Hunter had observed before. They weren't military, but that didn't matter much when it was eight versus one.

Hunter peeked over the lip of his crate and watched the ISB agent—whose uniform was somehow still obscenely white—direct the authorities with sharp hand gestures. Two pairs were moving from cover to cover on his left and right, flanking Hunter. The ISB agent shouted, "Drop your weapon and come out with your hands up!"

Well, that wasn't happening.

The agent issued orders to the authorities on the ground and through his comms device. "This is a capture mission. I want him alive."

If there was good news here, it was that they weren't trying to kill him. The least he could do was return the favor.

He popped up and put a bolt in each knee of the point man on his left. He went down screaming. Hunter caught his partner in the shoulder, spinning him and sending his weapon skittering across the tarmac.

Stun rings struck high over Hunter's head. These cops moved well, but their aim left something to be desired. Not that Hunter was complaining. Feeling somewhat sorry for them, though, he toggled his rifle to stun before returning fire. Two more went down.

The rest maintained distance and fired from cover, pinning Hunter in place. They didn't have to advance—probably recognized that tactic wasn't in their favor. Backup was coming. Eight against one might not have been insurmountable under the right circumstances, but what about fifteen or twenty to one? And the reinforcements weren't just local police . . . they were actual soldiers, co-opted by the ISB as it was known to do when in need of "enforcers." If he was captured, he'd become bait to snare Wrecker, Tech, and Omega. Because his team would risk everything to rescue him, as he would if the roles were reversed. Hunter couldn't bear the thought of being a liability to his family. A risk to himself was more than acceptable. One for the others he would not allow.

Funny, he thought he finally understood Phee's point about the burdens he carried unbidden.

Hunter had a single thermal detonator on him. He could lob it at his enemies to create a momentary distraction. They'd scramble, and one or two might get caught in the blast radius and take some shrapnel. The detonators were notoriously imprecise weapons, though. Not enough to give him a path to the *Marauder*. There was another way to use the detonator if the situation became unassailable. Plan 99.

The plan was crafted before their first mission: If something went wrong, one of them would make the ultimate sacrifice so the others might fight on. Somehow, someway, it had yet to come to that, but Hunter never felt encouraged by his team's long, unbroken streak of improbable wins. He felt the weight of an unseen countdown, where you heard the chronometer ticking but couldn't see its face.

More blasts struck his cover, sending vibrations through his body. Unless something changed, he'd have to decide quickly. His fingertips grazed the detonator's trigger, but as he peeked around his remaining cover he detected movement beyond his attackers, at the *Marauder*.

The loading ramp lowered.

Hunter's fingers retracted from the detonator. Because of the continuous air traffic and semi-deafening blasterfire, none of the cops noticed the ramp bump the tarmac, fully extended. Nor did they see Kuuto lumber down the ramp, the muscles in his organic leg quivering from the heavy load he carried.

The ISB agent, the most intuitive of the bunch, turned, saw, and his eyes bulged.

"Down! Down! Down!" he shouted while on the move, getting far away from the Dallow authorities who were most likely to draw fire.

Kuuto wielded, with great effort, the DC-17m blaster rifle, Wrecker's biggest, most destructive gun. The monstrosity looked more suited for the hull of a battleship than for wielding by hand, and it let loose a streak of blaster bolts so furious it seemed like a solid laser beam, scarring the air in a sweeping blur.

Dallow officers fled, dived, and cowered while the rounds shredded the ground, storage crates, and other ships. As chaos erupted, the *Marauder*'s engines flared on.

Debris and dust created a dense fog. Hunter recognized what Kuuto had done, the chance he'd provided, and sprinted the clear path to the ship, bounding up the ramp on Kuuto's safe side away from the barrel of the DC-17. As he passed, he clapped a hand on Kuuto's shoulder, a silent signal that they could both retreat. Kuuto reacted instantly, maneuvering backward while maintaining a steady stream of cover fire until the ramp was completely sealed.

Hunter thought, *Good job, soldier*—both a compliment and a deduction.

Then he was on his way to the cockpit to take control of the *Marauder*—from Sohi, because who else could be piloting? On his way, he came upon a dormant MEL-222, noticing the restraining bolt affixed to her frame—the reason she hadn't answered his distress call. He knocked the bolt off, and MEL-222 twitched into consciousness.

The cockpit door was open, and the back of Sohi's head was visible in the pilot's seat. Hunter thought about snatching her up and away from the controls but reconsidered as blasterfire from the recovered Dallow officers pinged off the hull. Surely, those ISB enforcers were on the way.

"Can you fly this ship?" Hunter asked.

Sohi pulled back on the throttle. "Buckle up and find out."

Hunter leaped into the copilot's seat and strapped in while Kuuto secured himself in the navigator's chair.

The *Marauder* lurched up, wings unfurling, off-kilter but rising. Sohi wrestled the controls at first but adjusted quickly. It was a stomach-dropping ascent; they always were when you flew out of a combat zone. Either Sohi was a piloting prodigy, or she'd done this before.

A good pilot. A good soldier. So-so thieves, but they hadn't been caught yet, so they weren't horrible at that, either.

Who exactly were these two?

Hunter could save that for later. "We need to go get my team."

"I figured," said Sohi.

She performed a swift 180-degree turn with the *Marauder*'s nose tipped down. That angle gave them a view of the menacing ISB agent, who stood upright, defiant, staring. It was as if he could perform a mighty leap to propel his body through the *Marauder* like a torpedo, ending this whole fiasco in even more rapid violence.

Sohi spoke under her breath. "Not today, Crane."

The *Marauder*'s nose angled skyward, and they were blasting away from the spaceport, just as Hunter spotted a *Gonzati*-class cruiser descend from the clouds.

It was fine. That lumbering thing wasn't a match for the *Marauder*.

As if to answer Hunter's silent boast, a trio of V-wings, sleek, speedy, and armed to the teeth, swarmed from the cruiser's belly in fast pursuit.

CHAPTER SIXTEEN

MOTEN ESTATE, DALLOW

A model of a fifty-story ultraluxe residential building on Vardos caught a stray blaster bolt and disintegrated, showering a crouched Phee with its dust. She coughed and rasped, "I will take any idea from that big brain of yours, Brown Eyes."

Tech and Omega knelt together behind the model of a hyperspace engine factory. Omega leaned sideways periodically to shoot her energy bow in a stalemate of suppressing fire that would soon see the trio lose their meager advantage. More guards were coming.

Tech peeked at the next big display table that marked the room's center. Another gargantuan model sat on top—one of Cellia's monuments to herself. But the table also featured a projector broadcasting the insufferable holovid they'd caught on the way in. More interesting than the projector or its feed was the scomp access port on the terminal controlling the media.

"Omega!" Tech motioned that way.

Omega saw and understood immediately. "I'll cover you."

She did, showing off near mastery of the close-quarters combat training drilled into her by Hunter. While her energy bolts forced their attackers to take cover, Tech advanced to the terminal and plugged in.

Tech combed through the system code until he came upon the function he sought: the comms jammer.

He said, "I'm deactivating the signal scrambler so we can communicate with Hunter and Wrecker."

"Excellent," Phee said, extending her blaster to fire at their attackers. "Tell them to hurry up."

An incoming bolt struck the metallic table Phee was using for cover, ricocheted high, and brought a crystalline chandelier crashing into the model of a Corellian castle. The collision echoed inside the vast hall, a nearly deafening racket when mixed with the nonstop rifle fire.

Tech began the distress call. "Hunter, Wrecker, come in. We're taking heavy fire inside the estate house. Over."

There was no immediate response, and the door at the far end of the hall opened, revealing a quartet of incoming battle droids.

That end of the room was crowded with assailants, forcing the droids to bottleneck in the doorway. Tech navigated more estate systems. He turned off the safeguards on automated doors. Two made it through unscathed, but the third was chopped in half by the rapidly shutting durasteel plate. Its torso, still holding its rifle, slid across the floor, a finger involuntarily squeezing the trigger, and the force of its shots sent it into a death spin. Blaster bolts hit three of its fellow estate guards, taking them out of the fight.

Sometimes fortune smiles on us, Tech thought.

Inspired by Tech's environmental intervention, Phee stopped blind firing and targeted a wall-mounted statue five meters off the ground. It was the visage of a Wookiee warrior wielding a massive war hammer. Antique, most likely pillaged. Phee hated damaging it, but desperate times.

She shot the statue's arm, severing its grip on the hammer. The meant-to-be-decorative weapon fell on a gray-skinned Aqualish guard, crushing him.

Effective, but also motivating. The contingent of guards saw the error in waiting for increased numbers when they were already the larger force. They moved up, willingly taking sporadic hits from Omega's bow and Phee's blaster while Tech continued the urgent distress call.

"Hunter! Wrecker! I do hope you're comms silent because you're stealthily flanking the guards attempting to murder us. Over." The bleak truth was he wasn't confident there'd be a response, and it could've been for any number of reasons—including Hunter and Wrecker already being captured or killed. He wouldn't allow himself to believe that, though. Even if the odds weren't with them—this would not be how Clone Force 99 went down.

The comm crackled with Wrecker's voice. "Sounds like you're having a good time in there."

"We have vastly different interpretations of the word *good*," Tech responded.

"Are you standing by the eastern wall, approximately seventy-five meters from the main entrance?"

Tech did an instant assessment. "No."

The ear-piercing barrage of blasterfire was immediately swallowed by the even louder sound of the eastern wall blowing inward with concussive force. A few estate guards had been standing in the wrong position and were obliterated by the debris.

In the resulting swirl of smoke, Wrecker stepped through the newly created exit, firing his rifle with gleeful laughter.

"Hunter told me to be quiet," he shouted to Tech, "but everyone else was loud, so I gave up."

Tech unplugged and popped from behind cover, then dragged Omega by the arm, covering Phee as she moved. He said, "I'm glad you did, Wrecker. Let's get out of here."

Intermittent streaks of deadly blasterfire volleyed back and forth as Tech and company took Wrecker's new door to the estate's exterior. Dusk was settling in, but the end of the day did not inspire Cellia's guards to take a breather. Tech and company would have to make a run for it.

"The stables!" Omega shouted. It was as good a suggestion as any.

It was a hundred meters or so through a topiary of immaculate beasts shaped from lush hedges—rancors, acklays, dianogas—broken up by looming bronzium statues of figures who must've been of massive importance to Cellia. In some cases, the effigies were ten meters high. The statues gripped golden chains running to thorny collars cinched around the hedge creatures' necks. The cruelty incorporated into Cellia's decor was unmatched. Whoever the hedge animal masters were, their bases offered suitable cover.

Crouched, Wrecker armed two thermal detonators and lobbed them toward their pursuers. The resulting explosion hurled bodies and kept the big guy grinning.

"I know you're having a great time," Phee told him, "but we've already overstayed our welcome at this party."

"I concur." Tech kept moving.

Omega sprinted past him into the stable entrance, where a trio of petite Ugnaught servants cowered in the corner, clutching the brushes they'd been grooming the fathiers with. The beasts were aggravated, whinnying with fright and rearing up inside their stalls.

Wrecker brought up the rear and sealed the stable entrance before putting a bolt into the lock panel. Heavy fire kept buffeting the door. "Now what?"

"I have an idea!" Omega piped.

Tech, Phee, and Wrecker spoke in unison. "Free the animals?"

Omega's cheeks reddened. "I have more ideas. But, yes, that's my preferred one."

Tech was already in the stable systems, working. "As you wish."

The flickering blue energy fields keeping the fathiers in their stalls crackled off, and the glossy-coated beasts ventured into the center aisle, cautious at first, then with something like eagerness as they gathered at the stable's far door, away from the increasing blasterfire. The creatures exchanged looks with each other, seeming to communicate in ways they surely understood, even if Tech didn't.

Omega, sensitive to such things, would've said the creatures were expressing hope. Oh, what must they have endured in this awful place?

Tech spoke to Wrecker. "Can you get Hunter on comms?"

"Raising him now."

Before Wrecker could make the call, a high whine keened through their receivers, then morphed into Hunter's welcome voice: "Team, we're on the way."

It should've been a relief, but Tech heard the tension in his brother's voice. "What's wrong?"

"Bad news is we've got a tail."

Tech said, "Is there good news?"

"No. Because we're not going to be able to land."

Phee said, "Well, since we can't fly, that's a problem."

"There's a cliff east of you," Hunter said. That's all he said. Because Tech, Wrecker, and Omega knew what that meant.

Tech took a deep breath. "Plan Eighty-Six-B."

Phee was concerned. "What's Plan Eighty-Six-B?"

"It's an addendum to our emergency escape protocol, Plan Eighty-Six."

"What's the *B* mean?"

No longer jovial, Wrecker said, "A worse emergency escape."

Omega inhaled sharply. "Oh boy."

No time for hesitation. Tech checked his gear. He had what they needed. They just had to reach the cliff quickly.

He asked Omega, "Do you think we can ride these creatures?"

"That's the best question I've heard all day. Saddle up!"

CHAPTER SEVENTEEN

SKIES ABOVE DALLOW

With the V-wings in pursuit, Hunter wondered if he'd sold his team a bill of goods on Plan 86B. They couldn't execute the tricky maneuver if the *Marauder* got shot out of the sky. *A distinct possibility,* thought Hunter as laserfire sizzled by just meters off the hull.

MEL-222 emitted a long, fearful chirp.

Hunter, grim, said, "I'm surprised you're so worried when Phee can rebuild you from a backup file like she always does."

The droid booped, a cheery sound.

"You're not supposed to be *that* happy about it!"

More blasts rattled the hull and Hunter's teeth. Close, but at least it wasn't a direct—

The impact of a spot-on laser knocked the *Marauder* off its course; it felt like getting sucker punched by a god. Its force yanked the controls from Sohi's hands, and Hunter had to grab the copilot's stick to help her rein the *Marauder* in.

Sohi reestablished her grip on the yoke and calmly said, "The rear deflector shield ate that but won't survive another hit. Their ships have agility yours doesn't. I'm going to have to get creative." She yanked the controls left, forcing the *Marauder* into a hard bank that saved their lives as they narrowly avoided more shots.

"And you're going to need help," Hunter said, undoing his harness and exiting the cockpit on the run.

The *Marauder* bounced and listed as Hunter sprinted aft to the gunner's perch behind the ship's double laser cannon. He made it into the seat—was *thrown* into the seat—as Sohi executed a steep diving maneuver to, yet again, keep them alive. The V-wing pilots giving chase did not seem too concerned with apprehending them, and Hunter wondered if that was by order of the agent he'd had that wonderful blade-to-blade conversation with earlier.

The man had called Sohi family. He seemed to want *her,* not want her *dead.*

If the pursuing pilots were insubordinate, Hunter was about to do his best to ensure they never made it back to their superiors to answer for their disobedience. He deactivated the laser cannon safety and proceeded to light up the sky.

Perhaps the pilots had gotten lax in their pursuit since there'd been no offensive resistance until now, a horrible mistake on their parts. Hunter locked onto one of the trio and shredded it with cannon fire. The black smoke explosion forced the other two to list away from flung debris, then reestablish course.

It was a dogfight!

With Hunter returning fire, even his misses forced the pilots out of position for good retaliatory shots. He was skilled enough to keep them off-balance for a bit, but they were already positioning themselves for a dual vectored thrust maneuver meant to split Hunter's attention. They pulled apart far enough to force his attention on one or the other— whatever choice he made would leave him exposed. So Hunter shot into the future. He locked onto empty air and fired where he *anticipated* the left-flank V-wing would position itself. His bet paid off, and the V-wing disintegrated into flame and dust.

As soon as he confirmed the kill, Hunter jerked his crosshairs to his right flank, where the remaining V-wing was scrambling to recover from the failed maneuver and lost wingmate. "Two down, one to go."

Sohi's voice crackled through the comms.

"That's great. Keep him off us for a few more moments," she said. "I'm going to try something."

Hunter didn't like the sound of that.

The remaining pilot got off a shot that didn't make contact. Still, the artillery explosion was close enough to vibrate Hunter's bones and temporarily jam the laser cannon's servos, locking Hunter into a fixed position that had him firing ineffective, easily avoided shots.

"Come on, you bantha-piss rust bucket!" he shouted at the controls as if they could be intimidated the same way as MEL-222, but they were much less responsive to his aggression. The targeting computer started a reboot cycle. The seconds it would take for the system to come back online might get them all killed. The V-wing regained a can't-miss position, lining up a clear shot.

"Whatever you're going to do, now would be nice!" Hunter shouted.

"I'm routing extra power into the rear deflector shield," Sohi said. "I estimate it can take one more significant hit."

"Fine," Hunter said. "Then what?"

Sohi's answer was a sudden ninety-degree ascent that had the *Marauder*'s engines shrieking and Hunter's harness digging painfully into his chest as it fought gravity for possession of his body. This position gave him a view of Dallow's woodland surface pulling away as Sohi climbed. His focus shifted as the V-wing followed their lead, beginning its ascent, its nose pointed directly at Hunter like a taunting finger.

The V-wing fired another torpedo, but Sohi performed a corkscrew maneuver that spun them out of the projectile's path at the last second. The V-wing cut the distance between them and fired another torpedo. Sohi outfoxed that one, too. She wouldn't be able to keep this up for long.

What was she doing? If they took even one hit, they were done. "Sohi!"

"I'm sorry!" she called back.

No! There had to be a way. "Don't you give up on me, *Gayla*!"

He hoped using the name the ISB agent provided would jolt her back into the fight.

"I'm not giving up," she said with a snap. "I'm apologizing for what you're about to experience."

"What in the blazes does *that* mean?"

The *Marauder*'s main engines cut off.

The sudden silence was jarring, but their skyward momentum continued momentarily as the V-wing drew closer. A split second before gravity reclaimed the *Marauder,* a sense of weightlessness gave Hunter a brief reprieve from the viselike pressure of his harness. Then he slammed into his seat as the full weight of the ship began free fall.

Hunter let loose a string of curses as Sohi fired the forward thrusters, transforming the *Marauder* from dropped tonnage to a propelled meteorite.

The V-wing pilot, having given up maneuverable distance for the chance of a close kill, had room to make only one move. He ejected just in time to avoid the battering-ram-like deflector shield on the back end of the *Marauder* colliding with and obliterating the V-wing with flaming force.

The shield protected Hunter from the heat and impact, but his view was of the fireball's guts, and he'd do well never to have that particular experience again. They were still falling, though.

No, not just falling, rocketing toward the ground, thanks to those forward thrusters.

"Hang on!" Sohi yelled.

The *Marauder* spun 180 degrees, so Hunter's view whirled to the sky instead of land. The forward thrusters pointed down now, too weak to cut their speed. They were still on a deadly collision course with the forest.

Hunter's gunner seat listed back and down as Sohi used the *Marauder*'s flaps to angle the nose up. She cut the thrusters and fired the main engine, sending a wicked vibration throughout the ship, making Hunter believe they might tear themselves apart before hitting the ground.

Their descent slowed, then ended, and a couple of jerky maneuvers had them flying straight again, on course for Omega and the rest.

Hunter had seen some amazing things in his time. So much that he'd forgotten many of them. This experience would not be one he'd forget anytime soon. If ever.

"That was some impressive flying." Hunter decided to prod her again, if for no other reason than the absolute horror she'd just put him through, and said, "Gayla."

"If you don't want me to eject you from that gunner's perch, don't call me that again." The seething menace in her voice was unmistakable.

Kuuto nodded approvingly.

She said, "Now, let's go rescue your friends."

CHAPTER EIGHTEEN

MOTEN ESTATE, DALLOW

They could not ride the fathiers. At least not all of them.

Most of the creatures were skittish despite Omega's efforts to soothe and persuade, and there wasn't enough time for intense bonding, with the Moten guards set to burst in any minute.

One beast—the largest (and oldest of the bunch based on the stripe of gray hair running from its crown down the length of its neck)—had a seen-it-all, done-it-all demeanor that spoke to Wrecker. "I like this one!"

The feeling must've been mutual, because the creature didn't buck when Wrecker climbed on its back. "Come on!"

Omega grasped Wrecker's beckoning hand. He swung her up and onto the fathier, placing her in front of him so she could better hug the beast's neck. Wrecker offered his hand to Phee next.

"All of us?" Phee said, wary.

"Fathiers are strong," Omega said like she'd been around them her entire life. "You're strong, aren't you, Lady?"

"It's a girl?" Phee said, hinging at her hip in search of confirmation.

Tech prodded her along. "We don't have much of a choice. She does look very strong, and it'll be a short ride." The door groaned from the stress of repeated blaster barrage. "One way or another."

Phee took Wrecker's hand and yanked herself onto the fathier's back behind him. Tech hopped up, cramming in behind Phee. He gingerly grabbed her waist. She gripped his wrists and tugged him into a tighter embrace. "Gotta lock in for safety, Brown Eyes."

The stable's rear door swooshed up, and the diminishing light of late day poured in. The boldest of the fathiers galloped off, veering either north or south toward tree lines. Omega squeezed their fathier's neck and urged her straight ahead, where the sea and sky met at the horizon. Once you passed the cliff.

Wrecker raised Hunter on comms. "We're moving!"

"En route!" Hunter said.

A few bounding paces beyond the stables and the sound of an explosion and crash caught up with them. They all craned their necks and spotted Cellia Moten's goons rushing into the freshly abandoned building. A couple fired wild blaster bolts that didn't even come close to hitting. Good news.

Bad news: Two guards yanked drop cloths off something Tech and company had missed while formulating their plans.

"Oh no," Phee said on all their behalf.

In the training and corralling of such swift beasts, the staff would want an easy way to catch a runner. So speeders made sense. Their fathier was no slouch, having already put fifty meters between them and the stable. That wasn't far enough to escape the sound of two ignitions firing up.

"How far to that drop?" Wrecker shouted.

An augmented-reality reading appeared on Tech's display. "Two hundred and fifty meters."

The pair of speeders rocketed out of the stable. As strong and determined as their fathier was, she wouldn't outrun them.

She wouldn't have to.

Tech spotted the *Marauder* in the southern sky, its timing nearly impeccable. It seemed to swell in size as it drew near. Their fathier was two hundred meters from the drop now, with the speeders fifty meters off their tail. Cellia Moten's minions rode double, a driver and a shooter. Blaster bolts sizzled the air, close enough for concern.

The *Marauder*'s engines roared, then throttled down as it swung its tail into position off the cliff's edge. The loading ramp lowered, revealing the passenger Kuuto beckoning them on. Hunter was in the rear gunner seat. He lay down bursts of cover fire that exploded dirt and rock, forcing the speeders to detour. The chaos had the unintended side effect of spooking their mount. The fathier skidded to a stop abruptly enough to nearly hurl Omega, Wrecker, Phee, and Tech off. Only Wrecker's incredible strength kept them on the beast, but it was now more of a chair than a ride. The fathier refused to budge. They had a hundred meters to go.

"Come on!" Wrecker ordered, dismounting and taking the entire team with him.

Omega said to the fathier, "It's okay, Lady. You took us as far as you could. Thank you!"

And they ran.

A hundred meters became seventy-five, then fifty, but the run was more dangerous as the speeders established positions to take shots at them. Hunter could cover only one side at a time, leaving them open on the unprotected side. They weren't going to make the last thirty meters at this rate.

Tech reached under his tunic, grabbing for the one thing that might get them out of this. "Wrecker!"

He tossed his hulking brother the tool.

"Got it!" Wrecker said, understanding instantly. Through the comm, he said, "Whoever's piloting, get ready to punch it."

Wrecker aimed at the *Marauder* and fired. The grappling hook shot into the cargo area like a tiny quadanium missile, affixing firmly to the ship's durasteel. The servos in the grappling gun's body drew the cable taut.

Tech said, "Everyone grab Wrecker."

Omega hopped on Wrecker's back first, gripping the grooves in his armor for purchase. Phee did the same. There was no more room on Wrecker's back, so he handled the grappling gun with one hand and grabbed the thick waistband of Tech's trousers with the other.

"Go!" Wrecker shouted.

The *Marauder*'s engines screamed, and they were away, towed beyond the cliff's edge, over the ocean, into the open sky, well out of range of the final volley of blasterfire.

The grappling gun servos worked overtime to pull them into the cargo bay, but they made it, collapsing on the floor, gasping, and recovering from several near-death experiences.

Wrecker returned the grappling gun.

Tech caressed it lovingly. "Hasn't failed me yet."

They broke clouds and then the atmosphere, and then they jumped to hyperspace.

Destination: anywhere but here.

Sohi willingly gave up the pilot seat to Tech, who inspected the controls as if searching for signs of betrayal. The *Marauder* flew beautifully for someone other than him or Omega. He might need time to get over it.

Hunter, though, had more pressing matters on his mind. He tailed Sohi to midship, where she sat on a bench with her neck craned, eyes closed, massaging her belly while executing some controlled breathing.

"Hey!" Hunter said, unconcerned with her needing a breather. They'd almost died because she hadn't been completely upfront with them. "No time for that now. You've got some explaining to—"

Kuuto blindsided him. A full-body tackle that sent Hunter sprawling. He'd let his anger get the best of him and gave the masked man an opening.

Kuuto attempted to flip Hunter onto his stomach and initiate an armlock, but Hunter read the move and countered it. He swept Kuuto's prosthetic leg with his own, bringing him to the ground. He spun to his knees, and as Kuuto attempted to launch a counterattack, Hunter's vibroknife pressed against Kuuto's throat.

Hunter said, "Doesn't seem like I can do much more damage to your vocal cords, but there are plenty more parts to work with. So settle down."

Kuuto's chest heaved and he tensed, perhaps considering unwise options. Wrecker loomed behind him. Tech had left the ship on autopilot and had his blaster leveled toward Kuuto's chest.

Omega, Phee, and MEL-222 were on the sidelines, and though they weren't involved in the standoff, none of them objected.

Sohi, who hadn't opened her eyes, said, "Sit with me. We owe them answers."

Kuuto made the smart decision and did as he was told, joining Sohi on the bench.

Wrecker backed off. Tech holstered his blaster. Hunter slipped his knife into his forearm sheath. For now. "Did you two rob a casino on Canto Bight?"

Sohi opened steely eyes and met his gaze. "Yes."

"And the ISB is after you?"

"That part's new, but apparently."

Phee whistled. "Whoa! And I thought my botched jobs were the worst news of the day."

Hunter ignored Phee and pressed Sohi. "Apparently? That Crane guy sure seems eager to bring you in. More eager than I'd expect an ISB operative to be for some out-of-favor political aide. The bureau protects the Empire from threats to the state. If they consider you dangerous enough to be on their radar, then we need to know why. Talk!"

Sohi's demeanor changed. It was minuscule. Perhaps unnoticeable to everyone but Hunter and Kuuto, whose chin pivoted her way. Her defiance melted and became something he hadn't seen in her before, even when she was piloting the *Marauder* with reckless abandon. Fear.

"How much," she said, swallowing hard, "did Crane tell you?"

"Not enough. Who is he to you?"

She scowled but was slow to answer.

Hunter decided to be blunt. "Is he the father of your child?"

Her scowl became disgusted, and her chest heaved as if she might retch. "No."

While her body language said Hunter had suggested something deplorable, Kuuto—with his shoulders raised to his ears and his fist clenched—radiated aggravation. He looked poised to attack again, but his rage wasn't directed toward Hunter.

Hunter took all this in and tried a different tactic, a calm one. "You need to tell us what's going on here. All of it. It's the only way to determine if we can help or if we need to kick you off this ship at the next planet spinning. We've had too many surprises lately to ride with walking, talking mysteries." Hunter looked at his team. "Agreed?"

Everyone nodded their agreement except for MEL-222, who was incapable of nodding. A quick blurp cosigned its sentiment.

Sohi considered. She turned to Kuuto and stroked his mask lovingly. "It's okay," she said.

His shoulders slumped, and he undid the clasps securing the mask.

"Sendril Crane is not the father of my child." Sohi motioned to Kuuto. "He is."

Kuuto removed his mask.

Hunter took a step back. Omega, Wrecker, Tech, and Phee had similar shocked reactions.

Kuuto's face was not scarred, burned, or missing necessary tissue as they'd been led to believe. It was smooth, unmarred by anything other than a beard. And familiar.

Kuuto . . . was a clone.

CHAPTER NINETEEN

DALLOW, DALLOW SYSTEM

endril Crane, accompanied by junior ISB operatives (a compulsory team assignment Crane could've done without), tracked the V-wing's distress beacon. The pilot had initiated pursuit of Gayla and the clone Hunter on his own, apart from any order Crane had given. This had come to be a common annoyance whenever requisitioning regional forces in service of a mission. The military grunts could rarely resist their skull-cracking proclivities, Crane found. They'd rather maim a target than detain them. Now, instead of Crane having competent assistance in pursuit of his mission—and its loose, perhaps exaggerated, intersection with the ISB's goals—he was dealing with two casualties and the need to retrieve a willful subordinate.

The surviving pilot's beacon placed him twelve klicks from the spaceport in dense forest, dangling from a tree by his parachute straps. His leg was twisted awkwardly, broken. He mewled from the pain.

"Cut him down," Crane ordered. "And don't let him pass out. I have questions."

The four operatives he'd been assigned (or burdened with, depending on the hour you asked him) were a young bunch—a bit brash. But they followed orders, and with the injured pilot on the ground, Crane began the debrief.

"Did you shoot them down?" he asked.

"No," the injured agent said between whimpers. "Whoever was flying that ship is unhinged."

"Not unhinged. Well trained. Exceptional improvisation skills. Better than you."

He grimaced in agony. "Is there a medic nearby?"

Crane stepped on the man's broken leg right at the bend. He screamed.

"You pursued on your own. When I gave an order to track without engaging, you did not respond." Crane lifted his boot so the insubordinate cretin could speak.

Wheezing, the pilot said, "The perpetrators fired on ordained law officers. SOP authorizes a return of lethal force."

"Standard operating procedure does not supersede the ranking agent on-site."

Defiance sparked in the injured man's face. "Why *wouldn't* you authorize lethal force in this situation?"

Crane considered what had been asked. "Fair question."

He drew his blaster and fired twice into the pilot's chest.

Three of the four young operatives in his charge drew weapons and sighted him, taken aback by the execution.

One shaky-voiced agent said, "You—you killed him."

Crane lowered his blaster and explained. "Standard operating procedures have been updated by the Emperor's order. To disobey a ranking agent's directives in the line of duty is an act of treason, punishable at that agent's discretion up to and including summary execution. Feel free to check if you don't believe me. Before you do, I'm ordering you to lower your weapons. Does anyone care to disobey?"

There was a moment's hesitation, but ultimately, no. No one did.

"Very good. Feel free to file an incident report and describe, in detail, what happened here. I feel buoyed by the rule of law as I have interpreted it, and if a tribunal were to find I'd acted beyond my purview, I would gladly accept their verdict and sentence. In the meantime, to answer our late teammate's valid question, these targets require a different approach because they are Clone Force Ninety-Nine."

Wide-eyed nods of recognition were exchanged among the young investigators.

One of them said, "They're alive?"

Crane let the question hang a moment.

Many of the older, lazier holdovers who'd transitioned from Republic Intelligence to Imperial Security focused solely on their assigned caseloads and didn't stay abreast of recent developments throughout the galaxy, updated wanted lists and such. That's why they missed opportunities to show the kind of initiative that let Crane make high-profile arrests and quickly carve his way toward autonomy. If there was a benefit to having a bunch of upstarts placed in his tutelage, it was that they were especially excited about the shift and attuned to the massive shifts that might arise under the new regime. From the Jedi Purge to the Delegation of 2,000, this group was well schooled on new and notable enemies of the Empire. They were already calculating how apprehending fugitives—who'd either faked their own deaths or been the beneficiaries of false reporting in the bureau—like Clone Force 99 would aid their careers.

"Need I say more?" Crane said.

The consensus was no, as Crane hoped. Though he hadn't lied, he did not want to discuss Gayla or their history with his underlings. The Clone Force 99 connection she'd fostered, while fascinating even to Crane, was enough need-to-know information to keep his team focused and obedient. His personal matters need not interfere.

"Now, does anyone have useful information for me?"

Drand—the one who'd waited to assess the situation before drawing a weapon, which Crane liked because it showed a sense of foresight worthy of honing—cleared her throat and swept a lock of blond hair behind her ear. "We've detained a spaceport employee who claims passengers from that ship were picked up earlier by a resident's chauffeur."

Crane raised an eyebrow. "Chauffeur? Interesting. Do we know where this resident lives?"

"We do, sir."

"Let's pay them a visit."

As they loaded up into their transport, Crane was already considering aiding and abetting charges he could level against anyone who may have assisted the fugitive clones . . . and Gayla. Given the excessive wealth that residents of this system were known for, fantasies of property seizures on behalf of the ISB danced through his mind. Command would love that.

Cheerfully—optimism none of the other investigators shared—he said, "Today may not be a total loss, after all."

⬦⬦⬦

Drand began, "This is . . ."

Crane was sure each of them had some almost suitable descriptor of the palace before them in mind. Grand. Excessive. Disgusting.

Aspirational?

That was one Crane could see some of his young colleagues gravitating toward, not understanding that the degree of wealth that acquired this kind of home could not simply be aspired to. It had to be handed down. Or taken.

"Who lives here?" Crane asked.

Drand tapped her datapad. Her brow creased. She tapped some more. "Records have a corporation listed as the owner. DuraCorp. But that's a subsidiary of another corporation, which is a subsidiary of another corporation. It's like nesting dolls."

Crane was familiar with this sort of enterprise camouflage, popular among executives and criminals alike. Any flaw in those business filings, he could exploit. Any hint of fraud, and he could take all that was dear to the individuals basking in this deception. The law was the law.

"Let's introduce ourselves," he said, exiting the transport.

The massive double doors parted before Crane and company could announce themselves, and a Kiffar with a bruised face greeted them. "How can I help you?"

"Is the owner home?" Crane said, laying a rhetorical trap. If the answer was yes, Crane could press the falsehood of corporate ownership angle, expanding his legal options.

The Kiffar said, "Mistress Cellia Moten resides here."

Ah, elusive. Skillfully so. This might be fun.

Cellia Moten. Why did it sound familiar?

Crane tipped his chin toward Drand, an indication to run that name. She went to work on her datapad.

Crane said, "Is Mistress Moten available for a conversation? It involves dangerous fugitives and could be a matter of her safety."

The Kiffar remained stone-faced, but a soft, high voice keened from beyond the entrance.

"Parlin, Parlin! Is that the authorities? Thank goodness. I didn't expect them to get here so fast." The woman, her luxurious gown sullied with dust and muck, her hair mussed, her hands shaking, emerged from the shadows of the entrance. Her eyes were wide with relief, but the look shifted to confusion. "You aren't the local police. You're ISB."

"Cellia Moten, I presume." Crane kept his voice light. He wanted her to trust him. Easier to catch her in a lie that way. Under Imperial statutes, lying to an ISB agent was punishable by up to ninety days of detention.

"I am." She extended her hand daintily, fingers down, the back toward the sky. Crane associated this gesture with royalty, beings who were accustomed to people grasping those fingers before kneeling or kissing rings. He remained upright while squeezing her fingers. It looked as awkward as it felt.

Cellia retracted her hand, unfazed. "Did the Dallow police send you?"

"No," Crane said, his original line of questioning lost in his own confusion. "Why would they?"

"Because I've been robbed!"

"You've been—" Crane was taken off guard here, though usually quick to control a situation, especially an interrogation, even if unofficial. He'd expected an inept adversary, but was this woman a victim? "May we come in so you can tell us what happened?"

The Kiffar tensed, but Cellia remained eager. "Of course. Do excuse the mess. The thieves went on an absolute *rampage*."

She led them into the palace, and Crane was taken aback again. This wasn't a mess. It was a war zone. Evidence of blasterfire. Bombs. Was that a pool of green blood in the corner?

Clone Force 99's work? From what he'd read, they were capable of this level of destruction.

Crane's operatives murmured among themselves while more beings entered from the opposite end of the room. There were various species and some droids, all armed with illegal weapons. Military-grade hardware came with serious jail time should Crane decide to charge the wielders—a right he reserved while he ascertained what happened here.

Cellia Moten said, "I was tricked by con artists masquerading as antique dealers. They wormed their way into my home under the guise of a simple transaction. Once they were here, they threatened my life and the lives of my workers."

"So you fought them," Crane said—a statement, not a question. The evidence of a battle was unmistakable.

"We do not wither here."

"What were you attempting to buy?" Drand asked.

"Pottery," Cellia said, and nothing more.

Crane would've preferred to be the sole interrogator here but took Drand's eagerness for a chance to examine their surroundings more closely.

Several lavish models, now mostly blown to smithereens. Red veins in white marble still screamed opulence through the dust and debris. Floor to ceiling, none of the finishes would have been affordable on a hundred ISB salaries. Crane's sympathy for Cellia Moten's tumultuous day diminished as the running credit count in his head increased.

"What were they trying to take?" Crane asked.

Cellia scoffed. "There's nothing in here that isn't valuable."

"I can tell." Crane continued down the corridor, prompting Cellia, her guard, and Crane's team to follow. "But, specifically, for the con artists, as you put it, to concoct a scheme convincing enough for you to shuttle them to your home, they must've had a specific payday in mind."

"I can't speak to their motivations. I don't think like a criminal."

"How many of them were there?"

"Three."

"All clones?"

Cellia took a moment before answering. "One of them resembled a clone. Somewhat. Another was a pickpocket child. The third was a pirate known as Phee Genoa. I'm sure her name's somewhere in the extensive files of the ISB."

Even more players than Clone Force 99 and Gayla? A pirate? And a child?

In the next grand room, there was more destruction. Crane pointed to a gaping hole in the wall. "What happened here?"

"My security attempted to corner the thieves before they could harm me and escape with any valuables, but they blasted their way through the wall."

That . . . was a lie. The explosive charge was triggered on the exterior, and the evidence was clear. Crane was so pleased to utter his next words. "Cellia Moten, by the authority of the Imperial Security Bureau, I'm placing you under—"

Cellia interrupted him. "Does Sheev know you're here?"

"Sheev?"

"I'm sorry. *Emperor* Palpatine. We're old friends, and I forget most of you may not refer to him by— You know what, never mind. I'm going to contact him and let him know that . . . I'm sorry, what's your name again?"

"I'm Agent Sendril Crane."

To the Kiffar, she said, "Yes. Parlin, please get in touch with Mas's office and inform them that Agent Crane and his team are assisting a close friend in a most personal matter."

Had Crane heard her correctly. "Mas?"

Sheev Palpatine. Mas Amedda. Crane knew the names, of course, but in the way he knew the names of longtime holodrama stars. He could maybe argue a closer connection because of the ISB's inherent political roots. Still, Crane could barely fit the grand impression of the Emperor and his closest confidant in his head, let alone refer to them as casually as *Sheev* and *Mas*.

Parlin tipped his chin to Cellia. "I'll notify Grand Vizier Amedda right away, Mistress."

He left them at a clip, and Cellia met Crane with a smile that was just below malicious. "Once the Emperor knows you're assisting one of his dearest companions, you'll be provided any additional resources you need to bring the vandals who desecrated my home to justice."

"Thieves," Crane said before he could think better of it.

Cellia said, "What was that?"

"Earlier, you said 'thieves,' not 'vandals.' "

She sucked her teeth and let the low click echo. "Two things can be true."

Not two lies, Crane thought but controlled his tongue. He sensed the danger here. It didn't scare him—he didn't feel much fear anymore. It intrigued him. In a little more than a breath, he'd gone from attempting to arrest her on conspiracy charges to questioning his safety in her presence. Being in this home, with this woman, felt akin to drifting in deep waters with an unseen leviathan skulking just below the surface. Was she *really* an associate of the Emperor?

She said, "I am under the impression that a ranking agent like yourself is not so beholden to semantics that it distracts you from the necessary truths that you, me, and the galaxy depend upon. Correct?"

Crane was slow to answer, somewhat in awe of her foreboding eloquence.

"Is that correct, Agent Crane?" Cellia asked, pressing.

Crane chanced a glance at Drand, who gave the slightest nod. She'd found something in her search. It better be worthwhile for her sake. He told Cellia, "Yes. Any friend of the Emperor is a friend of the bureau."

For now.

CHAPTER TWENTY

THE *MARAUDER,* HYPERSPACE

Hunter, Omega, Tech, and Wrecker were crammed in the cockpit—a tight squeeze but necessary. Phee and MEL-222 remained outside, their eyes on the troubling passengers with even more troubling secrets. Phee didn't even object to being excluded from the conversation in the cockpit. That was clone business.

"We've seen it before," Wrecker said, though not as confident or boisterous as usual.

Omega said, "Cut and Suu?"

Wrecker nodded, but even that lacked conviction.

Cut and Suu Lawquane were allies, friends, who'd offered some cover for Omega and Clone Force 99 on the planet Saleucami in their early days on the run. Cut was a clone and a deserter. He'd married the widowed Suu, a Twi'lek, and her children became his. The Lawquanes forged a family from the flames of war.

Tech spoke to Wrecker's apprehension. "It's not quite the same. Even if it were, the ISB aren't tracking Cut and Suu for robbery."

"Cut and Suu never lied to us," Hunter said through clenched teeth. "How'd the bureau even find us?"

Tech said, "I've been considering that very query. My best deduction is something specific to the casino they robbed. Perhaps they got tagged with some sort of tracker?"

Wrecker pressed his hands together as if pleading for all of this to make sense. "Why not snatch them on Mygeeto, then?"

"Also a query I've been pondering." Tech seemed to chew over a potential answer. "Perhaps it was something with the credits, though I can't quite make sense of how."

Hunter chuckled, a humorless sound. "If you're even close to the right answer, the funds are worthless, then." He rose from his seat with purpose. "Hopefully, Sohi and Kuuto can find some workaround for that problem when we drop them off on the next planet."

Omega blocked his path to the door. "You can't kick them out. The baby."

"You care much more about them than they do about us."

"I just—"

"They *lied* to us, Omega. Sohi's manipulations put our entire family in danger so she could protect her own. If she'd been halfway honest about who they were and what they were running from, not only would we have had a choice about throwing in with them, we could've made a real plan to prevent the mess that just happened. Also, and think about this very carefully . . . you know what our lives are like. We can't seem to stay out of trouble any more than they can. We're as big of a threat to them and their baby as they are to us. Tell me I'm wrong."

The thing was, she couldn't.

The veil of disappointment that fell across Omega's face wounded Hunter in a way a thousand battles never could. Fighting through injuries was part of the job, though. "It has to be done."

"Wait," Tech said, always reasonable amid the unreasonable. "Information may be worth what those credits aren't now that we're on this Crane's radar. Everything you've told us suggests there's more to his pursuit than capturing a casino robber. Something personal. If it's personal, it can be exploited. We might want those details before we send our passengers on their way."

It wasn't illogical. Nothing Tech said ever was. Hunter still hated it.

He looked at Omega. "I know *you* agree with him." He turned his attention to Wrecker. "What about you?"

Wrecker said, "The ISB already knows they're on our ship. We kick them out now, the bureau's still going to be looking for us. So more intel doesn't hurt."

"Very well," Hunter said, "but I'm asking the questions. If I don't like the answers, they're off this ship immediately. Got it?"

He mashed the door control, unsealing it. Phee and MEL-222 eyed him, wary.

Phee said, "You look cranky . . . *er*."

"Well, that's your fault now, isn't it? How, exactly, are you coming by these blasted jobs?"

Phee feigned offense. "Because I'm reliable. And trustworthy. Everyone knows if you want discretion, you come to Phee. It's pretty much my middle name. Phee 'Discreet' Genoa."

Tech said, "You frequently recount your adventures in great detail to anyone who listens."

"I change the names to protect the guilty."

"The names and the facts," said Hunter.

"I think your stories are great, Phee," Omega said. "I'm going to tell all kinds of stories like that one day."

"Is that so?" Hunter asked. "Come on. There are other stories I'm interested in today."

He found the thief couple midship, much like he'd left them. She was in a state of near-meditation, massaging her midsection while the unmasked clone fiddled with his cybernetic leg. He straightened as Hunter approached, on guard and unflinching.

"What's your real name?" Hunter asked.

"CT-804."

"No. We don't do that here. What's *your* name?"

The clone smirked and nodded. "Ponder."

Hunter shifted to the Keshiri. "No need to introduce yourself. *Gayla*."

She didn't open her eyes. "Told you not to call me that."

"Why? Are you allergic to the truth?"

Now she opened her eyes. She looked exhausted. "I'm over the past. I'm not that person anymore."

"Is that person worse than a robber?"

"Yes."

Hunter hadn't expected such an answer. He was especially attentive to every tic and tell now, and that felt like . . . truth. He'd be careful not to get lulled by it. A liar's best tool is intermittent honesty—time to set boundaries.

He said, "I want to throw you out of the air lock."

It was an exaggeration, but he was going for intimidation. It didn't work.

"No, you don't," she said, sounding almost annoyed. "Nothing in your file indicates an aptitude for cold-blooded murder. CT-9904, perhaps, but not you. Where is Crosshair, by the way?"

A chill fell over the cabin. They rarely spoke of him these days, but for a stranger to mention him so . . . so . . . smugly. It was out of line. Of course, Sohi meant it to be jarring, but to what end? It certainly didn't endear her to Hunter, and it might've lost some of the goodwill that Omega had maintained since they first met.

She stepped forward, the tiny dynamo she was, her arms crossed and her voice stern. "Tell us who you are and how all of this happened. Now."

Tech backed Omega. "You heard her."

Sohi looked to Ponder. His hand slipped into hers, and their fingers interlocked. He said, "I think you should. We owe them."

She considered and inhaled deeply. "Most of what I said before was true. I worked in Senator Cadaman's office. I fled when the Empire rose. I . . ."

She trailed off, but Ponder squeezed her hand again. "I'm here with you. I always will be."

Another heavy breath, then Sohi said, "I worked in Senator Cadaman's office because it was my cover. I was a spy."

Phee's head cocked, her mouth turned down. "Wait, if you were spying on a Republic senator, then that means—"

Sohi confessed before she could be outed. "Yes. I worked for the Confederacy of Independent Systems." She looked Hunter in the eye. "I was a Separatist."

It felt like the oxygen vented from the cabin. It was a wonder the life-support alarms didn't go off. *A Separatist,* Hunter thought, *on our ship?*

Wrecker's expression was shadowy, far from his usual boisterous nature. "You fought clones."

Tech's face was unreadable when he asked, "What sort of information were you acquiring in the senator's office?"

Sohi looked Tech in the eye. "Senator Cadaman was on the Intelligence and Armed Services Committee that often received briefs on reconnaissance, weapons development, and troop movement. They were difficult to access, so I could acquire maybe one out of every six or so detailed reports, but the information in those briefs was what I sent to my handler."

"Troop movements?" Hunter said.

Sohi's face was stony when she responded. "Yes."

"You didn't help *fight* clones." Hunter stood, his demeanor cold. "You helped *kill* us!"

He charged, but Wrecker's massive hand slapped his chest plate, as effective as a suddenly raised ray shield. Even if his brother hadn't stepped in, Hunter would've had to go through the clone Ponder, who was now between him and Sohi. Hunter hadn't meant the woman any harm; he only intended to get in her face and confirm that she was off the *Marauder* at the very next system they reached.

He was furious, though, and since Ponder was set on protecting a clone killer, when it came to releasing the pressure valve on Hunter's anger, Sohi's misguided partner would do.

Hunter backed away from Wrecker, then ducked under his arm, too quick to be stopped. Still low, he launched a sweeping kick into Ponder's organic leg, grabbed the clone before he hit the deck, and launched him into the wall with a hip throw.

Ponder said, "*Oof,*" as the wind exploded out of him. He collapsed to the floor, dazed. It all happened fast, but everyone was reacting.

MEL-222 beeped, appalled.

Omega sulked, disheartened.

Wrecker tensed to intervene.

Tech shook his head, disappointed.

Phee said, "This is why it's hard for you guys to make friends."

But the only thing that stopped Hunter from dishing out more pain to Ponder was the blaster suddenly aimed at his temple.

"Enough," Sohi said, sounding tired. "I don't want to shoot you, and you don't want to be shot, so let's finish the conversation and get on to whatever comes next. Shall we?"

CHAPTER TWENTY-ONE

MOTEN ESTATE, DALLOW

Parlin swept an arm over the vast space Cellia Moten had allotted to Crane and company for the duration of this new, prioritized "robbery" investigation. Crane steamed. Furious.

Whatever communiqué had made it to the Grand Vizier's office resulted in near-immediate action in the form of new orders from Command. Crane suspected the only actual robbery here was Cellia Moten stealing his autonomy for her ends.

"Any amenity you desire is at your disposal," Parlin said.

Crane hadn't planned on keeping his team in this planetary system for even a day. Gayla's options for eluding him increased exponentially the longer she was on the move. And here he was with his boots stuck in Dallow mud.

His superiors had directed him to set up a temporary staging ground on the Moten estate at Cellia's request. The structure they now occupied she'd called a "guest dwelling," but it would've rivaled luxurious homes of the galaxy's mid-tier elite. That this was a domicile Cellia kept empty and available on the off chance of company was another boast of her superior fortune.

The architecture and design of the main palace were echoed here but with slight differences. Gone were the white-and-red marble floors, re-placed with stained wooden planks—perhaps from the local forest. None of the extravagant models were present here, and decorations were sparse. This structure seemed like a model in some ways—perhaps an early palace design that Cellia found too minimalist for her personal quarters.

"Explore the dwelling," said Parlin, "and if there's something you can't find, simply activate any communications panel, and your needs will be met."

Crane hid his aggravation in the face of such hospitality. He gave Parlin a cordial nod. "Thank you."

One of his team, a leathery, tanned boy named Weilan, could not resist the Kiffar's offer. "Would you happen to have any Dallow sand claw cakes? I've heard they're a must-have in this system."

Parlin smirked. "I'll have the kitchen prepare some for your party."

"Excellent," Weilan said. "I'm starved. Aren't we all?"

He looked to his colleagues for confirmation. They remained silent. They knew better.

Parlin said, "If there's nothing else at the moment . . ."

"That will be all," Crane said.

Parlin exited. The door sealed behind him. Crane motioned for Weilan to come closer. He did.

"Where did you hear about Dallow sand claw cakes?" Crane asked.

Weilan said, "My mother is a chef on Naboo, and she once told me—"

Crane's hand whipped forward and pinched the tip of Weilan's wagging tongue between his thumb and forefinger, stretching the muscle to its absolute limit and forcing the subordinate into a distorted shriek.

"If you ever want to enjoy your mother's cooking again, don't fight. Listen." Crane crouched and tugged downward, dragging Weilan to his knees. "Everyone may not be familiar with the policies on civilian aid. For however long we're here, the bureau will pay the property owner a per-night rate equal to the average price of a local hotel. For any damage to the property, the bureau will reimburse the owner within ninety days of receiving a detailed invoice with corroborating images. Any meal"—Crane squeezed Weilan's tongue harder, eliciting a whimper—"our host provides will also be reimbursed, and *we are not to request or accept any-thing of extravagance when it can be helped.* Is anything I've said unclear?"

Drand and the others nodded and confirmed they understood.

Crane said, "Do *you* understand?"

Weilan was in tears, only nodding within the short range of motion that kept Crane from ripping his tongue from the root.

"Good. I hope those sand claw cakes are as delicious as you claim." Crane released him, and Weilan hurried away with his hands pressed to his trickling bloody mouth.

"Drand, a word," Crane said.

The others went about preordained duties while Crane consulted with his most promising upstart. At least she'd better be. She was about to get promoted.

"Yes, sir?"

"Would you feel comfortable handling the investigation into the incursion on this property without my assistance?"

"Yes, sir."

By not hesitating, she passed a critical test. A no would indicate a damning lack of drive and confidence. The yes she gave came with its own risk from her perspective. What if Crane were power mad, or egotistical? He could see her as a threat and possibly maneuver to stunt her advancement in the bureau. In spite of that possibility, she'd made a smart, calculated move.

Then her curiosity got the best of her.

"Agent Crane, our primary target, this Gayla Reen, how, exactly, is she a threat to the Empire? The mission briefing didn't offer much in the way of detail beyond labeling her"—Drand referred to her data-pad—"'a known fugitive with high potential for dissidence.'"

Crane bristled. He'd purposely avoided extraneous details in the official records. A "threat" to the Empire was a fluid concept, encompassing anything from slanderous speech to attacks on government facilities. That sort of flexibility allowed Crane to prioritize his pursuit of Gayla without exposing the personal nature of the chase, or his ultimate goal—to recruit Gayla to the bureau. After a thorough, perhaps painful, re-education process, of course.

He'd done much for the bureau in his short time there. Had earned the right to dictate his caseload. Drand was very close to exposing his abuse of that power.

How excellent.

She *was* a threat, but in the best way. He loved knowing he played a hand in sharpening weapons, even if it meant he might get cut.

Let's redirect her aim, Crane thought. He said, "I'm going to contact Command and request you remain here as lead investigator. The team will be yours to direct."

"Thank you, sir. But the Gayla Reen file?"

"It seems like it will be difficult for you to properly lead this team if you're focused on a file that will no longer be your concern. Perhaps I should speak to one of the others about taking over?"

She made the correct decision again and did not press further. "No need, sir. I'm ready and willing to lead."

"Very well. What did you find on our host? A good update, credited to you, will help me make my case to delegate."

Drand raised her datapad to Crane, a mix of excitement and uncertainty wafting off her. "Fascinating file here. Or, rather, a lack thereof."

Crane took the pad from Drand and understood immediately. Most galactic citizens with registered chain codes had files containing limited information. Data collection efforts were underway to fill out *everyone's* file. In the meantime, anyone accessing a bureau record could expect to find standard identifying data: name, species, system of origin, and system of residence (if those differed), gender, height, weight, profession, documented criminal history (if that existed), and known associates. Those were typical.

Then there were the other files.

Data collected by means some in the former Republic Senate might've taken issue with—thank goodness that archaic, ineffective institution was neutered now. These other files—some with designations like green (mild surveillance, reference only), yellow (elevated surveillance, regularly reviewed/updated), and purple (constant surveillance, possible threat)—required clearances that Crane and most of his team had. Which is what made Cellia Moten's file more . . . concerning?

Crane had never seen a designation like hers before. *Red.*

More concerning, he didn't have clearance for the designation. Drand was already denied access, and Crane's clearance code got the same results. Here he was, working from the property of a person with the most secure bureau file he'd ever seen.

Who in the blazes was Cellia Moten?

Crane told Drand, "Start working up a dossier on the pirate she named. I will speak to a colleague about the nature of a 'red' file. Many mysteries today. Many mysteries."

He wished he was excited about the challenge, as he usually would be, but this was the strangest thing he'd encountered since transitioning to the bureau from his previous role. It felt like trouble. While adaptation was a skill he'd honed—and taught—apprehension buzzed at the base of his skull.

"Everyone," Crane said from his diaphragm. They snapped to attention as if he'd snatched them *all* by the tongue. "Drand's got her assignment. The rest of you—pick any one of the guards we met today and work up background on them. When you're done with one, move on to another. I need to reach out to headquarters." He cut a searing glance Weilan's way. "We'll reconvene when dinner arrives."

Crane grabbed a portable communications array from the gear they'd stacked near the entrance, then found a private room deep within the dwelling where he could make the call.

While a records request could be made through any agent in the Surveillance Branch, Crane chose to go directly to one of his longtime colleagues, another transplant from his old world. Someone he trusted and who trusted him. Still a rarity in his new role.

Crane set up his mobile communications array on the nearest table. The boxy piece of tech carried like a briefcase. With a button push, the device bloomed open like a metallic flower, the "petals" representing some of the most advanced comms systems available, sized for portability. A compartment opened and ejected a slim visor that Crane slipped on, initiating the secure transmission protocols.

"This is a special records request for Investigator Olyen Brey from Investigator Sendril Crane, confirmation code 72-AU897." Crane's voice had a slight warble, resulting from the visor scrambling his words so no unauthorized listeners—either in person or on the other side of a hidden surveillance device—could decipher his speech. Intended parties using the same secure protocols would detect no distortion.

A hologram materialized, tinted yellow instead of the standard blue—another security measure. That color created a visual frequency aligned to Crane's visor that meant even if another being was in the room they could not see Brey's projection. Overkill, perhaps, but given the nature of the red file in question, caution seemed in order.

Brey appeared. "Request line open, confirmation code 09-AU654. Proceed."

"The subject is Cellia Moten. Her file has a red designation that I've never seen before. Can you explain?"

Brey's hologram glitched in and out of existence, consistent with the secure protocols as Brey worked silently on the other side. Brey then disappeared altogether, though the call remained active. The dead air stretched Crane's patience.

Finally, Brey returned. "Apologies. I had to request additional clearances for both of us. It seems Command is aware of your current situation and has granted us access to the red file on Cellia Moten. This is classified information not meant to be shared with your ground team. Confirm?"

Crane hesitated.

"Confirm," Brey repeated.

"I have an officer with me, Drand, whom I'd like to cede authority to for the duration of this home invasion investigation."

Despite the glitches, Crane read the confusion on Brey's face.

Crane said, "I think leaving my team here to attend to Mistress Moten while I pursue the original target is the best use of bureau resources."

"Orders don't require you to think about what's best."

"Yes, but—"

"I will inform Command of your request, but in the meantime confirm that the red file information won't be shared with your team."

Begrudgingly, Crane said, "Confirmed. What am I dealing with here?"

"Something terrible. An aspiring politician. Cellia Moten wants to be a regional governor."

Crane groaned and squeezed the bridge of his nose. His temples throbbed with new stress. Of course. Boasting about a friendship with the Emperor. Throwing her weight around and bending the ISB to her will. Her extreme wealth wasn't enough. Cellia coveted power and wielded what she already had to gain more.

Oh, how Crane wished he could've arrested her.

Crane said, "Does a red file mean she's being vetted for the role? She seems to have an in with the Emperor already. Is an appointment likely?"

"That is unclear. The red file isn't about her being vetted. It's about her being investigated. By Krill Sans."

Crane's spine went rigid. Everyone in the bureau knew the name Krill Sans since she'd gone missing nine months ago under mysterious circumstances.

"Explain," said Crane.

"I'll unlock the red file for you to review on your own, but from what I'm seeing, someone wanted eyes on Moten."

"Does she have ties to any dissidents or insurgent upstarts?"

"Nothing known. It seems she was being surveilled proactively."

Crane nodded. Not unheard of. Every government he'd ever worked for or infiltrated loved knowing the secrets of its more powerful citizens, in case such information ever became useful.

Brey said, "Sans was undercover in Moten's security detail around the war's end. The assignment progressed as expected, with no actionable or interesting intel on Moten. Sans filed a final report en route to headquarters but never showed up. Witness accounts say she was last spotted in the Lothal system. Then, nothing."

Crane had heard some of the story, of course. Not the details surrounding Sans's target. He was flabbergasted.

"How is it the bureau didn't come down on Moten like a hydraulic press? She's clearly a suspect here."

Another extended silence from Brey that turned Crane from impatient to aggravated. What was the holdup?

Crane was not prone to rash emotions—at least not prior to throwing in with the Empire—but he was tempted to put his fist through the comms terminal.

Brey returned. "Apologies again. Your last question confused me. I needed to get clarification from Command."

"About what?"

"The reason Moten's request to have your team remain planetside was granted," Brey said. "*You're* investigating her now."

Frustration pressed Crane back in his seat. His own exemplary record was working against him here. The bureau wanted *him,* specifically, to pick up where Krill Sans left off, because he'd been so good at his job. The privilege to identify and track personal targets—a privilege he'd earned through demonstrations of dogged obedience—did not supersede the bureau's wants. How likely was it that Command would allow him to continue his pursuit of Gayla before he'd satisfied his orders? Not very.

Brey said, "Find out what happened to Krill."

Crane nodded. What else could he do?

"I'm here if you need me. But I hope you don't. Watch your back." Brey ended the transmission.

Crane did not hesitate. Even as the meal that fool Weilan requested arrived and dusk became full dark, he read through the declassified file on Cellia Moten, growing troubled.

One ISB agent had already vanished after getting close to Crane's current host. From what he ascertained of her file, it wouldn't take much for another to disappear.

Watch his back. In other words, be careful. Be slow.

No.

If Crane needed to do the bureau's bidding before he was allowed to leave Dallow, he wasn't going to drag his feet. He'd been so close to Gayla today. He would not delay their reunion longer.

"*. . . simply activate any communications panel, and your needs will be met.*"

Crane found one such panel in the corridor outside his room. He activated it, and Parlin answered.

Crane said, "Is Mistress Moten available? I have a few questions."

CHAPTER TWENTY-TWO

THE *MARAUDER,* HYPERSPACE

Thanks to skillful diplomacy on Phee's part, Tech now held Hunter's knife and Sohi's blaster. He sincerely hoped that neither of them concealed other weapons that might emerge in the heat of discussion.

The clone Ponder retook the seat next to his partner. Hunter might've bruised his ego a bit, but he was no worse for wear, finding comfort with his fingers intertwined in Sohi's. Sometimes, he reached over to caress the side of her belly with his other hand. It did not seem to be a conscious motion. Something like reflex met with hope?

Tech glanced at Phee, who was focused entirely on the exchange between Hunter and Sohi. She didn't notice him watching her. That was fine. Tech didn't care for attention in moments like this. Moments he didn't allow himself often. His focus was generally problem-solving on behalf of the team. He rarely thought of himself apart from Clone Force 99. Yet, right then, with Phee in sight, he skirted . . . possibilities?

MEL-222 bumped his hip, beeping and booping misplaced concern.

"I'm fine, Mel," Tech said, the moment gone. He refocused on the main conversation.

"How many?" Hunter pressed, refusing to let this point go. "How many clones are in the ground because of what you did?"

"I have no way of knowing that," Sohi said, content to take Hunter's verbal lashing. "When I can't sleep at night, I imagine it's millions. That's how the weight of my choices presses on me."

"Are we supposed to feel sorry for you?"

"No," Ponder said. "She's simply saying that she feels remorse."

Hunter huffed. "And what about you? How long have you known that she traded information that got your brothers killed? How could"— Hunter motioned at Sohi's bulging midsection, the child gestating there— "*this* happen?"

Ponder did not flinch when he placed his full palm on Sohi's stomach. "Love is how this happens."

Hunter surely had more to say, but Omega intervened. "What's your story, Ponder? How did you two meet?"

"I didn't die when I was supposed to." Ponder flashed Omega a small smile. "I was in a squadron on Metalorn when our transport took fire and went down. I was the sole survivor." He rapped knuckles on his cybernetic leg. "Most of me anyway.

"A Jedi general called in medevac for me. They shuttled me to the orbital clinic, where I got this leg and orders to return to Kamino— shamed and shunned. If there was a bright side, I got a private bunk. Never had that before."

Phee said, "Well, that's more compassion than I was led to believe your Republic Army showed clones. I thought they patched you guys up and threw you back in the meat grinder."

"Regs get superstitious," Wrecker said with much disdain.

Phee's lips pursed, confused.

Tech explained. "Merely being injured gets you patched up and redeployed. A squad that suffers a few losses gets new clones assigned and sent to the next battle. When you're the only surviving member of your team, others aren't often welcoming. They consider you bad luck. I won't bother with explaining the fallacies in that thinking. But it's simply how things are."

Ponder acknowledged the truth with a nod. "Be thankful none of you know what it's like to be the only one who makes it home."

Hunter, Wrecker, and Tech all exchanged looks. They *were* thankful for that—every day.

Ponder said, "For the next half year, I was cooking meals in the mess for all the new clones training for their near-death experiences when a delegation of senators showed up like they sometimes do. One named Tyzdel came to the kitchen. I thought he would chew me out over some dietary restriction no one had informed me of. He had something else in mind."

"Senator Elem Tyzdel was newly elected and looking to make a name for himself," Sohi said. "He'd gained some traction on a clone rights platform and was looking to push his agenda further with his Wounded Clones Bill. He needed examples—"

"Props," Ponder said.

"—for the Senate floor. I was in Senator Cadaman's pod the day Tyzdel introduced Ponder and a few other wounded clones to the galaxy."

Sohi stopped speaking, perhaps thinking that was all anyone would be willing to hear. Not so.

Wrecker and Omega spoke in unison. "But how did you meet?"

Hunter looked unamused.

Tech was admittedly curious, but stayed quiet to not aggravate Hunter more.

Sohi said, "Ponder testified about what happened to him. I could tell it was hard, and he left out many details. His sincerity—how he spoke about his fallen brothers—touched me and everyone else present. Had that been all he said, maybe we wouldn't have met. But the senator from Naboo asked where Ponder suffered such a heavy loss. He said Metalorn. My chest seized. All the sound went away. I got so dizzy. I might've fallen from the pod if Senator Cadaman hadn't seen me swooning and tended to me."

She stopped again, but no one pressed for an explanation. Hunter spoke the truth for her. "It was one of the battles you'd stolen intel on. You may have been the reason for what happened to him."

She nodded. "That's the thing about being a spy. Do it right, your victims don't see you, and you shouldn't see them. My fate was sealed when I looked into where the injured clones were staying, where they were eating meals. Where they were dealing with the pain I likely caused them."

Ponder squeezed her hand and took over. "She was very good at the spy stealth thing because, for the longest time, I thought I saw her first.

"I'd go to dinner, and she'd be at a table alone, scrolling through something on a datapad. I'd occasionally stroll through a park and see her doing the same. It never struck me as odd. I thought I was lucky. I still do."

"When he asked to sit on a bench next to me," Sohi said, "I halfway expected his next move would be a blade between my ribs. I thought that's what I deserved. When he didn't kill me, I forced myself to sit in his presence and assess what I'd played a role in. My betrayal wasn't the sole betrayal for Ponder, I learned."

Ponder picked up where she'd left off. "I didn't realize she'd seen me speak in the Senate, so I told her a bit of why I was on Coruscant. More than a bit. I told her things I didn't bother to say in the Senate chambers because, as far as I could tell, the majority of that chamber didn't care about injured clones at all. We're tools to them. How many people care about a damaged hammer? I didn't linger, though. Even I know it's best to listen instead of talking about myself all night. We discussed books, music, holodramas, and wonders of the galaxy."

"We've never stopped talking about those things," Sohi said.

"Tyzdel had us injured clones stay on Coruscant for weeks of debates that didn't go anywhere. Eventually, the whole initiative faded in the wake of another, more attractive, career-making cause. I became a cook. The senator had thanked us for our service and got ready to send us off, but by then, I had no intention of leaving Sohi's side. The Senate had several kitchens. I asked Tyzdel if I could stay. He seemed annoyed by the request but maybe figured it was the least he could do since we starred in his little sympathy play. He made the arrangements."

Sohi said, "We haven't spent a day apart since."

Hunter asked Ponder, "Not even when you learned what she was?"

Ponder looked ready to take another swing at Hunter, but Sohi said, "If I knew then what I know now, I would've made different choices."

Hunter threw his hands up and cackled an exaggerated laugh. "Because the Empire's after you! Because your side lost!"

Anger flashed across her face like lightning in a cloud. "Because it didn't mean anything!" Her gaze swept the room. "Did the Separatists gain their independence? No. Did your Republic's democracy survive? No. Who really wins when a monster none of us saw coming springs from the darkness and consumes us?"

Wrecker, quieter than usual, said, "You might have a point there."

Hunter stood, stoic. "Agreed. It gives us much to consider when we drop you at the next system. You're off the *Marauder*." Before Omega could protest, he shot a silencing look in her direction. "And that's final."

Sohi didn't fight the verdict. "May I go rest, then? I'll need my strength if we're to make our way on some random world."

Hunter waved a dismissive hand.

Sohi got to her feet slowly, squeezed Ponder's hand twice, and departed for her assigned bunk. Ponder remained in his seat, staring Hunter down.

"Something you want to say?" Hunter asked.

"It was my idea to reach out to Phee because of you all. People say Clone Force Ninety-Nine denied Order Sixty-Six. A Jedi saved my life, so that means something to me." Ponder shook his head and retrieved the mask he'd worn in his Kuuto guise. He placed it on.

At first, Hunter thought it was some pin on the conversation. A way for Ponder to punctuate his disappointment over Hunter's decision. Then he picked up Sohi's footsteps behind them, heard the canister pop, and the resulting hiss. He understood too late to do anything other than yell, "Everyone! Hold your breath!"

Futile words. The gas was already filling the cabin.

Wrecker got the first big whiff of the dirty blue vapor, coughed twice, then collapsed. It hit Tech and Phee next. They fell together. Hunter reflexively clamped a hand over Omega's nose and mouth. Still, the sweet burn of the gas was already in his sinuses. He fought to keep consciousness even as his hand dropped from Omega's face and her fearful eyes rolled to the back of her head. She buckled.

Hunter went to one knee. Sheer rage was the only thing that allowed him to last this long—his lungs *burned*. As he stared at a freshly masked Sohi who moved through the vapor cloud she'd unleashed, his clumsy, half-numb fingers reached for a knife that wasn't in its sheath because he'd handed it to Tech an hour ago.

MEL-222 skirted forward, attempting to help, but Ponder intercepted, freeing a restraining bolt from beneath his tunic. He slapped it on the droid, shutting her down.

Sohi kept a safe distance from Hunter and said, "We could've taken your ship and left you. For what it's worth."

The world contracted to a sliver, then nothing else.

Hunter passed out.

CHAPTER TWENTY-THREE

MOTEN ESTATE, DALLOW

Crane sat in the only office chair that hadn't been obliterated in the earlier firefight while Cellia paced the room, assessing the damage done to what looked like fancy junk to him. He knew nothing of art, antiquities, or any of the arbitrary things the wealthy prided themselves on acquiring. Certainly, he wasn't one of those whiny types who proposed a theoretically better way for the rich to spend their credits. It was their money; they could do with it what they wanted. He did acknowledge that the ability to purchase anything in the galaxy seemed to activate desires and instabilities (as he suspected was the case for Cellia) that were mysterious to everyone but them.

One thing that wasn't mysterious was that Cellia's collection skewed toward violence and dominance, evident in the various weapons and religious iconography that survived the day's assault. This detail was missing from her red file. He'd be sure to add it when it was safe.

"You'd mentioned the thieves made a ruse of trying to sell you pottery," he said. "Would you mind being more specific? We never know what details can expose an unexpected lead."

"Is that so?" She pulled a macabre piece from a high shelf for inspection. It appeared to be a fossilized nexu skull with the jawbone missing.

"If what they proposed was attractive to you, your tastes might give some insight into how they engineered a scheme against you. Do they have a source? Could it be someone you know? Someone in your employ?"

She blew dust off the skull and returned it to its shelf. "An inside job. That would be nasty, nasty business."

"Are there any workers here who arouse your suspicions? Perhaps someone who'd moved on in recent months? We could try to track them down."

Cellia strolled behind Crane, forcing him to twist in his seat to keep an eye on her, and he wanted to keep an eye on her. She'd moved on to an archaic sword, lightly drawing her thumb across the meter-long blade. "I'd have to give your questions deeper consideration. The possibility never occurred to me."

"If you allowed my team to access personnel files, we could assist in determining likely suspects." Considering what he'd really been tasked to investigate, this approach might be too aggressive. His impatience overwhelmed his subtlety.

She was silent when she moved on to her next trinket.

What could be going on in that head of hers? Paranoia? Fear? *What are you hiding, Cellia?*

"Have you ever seen one of these before?" She recovered what at first appeared to be a damaged piece of masonry, misshapen and pock-marked. She swept dust away, turned it over, and revealed it depicted an agonized face chiseled into rock. She passed it to Crane.

He took it, faking intrigue. "It's heavy."

"Indeed. It's a Savarian priest who stood up to a local crime syndicate and had his tongue cut out. Many Savarians still speak of him as a martyr, if only in whispers."

Crane turned it at angles, taking in the detail. "It's a very realistic sculpture."

"*Sculpture?*" Cellia sounded appalled. "I only collect genuine artifacts. That has been treated with a rapid fossilization process that has come in vogue among more esoteric collectors."

Crane reexamined the incredibly detailed face of suffering in his hands. Details too fine for any artist to replicate, perhaps. Crane gently placed the face on Cellia's desk as if his handling mattered to that wretched priest. Then he wiped his hand on his pants leg—several times. Even after, he still felt that cold, eternal stone. He would for a long time.

Cellia said, "The item those con artists offered me was a Caridan mortar—an ancient instrument used in religious ceremonies. As for the personnel files, I'll have Parlin provide you and your team access. If that's all for the evening, you can imagine I've had an exhausting day."

She moved to the ajar door, still damaged, indicating he should do the same. Before he crossed the threshold, he had to ask, "That Savarian face . . . did you show it to me because you believe it has some significance to the investigation?"

Cellia's smile was tight. "Not at all. I thought you might be intrigued by the punishment—the whole thing with the tongue."

She let that hang between them.

"I see," Crane said.

"You and I don't know each other well. Yet. While I have a deep, long-standing relationship with Sheev Palpatine, I'm never opposed to making new friends, and friends should understand one another. Don't you think?"

Crane stepped lightly. "I believe so."

"Good night. I look forward to your findings."

From the shadows, Parlin appeared, a rifle slung over his shoulder, to escort Crane back to his quarters.

<hr />

"Listen up!" Crane said the moment Parlin left the guest dwelling. "I want intel on Caridan ceremonial mortars—"

"On it," Weilan said around his swollen tongue. He was desperate to please.

"Comb through the estate's personnel files and flag any employees with anything more than a speeder citation in their past."

Another affirmative from a pair who immediately hunched over their portable terminals, on task.

"And you," he told Investigator Drand, "this may be nothing, but look for reports of missing priests from Savareen. Send me whatever you come across."

"Will do. Did you learn anything from your time with Cellia?"

I thought you might be intrigued by the punishment—the whole thing with the tongue.

"Nothing of note." Crane considered telling Drand that he suspected their dwelling was being monitored and Cellia's crew could see and hear nearly everything they did, but he held on to that bit of intel. The former spy in him was reserved that way. Besides, it would only make the team paranoid, and they still needed to do their jobs.

In the meantime, now that they had access to the personnel file, there was a name he wanted to check himself—the alias Krill Sans used while undercover.

Crane said, "I'll be in my quarters. Notify me if you need me."

The team spent the remaining evening hours compiling relevant information, agreeing to review the findings in the morning. As they all retreated to personal quarters for the night, Crane made a discovery—one he was meant to make. Cellia's account of what happened in her home was nonsense. She knew that he knew. She'd put his team in a dwelling she was monitoring and gave up access to her estate's files too easily. When he backtracked Krill Sans's time on the property, he came across a security program that assigned and limited estate workers' security access. A token they were instructed to keep with them at all times not only granted them entrance to any areas they were approved for but tracked their positioning while anywhere on the property.

Krill Sans's token was still active.

The positioning pinged an area about a half kilometer away from any structures, the forest's edge.

Crane pressed back in his chair, considering all the possibilities before deciding.

He took the bait.

With a setla lantern and his blaster, Crane left the dwelling without informing his ground team, though he did send Brey a single secure message before leaving.

Following a lead. If I don't check in by morning, send help.

The night views of Dallow were something to behold. The entire galaxy was on display in the tapestry of constellations stretching across the unmarred sky, with bands of multicolored celestial gasses draping the cosmos in translucent ribbons. But Crane took little note of beauty, focusing on the weak signal pulsing on his hand display. Nocturnal forest creatures scurried and cawed, their positions given away by occasional rustling foliage. He was close.

A few more paces brought him to a grove of young trees. There were dozens, and near the central-most point, Krill Sans's signal presented the strongest, eliciting a high keen from the tracking device. Crane tapped his foot on the root of a tree that had been there awhile. Understanding.

Krill Sans was no longer missing.

Cellia spoke behind him. "Did you know Agent Sans?"

Crane turned, reaching for his blaster, but Cellia was not alone. Parlin and two cronies trained rifles on him. They kept their distance. Not outside the range of a throwing spike, but he couldn't possibly take all three before one of them—the lucky one—got off a shot. This encounter would go the way of Cellia's choosing.

Crane answered her question. "Not personally. She had an outstanding reputation."

"Yes. A shame. We'd deduced her true identity weeks before I was forced to take action. My feelings were hurt because installing a spy in *my* home had to be the work of *someone* elite. *Someone* I've certainly conversed with at some gala or fundraiser. *Someone* with a great deal of access to the levels of government. Perhaps *ultimate* access." She shrugged, then asked, "You wouldn't know anything about that, would you?"

As much as she'd tossed around the Emperor's name before, she played coy now. *Why?*

Crane said, "I don't."

"I was content to play out the charade," she said, "because I saw strategic value in feeding her information I wanted to reach her handlers. Also, Krill was an excellent worker. The beauty of my garden topiary began with her. She would've done well as an artist."

"Certainly better than she did here," Crane said, refusing to blanch at the possibility of death. He'd trained many operatives to face this moment with pride and defiance. *We all end, so end well.*

"Thus our joint misfortune. She stumbled upon my grove, and I couldn't let that make it into her reports. You do understand."

Crane said, "You wanted me to find her. You just about led me here by the nose. So, no, I don't understand. Why walk me here if she died for stumbling over these roots?"

"Part of my success in this galaxy hinges on recognizing the inevitable. My little nature project can't stay hidden from the likes of the ISB forever. Not without the help of a friend, that is. Have I told you how much I value friendship?"

"I've gotten an impression."

Cellia tipped her chin toward Parlin. He and his crew continued to aim their rifles at Crane. "Friendship or fertilizer? It's your decision."

Crane smirked. "Friendship flows in two directions. You haven't been much of a friend to me, keeping me here, away from my mission."

"And what would that be?"

"Bringing a rogue operative in from the cold."

Cellia considered his words, then motioned for Parlin and the others to lower their weapons. "Go on. I wish to hear more."

"I trained spies in my former life. Was mostly aligned with the Separatists. Not out of any passion for the movement, or disdain for the Republic. Spies must have some allegiance even if it shifts eventually."

"As yours clearly did."

"Again, no passion. Preservation. I saw what was coming. You can't be responsible for placing eyes and ears into shadows throughout the galaxy and not glean a larger perspective. The Separatists were bound to fall, and punishments would be harsher for stalwarts *after* defeat. I made a calculation and defected."

Crane stopped speaking. There was no shame, or difficulty, revisiting a painful—physically and psychologically—piece of his past. He needed a moment to evaluate Cellia's reaction, determining the exact amount of truth needed to save his life.

It had been a gamble for Crane to confess that, for all intents and purposes, he was a traitor, but he'd spent time with enough murderers to know they were rarely righteous in the presence of other wrongdoers.

Cellia's eyes were wide. Curiosity piqued. "It's quite an impressive leap to go from an enemy of the Republic to agent of the Empire, isn't it?"

"I suspect had the Republic remained as it was it would've been an *impossible* leap. We're in a new age now. Skills honed as a Republic fighter or a Separatist spy are skills the Emperor uses as he sees fit." Crane decided to gamble a bit more. "But I'm sure you know that about your friend."

Cellia's enthusiasm for a good story cooled. "That I do."

Silence stretched. He may have soured her mood and that was bad. Too much time for Cellia to consider the benefits of disappearing him. He had to give her something *new to* exploit, feed her hunger for power and control.

Crane said, "The operative I'm chasing is the best I've ever trained. Someone who'd be a true asset to the bureau and the Empire. But she's scared, and spiraling, and it needs to be me who brings her in. Or else . . ."

He let his breathing rasp, let her perceive weakness.

Cellia said, "She means quite a bit to you."

Yes. That much was true. He must step lightly here. "One allegiance that has never shifted is to those I've trained. I put her on the path she's on. I need to see her home. If there's some way our friendship can aid that mission, I'm more than willing to return the favor in kind."

Cellia grinned wide. "Friendship flows in two directions indeed."

Crane continued selling Cellia on his desire to do what was necessary for her benefit, and his. He dispensed the exact amount of truth needed to survive Dallow. No more or less. By the time the sun rose, Cellia knew much about his history with Gayla, but not the most important part.

That she was his daughter.

CHAPTER TWENTY-FOUR

BATUU, THE OUTER RIM
Before . . .

"Are you tired?" Father Crane asked.

Gayla *was* tired. They'd been hiking for hours at a steady clip. She was responsible for carrying a heavy satchel of supplies plus the new rifle Father gifted her that very morning. The excitement of going out with him alone for the first time ever while the others were left to menial chores provided ample energy at dawn, but by midday with the sun beating down on them, her reserves waned.

She said, "No, Father. I'm fine."

"Good. Let's keep checking the traps."

Their training grounds rested in the jungles of Batuu's southern hemisphere. The more populous segments of the planet were known as Separatist smuggling hubs, far from the gaze of Republic enemies, but the home Father Crane had built for Gayla and her siblings was away from the bustle of unregulated trade. It was secluded and humid and sometimes stinky. It was dedicated to honing all of Father's children into the weapons they'd need to be to survive—and thrive—in a harsh galaxy. Part of their training involved mastering one's demeanor to show only what you *wanted* others to see. Gayla worked hard to show Father she was unbothered by the day's exertion, afraid that if she displayed any weakness whatsoever, he might choose another sibling over her next time and every time thereafter.

They pushed through thick foliage, hacking at vines that hung like curtains and branches that formed a netlike mesh across their path. Father told her these routes were well traveled but the nature of the foliage here meant what you cut today would be back tomorrow. Gayla's arms ached from wielding a vibromachete—one of the many edged weapons they trained on—yet she persisted, imagining her older siblings had severed these very vines once and gained favor.

Long, quiet intervals of bushwhacking were broken up by longer lectures reiterating Father's thoughts on subjects he deemed essential at the moment. Since Gayla could recite most of them by heart, she preferred quiet, though she'd receive no such gift. She worked to exhaustion clearing their way and made a game of predicting Father's favorite lines before he said them. Next was the part starting with "*The Separatist cause is today's cause, but . . .*"

Crane said, "The Separatist cause is today's cause, but a day would not be a day if it did not end. And as days end, so will our service to this cause or that cause. Our skills are boundless."

Gayla sliced through a coiling, thorny vine as thick as her wrist. Now he would talk about "*Power shifting like energy pulses from a dying star . . .*"

"Power," Father said, "shifts. Like the energy pulsing from a dying star in its last . . ."

She suppressed a giggle over how good she was at her new pastime.

Game grazed the brush, and the traps set around their compound's perimeter provided half the meat they consumed. The other half came from more aggressive hunting, done by siblings in their final year of training. Every trap they'd checked so far had been undisturbed, still set and baited with blumfruit. "Often the case," Father assured.

But the pitiful mewling Gayla heard before piercing a patch of interlocked vines let her know they were about to break their streak.

Several meters ahead, in a clearing covered in dried brush to conceal a very effective trap, lay a dugar dugar with its leg caught painfully in the pressurized clamp. Even from a distance, Gayla recognized it was a young creature, and if its leg wasn't broken, they would need to release it so it might grow, mate, and continue life's cycle. She hoped it wasn't hurt too badly.

Father approached first and stood over the creature with his arms folded behind his back. He gave the creature a once-over, then locked eyes with Gayla and lifted one eyebrow. She hurried to the animal without needing to be told.

The dugar dugar bleated when she knelt beside it, its eyes wide with fear.

"I won't hurt you," Gayla whispered.

The blumfruit that had served as bait was a meter or so away, uneaten. Likely flung when the trap snapped. Gayla grabbed it, its sticky juice running between her fingers, and held it before the dugar dugar's mouth. The creature was reluctant, so Gayla stroked its ear. "You can have it."

It took a tentative nibble, then greedy bites. While it ate, Gayla examined its snared leg. Their traps were blunted, not sharp or grooved. Painful, but a decent-sized animal could be released with no more than a bone bruise, if it were lucky. This dugar dugar had been lucky.

Gayla touched the mini-display on the trap, intending to enter the release code.

"What are you doing?" Father asked.

"Releasing him. He's a baby."

"Yes, that's what we'd typically do." Father gazed into the distance as if he saw something more interesting than what was happening between them. "But you told it you weren't going to hurt it."

Gayla was confused. "I did."

"This is a perfect lesson in necessary deceit. Since you've set an expectation, you need to counter it. Without conscience."

Gayla's head snapped back and forth between the helpless dugar dugar and Father. "But—"

"Without hesitation!" he snapped. An unmistakable command.

Gayla rose to her feet, spinning the rifle off her back into a shooting position. She aimed at the creature's head, squeezed, but just as her finger tugged to the trigger's break point, Father knocked the barrel aside, making the shot go wild.

"Your reluctance cost you your first and best opportunity," he said, speaking fast, painting a scene with words. "Now, your enemy is upon you. Your rifle is useless. Use your blade."

What he said was horrific. The absolute last thing she wanted to do. She knew better than to hesitate a second time, so she gripped the vibro-machete's handle and finished the dugar dugar. It was quick. In her mind it would always seem slow. Close to eternal.

She breathed heavier than she had when forcing her way through the thick brush. She didn't dare look at Father, ashamed of her actions and ashamed she needed to be prodded so hard to do what she'd been trained to do.

To busy her hands, she entered the trap's release code, and let its hydraulics reset the half-circle pincers to the ready position. Then she moved the dugar dugar's body aside, awaiting instruction.

Father let the silence linger. He had to know it was torture for her, and she accepted the quiet punishment. She was grateful that was all she'd earned. When she couldn't take it anymore, she said, "Should I carry the carcass back to the compound?" Since they didn't usually bring home game this small, she wasn't certain.

"It will feed only half of us," Father said. "You will not be among the half."

Understood. She'd gone hungry before. "Very well, Father."

She unspooled a length of rope from the satchel, intending to tie the dugar dugar's legs and make it a more compact bundle for the long walk home, but Father knelt and gently took the rope. "I'll do this. You have one more difficult thing to do."

Gayla had no clue what he meant, so she said, "Yes, sir."

Father said, "Stick your hand in the trap."

She knew she hadn't misheard him. More often than not, punishment and pain were a complementary pair in their compound. She also knew any more hesitation today . . . well, that just wasn't an option.

Gayla thrust her hand into the trap. A flock of pipa birds were startled to flight. Whether it was the blaster-loud snap of the trap springing or her screams that sent them airborne, Gayla didn't know.

Father Crane knelt beside Gayla, stroking her hair lovingly. "We all make mistakes. I'm glad you're making yours here and now. In the field, it could cost you much more than the use of a hand. The value in the pain you're feeling . . ."

The throbbing in her half-crushed hand kept her from appreciating the good this would do her down the line, and the precision of Father's wise words were drowned by blood whooshing in her ears. Yet, somehow, the lesson stuck.

THE *MARAUDER*, HYPERSPACE
Now

Sohi released the *Marauder*'s yoke and flexed her hand, attempting to shake loose a phantom ache from some youthful injury and distract herself from the creeping nausea that was growing from uncomfortable to painful. She focused on the guilt she felt for betraying Clone Force 99, savoring the sensation of *knowing* she'd done something wrong, because, for too long, spycraft had dictated that she make no such distinctions.

"How are you, love?" Ponder asked.

"I'm persisting."

She felt his scrutiny and sensed his worry. She wanted to comfort him, but truthfully, she was worried, too. Something didn't feel right.

Admittedly, she'd been doing too much. This close to delivery, the stress of everything from Canto Bight and Dallow to now was riskier than she'd wanted to admit. What choice did they have? There was no downtime when on the run.

A vicious cramp sliced right across her abdomen, and she couldn't rein in a hiss that might've been a full-throated scream for someone without her high tolerance for pain.

"Sohi!" Ponder said, out of his seat now, trying in any way he could to assist.

She ignored him and began rapidly punching commands into the flight computer because she felt lightheaded and feared she might faint. "Ponder, listen. I don't think I'll have the strength to say this twice . . ."

Hunter awoke coughing and gagging but in motion despite the searing pain in his chest. He crawled to Omega, raising her head and torso, using his limited, ragged breath to scream, "Be okay! Be okay!"

He shook her hard and she spasmed; her eyes popped open like stellar shades. She began a violent coughing fit but caressed his shoulder, letting him know she hurt but was recovering. He left her to it, rousing Tech and then leaving him to get Phee up while Hunter worked on the big guy.

Wrecker had fallen flat on his stomach, his cheek pressed to the hard deck while he snored like a rancor. Hunter didn't try flipping him but prodded his armor with hard-toe nudges. He roused, coughing slowly.

Phee was up and about, wincing, as she knocked the restraining bolt off MEL-222. The droid lit up, aware and angry, sounding a litany of rapid-fire curse beeps.

"I couldn't have said it better myself," Phee rasped. "Where are they?"

The same question Hunter had been wondering. "Only place they could be."

The crew hobbled toward the front of the *Marauder*, getting stronger by the second, but when Hunter tried the cockpit door, it didn't budge. Tech punched his code into the jamb's keypad, and an angry buzz indicated he would need a new code. He growled. "They've been busy."

The *Marauder* lurched, followed by the familiar sound of the hyperdrive powering down.

Tech said, "We just dropped from hyperspace."

Why? Hunter thought. *And where?*

Hunter told Wrecker, "Rip it open. Now."

Wrecker, happy to oblige, nudged his way to the front of their raiding party and hooked his fingers into the durasteel, creating a set of ten divots as easily as a child plunging their hands into clay.

"Wait!" Omega said. "We have to be careful. Regardless of what Sohi and Ponder did, the baby's family."

Hunter gave a heavy sigh, then told Wrecker, "Rip it open *gently*."

Wrecker strained against the servos securing the door. He grunted from exertion, and for a moment, it seemed like he'd lose this particular battle.

Then the door groaned and began to give—millimeters at first, but Wrecker reasserted his grip and shifted his stance, allowing for more leverage. The gap peeled open faster. When Hunter got a sliver of a view into the cockpit, his blaster ready and set to stun, Sohi screamed.

Omega slid to his hip. "What's wrong? Why's she sound like that?"

Hunter didn't know. Another trick?

A whisper in the back of his mind, beneath the anger and the combat readiness, said, *I don't think so.*

He nudged Omega behind him. "Stay back until I clear it."

The gap widened, enough room for the blaster's barrel and a careful shot if necessary. Hunter had a better view of the pilot and copilot seats. They were empty.

Sohi writhed on the floor between the seats, clutching her stomach. Ponder was on one knee, wedged between the copilot's and navigator's seats, attempting to comfort her. The clone did not look up when he begged, "Don't shoot. Please. She needs help."

In a final mighty yank, Wrecker slammed the door into its recessed groove. At Ponder's request—and against his better judgment—Hunter did not shoot. Instead, he let Tech and Phee into the cockpit, where they assessed the situation.

"What happened?" Phee asked, pressing the back of her hand to Sohi's cheek before checking her pulse.

"Sharp . . ." Sohi winced. "Pain. Something wrong with . . . baby."

Phee looked to Tech, her panic evident. "You got a plan for this, Brown Eyes?"

"Beyond getting her off of the floor to a more comfortable position, I do not."

"We're in the"—Sohi whimpered but gutted through the pain—"Garel system. There's a planet called—"

Sohi cried out one last time before fainting.

"Oh no," Ponder said, clutching her face. He looked desperately to Phee, the most sympathetic adult present. "The planet is Tryth. She set a course when the pain first started. She knows a medic there—a relative of sorts. We have to get her to him."

Hunter said, "You're seriously asking us to help you."

"I'm *begging* you to help my partner and our child. I have no expectations. I know what we've done, and you have no reason to trust us. We are at your mercy." Resigned to whatever fate was decided on their behalf, Ponder clutched Sohi's hands and began to cry. "Please be all right, love. Please."

All eyes fell on Hunter. He'd been against everything that had inevitably gone wrong, yet he took no comfort in having his pessimistic reservations justified. Not now.

He cursed, holstered his blaster. "Tech, get us to Tryth. Omega—"

"I'm staying with Sohi," Omega said. "Wrecker, I'll need the medpac."

"On it," Wrecker said, bounding to the back.

Entry into Tryth's atmosphere was by the numbers until the *Marauder* broke the gray-black cloud cover and injected them all into a vicious electrical storm.

Hunter and Omega helped Ponder get an unconscious Sohi upright and secured while the ship bounced unnervingly through the turbulent maelstrom. Even through her gown and his armor, Hunter detected the fever baking her. A moment after they got her harness buckled, the ship bounced hard enough to hurl Hunter into Wrecker and toss Ponder in the galley's direction.

Ponder worked to get his cybernetic leg under him, and Hunter might've lent a hand, but his willingness to assist the duo who'd drugged him and his family was spent. Ponder could make it to his seat on his own.

Wrecker must've been in a kinder mood because he assisted the hobbled clone, so Hunter left them to it and took a seat in the cockpit.

"What are we looking at?" he asked.

Wicked forking lightning of a purple hue crackled ahead, and the ship took another turbulent blow.

"It's bumpy," Tech said.

"Do we even know where we're going?" Hunter asked.

"Sohi punched in coordinates before she got sick," Tech said. "Getting there is going to be the difficult part. This storm is ionized."

Phee said, "Say it in a way everyone understands."

"It's not only air currents disrupting flight. Unpredictable magnetic fields are jostling us. I don't know why. Perhaps when we can see—"

Another jolt was followed by a sound of distressed metal that Hunter didn't like. The *Marauder* listed left.

"Oh," said Tech. "We lost a flap."

"Can we land without it?" Hunter asked.

"Let's hope so."

Another lightning bolt sizzled before them. Tech pitched them down and right, compensating for their lost flap. It was a stomach-lurching, panic-inspiring maneuver that had them skirting between lightning bolts with zero forward visibility because the cloud banks were so dense. The thrusters roared, and Hunter's jaw clenched. He trusted Tech with his life, but this was a bit much.

The drop lasted another horrible minute before the clouds thinned into mist. The overcast topography of Tryth revealed itself in stark flashes of electricity that made Hunter think his eyes deceived him. Some rivers looked silver under the effects of a nighttime storm.

Except they still looked silver when the lightning receded for lengthy periods. Not water, but . . .

"Is that mercury?" Phee said, voicing Hunter's thoughts.

"Possibly," Tech said. "Might explain some of the strange magnetic phenomena."

"Tech, are we near Sohi's coordinates?" Hunter asked.

"We're at least an hour away."

An hour?

Was that time Sohi could spare?

If Hunter had steeled himself against any empathy for Sohi, Ponder, and their situation, it would've been justified given the lies and betrayal the couple brought. But Omega just had to go and remind everyone about the baby. She'd called them family.

She wasn't wrong.

"Do what you can," Hunter said to Tech and maybe himself.

Family.

The storm raged on.

CHAPTER TWENTY-FIVE

MOTEN ESTATE, DALLOW

With the secure protocols, Crane checked in with Command to assure them all was okay. "This is a special records update for Investigator Olyen Brey from Investigator Sendril Crane, confirmation code 72-AU897."

Brey said, "Update line open, confirmation code 09-AU654."

"The subject is Cellia Moten."

"The red file is open. Proceed with the debrief. I'm glad I heard from you when I did. I was moments away from dispatching an enforcer squadron. How was your night?"

"Uneventful."

"That's surprising," Brey said, his hologram glitching as he recorded notes. "I've never known one of your leads to shake loose dust."

"I had a brief conversation with the subject—I'm hesitant to call it an interrogation. She's an older woman who needs rest. She was cooperative in providing personnel files, which my team combed through while also researching the assailants Moten named in her home invasion. Plenty of background on one Phee Genoa and the rogue members of Clone Force 99. But the bureau was already privy to all that."

Brey glitched again. "A shame. Nothing of note on Krill Sans?"

"Nothing."

"Very well. Command says to gather any intel on Moten until you have actionable leads on the pirate and the clones."

And Gayla, Crane thought.

"Understood," Crane said. "Will report back soon."

Crane deactivated the comm unit, removed his visor, and squeezed his eyes shut to stem a stress headache. He'd been engaged all night in what might've sounded like civil discourse but was really negotiations for his survival. The same way Cellia recognized having a contact inside the ISB was beneficial—as opposed to another officer disappearing on her watch—Crane realized that honoring the terms of his defection—absolute loyalty to the Empire—wasn't in anyone's best interest (particularly when three repeater rifles were near).

That was what drove his willingness to deal on Cellia Moten's terms for now. While Crane didn't fear death, he loathed the thought of dying when he was so close to getting Gayla back. And her baby. *His* grandchild.

For all intents and purposes.

He stepped into the corridor and heard his team stirring in the common area, already hard at work, crunching the available data. They stood at attention when he entered the room, an unnecessary show of respect and subservience he'd never tire of. "As you were," he instructed before making a show of sniffing the air. "I don't smell any caf."

Weilan sprang from his seat to initiate a brew.

"Drand," Crane said, "where are we?"

Drand approached with her datapad and began her report.

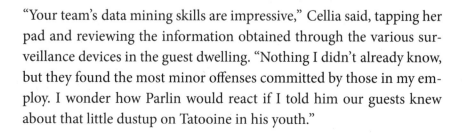

"Your team's data mining skills are impressive," Cellia said, tapping her pad and reviewing the information obtained through the various surveillance devices in the guest dwelling. "Nothing I didn't already know, but they found the most minor offenses committed by those in my employ. I wonder how Parlin would react if I told him our guests knew about that little dustup on Tatooine in his youth."

Crane sliced into his juicy steak and brought a dripping, bloody chunk to his lips, savoring the aroma before popping it into his mouth. He said while chewing, "Violently would be my guess."

"So insightful." Cellia grinned. "Did you file a report about me?"

"I did. I'll need to gradually nudge Command from their suspicions about your role in Krill Sans's disappearance, but I don't see any problems in the misdirection we agreed upon."

"Excellent!"

They sat at opposite ends of a long quartz table accented with gold filigree. Seating for sixteen lined the sides, but only Crane and Cellia were present. The space was so grand that on initial entry, Crane wondered if they'd have to shout to hear each other, but the room's expertly engineered acoustics made that a moot point. Crane could hear her breathing, quick and excited.

She looked up from the datapad, beaming. "I cannot tell you how happy I am that we found common ground in our desire to do what's best for the galaxy."

"The greater good," Crane said through more meat.

She often rambled and went off on tangents. She sometimes made wild leaps between thoughts like a droid with a scrambled processor, though Crane discerned a common thread throughout the nonsense.

Her.

There was no more tremendous admirer of Cellia Moten than Cellia Moten. In that, Crane found a path to stay among the living. He would agree with her or plant seeds for good ideas she could later claim she originated.

Like this one. "If we use joint resources to find Phee Genoa and her cronies, we can still get that mortar you covet."

"Won't the credit-tracking program you described eventually point us to them?"

"If they haven't already deduced how I found them in the first place. If they put it together, they won't use those funds again."

Cellia nodded. "I see."

She summoned Parlin through a comlink. He emerged through the automated doors a moment later. "Yes, Mistress."

"I want my mortar, and I wish to punish Phee Genoa and her clones for not dying quietly here. Let's combine efforts with our friends at the ISB to accomplish that goal."

Crane smirked while finishing his meal.

"Of course," Parlin said. "Do you have a specific plan in mind?"

Cellia focused on the datapad again. "Crane, can you tell him what we were thinking here?"

"Cellia thought we might put out feelers to ISB informants, my contacts, and the various loyalists she cultivated throughout the galaxy in her bid for the regional governorship."

"Low level, though," Cellia said without looking up. "I'd hate to disturb busier friends occupied with pressing business matters."

Or pressing criminal *matters,* Crane thought, recalling the infamous list of known associates in her red file, in addition to the ones she'd obliviously bragged about once she decided Crane was an ally. Who boasts about fraternizing with Hutts?

Parlin dipped his head. "Understood, Mistress. I'll connect with our contacts immediately."

"I'll do the same," Crane said.

Parlin left the way he came, and Crane waited for whatever else Cellia wanted to discuss. He hoped it wouldn't be too long of a rant. He'd yet to try the bed in his quarters and was nearing total collapse after spending all night in her grove.

Cellia, for her part, couldn't have gotten much more rest than him, yet her energy seemed boundless when she said, "Can we speak about Sheev?"

Crane would never get used to such casual use of the Emperor's name. She wielded it with the same weight as discussing her Hutt friends. He said, "I'm happy to talk, though I don't know how much I have to say."

"Don't sell yourself short. You have a fantastic team at your disposal, so perhaps you can satisfy a lingering curiosity of mine."

"I'll try."

She leaned forward, her smile laser bright. "What's Sheev building?"

Crane's face creased. He had no clue how to respond other than honestly. "I don't know what you're referring to."

"Exactly. He's building something *big*, and thanks to your confirmation, I know it's a *secret*. Even from the ISB." She clapped her hands like an amused child. "Such a sly fellow."

"Keep in mind, my role in the ISB wouldn't necessarily expose me to any of the Emperor's projects. Nothing I'm involved in has been construction-related until I met you. But to that end, it can't be so secretive if you know about it."

She pushed out of her seat as spry as he'd seen her and just about trotted to Crane's end of the table clutching her datapad. He might've feared an attack if she were more intimidating and less nettling. As things stood, he only feared another hour or two of ranting.

Dragging the nearest chair next to him, its legs screeching against the floor, she turned the pad so he could read the documents displayed there.

"I'm not supposed to know. Nobody is. These are invoices from supply companies I use for my largest projects. The same companies I used when I constructed three of Sheev's homes. You should see the one I built on Byss. It's truly a marvel."

Crane reviewed the data. Large—gargantuan, honestly—purchases of raw materials. But nothing indicated a purpose or any overt connection to the Empire. Might she be mistaken? Or deluding herself?

Cellia read his perplexed expression and clarified. "The purchases are through shell companies. Some are new, but some are the ones I was instructed to bill when I worked on his homes. I recognize the pattern—though it's on a scale I've never seen, and I've built Star Destroyer factories. So, my question is, what could it possibly be?"

Explained that way, it wasn't a horrible inquiry. Crane bet it wasn't her only one. He asked, "Are you also curious why he wouldn't have contracted this massive project to you? His dear friend."

"Are you reading my mind, Agent Crane?"

"I simply understand your frustration. You want to serve, as do I. You need information to do it well."

Cellia said, "You truly understand the needs of the galaxy. Now get me answers, and I'll see what my sources can piece together about your missing protégé. I look forward to discussing our discoveries soon."

CHAPTER TWENTY-SIX

APPROACHING FELLIAN OUTPOST, TRYTH

The cloud deck dropped lower the longer they flew, a great sky leviathan stalking their descent, closing to swallow the *Marauder*. Finally, Tech pointed. "There, I see it."

The crew followed his gaze to pinpricks of light—evidence of a small city—piercing the swirling mist and rain that pelted the viewport. Tech exhaled all the tension he'd been holding inside. He'd already calculated the probability of them reaching their destination intact, and his assessment was encouraging, but still, he loosened his grip on the yoke, allowing hands that had been cramping for the last several minutes some relief.

Sohi hadn't regained consciousness, so they still relied on the coordinates she'd punched in before her episode, hoping that in her pained state she hadn't mistyped. With the swelling colony in view, it was clear she'd managed an accurate heading. The destination was a far cry from the posh modern spaceport they'd fled on Dallow or even the crowded hub on Mygeeto. The structures and spires fanning out for kilometers in every direction were industrial. Smokestacks chugged undulating columns of white-blue exhaust. Immeasurable lengths of piping ran from one scaffolded building to another, many hissing steam or dripping unknown liquids at the joints.

Wrecker stood at the cockpit's door, abandoning his harness and relying on his strength to keep him stable during the frequent bumps. He leaned over Hunter's shoulder with something like awe in his voice. "What is this place?"

Despite his disdain for Sohi and Ponder's deception, Hunter said, "Somewhere that can help them. I hope."

The local spaceport tower hailed them. Tech opened the comm, and a gruff voice initiated docking procedures in a most unorthodox way. "Hey, ship! Who are ya?"

Tech frowned. "We are a merchant vessel," Tech began, "making an unscheduled landing due to a medical emergency."

At the sound of Tech's voice, Ponder burst into the cockpit—at least as far as Wrecker's bulk allowed. He shouted to be heard through Tech's open line.

"We need a medic by the name of Jatil Omstock. Do you know him?"

"They're looking for Jatil," the traffic controller told someone in the tower.

"Who's looking?" A lower, more guarded voice joined in the background.

"What's your clearance code?" the controller demanded. Tech broadcast one of the counterfeit identification codes they rotated as needed, then muted the line to chastise Ponder. "If you want this to go well for her, we must reach the ground without arousing suspicion."

"Too late for that," Omega mused, having joined them at the front.

The controller checked back in. "Yer code's good, but who are ya, and what business do you have with Jatil? I ain't clearing ya for landing till ya tell us!"

Hunter's gaze was cold when he told Ponder, "You got us into this."

"Tell them . . ." Ponder's face scrunched. He pressed fingers to his temple as if trying to push the correct response out of his brain. "Tell them '*Zellias bloom unseen but by few*.'"

A new voice came on the line. Softer, more refined. Perhaps angry. "I don't recognize your voices. Who are you, and how do you know that phrase?"

The *Marauder* shuddered around them, a prelude to total failure.

Tech said, "If we could land—"

"Tell me how you know that phrase, or the moment you touch down, I'm going to have my mechanic droid friends fire a hundred long nails through your viewport, which will likely negate your need for further assistance."

"I would say so," Tech mumbled under his breath.

"Jatil, the phrase came from Gayla Reen," Ponder said. "She's with us and she's in trouble."

"Put her on."

"She's unconscious."

Extended silence on the line. The *Marauder* listed, and the engines whined.

Hunter leaned over Tech. "Tower! What's the verdict here?"

"Land," Jatil said. "And tell me what's going on with Gayla while you do."

Ponder did.

Tech made the wobbly touchdown, straining against the hobbled ship.

He dropped the landing ramp, and before it bumped the tarmac, Ponder was moving. He freed Sohi from her harness and carried her to the landing crew droids, which had a levitating stretcher waiting. With them was a stoic-faced, tanned Lothalite that had to be Jatil. As soon as Ponder had Sohi resting, the supposed medic directed the droids to a bulky transport that was half loaded with what appeared to be broken stones with silver veins peeking through the surface. The propulsion on Sohi's stretcher stirred up a cloud of mine dust as it settled in the transport's cargo compartment. Ponder hopped in next to her, utilizing one large stone as the galaxy's most uncomfortable seat.

"Let's go!" he urged, desperate.

Jatil looked to Hunter, Wrecker, Tech, Phee, and Omega, who'd crowded the loading ramp to assess the situation. The medic yelled, "We'll be at my clinic in the merchant district. You can follow us or ask anyone. They'll point the way."

Jatil didn't wait for a reply as he leaped behind the transport's controls and accelerated out of the spaceport.

Hunter had no plans to follow or ask about the clinic. Instead, he said, "How soon are we air-ready?"

Tech's expression was flat. "We know about the missing flap but have no indication of other problems. I need to run a full diagnostic— that's half a day—and complete the most critical repairs. Minimum, two days."

"One day," Hunter countered.

"He can't promise that," Omega said.

A nearby ground crew droid was eavesdropping and offered unsolic-ited advice to MEL-222, who trekked over and relayed the message in apprehensive beeps.

Phee translated, "Ground crew's saying we should let the storm pass. Could be three days."

Hunter's response was inappropriate and colorful.

MEL-222 chirped an extended indignant tone.

"I will not apologize," Hunter said, directing his ire at Phee. "This is all your fault. We never should've agreed to any of this!"

"Any of what?" Omega asked, her arms crossed. Her frown and de-meanor making her look older than she was.

"Following Sohi's mysterious coordinates. These missions. Pabu!"

Omega's face went slack, stunned.

Phee didn't mince words. "You know, you seemed pretty grateful about my bringing you to Pabu when you didn't have anywhere else to go. But, whatever. We're doing this. When are you going to stop this whiny blame game? You *did* agree—to all of it—so that's on you, Hunter. I don't have any power over your decisions, Wrecker's, Omega's, or Brown Eyes's. So stop making me the scapegoat because your little ego's bruised."

"You think this is about ego? Are you mad?"

"You make this about you *all the time*. But guess what? Nearly every-thing Clone Force Ninety-Nine does takes a turn that requires some wriggling to set right—no matter whose bright idea the mission was. It doesn't bother you that you're in a tough situation. It bothers you that you weren't the one that led us into it!"

A coldness swept over Hunter. Partially from the storm winds and partially from the general sense of agreement he felt coming off Omega, Tech, and Wrecker. It wasn't a sensation of anger or even frustration. His team—his family—just heard words they may have wanted to say themselves. And they were relieved.

He turned to the group. "Something you'd like to add?"

Tech said, "There are instances when your assumptions overpower your assessments. Particularly as of late."

"I don't know what that means."

Wrecker spoke softly. "You're trying to make the best choices for us."

"What's wrong with that? We don't like good choices now? I've reached my limit of bad choices this trip. You haven't?"

Omega clarified. "*For* us. Not *with* us. What *you* think is right isn't always the same for us."

Hunter fought to keep his voice measured when he made the point they must be missing. "We're here. We're alive. We're together."

"Not all of us, brother," Tech said.

That stopped Hunter as effectively as a stun blast. Bringing up Crosshair—even without saying his name—was a low blow. "Well then, I guess you've made your point."

Phee said, "Are you going to throw a tantrum now? Stomp off to sulk in the rain?"

"I'm a soldier. I don't . . . *tantrum.*"

Omega, sheepish, drew closer. "I want to make sure that Sohi and the baby are all right. We're going to have to be here awhile anyway. Right, Tech?"

Tech nodded.

"So," Omega continued, "let's scout the area and figure next steps. Take some time to think."

She meant time to cool down, and Hunter knew she was right. They'd been cooped up in the *Marauder* for too long, and that wasn't helping anyone's mood.

Tech said, "Mel and I will begin diagnostics immediately. I'll establish rapport with the spaceport crew to source potential parts. It would be helpful if Hunter and Wrecker could secure provisions since we will exhaust our rations by tomorrow."

"I can go alone," Hunter said.

"No," Wrecker said, "I'm coming, too."

Now who was making choices for who?

Wrecker elaborated, "We'll make food happen."

"Remember, if 'making food happen' requires a purchase," Tech said, "don't use any of Sohi's credits. I'd like a closer look at them first."

After all agreed, Hunter addressed Phee: "As you've pointed out, I don't have much say in our current situation. So, may I ask if you're going to accompany Omega to the clinic?"

"Yes. I also want to see how Sohi and the baby are doing."

"Keep your comlinks in reach. Any trouble anywhere, sound an alarm." Hunter begrudgingly added, "Unless there are objections? Are there?"

No. That was an order everyone agreed with.

CHAPTER TWENTY-SEVEN

MOTEN ESTATE, DALLOW

"This is a special records request for Investigator Olyen Brey from Investigator Sendril Crane, confirmation code 72-AU897."

Brey flickered into view. "Request line open, confirmation code 09-AU654. Proceed."

"I had another meeting with Cellia Moten. No new information on our investigations was garnered, but she proceeded with an odd line of inquiry, and I want to find answers."

"You're asking questions on *her behalf*?"

Crane sensed apprehension on Brey's side and altered his tone. "No. That's not what I mean. She asked me an odd question I'd like to clarify as a way of better assessing her motivations."

"Understood," Brey said. "Proceed."

"She indicated the Emperor has some secret construction project in the works. She's pieced this together from a convoluted documentation trail. Is there any validity to this?"

Brey glanced at his console, searching whatever records he had access to. "Unclear. What kind of project?"

"She couldn't say, only that it's utilizing a massive number of resources."

"Interesting. I'll raise it to Command and see what we get. Hold."

The secure hologram shifted from Brey's face to a flat haze. Crane waited for Brey to continue. Time stretched, then stretched more. Crane knew some records requests could get tedious when the person doing the gathering didn't have advance notice, but this wait was excessive. And concerning.

Crane spoke to the holographic static. "Are you there?"

The comm disconnected as if the call was over.

Crane leaned forward, checking the terminal for malfunction. The console beeped with an incoming call. Brey reestablishing the connection. A glitch, then. Crane answered.

The holographic face on the other side of the transmission was familiar and startling . . .

"Colonel Yularen?" Crane gasped. He was so surprised—a rare occurrence—that he forgot his station. "Where is Brey?"

The silver-haired, mustached commander spoke quick and clipped. "I will be your line to special records requests for the remainder of your time away. You mentioned one Cellia Moten making erroneous connections between the Emperor and some materials acquisitions. Elaborate."

Every alarm in Crane's head sounded, scoring the obvious question: *What dirty secret have I stumbled upon?*

He knew better than to ask another question without answering the one posed. He detailed what he would have considered a half-baked conspiracy theory if Brey had returned and dismissed the notion in a normal fashion. That Crane was communicating with a high-ranking officer like Yularen proved Cellia Moten's hunches were spot-on. Did the bosses know they'd bolstered her credibility? And should Crane be concerned if they did?

Yularen seemed to be reading off a datapad when he said, "These companies Moten acquired the invoices from, Konsmata and Incostar Systems. Are they the only two?"

"There were more, but I didn't note them, because I didn't believe they were relevant to my current investigations."

"Get the names. I'll expect them in your next report."

Crane swallowed hard, then said, "May I ask about the urgency of this request?"

"It's an order, not a request. And no. You may not."

"Understood."

Yularen said, "Do you have further questions?"

Of course, he did! He was wise enough not to ask them.

"No, sir."

The transmission ended.

Now, this was disconcerting. Cellia was digging into a deeper gravity well than he'd anticipated, and his primary question was, Would they all get sucked in?

His carefully threaded survival tapestry might be overwhelming to some in its complexity, but this was a familiar stress to Crane. He was undercover for the bureau, pretending to be a willing operative for Cellia, while realizing the bureau may not be so fond of him after digging too deeply into very important beings' affairs.

Most seasoned operatives would see the danger here. He did as well. He also saw *options*.

Once a double agent . . .

FELLIAN OUTPOST, TRYTH

A local taxi transported Omega and Phee to the clinic. It was supposed to be a short ride from the spaceport, but it felt longer because the driver, a broad-faced Snivvian named Burk, talked the whole time. Phee rarely enjoyed a chatty cabbie—it often put her cover story through unnecessary rigor when she was somewhere she shouldn't be—but this driver filled them in on crucial details they hadn't pieced together in their short time onworld.

"Fellian Outpost is a processing town," he said, in his deep, melodic voice. "Mercury refinement is a base additive for various fuels."

Phee said, "How long has that been your main industry?"

"Centuries, I guess. My parents left their homeworld for the opportunities here. As the saying goes, 'The plant is always hiring.' "

"You're just that busy, eh?" Omega asked.

"Always. We thought the war effort was demanding. But peacetimes haven't slowed down demand at all. The Empire must have places to go! That, and folks keep falling into the merc vats."

Phee couldn't tell if he was joking. He didn't sound like he was joking. She turned her attention to the scenery scrolling by and left Omega to be the charming conversationalist.

It was an oppressive night, compounded by storm clouds roiling overhead. The entire city was grimed by factory dirt, and muggy humidity gave every inhalation a mildewy tinge. Phee had seen many worlds like this, full of decent beings braced against the ever-encroaching pressures of living. A routine so strenuous it made the buildings sweat.

Various plasma lights and signage bordered their route—food, drink, and entertainment of the seedier variety. Gruff workers of different sizes and species milled about either in the direction of the steaming refinery or toward their homes and the night district, to rest or play before the industrial wheel rolled them back around.

"We're here," Burk said, jovial to get paid.

They reached a modest storefront, its signage dark, though even unlit the universal symbol for medicine was easy to read.

Omega climbed out, and Phee paid (with clean credits) just as a fresh round of mercury downpour began. Whatever had happened to this atmosphere, it remained breathable, and the droplets maintained the feel of water, but they were slightly heavier and shimmered like silver splinters falling. The rain pattered loudly off Omega's poncho.

Burk took his fee and a healthy tip, thanked them for being good riders, then said, "If you need more help getting around, call dispatch and ask for me!"

Omega and Phee entered the clinic's empty, dingy waiting room. Ambient lighting fostered a gloomy feel, but brighter lights seeped from a back room.

"Let's get this hydration solution in her immediately," Jatil Omstock said from down the corridor, his voice firm but not panicked. Phee took that as a good sign. When she followed Omega into the examination room, the child recoiled, her hand pressed to her lips to wrangle a gasp, and Phee reevaluated her enthusiasm.

She turned the corner and saw what Omega saw: Sohi prone on an examination table, her blue complexion gone a dusky gray. Luminescent diagnostic rings encircled her from collarbone to thigh, obscuring the view of her torso and hips. A levitating medical droid assisted Jatil in loading medicinal vials from a cabinet into injection ports on the exam table.

Ponder stood in the corner, hugging himself, tears cutting down his cheeks. He looked as helpless as anyone Phee had ever seen.

Jatil noticed he had an audience. "It's good that you got her to me when you did. It's going to be touch and go. But . . . maybe. Maybe."

"The baby?" Ponder said.

Jatil seemed slightly annoyed but spoke to the droid. "Bring up the monitor."

The droid projected a display onto the wall with myriad readings Phee could not possibly understand.

Though Omega did.

The child squinted, scrutinizing the charts and figures, rapidly scanning information.

Finally, after checking a few of the readings, Jatil addressed Ponder's question. "The same as the last time you asked, friend. I don't know yet."

Omega stepped fully into the room, resting her hands on the examination table. She leaned in, scrutinizing Sohi while doing double takes over the monitor readings.

Jatil said, "You all should step out of the room while I—"

"Have you administered cardinex yet?" Omega accessed the hologram's augmented reality menu with a sturdy finger and rapidly punched commands.

"Excuse me? What are you doing?"

"Checking your work."

"I . . ." Jatil was taken aback, but he answered the challenge. "Cardinex is only moderately effective for Keshiri. It won't bring her out of her shock state."

"Not true." Whatever Omega had done in the menus, new readings appeared, along with an image of some chemical bonding process. "Cardinex in a ninety-five percent saline solution will help regulate vitals almost immediately."

Jatil looked over Omega's work, considering. "This is an odd mix. Why are you so certain it will work?"

"It's because of the baby," Omega insisted. "The child is half-clone, and that's why your current approach isn't working. Most likely, enhanced protein markers have been passed to the child from Ponder, so its optimized biology is siphoning the beneficial effects of your current treatment and keeping Sohi in shock."

"How could you possibly know that?"

"I assisted in a bunch of medical procedures on Kamino. All our patients were clones. I know their biology as well as anyone." She knew *her* biology as well as anyone was a more appropriate way to say it, but it was best to keep discussion of her clone heritage between her and her brothers.

Phee watched Jatil's face shift from curiosity to respect. "All right. Everything you've said so far tracks." Jatil looked to Ponder. "Any objections?"

"None if you can help my family."

Jatil told Omega, "Show me more."

Omega went to work. First talking Jatil through the intricacies of clone biochemistry, then taking full charge while the local medic and his droid played dutiful assistant. When Omega retrieved an intimidatingly long syringe from Jatil's supplies with the intent to use it, Phee, apparently, had had enough. The pirate backed out of the room and said, "I will leave you to it."

CHAPTER TWENTY-EIGHT

FELLIAN OUTPOST, TRYTH

P hee noted her surroundings. There wasn't much else on this level besides the waiting room, Jatil's cluttered office with the door ajar and his name placard over the jamb, and a staircase going up.

She followed the path past a second-floor corridor, then kept on to a rooftop landing overlooking fields of piping. The metalwork ran from the processing plant and beyond, toward silhouetted mountains that sat like distorted sleeping giants on the horizon. The rain had stopped, leaving silver puddles in the worn, even areas of the roof, and the metallic smell in the air reminded her of new machine parts, system components, and the man who'd see such things as puzzle pieces in need of assembly.

Phee opened a comms channel. "Hey, Brown Eyes. You're missing an impressive view."

Tech said, "Somehow, I doubt that."

"I was talking about me."

Back in the *Marauder*, Tech sat upright, breaking away from the console he'd been hunched over. MEL-222 was on the other side of the cockpit, running the *Marauder*'s diagnostic program. Tech thought the droid might not have heard Phee's provocative comments, but MEL-222 let loose an undulating wolf whistle.

Tech said, "While your self-appraisal is not without merit, I've got my eyes on the credits Sohi paid us with."

"Really? Find anything interesting."

"Not so much interesting as discouraging. There's embedded coding that pings the locations of terminals where the credits are spent. I suspect the intended purpose is clandestine data mining, but in our case it's as effective as a homing beacon if we were to use any more of these funds."

"Can you nullify the code?"

"Not without the proper encryption key."

"Seriously? *You* can't get around *that*?"

"I could if I worked the problem, uninterrupted, for anywhere from two to five centuries, but that hardly seems like a feasible approach."

"Fair point." Phee's tone became downtrodden. "Pabu really needs those funds."

"I am aware. Which led me to reexamine Mel's erroneous auction house code."

MEL-222 chirped something rude.

Tech ignored it and continued. "I wondered if the credits we'd siphoned from the other bidders might still be accessible to assist in a workaround for the island."

Phee said, "Are they?"

"No. Once our ruse was revealed, the attendees had a slew of personal slicers working the problem and retracted their funds before we jumped to hyperspace."

"Not that I don't love that velvety voice of yours, but why are you telling me this?"

"I corrected the code."

Phee shook her head. "I'm happy for you, Brown Eyes. A small victory is still a victory, I suppose."

Tech nodded, satisfied, then changed the subject. "Do we have a status on Sohi?"

Phee's flirtatious lilt fell away. "She's in rough shape. Omega's helping."

"Then her chances of recovery are vastly improved."

"On that, I'd have to agree. Have Hunter and Wrecker checked in?"

"Not yet, but nothing's exploding, so I'm confident they're doing fine."

"We passed a hotel on the way. Should I get rooms?"

Tech glanced at MEL-222's console, noting where they were in the diagnostics routine. "It would be for the best."

"Hopefully, they have enough for everyone."

"Then why does it sound like you're hoping for the opposite?"

"It would be a shame if, after all that time in space, some of us might be forced to double up with absolutely no privacy." She was not being coy about her entendre. "I wonder who might have to make such a sacrifice?"

"Go. I'll wait to hear about the outcome," Tech said, refusing to reveal his preferences on the matter.

It was a fun little game they played.

Wrecker and Hunter perused the merchant district to get supplies for the trip back to Pabu. They found a strip of road lined with storefronts run by locals barking their wares.

"Come see, come see. My meiloorun's better than what's up the block. You'll be back to me overpriced and underwhelmed."

"This honey-wine is fermented using an ancient family recipe. The best around."

"You two seem like you know good cooking. Whatever you like gets better with my Trythian redsprout."

Wrecker sensed the air of routine competition with underlying desperation. There were more merchants than shoppers. More goods than people in need of them. The massive amount of credits that flowed toward this world as its mercury flowed out seemed to stop inside the processing plant's walls.

Turning a corner, they came across a mural along the side of a building. It was of clone troopers—Regs—five meters high in formation, their visors tipped toward the sky with a single robed figure leading, face in shadow, a lightsaber ignited with a golden blade, and the Republic sigil in the background. A famous war slogan was stenciled over their heads: UNITE.

Wrecker never cared much for the simple and overused slogan, particularly when they fought beside Reg squadrons that had adapted it as a war cry. Who was it for? The clones were already united—they'd been bred for that. They certainly weren't uniting with the droids and enemy combatants they dismantled in combat.

The mural was a stunning, ominous piece of art despite the graffiti that sullied it now: Huge red slashes across several troopers' necks. Eyes painted over with Xs or shaped into silly caricatures. The foul language over most of the image indicated a clear Separatist alignment among these working folks. And it didn't bother Wrecker one bit—the old ways didn't matter anymore. He got why locals defaced war propaganda from their enemy. The art wasn't inspiration to *unite*; it was an order to *submit*. These people didn't comply. Wrecker had a lot of respect for that these days.

He said, "Good thing we left the armor on the ship, eh?"

"You're not wrong," Hunter agreed.

They worked through their supply list, filling a massive satchel that might've required droid assistance if anyone but Wrecker was doing the lifting. He trod beside Hunter, the heavy sack hoisted over his shoulder as he chewed a meiloorun fruit to its pit, attempting to keep conversation between him and Hunter light after the tense exchange back at the *Marauder*. "That Bith vendor wasn't lying. It is good, and the price was reasonable."

"I'm happy you're happy," Hunter said, his voice low and distracted.

Wrecker craned his neck as they walked the block, taking inventory of the sellers in their vicinity. "We should probably get more soap. We haven't exhausted our stockpile, but given the extra days and tight quarters, there's nothing wrong with being proactive here."

Hunter said, "I don't have a problem *not* leading."

Wrecker sighed, took a final bite of his fruit, and tossed the rind in a refuse receptacle. He'd known this would come out eventually. "Okay."

"I do know what *good* leadership looks like, though."

Wrecker pointed several stores down. "Is that a soap seller?"

"That's a basket stand. Are you trying to change the subject?"

"I thought those baskets had soap in them."

That was true, but he *was* trying to change the subject. It wasn't that Wrecker shied away from tough topics, though he'd prefer it if tactics were involved. Hunter's discomfort with what Phee had implied was not something Wrecker had a strategy to solve. Sometimes they all needed to hear tough stuff, then sit with it. As good a leader as Hunter was, he wasn't so good at that.

Wrecker said, "Come here."

He led them back to an intersection they'd passed through earlier. Looking one way down the cross street presented a mountain view beyond the city's borders.

Wrecker said, "When you asked me about staying on Pabu, it's fine, the sunshine and water. Most like that sort of thing. But give me this view any day!"

The occasional silver spout of a mercury geyser broke the darkness like a blade run through the planet then suddenly yanked free. Unsettling but beautiful. Very Wrecker. What was he getting at, though?

"So you want to stay *here*?" Hunter asked.

"No. I don't want to *stay* anywhere. But I can *live* anywhere. You should know that better than anyone."

Hunter's exasperation ramped up. "Yes, we're made to survive anywhere, but that's not what I meant about Pabu."

"It's not what I mean, either. *I* mean it's okay if we're not 'one mind, one weapon' or any of the other regimented fighter think that got drilled into us."

Hunter's face pinched. A war within him.

Wrecker clapped a hand on Hunter's shoulder. "I mean it. It's okay."

Wrecker pointed to a vendor stand a few storefronts down. "There's some soap."

This time, he wasn't wrong.

Back at the *Marauder,* Hunter and Wrecker stowed all the provisions and checked on Tech in the cockpit. At the sound of their approach, he rattled off updates.

"The spaceport machine shop fabricated a replacement flap that I finished installing moments before you arrived," Tech said. "There's carbon scoring from blasterfire we'll need buffed off the hull, but there's a sandblaster crew servicing vessels in the area tomorrow. I've already contracted them. Mel's still reviewing systems, but it appears that we'll be shipshape to take off once these ion storms clear."

Hunter, fighting to keep the hope from his tone, said, "Do we have a more precise estimate on when that might be?"

"We are still looking at two days minimum."

Hunter refrained from foul language. "What's the status on Omega and Phee?"

"Omega's at the clinic with Sohi and Ponder. Phee's secured lodging." Tech hoisted a small bag packed for a night away.

"We're not staying with the ship?" Hunter asked.

"Mel is," said Tech.

MEL-222 chirped, the sound of self-pity.

Tech said, "You don't sleep."

MEL-222 retorted. And it wasn't nice.

Hunter insisted they go to the clinic first. He wanted eyes on Omega, and then they could hunker down for the night. It was late, and foot traffic slowed considerably along the mud-crusted walkways of the town. Sure, a pub or two were available for those who preferred staring into an empty bottle after midnight. Mostly, these were working citizens who needed their rest.

A couple of days of this kind of calm might do them some good, Hunter thought, trying to make right with the things he couldn't change, something his family seemed insistent on him doing.

At the clinic, they found Phee in the empty waiting room, her feet kicked up on a table and a phaseball game on the holonet.

"Where's Omega?" Hunter asked.

"I'm doing well, Hunter," Phee said. "And how are you?"

He stared.

"She's with the patient. Kid's got skills."

Hunter was already on the move, walking the corridor in the only direction that made sense until he found the examination room. While he acquired proof-of-life on Omega, Tech sat next to Phee.

He said, "I once met a Reg who thought the outcome of all phaseball games was predetermined."

"I've heard that one," said Phee.

"I used to think it was an illogical conspiracy theory. There were too many variables to execute the ruse on such a large scale."

He let that hang without saying the rest. The same thing could be said about war. Before.

Phee touched the control resting on the arm of her chair; the holo-feed winked away.

Tech said, "I didn't intend to discourage your viewing."

"Eh. I don't like either of those teams much, anyway."

She placed the control on a nearby table, and when her hand returned, her fingers grazed Tech's. Two thumbs, barely touching. Tech thought the room got awfully warm.

"Wrecker," he said, a little too loudly, "what are you doing?"

Wrecker's back had been to them, but he turned, cradling a candy dish in the crook of his elbow while stuffing a freshly unwrapped styro-taffy in his mouth. "These are free, aren't they?"

Hunter found Omega, Jatil, and a medical droid conversing calmly before a projected display of Sohi's vitals while Ponder sat next to her, gripping one of her hands in both of his. She was awake but haggard. Her cheek-bones protruded, and the circles under her eyes were the darkness of space itself. A grim question bloomed in Hunter's mind, but he answered it himself when he spotted *two* heartbeats on the monitor. The baby was as it should be. Good news, despite Hunter's lingering disdain for the mother.

Sohi noticed him lurking in the doorway. "Hunter, you could probably take me now if that makes you feel better."

"It doesn't."

Omega greeted him with giddy, sparkling eyes. "Hey there, Hunter. I used some old Kamino know-how to care for Sohi and the baby. It was amazing!"

"You're amazing," Hunter said. And meant it.

Jatil said, "I concur. My medical training came from the battlefield, and I never had the occasion to work on a clone. The knowledge Omega shared is fascinating."

As much as Jatil marveled over Omega, the unspoken detail of Jatil's admission stuck with Hunter. He hadn't worked on clones, because he'd been in a Separatist detail. He'd fought on the other side. "How is it you know our friend Sohi?"

Sohi grimaced and twisted toward Jatil, perhaps to warn him not to speak so fast, but the severity of her condition prevented swift action.

Jatil said, "Gayla and I were in military school together. We—"

"Are both spies?" Hunter said.

Jatil caught Sohi's pointed stare too late. "We are old friends. Though it's been some time since we've seen each other. Congratulations, by the way."

"Thank you," Sohi said, squeezing Ponder's hand.

"Yes," Ponder offered. "You and the young one have our eternal gratitude."

The enthusiasm on Jatil's face slid a bit. "Gayla and the baby are stable for now. But I'm concerned about the level of medical care you've received throughout your gestation period. You seem underweight with elevated cortisol levels, indicating long periods of heightened stress. I've seen something similar among women who work in the processing plant. Stress puts strain on a pregnancy."

Sohi cleared her throat. "We've been forced to travel."

"I advise you stop that as soon as possible. Was Tryth your intended final destination?"

Ponder said, "No, Felucia. Do you think it would be a problem to make that trip?"

Sohi flashed wide eyes at Ponder. Hunter wasn't sure how to read it.

Was she displeased that he was asking questions on her behalf, or was she worried he'd said too much?

Jatil said, "Hyperspace travel is risky this late in gestation; there's a high chance of—"

Sohi clutched her stomach and groaned. She bit her bottom lip hard enough to draw blood. "Something's wrong."

Alarms rang from the monitor, and the display flashed red. Jatil sprang into action, tapping commands into the exam table console while motioning to Omega and the droid.

Sohi winced, then *screamed.*

Ponder was at her side in an instant, gripping her hand. Omega and Jatil glimpsed the flashing red monitor, the spiking numbers and undulating graphs displayed there. They looked at each other, and Omega said, "Is the baby coming now?"

"That would be my guess," Jatil said.

Ponder's voice raised with forced hope. "It's only a couple of days early. That's fine, right?"

Sohi squeezed his hand. Despite the agony she was trying to hide but couldn't, she tried to comfort him. "They're going to take care of me and our little one." Sohi cast a stern gaze toward Jatil. "Aren't you?"

Ponder couldn't see Sohi's face when she turned, but Hunter could, and he read the expression there as, *You better not indicate anything different, Jatil.*

Jatil understood and said, "We're going to administer the best care available in this system. But we're going to need the room."

Ponder's expression shifted to disbelief. "Wait. You want me to leave?"

Omega flicked a glance at the monitor again, then forced a smile that might've chilled Ponder to the bone if he knew her as well as Hunter did. She said, "This is not an official birthing room, so for us to maintain an ideal environment we need as few people present as possible."

It was nonsense. Merciful nonsense. Hunter grabbed Ponder's arm, expecting a fight, but Omega had sold the moment properly. "All right," Ponder said. "Anything to make it safe."

"Come on." Hunter guided him to the door.

"See you soon, my love," Ponder said.

"You will," she said.

Jatil said, "I'll call you when it's time to sing lullabies."

The door closed, and Hunter hoped all that'd been said would indeed come to pass.

But he wondered.

CHAPTER TWENTY-NINE

MOTEN ESTATE, DALLOW

"Did you know some Skakoans worship a god of innovation?" Cellia drank dark wine from a crystal flute while a blue plasma flame in her massive fireplace danced shadows across her face.

Crane considered it from the expensive, uncomfortable sitting room chair she'd directed him to. "I did not."

"Yes, what an admirable idea. For that god's followers, any progressive thoughts or technological advances are gifts from the deity. No autonomy, no credit, no pride for the beings themselves. Of all my religious studies, it's probably the closest to the truth."

"And the truth is?"

Cellia leaned forward in her thronelike armchair. "True innovators—the thinkers, builders, and leaders—are like gods bestowing blessings to their lessers. Don't you agree?"

"It depends. Do you consider *me* a 'lesser'?"

She leaned farther and patted his knee. "I said 'leader.' Is that not your role?"

"Would that make me a god of order? I like the ring of it. What aspect of existence would you occupy?"

A dreamy smile formed on her face. She'd considered this before,

Crane thought. She wanted to deliver it perfectly like she'd rehearsed in a mirror while counting all the former guests fertilizing her forest.

She said, "The God of Connections."

Crane had to admit that had a ring to it, too. He fought a shudder.

"All these years I spent watching Sheev work rooms and charm whoever needed charming, I had no clue of his grand aspirations. Viewing it through a lens of belief—of absolute faith—I have a better grasp of how he's accomplished so much. The results are something to behold. An inspirational blueprint, if you will."

"A blueprint to become an emperor?"

"No." She laughed, her eyes sparkling. "I suspect suggesting such might be considered treason."

"Perhaps."

"Naughty boy." Cellia winked. "We'll keep your little slip of the tongue our little secret."

We're racking up quite a few of those, aren't we, Cellia?

"Emperors require help, though—such a heavy burden," she said. "The best help is the kind you don't even know you need. The kind that solves problems you aren't even aware of. Sheev can expect that from me if he appoints me as a regional governor."

"I'm sure he appreciates that. You two being so close."

The humor and hope melted off her face. "You would think. He's so busy these days. Amedda's easy enough to reach, but I wonder if he's even passing along my messages. He was always very possessive of Sheev's time and attention. A sycophant who might come to do more harm than good."

"A problem the Emperor doesn't even know he has."

"Exactly!" Cellia's expression darkened quickly. Alarmingly. "Why are you still communicating with the ISB through secure protocols?"

Though the conversation had taken a dangerous turn, Crane did not react with any kind of concern whatsoever. In a calm and measured voice, he said, "It would seem strange if I were to abandon the secure protocols for an open line now. Especially given the information you're having me look into."

"That sounds true. It better be. What have you uncovered on Sheev's project?"

"Nothing. My contact is researching."

Cellia tapped the arm of her chair in an agitated rhythm. "That is not what I expected to hear."

"Funny. My contact said something similar when I told him there was nothing to report on you."

She stopped tapping, settling for silent contemplation. "Can we be assured of his discretion?"

"You don't seem to be assured of mine, so how much does anything I say right now matter?" Crane threw back the drink he'd requested upon arrival to this antagonistic meeting. "You didn't kill me last night, so there's no point in not trusting me now."

She stared into her wineglass as if the proper response could be found there.

Crane said, "I need to review those invoices you showed me for anything that might allow me to probe more judiciously. Away from watching eyes."

She was hesitant and irritated. She didn't like him speaking to her so directly. Good.

"The Gods of Connection and Order are not enemies, Cellia, so let's stop wasting time on unwarranted concerns. Let me see your invoices."

She faked a smile and ordered a droid to bring in her datapad. She accessed the information and passed it over.

Crane pretended to skim the entirety of each invoice while committing each company header to memory. Seven major firms in all. He returned Cellia's datapad. "I'm on it."

"Excellent." She had a different droid refill her wineglass.

"My turn," Crane said. "Have any of your galactic contacts gotten a lead on Gayla and the rest?"

Cellia tipped her head apologetically. "Nothing yet, I'm afraid. These things take time."

Perhaps. But Crane had the sense Cellia only worked in trades. If she did get a clue about Gayla taking some underground route or reaching some hovel of a destination, Cellia might not tell until her curiosity about the Emperor's machinations was satisfied. That was not optimal, but they'd yet to reach an impasse, so he let it go.

For now.

Parlin entered with his arms folded behind his back and his head bowed. "Mistress, the other matter of the evening requires your attention."

"No need to be coy. You can bring our guest in."

Parlin's chin ticked up, surprised. "Mistress?"

Cellia spoke directly to Crane. "You don't mind some additional company, do you?"

"This is your home. I wouldn't presume to have any opinion on who you allow in it."

She guffawed even though it wasn't funny, then made a come-hither hand gesture for Parlin to obey.

The Kiffar left the room briefly, then returned with a portly Sullustan. The being was awestruck by the extravagance of the palace, his neck craning to take it all in while his flaps undulated.

"I don't know what rancor crashed through the rest of the place, but this room's great."

Cellia's goodwill cooled by degrees. "Yes. I suppose so."

The Sullustan wore trousers and a faded leather vest with arms exposed. The tattoos marking his flesh were like a galactic thug's starter kit, indicating gang affiliations and boastings of criminal activities. As Crane noticed the Sullustan gangster's "uniform," the Sullustan noticed his.

"Hey!" The dewflaps flared. "What's a cop doing here?" His hand dropped to his hip, clutching for what Crane assumed would've been a blaster if Parlin hadn't already confiscated it.

Cellia attempted to de-escalate. "Relax, Jorm. He's an ISB agent, not a mere local officer. To be perfectly blunt, your lowly misdeeds are beneath him, so he should be of no concern this evening. Do you have what I asked for?"

Jorm relaxed *a little,* then lifted the sack he'd been carrying. He reached in and produced what looked like a petrified rectangle of sand with a bootprint in it. "An impression of the Lasat messiah walking on sacred soil. It took some doing, but it's all yours now. As soon as I get my credits, that is."

Cellia reached for it with greedy, clutching hands. Jorm passed it over, and she gave it a cursory examination before nodding her approval. "Very good." She next said to Crane, with malicious glee, "I hope you won't mind if we call it a night. I want to settle up with my friend Jorm."

"Of course." Crane couldn't get out of there fast enough. Not that speed was a factor at this point. He'd be an accessory to the Sullustan's murder no matter what. But he felt a need to put some distance between himself and Cellia's homicidal compulsions. Had she forgotten her lie to him about being done seeding her grove for the good of the galaxy, or had she decided she liked exposing her true self to him?

Neither option offered much comfort.

"A word outside, please, sir?" Drand said.

Crane entered the guest dwelling to find Drand waiting, almost at attention, while the others continued perusing their consoles and pretending not to listen.

He wanted to relay the corporate names from Cellia's invoices to Colonel Yularen sooner rather than later. Still, since he'd committed them to memory, he could spare a moment to deal with whatever this was. He waved her outside.

Their second evening on Dallow drew near with the dark bleeding into the sky at a side angle attributed to the planet's odd orbital tilt. Cellia's views were magnificent. Not enough to distract him from his disgruntled associate. "Yes?"

Drand let loose. "Why are we still here? We don't have leads on her robbers. We're rehashing old data and staring at the ceiling. Our talents can be of much better use doing almost *anything* else."

She did not mention that he hadn't come through with the promotion he'd all but promised before Cellia pressed a boot to his neck. He doubted Drand would be so agitated if she were wielding fresh power. Her disappointment was understandable, if not tolerable. "Command says stay, so we stay. I'm subject to their orders as you are to mine. Or have you forgotten?"

The snap in his tone was not lost on her. She stood straighter and did not look at him directly. "No, sir."

"Good."

"May I ask a follow-up question, sir?"

"Proceed."

"Is Cellia Moten so close to the Emperor that he's aware of us? Do you think he might know our names?"

Crane was surprised by the . . . *reverence* in Drand's voice. He wouldn't expect someone so young and early in their career to hold a figure she'd likely only seen through holovids in such high regard. Drand wanted to know if being in Cellia's presence might lift her name to the ears of the most powerful being in the galaxy.

The God of Connections would be pleased.

Crane was not. "It is unimportant if anyone knows our names, creeds, or contributions. Completing our mission is our only concern. If completion costs our lives, then it is a bargain price! Understood?"

"Yes, sir."

"If there's nothing else, I'll be in my quarters."

"Nothing else, sir."

Crane turned toward the guest dwelling entrance but stopped to ask, "What I said to you about completing missions? Did it sound familiar?"

"Yes, sir." Drand's voice cracked. She was lying. She'd forgotten he'd relayed the same principles to her on at least two other occasions. These young recruits did not seem to get it. The lot of them seemed more concerned about promotion than purpose.

Crane let out a long whistling breath, the most disdain he was willing to waste time on. What was the word Cellia used? *Lessers.* "Dismissed," he said.

He entered the guest dwelling not disappointed by the knowledge that his subordinates barely bothered to retain the wisdom of craft he offered freely. He was despondent. Grieving in his own way for Gayla, whom he'd been apart from too long.

He'd only had to tell her once.

CHAPTER THIRTY

FELLIAN OUTPOST, TRYTH

Hunter, Wrecker, and Ponder gathered on the clinic roof, overlooking streets gradually more void of citizens the later it got. Jatil had sent Phee and Tech on a supply run since the clinic wasn't necessarily outfitted for childbirth.

The deepening night did not bring peace or quiet. The air continuously thrummed with the nonstop production of refinery machines. The *whoosh-whoosh-whoosh* of hydraulics pumping mercury gave the impression of a great heartbeat, silver blood in grotesque veins, the city sitting like a rash on the planet's skin. Maybe one could get used to this place after some time, but Hunter could not conjure a scenario where he would want to.

Wrecker had brought up a stack of chairs from the waiting room and placed his by the door. It was an effective blockade every time Ponder tried to force his way back down to the examination room turned delivery room. After a third failed attempt, the father-to-be settled on the ledge and into his contempt for the rogue clones.

"The Bad Batch," Ponder said, spitting off the roof. "I got some more appropriate names for you dolts. Wanna hear them?"

Wrecker said, "I kind of do."

"That's my wife and child down there!"

Hunter said, "You two are our kidnappers and hijackers. Be grateful we don't throw you off this roof."

"Like you wouldn't do the same things for Omega."

Hunter leaned against a large cooling unit. He crossed his arms. Flexed his fingers. All sorts of small movements to keep himself from fulfilling his threat. "Watch yourself."

"Tell me I'm lying!" Ponder said, needing to redirect his anxiety. Needing a fight.

Hunter was happy to give him one. "You *married* that clone killer? Nice little detail you left out before."

The reminder of Clone Force 99's animosity doused some of Ponder's fire. "That part's new. We did it on Canto Bight."

"Before you stole a load of useless credits."

"Yes, that," Ponder said.

"Congratulations!" Wrecker said.

Hunter glared at him.

Wrecker said, "What? I'm impressed."

Through clenched teeth, Hunter said, "Why?"

Wrecker gazed upon Hunter almost sympathetically. "Because we know war. We can fieldstrip any weapon that's ever existed. We've seen more death than the galaxy should allow. What Ponder's talking about, for our kind, that's new. It's exciting."

"But—"

"But there will always be time for fighting. I can't stop you from fighting right now. But *I* want to hear about a clone's wedding." To Ponder, Wrecker said, "Did you have cake?"

Ponder blinked rapidly, as if disoriented by the twists of this exchange. "Yes. A small one."

"Walk me through it, Ponder." Hunter wasn't very enamored with nuptials, despite Wrecker's passionate argument. "How long before you knew what she was? Were you together for a while? Did she fill you in between loving hugs and kisses?"

"No. She told me who she was within days of our connection . . . blossoming."

"Really? Some poor spycraft there, wouldn't you say?"

"She was done with all that—the lies. Crane's manipulations whipped her this way and that, and she didn't want to follow in that monster's footsteps. She wanted to surrender to the Republic and atone for what she'd done."

"Let me guess. You stopped her."

"No. The Jedi Purge did."

That stunned Hunter silent.

Ponder said, "I still recalled the compassion of the Jedi on the day I lost my squadron. I talked Sohi into surrendering to them. We were going to walk into the Jedi Temple so she could confess her crimes. What was meant to be our final night together was the same night General Kenobi struck down General Grievous and ended the war. I take it you know the rest."

Wrecker shifted uncomfortably in his seat. He knew. Too well. The inhibitor chips embedded in clone brains, the mechanism that compelled them to kill the Jedi, had malfunctioned in his head. But while Hunter and Tech never felt a compulsion to kill on that day, Wrecker later lost a piece of himself when his chip activated spontaneously. It had sicced him on those, through the chip's influence, he'd deemed traitors to the Empire.

The chip was gone now, but the memory of what he'd nearly done would linger for the rest of his days. He would rather be talking weddings.

Hunter asked Ponder, "Did you . . . participate?"

"I didn't kill any Jedi. For weeks I didn't understand why so many of us did. Sohi still had access to information channels, and she discovered the truth about those implants in our heads. Turns out I got a lucky charm the day my squad died."

Ponder shifted his head and swept a patch of hair aside to reveal an ugly, long-healed scar.

"Piece of shrapnel, micron thin. The medical droids said it hadn't done any significant damage. They either didn't know about what was in my head or were forbidden to mention it. Sohi believes this is what allowed me to remain me during the purge. I'm grateful for it." He let the hair fall back in place. "It was horrific to see so many of our kind turn on comrades. I—I didn't want Sohi to surrender herself after that. It was selfish, but I clung to her. She felt steady to me, and I to her. I thought of the general who saved my life. I mourned him. And after, we ran."

"And after, we ran," Hunter repeated in a hushed tone of reluctant solidarity.

"Hurry up. We close soon!" The Toydarian owner of the only open mercantile shop Tech and Phee could find hovered behind his counter, his fluttering wings kicking up fine dust.

"We'll be out of your scraggly little hairs shortly," Phee said, sweeping a couple of drop cloths off the shelf into a levitating cart that was filling rapidly. Jatil had said blankets, but the rough tarps would have to do.

Tech spoke low when he said, "Might we try not to antagonize the shopkeeper since we caught him as he was closing."

"He wants credits in exchange for goods. We're going to make that happen. But if he wants to toss in some rudeness on the house, I'm ready to make that exchange, too."

They turned onto an aisle of foodstuffs and plucked ingredients for homemade baby formula off the shelves. Phee grimaced over a jar of Bestrum algae powder. "No one new to the galaxy should have to have this as its first meal."

Tech tossed a jar of viscous red gel in the cart. "It'll be tasteless when combined with this jaquira nectar. Regardless, the nutrients are the most important part."

Phee was glum when she said, "Yeah. I guess you're right."

But that wasn't true. The most important part was what they *weren't* saying. What if the birthing didn't go well? What if they were shopping for nothing?

"It's odd, isn't it?" Tech said. "We've known her for a little over two days. She's lied to us the whole time, knocked us out with unpleasant gas, and yet . . ."

"That kid needs its mother to be all right. The mother needs her kid to be all right. No matter how much of a scoundrel she is."

They moved on to the cooling vats at the back of the store and grabbed three jugs of milk.

Tech let the vat close, savoring the crisp, frigid breeze it created. His thoughts snagged on a query. "Have you spent time with many babies?"

"On occasion. I've lent a hand in the Pabu nursery a few times. Did some jobs with pirates who had families. This one Chalactan's kid threw up on me once. It was cuter than it sounds." She made room in the cart for a box of Lochi Flakes. Not on Jatil's list, but a lady had to treat herself occasionally. "Have you seen any caf powder?"

"Next aisle," Tech said. Then, "It was never clear if we clones could sire children."

Phee was annoyed at the paltry caf offerings but picked a powder that seemed the least offensive. "Seems like the mystery's been solved, Brown Eyes. How do you feel about that?"

Tech felt . . . a loaded question. "It proves a hypothesis I've held for some time. I'd love more data on the potential number of clone offspring throughout the galaxy, but I imagine that would be hard to come by."

"You're good at solving hard problems. The big question is, if you could gather that data, what would you do with it? What would it mean for *you*?"

"I . . ." Tech didn't know what to say. "I think we've completed Jatil's list."

"Wonderful!" the shopkeeper yelled. "Then you pay, and you go!"

"Good plan!" Tech shoved the cart toward the checkout in a hurry.

Hunter spotted Tech and Phee's approach from the roof and waved to get their attention. The street was virtually deserted by then and would likely stay that way until the next refinery shift change. It was quiet enough that Hunter didn't have to shout his eternal question, *Any trouble?*

"All's well," Tech called back.

He and Phee entered the clinic and parsed the acquired goods on the waiting room floor. Hunter soon appeared alone, inspecting the haul and ready to debrief.

"It seems very calm here," Phee said, keeping her voice high in a failed attempt to avoid the ominous insinuation of a silent childbirth.

Hunter said, "I'm going into the exam room. Ponder needs to know something. If it's bad news, me as a buffer might be best."

Tech exhaled a heavy breath. "You don't have to do it alone. I will—"

The examination room door swooshed open, and Jatil emerged, looking exhausted. His face was unreadable.

Phee said, "Well?"

A piercing infant's shriek sounded from inside the room.

Jatil flashed a small smile. "It's a girl."

When the medic didn't say more, Hunter braced for the worst. "Sohi?"

Jatil sighed. "We'll need to keep a close eye on her, but I think she'll be fine. Mostly thanks to Omega. She'll need rest, but I don't get the impression you all are leaving in a hurry."

More than satisfied with this outcome, Tech said, "Perhaps I'll deliver the good news to Ponder."

Phee joined him as he climbed the stairs. Hunter stayed with Jatil. Assessing. "You okay, doc? Seems like you got a win today."

But Jatil's attention was elsewhere.

"Doc?"

Jatil shook himself out of the trance. "Oh, sorry. I probably need some of that rest I'm prescribing, is all."

"You're not the only one."

Thunderous footsteps echoed on the stairs as Ponder just about fell through the doorway into the exam room. Wrecker filled the corridor next, with the others trailing.

Hunter peeked into the room, where an ecstatic Omega helped a weakened Sohi pass the swaddled, fussing infant to her father.

The hovering medical droid said, "She has expelled fresh excrement. Welcome to parenthood."

Omega backed away from the family, allowing them some privacy.

Hunter dropped a hand on her shoulder as the exam room door shut. "You're amazing, kid."

"No, that baby is. She's so strong, and her eyes are so big. It's like she wants to see the entire galaxy at once."

That reminds me of someone, Hunter thought.

A sweat-drenched Omega beamed. "This was an incredible day."

Despite how they got there, Hunter somewhat agreed.

He glanced to Jatil to see how the medic was holding up, but he'd already disappeared into his office without a word.

CHAPTER THIRTY-ONE

⟨═══════════════⟩

SULLUST SYSTEM, OUTER RIM
Before . . .

The *thunking* catch of a boarding tube fastening to the Skipray's air lock triggered an unexpected shudder of excitement in Crane. It'd been three months since he'd sent Gayla on assignment. A long time not to see his favorite child.

He'd been waiting in orbit since dropping out of hyperspace, mere hours after receiving her distress call. The particulars of the call were a mystery to him. This was supposed to be a short-term integration and data grab, set to go for at least another month, with a quiet dead-of-night exfiltration. Something had gone wrong. Whatever the circumstance, he didn't have a pupil more capable than her. He trusted she'd still completed the mission.

She'd better have completed the mission.

The air lock unsealed with a hiss of pressurized air. Gayla stumbled inside, her chest heaving. Her knees buckled a few steps beyond the threshold, and her hands skidded across the deck, slick from blood. A lot of blood.

Not hers, though.

She managed to get out of the prone position and sit upright, grimacing in pain. Her left arm hung oddly—clearly dislocated at the shoulder—

but Crane's attention was on the sack in her right hand. He tipped his chin. "Are those the data disks?"

Gayla nodded but did not meet his gaze.

He took the soggy sack from her, opened the mouth, and spilled the contents on the table. "You got them all?"

Another pained nod while she attempted to reset her shoulder on her own.

"Excellent, child! You truly are something special." He strolled to her, behind her, crouched so that his knee dug into her spine as a brace, then he assisted in popping the shoulder back into the joint. She howled as her bones snapped back into alignment. When she'd collected herself, Crane asked, "Do you have any other injuries?"

"Ribs might be cracked," she managed between rasping breaths, "maybe broke some toes."

"Still not kicking with the ball of your foot? Some lessons have to be learned hard."

"I messed up somehow. I don't know. They knew I wasn't who I said I was and came for me."

"How many?"

"Five."

"How many are still alive?"

She glared, then looked away.

"Good." Crane helped her to her feet and led her to the closest bench, where he sat her down, then joined her. "When I was your age, I fouled missions and had to improvise. Too often, admittedly. That is what our role requires from time to time. What's important is that you completed your mission."

"And survived?" There was tension in her voice that Crane wasn't used to and did not like. Something . . . rebellious.

"It's good that you lived, particularly since it was your own mistake that put you in jeopardy. Missteps have consequences, as you know."

"As you've said." Her lips pursed. A childish pout he thought she'd left behind in her adolescent years. Crane would be lying if he said seeing flashes of her youth didn't make him nostalgic.

"Are you hungry?" he asked, rising from the bench and gathering the precious data disks that he'd pass along to his superiors. He moved toward the galley. "Come. I can warm you up something."

Gayla rose and followed a few steps behind. Her bloody clothing squelched. "I'd . . . like to get clean, please."

Crane opened a pantry cubby and retrieved a can of stew. He popped the top and dumped the unappetizing, congealed mass into a stovetop pan. "Unfortunately, the showers aren't working. I'll have a mainte-nance droid inspect them once I return to Batuu. You can change gar-ments, though. Check the locker over there."

"I want to wash the blood off."

"I know you do. But we don't cave to our wants, do we? Besides, I'm not suggesting you wait an entire trip home to cleanse yourself."

The old youthful fire blazed in her eyes. "What option do I have?"

"Coruscant. That's your next mission. I've been lining it up for you for the last month. There are several safe houses to choose from, and you'll develop your new persona there."

"New . . . persona? I need a break. I . . ." Gayla trailed off.

"Is there a problem?"

She passed her hand over her torso and waist, indicating the gore splattered there. "I can't do this again."

Is this a tantrum? Crane thought she'd matured from this, too. It was so good to see her that he had a hard time maintaining a harsh reaction. So he simply reminded her, "You won't have to if you don't make mis-takes. This assignment's going to place you in the Galactic Senate. I'll brief you over our meal."

She raised her crusty hands. "I can't eat like this."

Crane nodded, understanding. He turned to a different cubby, then tossed her a pair of gloves. "Here. You'll be fine. Now, sit. I'll fill you in on Senator Cadaman."

Given Gayla's hasty exit from Sullust, space traffic was being heav-ily monitored, meaning the best course of action was to keep their two ships cloaked and in stationary positions until the heat died down. Fatigued from the impromptu trip, Crane retired to his bunk early and told Gayla he'd drop her at Coruscant after a few hours of rest.

He had dozed off for barely a moment when the air lock alert sounded in his quarters. He ran to the gangway to find Gayla's discarded bloody clothes and her ship gone, en route to Coruscant.

Crane hadn't seen her since.

MOTEN ESTATE, DALLOW
Now

Crane emerged from slumber to find the guest dwelling empty, the entire team of investigators missing. His immediate thought was that Cellia had them rounded up and murdered, but he understood the fallacy there. *He* was still alive.

No way she thought so much of their allyship that she'd escape his wrath after pulling such a brutal move. And she'd have been correct.

Not that he held a strong affection for the team he led. They were pale comparisons to other charges he'd trained over the years. But the disrespect of slaughtering them would demand annihilation. No, this wasn't her doing. The most logical conclusion was the team had all gone out together. But where?

Crane grabbed the nearest holocomm and raised Drand. "Where are you?"

Her flickering blue image hovered over the disk in his palm. "We couldn't stand another moment cooped up in that house. We're meditating seaside. Join us."

Meditating seaside? Since when— "Get back here. I want to do a morning briefing."

"We think it would be better by the seaside today. Join us."

Oh.

Crane understood.

This was trouble.

He feigned exasperation. "I'm on my way."

When he arrived at the seaside cliff and found his agents seated cross-legged in the grass, gazes on the horizon, he knew this was playacting. That his agents were taking such measures was alarming, not because of the reaction it might force from Cellia. Crane worried that they suspected he'd cut a deal with her.

"What is this?" he said.

Drand faced the ocean. "Our dwelling is bugged. Weilan found listening devices last night. We suspect cams, too, but didn't want Moten's detail to see us searching."

Crane had to be careful here if he was to maintain trust. He *could* have told them about the devices on their first night. "It's no crime for someone to surveil their own home."

"Correct. But people who quietly collect secrets often keep many of their own."

"So?"

"I snuck out last night, tailed Moten and her security detail."

More caution on Crane's part. "What did you see?"

"They had a Sullustan with them who'd been badly beaten." Drand's voice strained. Was she holding back tears? "I was too far away to help and probably couldn't have stopped what happened since there were four of them. They murdered him and buried him in a grove south of the property."

Crane was silent a moment, hung up on one word. "Did you say *south*?"

"Yes."

Crane had his datapad with him. He tapped through menus until he had a still image of an aerial view of the property. "Show me."

Drand zoomed in to the area she'd indicated. It wasn't the northern grove he'd discovered on their first night. Cellia had two killing grounds.

Or were there more?

He zoomed out of Drand's area and scrolled the image, looking for what he already knew he'd find. East. West. Southeast. Northwest. Numerous groves of young, recently planted trees pocked the land surrounding the vast property. Were they all . . . ?

"Agent Crane?"

"Yes. This is good work, Drand."

"Arresting her might be tough, given the size of her security force. If we call in reinforcements immediately and take them by surprise—"

"Wait," Crane said, more knee-jerk than reasonable. Drand wasn't wrong, but she also wasn't in charge. "I'm going to contact Command on a secure line, relay your findings, and ask them to advise."

"What do we need advice about? Cellia Moten is a *murderer*! We're in danger as long as we're here!"

Oh, she's worse than a simple murderer, Crane thought. Some drunkards drew blasters in bar fights. Some gangsters retaliated over being scammed or disrespected. Penal colonies all over the galaxy were full of those types. Cellia Moten was something else. Crane's estimates of how many bodies might be underfoot rose by the second. If she ever gained the inherent power and implied immunity of a high politician as she desired, her victims might be innumerable.

But the others were watching, and Drand had overstepped her boundaries.

"Quiet!" Crane barked. "Have you forgotten yourself? We're in danger if she knows we know. Don't let on. Any of you. I'll have answers for you soon, then we'll act. When I say! Understood?"

They all snapped to attention. "Yes, sir!"

"Now continue your meditations until you remember who the superior agent is here. As you were."

Crane left them to it.

FELLIAN OUTPOST, TRYTH

With a day or two more of ionic storms keeping them grounded, Hunter made the best of an annoying situation and slept in. The room Phee got him was comfortable enough. He'd spent countless nights dozing in trees, on rocky terrain, or in the frigid cold—whatever the mission demanded—so the lumpy, musty sleeper felt like Sulianan cotton. He bathed, dressed in simple garments, and checked the other rooms to find them empty.

With his comlink, he raised Omega first. "This is Hunter. What's your location?"

"At the clinic with the baby," Omega chirped back.

"Everyone there with you?"

"Tech and Phee are at the *Marauder*. Wrecker's here, though."

"Doing what?"

"Cowering at the sight of the baby's latest diaper."

Wrecker's voice crackled in the background. "I thought bog gas was bad!"

Hunter chuckled. Then, in spite of himself, asked, "How are Mom and Dad?"

"Good. Sohi's stronger today but has a ways to go. Ponder's a natural at mixing formula."

"Those kitchen skills don't go away, I suppose."

Now that he had confirmed the positive status of the family, some tension leaked from Hunter's shoulders. He wanted off this rock but was adept at recognizing what he couldn't control. He said, "I'm going to do some recon on the city. Wanna come?"

He already knew the answer. Omega never turned down the chance to explore. "Yes!"

"I'll be by the clinic shortly."

He waded into the street traffic, which had a significant uptick from the night before, and took his time covering the short distance to the clinic. Even though this system's sun was more like gray haze filtered through sporadic rain clouds, observing citizens under morning conditions was always different. Daylight exacerbated strain. It revealed who carried sagging shadows beneath their eyes and who trudged along slower than a good night's rest would justify.

Of the open businesses along his path was a laser tattoo parlor that had escaped his notice the night before. A Trandoshan large enough to give Wrecker a complex sat on a stool by the parlor's entrance, his scales heavily painted in impressive, intricate designs. At Hunter's notice, he waved a taloned hand centimeters from the left side of his face and spoke in a guttural voice. "Nice ink."

Hunter tipped his chin, accepting the compliment.

"You interested in something new? Some vintage Republic sigils to get you all nostalgic for the old days?"

Hunter tensed, unsure if Trandoshans dealt in sarcasm. "You joking or serious?"

"Serious. I mean, you got your own thing going on, but I can smell a clone a kilometer away."

"That gonna be a problem?"

"Not for me. Used to be I'd get run out of town for offering Republic anything. Times change, even if the bosses don't. As long as everyone's got their credits on payday . . ." He trailed off and spat a glob of goo on the sidewalk.

Hunter detected sincerity and let it be. "Not today, friend. But I appreciate the offer."

He kept it moving a few doors down until he came upon Jatil's clinic. The waiting room was still deserted save for one pitiful-looking patient wearing refinery safety gear that had failed at the only job it had. The woman's arm steamed from a chemical burn.

As Hunter entered, Jatil appeared to usher the patient in to be seen. "They're on the second floor," he said to Hunter in passing. "My backup exam room."

Hunter climbed the stairs and entered a corridor crowded with Ponder, Wrecker, and the baby cooing in Wrecker's arms. They hadn't noticed him yet, so he eavesdropped on Wrecker's conversation with the child.

"What you're going to find about this galaxy is a lot of beings will misunderstand you. Take me for example. Some think I only care about blowing things up and eating. I'm more complicated than that. I care about the size of the explosion and also how good the food tastes. I have layers."

Hunter couldn't contain his laughter. "Is that so?"

"Hey!" Wrecker said, mock offended by being spied on. "This is a personal conversation between me and Coru."

Hunter repeated the name. "*Coru*. That's beautiful."

"Beautiful name for my beautiful niece."

"Your *niece*?" Hunter and Ponder said together.

The baby gurgled as if to agree.

"See!" Wrecker booped the child's nose, and she responded with a coo. "You like the sound of *Uncle Wrecker,* don'tcha?"

Hunter said, "Omega in with Sohi?"

Ponder nodded. "Checking her vitals and such. That kid's a wonder."

"You don't have to tell me."

The exam room door slid open, frosting the warm corridor in cold, therapeutic air. Omega emerged, smiling. "Come in. Sohi wants you."

Ponder reclaimed his child and crossed the threshold. Omega waved to Hunter and Wrecker. "All of us."

Hunter wasn't expecting that.

Omega slid past him and yelled down to the clinic's main floor. "Jatil! Sohi needs to speak to us."

This room was larger than the one downstairs, which allowed for a more comfortable fit for the group. The medical droid reviewed a chart in the corner while Sohi muscled her way to an upright position in bed to retrieve her baby.

Jatil entered, wringing his hands, anxious. "Is everything all right?"

"It is," Sohi said, "thanks to you. All of you."

Ponder passed their child to Sohi, and she gazed at the infant with pure joy, which had to be the most honest thing she'd done since they all met.

She noticed Hunter watching. "First of all, Hunter, we should all note that I kept my promise. I did not give birth on the *Marauder.*"

"A spy and comedian," Hunter remarked. "Nice."

"Seriously, I asked you all in for a reason. I wanted to apologize for what I—"

"*We,*" Ponder emphasized, stroking the baby's cheek.

"—what *we* pulled you into. I owe you several debts, but the biggest, by far, is for getting us here so our child could be born safely."

Wrecker nodded. Omega did, too. They watched Hunter.

Was he angry about the deception? Yes. Was he disappointed they'd done so much work and still had nothing to help Pabu? Absolutely.

Could he understand the desperate drive to do the unthinkable for someone you loved? There was never a time he couldn't.

He said, "Don't concern yourself with debts, Sohi. Worry about heal-ing. We'll settle up when the time is right."

Sohi spoke to Jatil. "And you, friend. *Brother.* Look at us."

Jatil said, "Look at us."

"The people of this town are fortunate to have you. You were always meant to *heal.* No matter what we were taught."

Jatil winced. It was a shy gesture. He didn't like much attention on him. A good trait for a spy, Hunter supposed. But as Sohi said, his clinic work was noble work. Better work.

"I was worried," Jatil said. "You were in bad shape. A weaker being might have succumbed."

Ponder stroked his daughter's cheek, his pride and joy evident. "You and Omega aided her strength. We—all three of us—are grateful."

Jatil said, "Everyone but the happy family clear the room, please. I'd like to examine mother and baby."

"Do you need my assistance?" Omega asked.

"Not this time, little one. Enjoy the day. You deserve it."

MOTEN ESTATE, DALLOW

Sendril Crane was in his quarters, attempting another secure transmission to ISB Command. His first three attempts had gone unanswered, and he was troubled.

No. Enraged!

How was no one—*no one!*—answering his call? He and his team had been in a holding pattern for too long, and Drand's assessment, as misguided as it was in its delivery, was correct. The longer they lingered under Cellia's gaze, the more vulnerable they were to her psychotic whims. He needed direction from Command now.

His comm unit beeped with an incoming transmission. Finally!

According to the display, it wasn't Command.

When Crane and Cellia put feelers out across the galaxy, Crane had beamed messages to *all* his contacts—even the ones he'd considered dormant. It was a matter of thoroughness. And perhaps it had paid off. Crane accepted the call.

The hologram that materialized was a face he hadn't seen in years. One of his weaker students, assigned to a worthless outpost at the start of the war, and forgotten about by most after the war's conclusion.

Crane said, "This is a surprise. What can I do for you?"

"Father Crane," Jatil Omstock said, "I have someone you're looking for."

CHAPTER THIRTY-TWO

FELLIAN OUTPOST, TRYTH

The mercurial rain resumed, rattling in a staccato drumbeat over the ponchos Hunter and Omega had donned. Shimmering silver rivulets ran down the waterproof shells and puddled where the pair stood on the town's edge, admiring the mountain geysers and the murky sky beyond. The air was humid with a metallic twang you could taste in the back of your throat, like being in an engine room when a hyperdrive ramped up. It wasn't unpleasant. *If adventure had a taste, it'd taste like this!* Omega thought.

She said, "Wrecker likes it here."

"I know." Hunter laughed. "When the land explodes on its own, it's a guaranteed win for him."

"Pabu's nice, too," she said, feeling sheepish.

"It is. So why do you sound like you're scared to say it?"

She nudged a rock with her toe. "Ever since we left Cid, everyone's been into different stuff."

"What do you mean?" Hunter said, though Omega thought he already knew what she was worried about.

"You've seen how Tech and Phee are."

"I've seen how Phee is. Tech's playing it a little closer to the vest."

"There's something there, though. Right?"

"I think so."

"Is it a Clone Force Ninety-Nine *something*?"

Hunter shrugged. "I don't know. You could ask him."

Omega nodded, acknowledging she could have that conversation with Tech, but she had the sense he was still figuring it out himself. She kept talking. "Crosshair's gone. Echo's gone. Who's to say everyone won't decide to go off on their own?"

"Do you want us all together on Pabu? Permanently?" Omega could hear the hope in Hunter's voice, even as he tried not to let it weigh down the question.

She took her time answering. Then, "No. I don't think I want that. Not exactly."

"You've made friends there."

"They'll still be my friends no matter where I am. That's what friends are."

A shrill whistle blew, signaling a shift change at one of the refinery hubs. The thick foot traffic on the Tryth streets got thicker still. Omega turned toward the crowd. "Can we walk?"

They waded into the crowd. He remained quiet, letting her think.

She said, "Has any other world you've been on had mercury rain?"

"No. This is new to me. I've heard of a planet, Sevetta, that's more mercury rich than here. So much so, the air's toxic."

"Nothing can survive there?"

"I didn't say that. The beings who live there are fine. They're made of mercury, too. For the most part."

Mercury *people*? Anything was truly possible in this galaxy. "That's amazing."

"I'm not done," Hunter said, waiting a bit to build suspense.

He was a good storyteller and she loved anytime he told her something new.

He said, "Beings from that world can shape-shift."

"Holy happabore! No way!"

"It's true."

They passed through the town square, where street performers put on a scandalous show about a character with a striking resemblance to the Emperor offending his Royal Guard with his smell. They got big laughs from a lunchtime crowd. Omega felt herself getting quiet again.

"Is Pabu the problem," Hunter asked, "or is staying together the problem?"

Omega did not evade. "Staying together is not the problem. I mean, I want us all together. But I also want to see all you've seen and more. The galaxy is so big!"

"And dangerous," Hunter reminded her. Not for the first time.

Omega felt obligated to remind *him* of something he wouldn't like. "Pabu's part of the galaxy. It's dangerous, too. Didn't a tsunami almost kill us there?"

"A natural disaster is—"

"As risky as an unnatural one. We might as well keep doing what we've been doing. It's gone okay so far."

The performers wrapped their short play to casual applause and the clinking of credits in a refinery hat, then sloughed off the mocking Imperial robes to reveal imitations of traditional Jedi garb. One performer screwed a blue glow stick into a mock lightsaber hilt while making a *snap-hiss* ignition noise with his mouth, followed by a *vwoom* sound that somehow came from his armpit as he swung the weapon. Another performer projected his voice in a manner that could probably be heard several streets over.

"I am General Bandawain Blubberbond of the ancient, never-wrong Jedi Order. I declare victory in this Clone War here! We have freed you all!"

The performers who'd played the Royal Guard in the previous skit tossed aside their red robes and helmets, revealing all-white "armor" underneath. Now they were clone troopers, and Omega's stomach lurched. She watched Hunter from the corner of her eye, curious how he would take this part of the show.

The clone troopers wielded makeshift blaster rifles carved from wood and aimed at the Jedi, somehow also producing the sounds of blasterfire with their armpits.

The Jedi collapsed. General Bandawain Blubberbond uttered one last line with his dying breath. "Perhaps I spoke too soon?"

The crowd guffawed.

"Funny what goes for entertainment these days," Hunter said.

Omega sensed his discomfort and took his hand. "Let's see what else is going on around Fellian Outpost."

They continued their excursion silently for a bit. Then Hunter said, "Constant adventure isn't all you think it is."

"I know!" said Omega. "It's more! This last year has been the best of my life. All we've done. The people we've met and helped. I used to think Nala Se's lab and Tipoca City were everything there was. It was just a speck."

"A calm life can be a good one, kid. The constant danger, the never having one place to come home to. It's punishing. Trust me."

"I do trust you, Hunter. But I think it feels like a punishment to you because you didn't choose it. Like I didn't choose Kamino. It was all I knew, and it was calm, but it wasn't enough."

And there it was.

"Sure. I get it." He looked away as if seeking a quick and comfortable change of subject. "Let's see what they're selling over there."

He sped up a little, and she didn't try to catch him. Omega knew she'd stung him. Pabu was an iffy proposition. But it seemed Hunter liked the prospect of it more than he was letting on. Maybe more than all of them.

He'd told her of many fights, of times things went sideways over the years. Times he'd been hurt badly.

Why did this feel like she'd delivered the worst wound yet?

CHAPTER THIRTY-THREE

MOTEN ESTATE, DALLOW

"Move, move, move! Let's go!" Crane shouted.

"You heard him," Drand said to the operatives packing up the ISB gear double-time. "Pick up the pace, Weilan."

She backed his orders with energy and purpose. His sudden decision to leave, as far as she knew, came because he'd reconsidered her previous, passionate argument for distance and safety. In reality, he was voracious to act on Jatil's tip before he lost Gayla again.

He promised Drand that once they were in open space, away from Cellia's prying eyes and ears, *she* would be the one to notify Command of the crimes she'd discovered, free to take full credit.

If they answered, Crane thought.

He'd neglected to tell her he hadn't been able to reach Yularen or anyone else in Command. Given their level of concern about Cellia both before and after they became aware of her prying, the sudden silence made the back of his neck itch.

Then, as if the bureau had read his thoughts light-years away, his comlink beeped with an incoming transmission. Secure protocols.

He sneered. "Now they want to talk?"

"What's that?" Drand said.

"Nothing. Carry on. I'll be in my quarters."

With the door sealed, he activated the array's secure channel and found himself eye to eye with Colonel Yularen's flickering hologram.

Yularen said, "We monitored the tip you received from the Tryth system. Are you mobilizing now?"

Crane was taken aback. Command knew about Jatil contacting him, and he was just hearing from them now? That neck itch intensified. "We'll be space-bound within the hour."

The colonel's chin lowered, and his shoulders bounced as if noting something on an unseen datapad.

"Sir," Crane began, mindful of his tone, "I've been attempting to call in an update for most of the day."

"Solar flares in your area, disrupting signals," Yularen said dismissively. "Regarding the tip from Tryth, you can confirm Clone Force Ninety-Nine *is* still with your former charge?"

Crane was stuck on that "solar flares" bit. An obvious lie. Why?

"Agent Crane?"

"Yes. The clones are grounded due to local weather."

More quiet. More note-taking. "Very well. You may proceed, but the clones are your priority. Capture or kill."

No. The clones were not his priority, but if he saw an opportunity to apprehend them after securing Gayla, fine. No need to squabble over specifics. "As you wish, sir."

"A squadron of troopers will meet you at Tryth. The clones are formidable, but they won't be expecting numbers. It'll be in your best interest to utilize the element of surprise." Colonel Yularen looked up from his mysterious data and met Crane's gaze again. "One more thing. Before you jump to hyperspace, call in and confirm that you and your team are clear of the Moten estate."

"Sir . . . *why*?"

Yularen's gaze was durasteel. "That will be all. For now."

The hologram winked away.

Speaking with Command left him with more questions than answers. Thankfully, the call was not without direction. He had his orders, and they did not conflict with his desires. It was time to go.

Crane packed up the comms array and quick-stepped down the corridor to his team. "I want an ETA on—"

He stopped short at the sight of Cellia Moten, Parlin, and several of her armed-to-the-teeth guards crowding the exit.

Cellia said, "I've never been to Tryth. I hear they have a rich history I'd love to learn more about. Shall we?"

FELLIAN OUTPOST, TRYTH

At the *Marauder,* Tech tested the newly installed flap for responsiveness. It worked perfectly. All the repairs he'd commissioned during their time on this planet were perfect. He said, "These Fellian spaceport mechanics are quite skilled."

"Mm-hmm." Phee stared at a blank navicomputer screen.

"They are also celestial gods capable of faster-than-light travel with a mere thought."

"Mm-hmm." Then, the words registered, and Phee said, "What?"

MEL-222 booped loudly.

Tech said, "You're ruminating again."

"I'm not ruminating. I'm calculating. How long can Pabu go without aid? Everyone's stretched to the limit, and we're not going home with any relief."

"There's something to be said about trying. You made an attempt—"

"Two attempts."

"*Two* attempts to help. But you're not Pabu's only hope. Thousands live there. From what I've seen of the populace, they're all intelligent and resilient. Where our attempts may not have yielded the desired results, someone else's may have. That's the inherent benefit of community. Is it not?"

MEL-222 beep-booped.

"He does have a point, Mel," Phee said. "I needed that, Brown Eyes. More than you know."

Moments passed when it seemed like Tech might not say anything. In the past, he probably wouldn't have—particularly if some pressing task required his considerable brain power—but the *Marauder* was shipshape, no one was currently shooting at them, and it felt prudent to recognize Phee's statement with more than a nod.

"I haven't found much joy in this life," Tech said. "When I have, it's rarely warranted verbal acknowledgment. If a sunset inspires glee, there's no point in telling the sun."

"Agreed. I have never met a talkative sun. Where are you going with this?"

"When verbal acknowledgment is warranted, I have come to believe it imperative that the words be spoken. I enjoy putting your mind at ease. That makes me happy."

Phee grinned slyly and placed her hand over his on the console. Her touch was welcome.

She said, "Acknowledgment appreciated. You can keep going if you want."

MOTEN ESTATE, DALLOW

Cellia arranged for two vehicles to transport the ISB investigators to the spaceport where the *Jurat* waited. She insisted that Crane ride with her and her elite guards in the limousine.

Crane informed her it was highly unorthodox for civilians to tag along on operations, and she countered with more incessant name-dropping. "Do you know Colonel Celmack?"

"I don't."

"He and I go way back. I've donated to several ISB-sponsored causes at his cajoling. If anyone gives you trouble, he can smooth it over."

"Is that so? I need to check." But when Crane attempted to return to his quarters to make a call—about Cellia's hijacking the mission, not her suspect friendship with ISB commanders—one of Parlin's men cut him off.

"Oh," Cellia said, "we shouldn't waste time on technicalities. Not when you're so close to apprehending the dangerous criminals who invaded my home."

"Funny how you know that," Drand said, defiant. "Almost like you were in the room with us."

Cellia's smile was tight. "On your first night here, we made the spaceport comptroller aware that you were my guests. They alerted my staff about your ship being readied for liftoff . . . as a courtesy. I made a deduction. Not that I could handle an actual investigation the way you do."

Cellia stared Drand down, and Drand broke, her gaze dropping to her boots.

After that, Crane was not allowed alone time with the team; he could only communicate with Drand through pointed stares and silent hope that she understood what was true from the moment they stepped foot on the estate. They were captives—potentially hostages, depending on how Cellia wanted to play it.

A couple of battle droids ushered the ISB team into a large drone truck while Parlin, the obedient chauffeur, held the limo door open for Cellia, Crane, and three hefty (one smelly) bodyguards. As Parlin was sealing them in, Cellia said, "Wait!"

Parlin raised an eyebrow. Cellia wriggled her nose, then pointed at the brutish, wolfen Shistavanen guard—the stinky one.

"No, no, no," Cellia said. "You ride in the truck."

The other guards chuckled while the Shistavanen let out an embarrassed whine. Thankfully, he exited, and Crane fought not to feel gratitude toward his kidnapper.

Parlin closed the door, and they were on the move.

The rest of the trip was by the numbers. Nothing impeded their progress at the spaceport. The ground crew helped the ISB operatives load gear onto the *Jurat*—under the watchful gaze of Cellia's guards—and Crane's agents took their place on board. Crane attempted telepathic communication one final time, something he wasn't actually capable of. A pointed stare to Drand that he hoped she understood as a signal to contact Command and report everything.

But once she was on the *Jurat,* it was out of his hands. Cellia's guards ushered him back to the limo and sped them to an exclusive area in a different part of the spaceport.

Cellia said, "I know you would've preferred to stay with your subordinates, but you'll find my transport much more comfortable. I promise."

He didn't respond, only gazed at a sort of vehicle he'd seen in holos and nowhere else.

The spaceport ground crew fussed about the exterior of a SoroSuub 3000 space yacht, painted in the same red-on-white color scheme as the palace foyer. The boarding stairs were lowered. Parlin parked the limo and escorted Crane up the gangway, not quite at gunpoint but close enough. Cellia followed, and her guards brought up the rear.

When Crane crossed the threshold into the yacht, he found the opulence grating. He was escorted through corridors of polished wood and quartz. Every seat was the massaged-tender hide of some rare beast. The pilots stood at attention as if greeting a great general instead of a spoiled rich woman who saw others as insects to step on. The aggression with which Cellia and others of her ilk flaunted their wealth felt like its own kind of brutality.

Cellia had Crane and her guards seated in a gallery at the ship's midpoint: a trophy room with treasures posed in intricate display columns along the vessel's centerline. The walls were viewports, allowing passengers to see the stars beyond.

At Cellia's order, the spaceport control tower cleared the yacht and the *Jurat* for takeoff. Crane watched his ship, a few hundred meters away, match the yacht's ascent as they slowly climbed from land to stars. He wondered if Drand had contacted Command yet when Cellia surprised him.

She said, "*You* should contact your office and update them on our status. Don't you think?"

At first, he thought it was a trick. She brought him a personal comlink and motioned for him to call. He did, uncertain if this was the punch line to a joke where Parlin put a blaster bolt through his skull. But he made the call, and Colonel Yularen's face appeared in a fan of translucent blue light.

Surprised, Yularen asked, "Where are you calling from?"

Crane kept his tone neutral. "I am aboard Cellia Moten's yacht en route to the Tryth system."

Yularen did not falter. "Is that so? Is Mistress Moten near you now? If so, please tell her Wullf Yularen says hello."

Cellia beamed and leaned into the transmission frame so the colonel could see her. "Hello, Wullf. It's been too long. What was it? That diplomatic reception on Naboo?"

"Yes, I believe so," said the colonel. "Crane, the *Jurat* is also en route to Tryth, correct?"

"Yes, sir."

"We see it moving but have been unable to raise the crew. Do you know anything about that?"

Crane's mind whirled, certain he did know something about it, though he knew better than to say so in present company. "I don't, sir."

"Technical difficulties, then," the colonel said. "Very well. Our trooper transport is set to rendezvous with you. Keep us posted, and, most importantly, keep Mistress Moten safe. Carry on."

The transmission ended. Crane waited for Cellia to reveal what that was all about.

She sat silently, staring out the starboard viewport, which gave her a direct view of the *Jurat*. She stared so long that Crane had no choice but to follow her line of sight.

Finally, she said, "We're about to jump to hyperspace."

Crane nodded. "Yes. Of course."

"It's a terrible thing those criminals did. Sabotaging your ship before they fled Dallow. If only someone had recognized the impairment in the hyperdrive. A tragedy could have been prevented."

A chill shuddered violently through Crane. He pressed his palms to the viewport and watched the *Jurat*'s engine exhaust flare blindingly white, the clearest signal a vessel was about to enter a hyperspace lane. Instead of winking away as acceleration to lightspeed commenced, the engine ports grew brighter and brighter and exploded into a blue flame that devoured the ship and everyone on board.

"Such a shame," Cellia repeated as they made their successful jump. "No telling what value those bright young minds might've brought to the ISB in time. It'll be up to loyal agents like you and concerned citizens like me to see that their deaths aren't in vain. What do you say?"

Crane settled into his seat, burying his most prominent emotion—rage—as he'd been trained to do. "It sounds like a fine plan."

Cellia smiled and began rambling about this or that, but Crane barely heard. This "partnership" she'd proposed was not going to work, and his foolhardy attempt to play it to his advantage had gotten his young operatives killed. There hadn't been a year in recent memory where his hands weren't stained with someone's blood—enemy or ally. It had always, always, been of his choosing. Cellia's violation was worse than if she'd killed and buried him in her grove. That would've been a defeat. This was defilement.

Keep *her* safe. This vile fiend. An order from Yularen himself.

Is this what happens when a monster with means can call the Emperor "friend"?

It was clear, then, whose security the Imperial Security Bureau was truly concerned with.

Crane sat quietly, considering his options. Whatever path his life took after completing his mission, he'd very much like to see Cellia's heart cut from her chest.

Hopefully, sooner than later.

CHAPTER THIRTY-FOUR

FELLIAN OUTPOST, TRYTH

Hunter and Omega continued their walk through Merchant's Row on their way back to Jatil's clinic when Omega went wide-eyed and pointed at a particular booth. "Hunter, do you see that?"

She bounded between shoppers before Hunter could confirm, then stopped at a fruit vendor, giddy over a bushel of prickly green orbs.

Hunter caught up, confused by her excitement. He said, "Avedame fruit?"

"Yep." She pushed the overly ripe ones aside and seized a firm orb with a bright, verdant sheen.

"Why are you so excited?" Hunter asked, flashing back on the many, many, many bland meals he'd shoveled down as a young clone in the mess hall.

"Avedame are nutrient rich. It's why they came with so many meals on Kamino. Clone metabolisms are primed to absorb every bit of energy the fruit provides."

"Have you been feeling sluggish?"

"It's not for me. It's for Sohi. She's still pretty sapped from giving birth, so this will help her. We can use the nectar in the baby's formula, too. It will help them both get stronger, faster."

The vendor, a sad-eyed ginger-furred Gotal woman, gave an unenergetic sales pitch. "It's a good price. Buy four, get fifth free."

"We'll take ten," Omega said, then raised an eyebrow. "Won't we?"

Hunter sighed and counted out the credits. "I guess we will."

With a sack full of avedames and a heart full of enthusiasm, Omega angled for the turn that would put them on the same street as the clinic. Hunter snagged her by the sleeve before she got too far ahead. "Me and you, are we good?"

She hesitated. "Are you angry with me?"

"Because you told me the truth? No. Never."

"I'm glad. We'll never not be good, Hunter. I love you, and Wrecker, and Tech, and Echo. Crosshair, not so much, but I'm sure he'll come around one day. You'll see." She grinned and bounded through the milling crowd to deliver her natural remedy to the clinic.

At that moment, Hunter had the closest thing he'd ever had to a premonition when he foresaw with eerie clarity what an adult Omega might look like leaving him for her own adventures.

A Fellian citizen in a refinery uniform bumped his shoulder, and he snapped out of it, which was fine. He wouldn't forget what his mind's eye showed him, nor what he felt in the wake of it. Hope.

He strolled in the clinic's direction, anxious to see how everyone's day went.

Omega burst through the clinic door and found a couple of refinery workers in the waiting room, their patched and worn coveralls specked with mercury spatter from their shift. One sat with his head canted back, a bloody rag pressed to his nose. The other massaged his jaw and held what looked like a fang between his thumb and foreclaw.

"Where's the blasted doc?" Fang-guy said. "A malfunctioning magcrate clipped us. Knocked my tooth out and broke his nose."

Broken-nose guy grunted and nodded. "We've been waiting an hour!"

"Hang on, I'll check," Omega said.

She dipped down the first-floor corridor toward Jatil's office to see what was holding him up. When the door swished open, her focus was drawn to the brightest thing in the dark room: a hologram running on a short loop.

It was Sohi's face—different hair and flesh color, but her face—taken from a Canto Bight security recording. It quickly became Ponder's Kuuto mask, taken from the same footage. Both images were enlarged and enhanced to the standards of an ISB wanted alert. REWARD FOR INFORMATION flashed above the likenesses.

Omega's perception shifted to Jatil, who was hunched over in his chair, cupping his face in his hand, sobbing. Her empathetic nature nearly took over, her mind already swirling with questions about how she could help, until logic caught up.

"What did you do?" Omega whispered.

It was loud enough for Jatil to notice her finally. His red, teary eyes said what he wouldn't. She knew.

"Hunter!" she screamed. "Wrecker! Ponder!"

Hunter, who'd just entered the clinic, heard her and came on the run. He met Wrecker and Ponder as they bounded down the stairs. They all converged on Jatil's office. Hunter's vibroknife was unsheathed and humming.

He took it all in instantly. His reaction was swift.

He crossed Jatil's office, coiled fingers in his hair, and snatched the man to his feet. The knife blade was a micron from his neck. Hunter said, "How much time do we have?"

Jatil said, "Not enough."

CHAPTER THIRTY-FIVE

HYPERSPACE, EN ROUTE TO TRYTH

Cellia Moten understood the galaxy better than most. As her mother did and her mother before her.

"Take a look at any given system," her grandmother told her when she was very young. It was night, and they stood upon a family sail barge overseeing a massive land excavation on Dantooine. The plot would soon become a Moten hyperdrive engine factory.

Grandmother said, "It's not the planets and moons that constitute that system. It is space—the all-consuming darkness of it. Every planet and every star is a pinprick separated by light-years. Lint on the infinite gown of a sightless god. But even within the scale cosmic, some of us are more significant—more *godlike* than others."

Mercenaries employed by the Motens had corralled a vocal band of Dantooine locals who'd spoken against the factory development. Some had gone as far as to sabotage excavation equipment. Though worthy of punishment, those acts did not drive Grandmother Moten to give the order she was about to give.

"The truly insignificant," she said, "have the blessing of ignorance. They do not know they are nothing. In some, this fosters a misguided pride, and they blaspheme."

Grandmother was referring to a young local who'd splashed the older woman's beautiful white gown with mud in protest of the alleged "environmental damage" the factory would bring. The allegation was a lie, of course. Radical propaganda crafted by those who hated progress.

That local woman and her family were among the agitators who'd been forced face down on the leveled dirt. A former bodyguard of Grandmother's—the one who let that young woman get close enough to sling mud—lay there, too.

"When they blaspheme," Grandmother said, "we of actual galactic significance must smite them. As a lesson for all."

Grandmother gave a thumbs-down signal to her mercenaries. The night brightened with blaster bolts accompanied by screams cut abruptly short. Cellia remembered thinking it was like a fireworks show.

She did not recount all of that to Crane as she inspected her yacht's curated collection pieces, but she felt he might like some insight into her nonconformist tastes. She tapped the glass of the central column where a stone Ithorian goblet was suspended in antigravity. "These starburst gems set in the onyx represent—"

Crane interrupted her. "What will you do when you're a governor?"

"Use my wealth and influence to improve the lives of all the citizens in my region?"

He shook his head. "No. I mean, what are you going to do? Outside of the performance." Crane, it seemed, was in a reckless mood.

"I don't know what you're implying, but you might reconsider if our partnership is to flourish."

"If it's to flourish, we need to stop talking around things. You want me to be eyes and ears for you inside the bureau, but you want me to protect you, too. You can't stop your 'collecting,' can you? Even as you're cleaning up your act to be a face of Imperial rule for your friend Sheev, you can't. That's why you're so insistent on going to Tryth."

Crane was not like her. Significant in some respects, but not the same as a Moten. Perhaps she'd encouraged his boldness, which had led to him misunderstanding her intentions. How harshly might she have to correct him? "I'm going to Tryth because I want the mortar those criminals took from me."

Crane leaned in to her, intensity beaming. "Can you ask Parlin to step outside?"

Parlin was the sole member of her security force still in the gallery. He shook his head slowly at the suggestion of leaving.

Crane said, "Don't you want to speak freely for once?"

Cellia said, "You might attempt to harm me."

"If you thought me a danger, you would've let me ride on the *Jurat*."

Cellia smirked. "Parlin, leave us."

The objection was immediate. "Mistress, no—"

"Parlin! Leave!"

His bruised nostrils flared. His chest heaved. But he obeyed. He left the gallery.

Crane waited a beat after the door sealed, then lowered his voice. "You can say it now."

"What is it you think I've kept from you?"

"You've kept nothing from me. It's all clear. I'm giving you the rare opportunity to say it plain."

Cellia said, "You first."

He nodded, appreciating a good turn. "Very well. I've only met a few prodigies in my life. Gayla Reen is one of them. Her talents were wasted in a banal Senate assignment. Not only wasted. Softened. It turned a dagger into a seat cushion. I refuse to let that talent go to waste. I'll make her understand."

Cellia was disappointed and bored by Crane's aspirations. A man wanted to regain control of a woman who'd rejected him. Not in the romantic sense, but still so quotidian as to tempt Cellia to have him cast from the ship. The only thing that stopped her was her inability to do that in hyperspace. Also, she still needed him to quell suspicions at the ISB of the *Jurat* explosion and her other murders.

With that in mind, a deal was a deal. Cellia made her confession. "I am a god. I decide when to end life, and I collect souls. There."

Crane seemed startled, but Cellia felt like she'd taken the first full breath of her life. Perhaps there was something cathartic about saying the quiet things aloud.

Crane sat back, hands on his thighs. Seemingly satisfied. "Thank you for trusting me. Now, if souls are what you want, let's go get you some more."

CHAPTER THIRTY-SIX

FELLIAN OUTPOST, TRYTH

Tech and Phee arrived at the clinic to find Wrecker escorting a couple of bruised refinery workers to the exit with a sack of random therapeutics and a recommendation to put ice on whatever still hurt in the morning.

"What's happening here?" Tech asked.

Wrecker said, "Trouble."

They sealed the clinic and went upstairs to the larger exam room, where Hunter had Jatil on his knees. Everyone was present and deadly serious. Hunter guided the vibroblade with a surgeon's finesse, drawing a thin sketch of blood on the medic's throat.

Hunter said, "Who did you contact?"

Jatil looked at Sohi when he said, "Father Crane."

Sohi's bed was upright, with tiny baby Coru cradled and sleeping in her arms. Ponder had been resting a hand on the baby's head but separated from his family at Jatil's words, advancing on the man, intending to do him harm. Tech stepped between the clone and the medic. "Hold on, Ponder. There's more information to be gained."

Phee said, "Can someone fill me in? I'm confused."

Hunter yanked Jatil's hair, forcing him to wince and talk. "Gayla and I were raised by—"

"Conscripted!" Sohi corrected.

"*Conscripted* by Father Crane at the same time. We were trained to-gether. She excelled at spycraft in ways I could not. She was favored."

Sohi said, "Is that how you saw it? Favor. He never loved or respected any of us! He made me do monstrous things. He buried you here."

Jatil nodded. "It was the best thing that ever happened to me. I wasn't built for espionage like you and the others. Putting me here to suss out potential Republic saboteurs led to me assimilating into this commu-nity. I grew to care about the citizens of Fellian Outpost. I love them."

Hunter's patience thinned. He let the blade bite a few more microns of Jatil's flesh. Blood trickled, and the medic squirmed. "Why help us? Then serve us up?"

"When you arrived, Gayla was in bad shape. I didn't think she would make it. I *hoped* she wouldn't."

Sohi's face creased with rage. "What?"

Omega's face was something sadder. "I don't understand how any medic could say such a thing."

Jatil, who was a sneeze away from having his throat slit, got indig-nant. "Crane's wanted alert arrived hours before you did. I knew who you were when you contacted the spaceport control tower. When you said Gayla was in distress, I needed to see. If she'd died, I could've cov-ered up everything. Thrown her carcass in a mercury barrel and let the rest of you go about your business. I didn't want Crane looking in Tryth's direction any more than you. But now you're healing and plan-ning to run. He'll find you eventually. When that happens, if he deter-mines you were here, and I didn't notify him, what do you think happens to Fellian Outpost then? This new regime punishes with pride." His final words on the matter were aimed directly at Sohi. "I would've let you die if you weren't with child."

"Am I supposed to be grateful?" she asked.

"Yes!" Jatil insisted. "I helped deliver a baby that's strong enough to make it without you."

"Without me?" Despite her weakness and soreness, Sohi tried to leave the bed, murder in her eyes.

Jatil kept talking. "Crane wants *you*. It's always been you. If he catches you now, nobody else matters. Your child and her father can leave and have a good life away from Crane's machinations. I gave you a gift. You can now sacrifice your future apart from your child's."

Sohi stood on weak legs and took wobbly steps while Coru cooed in the crook of her elbow. Phee stepped in for support when it looked like she might fall. Sohi waved Phee away.

Sohi's voice was strong, even if her body wasn't. "You didn't have to tell him anything! You could've let us go without a word."

"As if Crane wouldn't have tracked you by other means. As if he wouldn't raze Fellian Outpost because he didn't hear it from me first."

"I should break your neck," Sohi said, wincing.

"Maybe later." Hunter withdrew the vibroblade from Jatil's throat, then snapped a vicious blow to the medic's temple with the knife's handle, knocking him limp. He said, "Tech."

"Already on it." Tech sliced into the nearest terminal.

Ponder slid into Phee's position, supporting Sohi's weight. "Is your ship repaired? Can we leave?"

Tech's fingers danced over the terminal controls. "The *Marauder* is functional, but we still need the ion storms to pass. That will likely happen within the hour, but I patched into the spaceport tower, and we have a problem. An Imperial *Sentinel*-class shuttle has dropped out of hyperspace. They're in an orbital hold because of the storm, but as soon as we're clear to lift off, they'll be clear to land."

Wrecker said, "Let's buzz them on the way out and jump to hyperspace before they know it's us."

Tech shook his head. "They've ordered the spaceport to impound the *Marauder*. We can't even get close to it without a fight."

Wrecker slammed his fist into his palm. "Then we fight."

"We'll have moments if we're lucky." Sohi passed the child to her father, grimacing from the pain the whole time.

Hunter and Tech exchanged glances that were a whole silent conversation. This was bad. Engaging, evading, and escaping the force coming for them would be difficult even if everyone was in fighting form—and everyone was not. Hunter hated this pragmatic part of himself, but he'd never known if it was training or his Kamino-brand DNA doing what it was designed for. He calculated their potential losses, and it wasn't difficult math to find their largest handicap. Who would be the first to admit it?

Sohi's face was unwavering when she said, "I know what you're thinking, Hunter. You're not wrong. If we're talking a smart, tactical exfil, I'm a liability."

Hunter said, "Are we talking about something else, then?"

She lurched across the room to a cabinet of pharmaceuticals, nudging aside the levitating medical droid to access the drugs.

"Is there something I can help you with?" the droid inquired.

"I doubt your programming would allow it." She plucked vials from the shelves, skimming the labels and shaking her head before returning them.

The medical droid protested. "You're not authorized to handle the controlled substances here."

"Ponder." Sohi jerked her head at him.

Ponder handed Coru to an eager Uncle Wrecker, who made cooing noises. Ponder then retrieved a restraining bolt from inside his tunic. He stuck it to the medical droid's shell. It immediately hit the floor, bounced, then remained still.

Ponder made as if to retrieve his daughter but saw the girl was doing fine with her current caretaker and let her be.

And Wrecker, for his part, was taken. "Your old uncle's going to get you your first thermal detonator once we get out of here."

The child gurgled and sucked her thumb.

Sohi continued scanning vials, making a satisfied noise as she palmed one filled with translucent purple liquid and quickly claimed another filled with milky green fluid.

She found two inoculation guns in a separate cabinet and loaded one vial into each.

"What are those?" Ponder asked.

"A stimulant and a painkiller," Sohi said.

Now Hunter was more worried. "Should you mix them?"

"No," Sohi said.

She shot one thigh with the first gun, draining the vial, then did the same with the remaining gun on her other thigh. The second vial was the stimulant, and it worked fast. Sohi's eyes bulged. She let loose a beast's roar toward the ceiling, startling Coru. To her credit, the baby did not scream. The infant examined her mother curiously.

When Sohi panned the room, Hunter felt like, maybe, he was meeting the real Gayla Reen for the first time. And he fought a shudder.

"Crane will not have me," she said, "nor my child."

"Worthy goals," Hunter said. "How do we make it happen, team?"

Tech said, "We'll need the *Marauder* ready to go before we board, or they'll simply blow the ship."

"Mel," Phee offered.

"My thoughts exactly. Let her prep while we work our way there."

"And how are we doing that?" Phee asked. "They know where we are and where we want to go. We need decoys, distractions, the whole she-bang!"

Ponder, who'd been contemplatively quiet, spoke up. "Decoys and distractions. What about the casino credits?"

Hunter perked. "Go on."

"We weren't counting on you allowing us back on the *Marauder,* so I brought all our possessions, even those credits, off the ship. If they alert Crane every time they're spent, then we should spread them around."

"Brilliant," Tech said. "Someone better get started."

Ponder retrieved the trunk holding the marked credits and divided them in sacks among himself, Hunter, Phee, and Omega. While Wrecker tended to the baby so Sohi could change and prepare, the others drifted onto the streets surrounding the clinic, making fast purchases and leaving exorbitant tips. To expedite the process, Phee found a bucket and dumped a bunch of credits inside. She made a FREE CREDITS sign and watched Fellians drift to it hesitantly at first, then with joyous urgency.

All was well until Omega looked up and saw Tryth's red sun peeking through the clouds.

The storm had passed.

CHAPTER THIRTY-SEVEN

IN ORBIT, TRYTH

The Moten yacht dropped out of hyperspace over Tryth a hundred kilometers from the *Sentinel* shuttle and established an immediate transmission.

"This is Agent Crane. Who am I speaking with?"

Head and shoulders materialized in a hologram. It was a tanned woman, her hair braided tight to her skull to accommodate her black hat. The matching collar and shoulders of her uniform's tunic were visible in the projection.

"This is Major Lessa Banebreak, the commanding officer of Squad 131. Are the investigators on the *Jurat* arriving soon, sir?"

Crane stood on the bridge of Cellia's yacht with Cellia watching. Best to deflect for now. "How many personnel are in Squad 131?"

"Ten, including myself."

Crane almost laughed. These were the "numbers" Colonel Yularen placed so much confidence in. "I trust you've been briefed on our targets."

"Yes, sir. Clone Force Ninety-Nine. We're aware of the reputation they've fostered—exaggeration, if you ask me. We're here to deliver a dose of reality, sir."

"Very well. Detail the op for me."

Major Banebreak began to speak when Crane received a signal. Out of hyperspace, all of his monitoring programs were reactivated. The credit tracker from the Ronik Casino pinged at a steady clip.

The major was patched into the same program. She tilted her head, concern evident. "Are you seeing this, sir?"

"I am."

The credits he'd used to track Gayla and company to Dallow were being spent on Tryth, in multiple locations across Fellian Outpost—dozens of purchases.

So they know we're coming, Crane thought. *Clever bunch.*

Banebreak said, "We were going to corner them at a clinic on the west side of the mercury refinery. Now, though . . ."

Now you're seeing why you should've brought more than one squad, Crane thought but did not say. Especially since he saw a unique opportunity here, one he'd been contemplating from the moment Cellia destroyed the *Jurat*. Clone Force 99's distraction might have been the best thing to happen to him in days.

Crane said, "This is an obvious attempt to confuse us, but they only have one play. Retrieve their ship or a similar escape vessel. The local authorities have the spaceport locked down. Split your squad, five to the opposite end of town where we see the highest spending frequency. Five with me. We'll box them in, one way or another."

Banebreak acknowledged the order. "Yes, sir."

"I'll see you on the ground."

FELLIAN OUTPOST, TRYTH

Clone Force 99, having grabbed their belongings from the hotel, switched from civvies to armor. They finished securing their gear and got ready to move.

"Everyone knows their job?" Hunter asked. It was a rhetorical question as far as Wrecker, Tech, and Omega were concerned. Any doubts, questions, or concerns would come from Sohi, Ponder, and Phee. They all nodded, confirming their readiness even though Hunter knew Sohi was lying. She was in bad shape.

Had her ill-advised painkiller-stimulant injection helped? Sure, she was standing. But her blue complexion looked grayish, like she'd died two days ago instead of pushing new life into the world. By contrast, baby Coru looked warm, chubby, and healthy. The child glowed like a power cell, and Hunter had to trust that energy would give Sohi enough strength and determination to get them both to the *Marauder*.

Tech gave Hunter a nod. "See you there, brother."

He and Phee exited through the clinic's main entrance. They were an advance team meant to approach the spaceport and scope out the situation. If anyone could find their way through whatever resistance awaited without being noticed, it was them.

Ponder, donning the light armor of his Kuuto disguise, embraced his wife and child. He stroked the baby's cheek and rested his forehead against Sohi's. A single tear raced down his jawline. The couple didn't say anything to each other. No I love yous and no goodbyes. Hunter got it. They were focused on their objective: to see each other again, safe and whole. No need for commentary.

Wrecker extended one massive fist. Omega bumped her knuckles with his, and Hunter did the same.

"See you there," Wrecker said. He clapped a hand on Ponder's shoulder. The clone pulled away from his family, then quickly stepped through the clinic doors without looking back. Wrecker followed.

Hunter addressed Sohi. "We have time, but we'll keep a steady clip. You start to lag—"

"I won't lag," Sohi said.

"If you do, I will carry you, and Omega will carry Coru. No argument."

She wanted to argue, Hunter could tell, but even that required energy she needed to reserve. She nodded.

"Before we go," Hunter said, "you must decide. What about him?"

Unconscious and tied to a chair, Jatil moaned. He was stirring more and more and would wake up soon. If the ISB came here, he'd have no intel on their plan, but the case of his betrayal deserved a response. Sohi would judge him, and Hunter had no problem with whatever verdict came down.

She shook her head. "Leave him for *Father* Crane."

"You sure?" Hunter said.

"I don't think he'll appreciate the reunion."

Enough said. "We're moving."

SPACEPORT, FELLIAN OUTPOST, TRYTH

Even with the storm clouds gone, the endlessly chugging smokestacks created a perpetual gloom ripe with deep shadows and camouflage to conceal Tech and Phee's spaceport approach. They'd made it to an alley a quarter kilometer away from the closest spaceport gate. Concealment wasn't the issue, though. Shadows alone couldn't grant them access—not when the location was as heavily fortified as this. A mix of local law enforcement and refinery security guards were stacked at every entry point.

Tech, who panned macrobinoculars over the perimeter, was instantly frustrated. The local spaceport had only bare-bones security measures, but what the facility lacked in sturdy fences it now made up for in alert personnel. This was a problem.

"What's rolling around in that big brain of yours?" Phee asked.

He passed her the macrobinoculars. "Concern."

She saw what he saw and sighed. Then, she angled the lenses up.

Two ships drew near—one, a luxury yacht that stuck out on this world like a swollen tentacle. The other was one perfectly suited for this world and their circumstances, a trooper transport. The transport descended within the spaceport perimeter, but, oddly, the yacht overshot the spaceport, touching down more than a kilometer away, beyond the secure area.

"You see that?" Phee asked.

"I did."

"Closer look?"

"After you."

Crane didn't want to offer Cellia advice considering his larger aims—
which he was mostly improvising at this juncture. But not stating the
obvious might read as out of character, and he needed to maintain a
charade of compliance, at least until he was off the ship. He said, "You
should park your ship inside the spaceport perimeter. It will be well
protected."

"My security detail is more than capable of protecting me and my
property," Cellia said confidently. "The common landing pads are too
close to those refinery exhaust stacks. It would strain my filtration systems, and I don't want to breathe that muck any more than I have to."

"Very well," he said, then thought, *May your hubris bring you all you
deserve.*

The yacht touched down in the spaceport's maintenance area, a vast
buffer of open field adjacent to where the bulk of air traffic approached
for landings or accelerated during takeoffs. Several domed hangars were
used for extensive repairs, and storage containers and heavy equipment
were littered about.

Cellia seemed satisfied with the exclusivity of the space. She told
Crane, "Remember, bring the pirate and my mortar here. Do what you
will with the rest of them."

"Of course, you have my word."

The yacht captain had already notified the trooper squad, so when
the ramp dropped, speeders were en route to pick Crane up and head
into the town of Fellian Outpost. Given all he'd seen and all Cellia had
revealed, Crane still wondered if her gift to him would be a blaster bolt
in the back before Parlin and company mowed down the troopers. With
every step, his confidence grew.

Crane faced her but kept walking backward, counting his steps until
he touched the ground. Almost free.

Cellia glided to the top of the ramp and said, "I want to meet your
protégé. If she's as much the talent as you, I think we'll all get along
nicely. Bring her, too."

He'd used every bit of spycraft to endear himself to her, to make her believe she'd instilled a fear-fueled obedience in him on par with that sycophant Parlin and the rest of their crew. As his boot dug into the soft Tryth soil and the speeder braked a few meters away, beckoning him, he buried his inner amusement over a truth only he knew.

He wasn't coming back. Not as the lap pet she wanted him to be.

But he would like Gayla to meet Cellia one day, so Cellia, with her loathsome god complex, might see, in her final, painful moments, the sort of disciple Crane was capable of producing.

"Hopefully, this won't take too long," he called to Cellia in the most reassuring voice he could muster.

Then he was off, clear of her for the time being. Free to reclaim his cherished daughter.

He never noticed two watchers in the shadows.

CHAPTER THIRTY-EIGHT

REFINERY PUMPING STATION, FELLIAN OUTPOST, TRYTH

Ponder fought the part of himself that wanted to stay with his family. That was pride talking. He'd wrestled with its reality-altering properties a lot since his injury. Pride told him he could handle another deployment and combat even though he had trouble handling the initial adjustment period with his new limb and the phantom pains that persisted beyond that. Pride assured him that, if he only got the chance, he'd win over squadmates who considered him a jinx. Pride said he was too good to slice mountains of kebroot for vats of stew.

That baby girl needed her father to put pride aside if she and her mother were to escape Sendril Crane. Hunter, or any member of Clone Force 99, was better equipped to protect his child if it came down to a fight, Ponder knew.

What he could do, with Wrecker's help, was distract the forces impeding his family's escape. And if it came down to it, Ponder could die to give Wrecker and the rest a chance to get off this void-damned world. If that part were still pride talking, it probably wouldn't be too long of a conversation. He'd seen the trooper transport land.

"So, how big is this explosion going to be?" Ponder asked.

Wrecker spoke with a child's glee. "Medium!"

"Compared to what?"

"Small and large."

They'd reached the edge of Fellian Outpost, where the closest mercury geysers sputtered mildly, their natural force diminished by a series of coiling pipes plugged directly into the silvery plume, running to the nearest refinery pumping station a quarter kilometer away. During the plan run-through, Ponder worried that blowing up any of the refinery operations would injure or kill civilians, but Wrecker enthusiastically explained, "This explosion destroys *things,* not *people!*"

Because mercury was such a vast and vital resource on Tryth, there were hundreds of automated pumping stations with several redundancies in the event of failure. Their plan would cause panic without permanent interruptions or casualties.

If it worked.

Wrecker and Ponder got as close as they dared, just out of range of sizzling hot droplets pattering the ground a few meters away.

Wrecker opened a compartment on his backpack and retrieved something shaped like a standard-issue thermal detonator, but it was larger and homemade. Ponder recognized the famous logo from a binkberry preserves can on one part of the grenade's shell.

"My own design," Wrecker boasted.

The giant thumbed the trigger and hurled the orb directly into the geyser.

They ran to a nearby rocky outcrop for cover. Ponder crouched, tensed, and waited for the explosion. He kept waiting. As the time stretched, Ponder lost his patience and stood upright next to a grinning, unconcerned Wrecker.

"Did it fail?" Ponder asked.

"Long fuse."

"How I—"

The pumping station erupted in violent blue-silver flame, with white-hot chunks of shrapnel whipping into the night. A refinery alarm sounded immediately, warbling into the residential parts of Fellian Outpost. Even from the border, Ponder heard citizens panicking. Within moments of that, the screaming sirens of emergency response vehicles.

"All right," Wrecker said, turning back to town. "Between those dirty credits pinging all over and our flaming beauty keeping the first responders occupied, the others should have a decent shot at reaching the *Marauder*."

"Good," said Ponder. "Let's move. If we double-time it, we can catch up to Sohi."

They began the hike back within the Fellian border, making it a couple of blocks in, passing flame-suppressor crews on a beeline for the pumping station. Ponder felt good about their part of the plan, as if the doom-and-gloom preparations he'd made before were for nothing.

Then the queasy feeling hit. The same feeling he'd had before his squad got blown out of the sky on Metalorn. It was enough to slow him down—and save his life. A blaster bolt sizzled the ground, a meter from his feet.

"Down!" Wrecker shouted and hurled Ponder through the window of a closed-down garment shop before diving through himself. Low and crawling, Ponder wedged himself beside the window frame with blaster bolts plinking the shop's exterior.

Wrecker stood on the opposite side of the window, concealed, but barely—very little could hide his bulk. He snuck peeks at the building across the street. "One shooter on the rooftop, but bet he's not alone."

Ponder surveyed the vacant storefront. Very little of use here. Several empty clothing racks. Some scattered tunics and dresses. A few dented refinery hard hats.

He had a hand blaster on him, a weapon ill-suited for range. The rifle affixed to Wrecker's backpack could do the job if they got a clear shot. The way that shooter was situated on the neighboring roof, they'd be wasting charge until his backup flanked them. If only they could get him to poke his head out.

"Wrecker," Ponder said, "would you mind lending me your rifle?"

"Are you any good?"

"I never mentioned my specialty before my injury, did I?"

"No."

"Sniper."

Across the street, from the high-ground vantage point, the storm-trooper called in status to his squadmates. "I have two combatants pinned down in the abandoned clothing store. Move in. Move—"

The trooper reacted before his brain processed exactly what was rocketing at him. It was a clothing rack hurled like a spear with the force of a missile. It hit the lip of the roof he'd been using for cover, forcing him to pop up and move, which was a mistake. A rifle blast made it so he'd never make another.

Ponder uncurled his finger from the rifle's trigger. "Still got it."

"Let's go." Wrecker hopped through the window, and Ponder followed. The big guy's powerful strides made it hard for Ponder to keep up. The servos in his cybernetic leg held fast, but his organic leg struggled, far removed from the twenty-kilometer hikes of his soldiering days. He didn't have to worry about making it that far, because when Wrecker turned the next corner, he took a blaster bolt to his right shoulder guard, halting the run. It was a glancing blow, barely singeing the armor, but it meant trouble.

Wrecker pivoted back to cover while Ponder went low, sliding the last couple of meters on his belly until he had a peek at where the shot came from. The trooper hadn't expected such a low target, and the time it took him to adjust was too long. Ponder put a round through his gut, dropping him.

He was not alone. Two more troopers took positions that gave them a bead on Ponder and Wrecker. A third combatant—an officer in uniform, not armor—shouted orders.

"Flanking formations!" she said. "Pincer maneuver."

Ponder backed up next to Wrecker. "You good, big fella?"

"Barely a scratch."

They both scanned the area and saw the optimal route at the same time.

"Suppressing fire," Wrecker said, arming a pair of standard thermal detonators, palming both in one hand like deadly fruit.

"On me," Ponder said and stepped out of cover, sending blaster bolts downrange, forcing the troopers to duck.

It was enough time for Wrecker to make a double fastball pitch, the two detonators angling apart, homing in on their specific targets.

One trooper saw what was coming and rolled out of cover, seeking safety outside the blast zone. The other was unaware, popping up to return fire and never noticing the explosive hit the mud by his feet. Perhaps not knowing was a mercy. He went up in a fan of fire and dust.

The officer barked, "Fall back, fall back!"

Wrecker and Ponder crossed the intersection and continued up the deserted street—apparently, the locals knew trouble and when to hide from it. Wrecker bounded forward like a tank, and Ponder had an adrenaline spike to thank for no longer feeling the fatigue of a hard run. His head was on a swivel, the old training kicking in. He saw every alley, window, and roofline that would give an enemy an angle on them. They were all clear.

This is good, Ponder thought. *If that was all of them, we make it to the next block, take a few quick turns, and we're free.*

His old training might have been his undoing. He had never been in a unit like Clone Force 99. Two-person ops. Four-person ops. Six-person ops. They were never a thing. He had been part of an entire clone squadron on every op until his last. Anywhere from thirty or more troopers in fixed positions. He was never the soldier bringing up the rear.

The trooper who'd survived Wrecker's detonator volley and who'd been ordered to fall back was the disobedient kind. Maybe seeing his fellow soldier go down drove him to the edge—understandably. Maybe he peeked around the corner and saw there were no eyes on him. However it went, the rogue trooper had a clear shot and took it.

Ponder felt the searing heat and went down screaming.

CHAPTER THIRTY-NINE

OUTSKIRTS OF SPACEPORT, FELLIAN OUTPOST, TRYTH

The Shistavanen and the battle droid sat at the foot of the yacht's ramp. The wolfman finished off a death stick and lit another while the droid rambled about little-known Tryth facts.

"A children's tale posits the planet's core is a giant kyber crystal, which is obviously fiction. However, many Trythian adults maintain the belief despite scientific evidence to the contrary."

"Folks believe whatever nonsense they want to believe," the Shistavanen growled, dismissive. "What a surprise."

"In the history of Tryth, there have been over one million murders attributed to disputes over the Kyber Core. One particularly bloody incident involved a citizen proclaiming himself the 'Kyber-Man' and inciting a riot against the—"

"Scuse me, fellas!" a voice called from the dark.

The guards stood, weapons raised. "Who's there?"

"Phee Genoa." She stepped into the yacht's landing lights, hands raised, dark glasses covering her eyes despite it being night. "I believe your boss is looking for me."

The guards got antsy. The Shistavanen swept his rifle in one direction while the droid panned his arm cannons the opposite way.

"Who accompanies you?" the droid asked. "I calculate a less than one percent chance that you're alone."

Another voice in the dark, Tech's, said, "I concur."

A metallic cylinder skipped end over end toward the guards, stopping between them. The Shistavanen said, "Oh crink!"

The flash grenade exploded, washing the sentries in a radiant burst that burned the furry guard's eyes and scrambled the droid's optics. Phee drew her blaster and stunned the Shistavanen while Tech snuck up on the droid and tagged him with a restraining bolt. With both guards down, Phee and Tech bound them, then ventured onto the yacht.

They traversed the long, bright entry corridor aft of the yacht, passing walls of framed art before taking a short winding staircase to the second level. They crept past closed doors, likely concealing sleeping quarters and other facilities.

"So what are we doing here?" Phee asked.

"I am still formulating a course of action. My inspection of this vessel's exterior revealed some oddities that might prove advantageous, though that will depend on our ability to take control of the bridge. And, of course—"

At the next staircase, the Kiffar Parlin descended casually, his rifle ready, cutting them off.

"—any further opposition," Tech finished.

"You know," Parlin said, "I'm glad you're here."

He fired his rifle. Tech and Phee dived to either side of the corridor, thankful Parlin wasn't a good shot at close range.

There was an intersecting corridor between them and him, though Parlin advanced while firing. The closer he got, the worse their chances, so Tech improved their odds by drawing his blaster and returning fire. He hit Parlin's rifle and sent it flying far behind him. Tech kept firing rapidly, but Parlin had wised up since their last fight, activating a wrist-mounted portable shield that absorbed the blast like a sponge.

"Go!" Tech told Phee. "I'll deal with him."

She dipped into the intersecting corridor and turned the corner, taking an alternate staircase as fast as she could. Meanwhile, Tech holstered his blaster, knowing it would do him little good against Parlin's defensive gear.

Parlin grinned. "I've read the files on your crew. You're the one they call Tech. Brains over brawn won't do you much good here."

Parlin deactivated his shield and cracked his knuckles. "Let me teach you a little something."

Tech sighed. "The crude way, then."

Parlin charged.

FELLIAN OUTPOST, TRYTH

Crane and his troopers arrived at Jatil's clinic amid frantic activity. The locals were still in a frenzy over the massive amount of "free" credits gifted to them by his quarry. It was sad, really. The gleeful spenders observed the Imperial armor with skepticism and outright malice in some cases. These troopers looked too much like the side this world had aligned against. Crane understood but fell short of empathy. These people's misplaced allegiances could classify them as criminals by default. Eligible for detainment and potential reeducation.

Though the same would likely be said about him by day's end.

"Switch your visor to enhanced mode," Crane instructed the troopers, still playing the role of hard-nosed operative so as not to tip his hand. "I want recordings of faces cross-referenced with chain codes for when we return with an appropriate prisoner transport."

"Roger that," a trooper confirmed.

Crane approached the clinic entrance. "Stand guard here. I'll call if you're needed."

Inside, he sensed near emptiness. He barely needed to search the first floor and never assumed any of his quarry would still be there. Yet he detected groaning upstairs and climbed. An exam room door whooshed open, revealing Jatil tied to a chair, a knot from a heavy blow swelling at his temple.

Jatil, with effort, raised his chin. "Father?"

"Do you know where Gayla has gone?"

Jatil shook his head, grimacing. "They knocked me out. I only woke up moments ago."

"How much of a head start do they have?"

Another head shake.

Crane sighed. "She can't move too fast with a baby inside her."

"Not—" Jatil vomited. Crane backed up, narrowly avoiding the splash. "Not inside anymore."

This piqued Crane's attention. "The child is born."

Jatil nodded. "A little girl."

The information hit Crane's mind like a chemical reaction. New thoughts bubbled up—alternate plans formed. "You've done good, Jatil. I'll see that you're rewarded."

"Can you untie me?" Jatil asked.

But Crane was already on his way outside.

He met his troops at the door and singled one out. "You. Detain the medic upstairs and prepare him for transport to a reeducation center. Charge: offering aid and comfort to fugitives."

"Yes, sir!" The trooper entered the clinic, unlinking shock cuffs from his belt.

One of the remaining four approached. "Orders, sir!"

Crane held up a halting finger and stepped into the muddy street. He angled his head toward the sky, noting drifting clouds that occasionally blotted out the stars. He tasted the humidity on his tongue. He considered.

Gayla had given birth within the last two days. She'd move with purpose but slowly. It would be all her body would allow. The baby would need to be soothed, but the unpredictability of an infant's mood would necessitate specific pathways to prevent being noticed: back alleys with low foot traffic.

Crane turned to the troopers. He opened his palm, activating a holo-projector. A map of the area appeared. "They'll be moving close to the refinery, in the shadows of the perimeter fence and the closest Fellian businesses. We'll likely be able to intercept here." Crane pointed to a refinery staging area where pallets of processed fuel additives were stacked and prepped for transport offworld.

The troopers nodded. "Excellent strategy, sir. Let's move."

She can barely move, Hunter thought. He looped Sohi's arm over his shoulder to prop her up. To drag her. She wasn't heavy, but she also wasn't helping. Her feet dragged like the blades on a plow. The shots she'd given herself were either too weak to maintain a steady clip, or they were reacting horribly in her strained system. They might kill her.

The arm holding the baby remained strong, though. It was as if she funneled every bit of strength into guarding the child—admirable but unsustainable.

"Sohi," Hunter said, "let Omega carry Coru."

She shook her head. Not even the strength to *say* no.

Omega said, "I'll take good care of her. Promise."

Omega slid in close and slipped Coru from her mother's arms too easily for Hunter's liking. "You still with us, Gayla?"

"Told you," she said weakly, "don't call me that."

That was a good sign. It wasn't a *great* sign, but the situation was workable as long as she could talk and move.

He tapped two fingers to the comlink on his helmet. "Tech, report."

He waited for a response. Got nothing. He double-tapped his helmet. "Wrecker, where are you?"

Nothing that way, either.

He knew his team. His thoughts didn't turn to the worst-case scenario. He did have to consider what might be necessary if Tech couldn't secure the *Marauder* or if Wrecker had gotten snared by ISB agents. There were no good options in either scenario.

"When are there ever?" he mumbled low enough not to spook Sohi or Omega.

They kept trekking along the outskirts of Fellian Outpost, sticking to a length of refinery fencing approximately two klicks from the spaceport. Hunter glanced through the gaps in the fence. Automated clamps lifted and arranged barrels in long chutes running from the refinery's interior, carrying them to massive pallets that would be loaded, stacked, and shipped as necessary. The barrels were slightly taller than Omega, rectangular instead of round, allowing them to fit together tightly. The corners were magnetized so, once activated, they'd snap together on their pallets like a child's building blocks, ensuring they didn't shift in transit.

The refinery never slowed production during the days of ion storms, so pallets were stacked as high as some of the minor Coruscant towers in parts of the lot. There were rows upon rows of deep crevices and shadows. Many places for Sohi to rest and regain a bit of strength while Hunter scouted ahead, solo, to assess their operational status.

"Hold," he said, lowering Sohi and propping her against the back wall of some Fellian establishment.

He produced a laser cutter from his kit, fired up the crackling-hot beam, and melted through select links in the refinery fence. He worked up, vertically, horizontally, then down again.

He was almost finished when he heard "Freeze. Hands up!" in the modulated voice of a trooper speaking through the audio emitter in his helmet.

Hunter turned.

Four troopers and Agent Crane blocked their path.

Crane said, "By the power vested in me by the Imperial Security Bureau, I place you all under arrest."

CHAPTER FORTY

MERCURY REFINERY, FELLIAN OUTPOST, TRYTH

Hunter rose from the fence he'd been cutting.

"Slowly," Crane said, "with your hands raised."

Hunter lifted his hands while tracking Omega and Coru. A trooper had them sighted with a rifle, and Hunter envisioned brutally taking that trooper down first.

Of course, it was a fantasy, no practical means to be found. There were ten meters between him and the weapons aimed their way. Any move, and they'd put him down. Worse, Omega, Coru, and Sohi were between him and the troopers, so any stray shots risked harming them.

This was Crane's game now.

The ISB agent drew his blaster. "There's a capture *or* kill warrant on you, CT-9901. I don't have a preference either way."

Sohi scrambled forward on her knees. "No, Crane. Don't!"

Crane fired.

Hunter's entire body lit up for a microsecond with the blue wave radiating from the stun blast. Then he went down, still.

Omega screamed but did not run to Hunter's aid. She had a bigger responsibility. She kept her body positioned between the troopers and the baby.

One trooper stayed sighted on Omega while the rest zeroed in on the weakened Sohi.

"Zap her or cuff her?" one impatient trooper asked.

Crane clapped him on the shoulder. "Hold."

The trooper relaxed, and Crane nudged past his armored guard to address Sohi directly. "Gayla—"

"Don't call me that."

"Fine. I won't call you by your name. That's how you feel about it today, and maybe you will tomorrow, but after I get you through the worst of some brief reeducation, you'll see there's much opportunity for those with our skill set."

She shook her head. "I'm done. With you. With the Empire."

"It doesn't have to be like it was. You won't have to become someone else. You won't have to betray people."

"I'm not joining the ISB!"

"I'm not talking about the ISB. Truthfully, I'm done with the organization myself. I knew it was a self-serving suckling on the Empire's teat, but the monsters it entertains because of their power and wealth are intolerable. Also, they send me to harsh worlds with incompetents."

Trooper helmets angled his way. "What's that supposed to—?"

Crane triggered the jolt disks he'd affixed to their armor, then stepped aside until they convulsed themselves still. Four dropped troopers, faces in the mud, meant Crane and Sohi could speak freely. He said, "It's time for something else. With our skills we have fine lives independent of the politicians and power brokers. There are no limits to what you and I might accomplish."

"How could you think I'd ever join you after all those years of torment mixed with tenderness to make me into something I didn't want to be?"

With a sincerity one might call monstrous, Crane said, "If not you, then what's my granddaughter's name, Gayla?"

Sohi grimaced. "Omega . . ."

Crane's face scrunched. "What kind of a name is that?"

"Run!" Sohi used her remaining strength to hurl herself at Crane's legs. She cinched his knees together and tipped him to the ground with the troopers he'd betrayed, soaking his white ISB uniform in good old Fellian mud. Crane squealed, more horrified by the dirt than the attack, it seemed. A short kick to Sohi's jaw freed him, but her aim had been achieved.

The blond child bolted through the hole in the refinery fence with Sohi's baby.

"Come back here!" Crane shouted, rushing after them. He kicked at the detached chunk of fencing repeatedly, widening the hole enough so he could slip through, too.

Meters ahead, the child turned the corner at the first row of barrels, looking to hide among the refinery pallets.

Crane chased.

The cybernetic leg Ponder had been given after his injury was not a top-of-the-line model. Nothing given to wounded clones was. Bonding to a mid-tier replacement limb came with several issues. The medical droids took a long time to calibrate proper balance and torque at the knee joint. The cybernetic foot was larger than his organic foot, so boots were a problem. The limb would often power down in his sleep and then suddenly reboot, causing a reflexive kick that was liable to propel him from his bed. All irritants he'd learned to live with. What choice did he have?

The worst drawback was the nerve connection. The best cybernetic limbs felt indistinguishable from organic limbs, refined to the point you could feel a feather graze a piston. Or so he'd heard. Ponder's limb was decent under ideal circumstances, but being on the run for so long led to neglected maintenance that left it in perpetual half-numbness over the last few weeks, like the sensation you'd get if you sat on your hand too long. Any form of touch—a caress, a punch—he sensed maybe 40 percent of what he should. He'd hated that until the trooper blew his leg off.

Because even at 40 percent, the pain shooting through his entire body was blazing, though not debilitating.

He flung himself behind the cover of a column and remained calm despite the sparking wires jutting from where his cybernetic leg used to be.

Wrecker's senses were in a heightened state. He heard Regs call it the "fog of war," but there was nothing foggy about it for him. He was attuned to everything, including when his dance partner for the evening went down in a heap. Wrecker found his piece of cover behind an old, abandoned food distribution transport and gauged the situation.

Ponder was pinned behind a column, down one leg. He still had the rifle, but his maneuverability was hindered; the remaining trooper and the officer were coming fast, pinging shots to either side of Ponder. They'd be on him. They'd finish him. Ponder knew.

"Go, Wrecker!" he shouted. "I'll buy you as much time as possible. Just take care of my family."

Ponder checked the rifle charge for his final blaze of glory.

But Wrecker yelled, "Coru would never forgive her uncle if I didn't bring her daddy home!"

Wrecker ripped the back door of the food distribution transport off its hinge and wielded it like a shield, charging the advancing enemies as their blaster bolts bounced off the durasteel. When he reached Ponder, Wrecker scooped the injured clone under one arm and began a sideways shuffle-sprint that kept the makeshift shield between them and those trigger-happy Imperials.

"This plan works, too," Ponder said. "I think."

Wrecker covered a lot of ground with his mighty bounding steps, but even he couldn't move at full speed carrying a full-grown clone and deflecting incoming fire. He said, "We need an explosion."

"You got more detonators?" Ponder asked.

"No. It don't have to be that kind of explosion. Take my helmet off."

"What?"

"Just do it!"

While being jostled about like a Jawa on a bantha, Ponder somehow managed to unclip Wrecker's helmet and grasp it under his arm. It seemed like the last thing one should do in a blaster fight, but Ponder was in no position to debate. "Now what?"

Wrecker's milky-white eye twinkled like a jewel against the scar tissue on the left side of his face. He grinned. "We're going to blow up the town square."

The giant sped up.

CHAPTER FORTY-ONE

MOTEN YACHT, TRYTH

The cruelty Tech discerned in Cellia Moten's presence was, apparently, a desired trait in those she employed. Parlin delivered a wicked flurry of punches and kicks gleefully. Blows that would've bruised organs and shattered bones if not for Tech's armor.

From the moment the fight started, Tech was on defense—blocking, dodging, wheeling away. The Kiffar's fighting style was a mix of arts, flashing traits of Echani, Rek'dul, and even some Velanarian boxing stances despite Parlin having only two arms. The onslaught of striking combos had Tech's weight on his back foot, forcing him off the corridor where they started and into the yacht's galley.

The pristine kitchen equipment gleamed silver and reflected warped versions of the combatants that looked like they were engaged in a hazy dance. Tech ducked a killing kick that dented a high-end oven, then leaped over a counter, putting the width of the prep station between himself and Parlin.

"Nowhere to run," Parlin goaded. "But this is as good a place as any to drop you. I like playing with my food."

"I was unaware the Kiffar diet skewed toward clone," Tech said, curious if Parlin seriously intended to eat him should he lose.

Parlin rounded the counter, massaging the knuckles on his strong hand. Tech backed away, aware the gap between them was closing.

"I've seen how you work," Parlin said. "You run your mouth to distract me while you work some techno-wizardry sleight of hand. Thing is, nothing in the galley can be sliced. Your little computer's useless here."

Tech had come to that conclusion a while ago. "You are correct."

Parlin tugged a long wicked-looking carving knife from a magnetized wall rack. "This'll do."

Tech sighed, raised his hands, and thought, *Phee, I hope you're making ample progress.*

Phee had made ample progress. She'd encountered only one being since making it to the yacht's third level—a young Twi'lek ship attendant who'd held up a drink tray like a shield when she saw Phee. "Please don't hurt me."

"Child, hide."

The girl skittered to a nearby cupboard and climbed inside. Phee kept going.

Further exploration brought her to a gallery where several items were displayed, most likely stolen and appropriated by Cellia. However, they could barely hold Phee's attention because Cellia was in the room, too.

She hadn't heard Phee approach, focused on the portside gallery window that overlooked the spaceport. Her expression screamed boredom. How could someone like her have to spend even a moment on a world like this?

Phee made herself known. "You planning on cleaning this place up once you become a governor?"

Cellia faced Phee. Her mouth formed an *O* before she screamed, "Parlin!"

"He's occupied. Where'd you get all this neat stuff, Cellia?"

Cellia grabbed the hem of her heavy gown and attempted to flee. She was slow, though. It was an awkward shuffle that got her nowhere fast.

Phee winced, embarrassed for her. She cut Cellia's escape off with a light jog.

"Not so fast."

Cellia did an about-face and tried to run the other way. Still slow and awkward. "I can pay you," Cellia called over her shoulder. "I can fund expeditions for you to recover artifacts on my behalf."

Phee caught up with her easily and snatched her by the collar. "I don't think so. You killed my friend."

Phee snatched Ven Alman's bracelet off the hag's wrist, then shoved her to the floor. "I doubt he's the only one."

Cellia's hair had come loose from its high bun and spilled messily across her face. She looked like what she was . . . ridiculous. It didn't stop her from trying to fast-talk. "I have influence and powerful friends. I—"

Phee held up a halting hand. "You're either going to offer me a deal you have no intention of honoring, or you'll lob some exaggerated threat. I think it's a fifty-fifty bet, whichever way you take it. But you can save your breath. You know why?"

Cellia's face pinched.

Phee drew her blaster and stunned Cellia. The old wannabe governor lay sprawled on the deck, unconscious.

Phee continued through the galley to the bridge, mumbling, "And I'm coming back to take all this stuff."

After a quick rush through the bridge door and a stun blast each for the captain and copilot, Phee tapped her comlink: "I have the bridge. Get up here."

◆

Parlin twisted Tech's arm into a painful leverage maneuver that threatened to dislocate the clone's shoulder, though the knife he planned on putting through Tech's spine would be of more significant concern. "I told you being the smart one on your crew wasn't going to do you much good."

"You did say that."

Phee's voice crackled in his earpiece. "I have the bridge. Get up here."

Finally, he thought.

Tech said, "Whatever file you read misled you. While my brothers and I each have our specialties, the things we're *best* at, relatively speaking, each of us is *good at everything.*"

Tech shifted his weight slightly—a k'Jtari technique that eased the strain on his shoulder. He slipped free of Parlin's hold to the Kiffar's wide-eyed surprise, then jabbed the extended fingers of his left hand into a nerve cluster on the right side of Parlin's abdomen—a Shon-Ju school technique.

They separated. Parlin backpedaled, but Tech stood his ground. "Shall we try this again?"

Parlin screamed and charged. He threw vicious combinations of kicks and punches that Tech easily evaded and countered with casually devastating strikes to various nerve clusters in Parlin's body. The soft tissue blows temporarily robbed Parlin of the use of his limbs, beginning with arms, then legs, until the Kiffar was a panting, quivering pile on the floor.

"How?" Parlin asked, disbelieving.

"I've mastered fourteen different styles of unarmed combat and am eighty-nine percent complete on the development of a signature style."

Parlin gaped.

"Honestly," Tech said, "in most situations, blasters are more efficient."

He stunned Parlin, then dragged his body into a meat locker.

Tech raced to the yacht's upper levels and joined Phee on the bridge. He stepped over the stunned and bound pilots and took the captain's control, immediately slicing into the ship's system with his forearm computer. "Ah," he said, "as I suspected."

"Speak on it, Brown Eyes."

"The oddities I'd mentioned before . . . tractor beam emitters. Military grade. I don't know why they'd be on this sort of vehicle."

Phee nodded. "I do. Tractor beams snatch up smaller, vulnerable ships. That sort of dominance is Cellia's MO."

"Your logic is sound." He punched up an ignition sequence. "In any case, let's see how strong they are."

"How you gonna do that?"

"By using them to clear a path to the *Marauder*."

Phee nodded, trying to project enthusiasm. "I thought tractor beams were meant to be used in space."

"Mostly."

"We aren't in space."

"Correct. So I suggest you secure your harness. This might get bumpy."

CHAPTER FORTY-TWO

TOWN SQUARE, FELLIAN OUTPOST, TRYTH

Wrecker bound into an active town square, immediately drawing attention as a massive armored being carrying a smaller one-legged being might.

Ponder noted the throng of people present. Horror dawned on him. "We can't set off a bomb here. Not with all these people about."

"They are the bomb!" The pair passed a fountain, and Wrecker threw his makeshift shield in the water, done with it. "Anger is the best explosive I know!"

Then he yelled for all to hear. "Soldiers are here! They tried to take my credits. They're going to try to take yours, too!"

Outrage flared in the individuals closest to them and spread like a contagion, rippling outward from Wrecker and Ponder. By the time the Imperials caught up, it had infected most of the square.

Wrecker, towering over the Fellians, was an easy target for the trooper and his officer. But with dozens of civilians between them, the Imperials had a problem. So they did what they always do—what Wrecker expected them to do.

The officer said, "By the authority of Emperor Palpatine and the Imperial Security Bureau, I order you to step aside and—"

A rotten melon splatted the woman's face, smearing her in slush and seeds.

The remaining trooper shouted, "Who threw that? Who dares assault an officer of the Empire?"

A hurled wrench bounced off his helmet, staggering him.

The officer skimmed melon muck away while screaming, "If the persons attempting violence against us do not come forward immediately, I'll arrest everyone in this square as accomplices and—"

Someone rushed up behind and smashed a goblet on the back of the officer's head. She stumbled, turned to retaliate, but more citizens closed in, shoving her and the trooper to the ground.

An unidentifiable Fellian shouted, "Damned soldiers think you can take and take and take. Don'tcha know the war's over?"

The Fellian crowd swarmed the Imperials with fists, blunt objects, and other painful weapons held high. The officer attempted to raise her blaster, but someone snatched it out of her hand. Wrecker began his sprint again, faster, unburdened by the weight of the shield. As he and Ponder turned a corner, they heard blaster shots and kept going.

"Put my helmet back on," Wrecker said.

Ponder did the awkward outfitting, then Wrecker tapped his comlink. "Tech, come in. Have you got the *Marauder*?"

"Working on it," Tech said. "Give me approximately three minutes and thirty-four seconds. Over."

A trio of local Fellian law enforcement officers huddled inside the spaceport perimeter near the *Marauder*. Their orders were simple: No one gets near that ship. They had permission to use necessary force, but truthfully, they all wanted to go home.

"Lemme bum a death stick?" one begged.

The death stick distributor of the bunch said, "I ain't got an infinite supply. You owe me for three already."

The third said, "If I have to stand out here babysitting an empty ship much longer, you can give me the death and keep the stick."

They laughed hard at that one.

The death stick holder said, "All right, all right. Seriously, these are my last, so I expect a whole pack—from each of you—when we're done here. Deal?"

His two buddies nodded.

As he pulled the metallic death stick case from his pocket, it got snatched into the night by an invisible string.

"What the—?"

Metal groaned as a three stack of shipping containers suddenly went airborne, hurled at the trio of cops with wrecking speed. They managed to dive out of the way and avoid getting crushed. Still, the tarmac became as dangerous as an asteroid field. Every loose item became a projectile whipping toward a gleaming space yacht that was doing wildly improbable maneuvers too close to the ground.

Tech worked the yacht's controls at its bridge like a maestro directing a symphony. The thrusters' firing and the tractor beam's strength created something like an invisible tether to the ground, but along its length was a swarm of projectiles drawn directly to the ship. That much debris threatened to shred the yacht's hull like a laser cannon. Tech cut various thrusters, making precise adjustments with the rudder before refiring reverse thrusters. This turned the invisible tractor beam tether into a debris whip that he swiped back and forth at everything around the *Marauder*, clearing a path while forcing all the Fellian officers to flee or be destroyed in the chaos.

Tech kept the ship bucking and bumping for roughly thirty seconds, but there was a limit to how much maneuvering such a large vessel could pull off with a wake of flying debris chasing it. An engine stalled, cutting the ship's agility by 30 percent and allowing a volley of scraps to shred one of the hyperspace boosters. The entire ship shuddered. Tech hit the tractor beam's emergency cutoff. All the litter was released back to Tryth's natural gravity and clattered to the ground.

Then Tech put the yacht down in a rough skid, not even bothering with the landing gear.

The bridge canted thirty degrees when the ship finally stilled. Tech undid his harness and adjusted his weight to make the lopsided trek off the vessel when Phee put her hand on his chest, stopping him. Tech recognized the look on her face; her eyes sparked with some new, bright idea.

She said, "This ship patches into Cellia's personal systems, right?"

"Yes."

"All of them?"

Tech didn't need to hear another word. He didn't know whether it was his analytical mind deducing a brilliant plan seconds after her or some shared sense of recognition honed by whatever bond they'd been not-so-subtly nurturing. Either way, Tech returned to the console he'd already sliced into and said, "9.2 more seconds should do it."

Thirty seconds later, they exited Cellia's yacht—Phee carrying a heavy sack with everything she had taken from the midship gallery— and were sprinting onto the unguarded *Marauder*.

Inside, MEL-222 burst from a cabinet, screeching terrified beeps and boops.

Phee said, "If you knew how to fly the ship you could've just picked us up."

MEL-222 sounded a long, warbling beep.

"No, I don't expect you to do everything around here!" said Phee.

Tech took his place in the cockpit and fired up the engines. "Wrecker," he called over comms, "coming to you."

"Roger that!"

Tech switched channels. "Hunter! Hunter!"

No response.

Phee said, "That's not good."

"No," Tech said, "it is not. Let's assess from the sky."

They left the trashed spaceport behind in search of new trouble.

CHAPTER FORTY-THREE

Hunter sat on the *Marauder*'s nose. His knees were pulled to his chest, his arms hugged around them. He was young. Crosshair, also young, sat next to him. A hyperspace tunnel coiled lazily around them, yet he felt the most stillness he'd felt in a long time. The peace and impossibility of riding on the outside of a spaceship moving faster than light-speed clued him in to this being a dream. Crosshair said, "That soft spot of yours is going to get you into something you can't get out of sooner or later."

Hunter chuckled, warmed by another contentious love-hate conversation with his brother. "That hard shell of yours is problem-free, I guess."

"I'm a good soldier. Good soldiers . . ."

"Follow orders. That all you got?"

Crosshair rolled a toothpick from one corner of his mouth to the other. "You aren't a good soldier anymore."

"Tell me something I don't know."

Crosshair took the toothpick out, flicked it into space, and said, "Being a good person is better."

Hunter faced his misguided, dutiful brother, his chest aching from what he'd never say aloud. Hunter missed Crosshair so much. *I'm going to tell him,* Hunter thought. But, in the way of dreams, he couldn't force himself to do or say the exact thing he wanted. Before he could get a word out, Crosshair said, "Time to wake up."

"But—"

Pain shot through every centimeter of Hunter's nervous system. His heart rate seemed to triple, pounding hard enough to rip through his chest and armor. His eyes popped open. Sohi leaned over him, retracting the long needle of an inoculation gun from his neck.

He sprang up then, crouched in a fighting stance with his vibroknife drawn, looking for Crane but observing the four unmoving troopers on the ground. "Where is he? What happened?" Sohi couldn't get a word out before Hunter shouted, "Where's Omega?"

Sohi remained on the ground, weak, but she worked a fresh vial of liquid into the gun. "She's in the stacks with Coru. Crane is after them."

Hunter was moving toward the hole in the fence when Sohi said, "Wait. I'm coming."

Hunter cut his speed, but not by much. "I can't carry you."

"You won't have to." She plunged the inoculation gun into her own neck and gasped.

Another stimulant? Hunter thought. He kept the worst-case scenario subdued in the back of his mind.

The effects hit immediately. Her eyes blazed. The veins in her neck and forehead stood in stark relief to her graying skin. She lurched to her feet but still looked weak and shaky. Hunter moved to leave her—if she could catch up, then she'd catch up. But instead of chasing, she worked another vial of liquid into the gun and injected herself again.

Hunter couldn't hide his alarm. "Was that a double dose of stimulant? That might kill you."

The way the drug was forcing her muscles to twitch gave her a deranged look. "Not for about twenty minutes. Let's not waste it."

She snatched a blaster and rifle off a downed trooper and led the way into the barrel stacks. Hunter pushed himself to keep up.

Omega ran with the crying baby deeper into the stacks, aware that she had moved parallel to the refinery building. She quickly turned and changed her heading so she could get inside. The machinery there ran perpetually, loud enough to mask the baby's fear. And Omega's.

She would've been somewhat frightened on her own, but alone, she could fight. Putting Coru down anywhere, leaving her for even a microsecond, never crossed Omega's mind. Holding a baby meant Omega could not confront Crane. She didn't have her bow, and even if she did she couldn't use it with Coru in her arms. So she'd evade. Factory plus noise would give Tech, Wrecker, or Ponder a chance to reach them if Hunter wasn't already awake and on his way.

She crossed an intersection with the factory conveyor belts in sight when a blaster bolt pinged off a pallet a few meters ahead.

"Stop!" Crane shouted.

Omega consciously controlled her breathing, as Hunter had taught her. She turned slowly. Crane approached at a stroll, his weapon aimed. "I only want my granddaughter. Cooperate, and I will not harm you."

She didn't believe that for one second. To buy some time, though, she said, "You mean it?"

Crane lowered the blaster, seeming to believe the false hope she projected. "I do."

He holstered the weapon, then tucked his hand inside his tunic to grab . . . *something*.

Omega had no plans to find out what.

She lunged for the nearest stack and smacked the button controlling the magnetized clamp on a single barrel. The green magnets turned red with a soft *clack* as the barrel detached from its neighbors. Quickly, she ran to a pallet on her other side, opposite the barrel she'd demagnetized. She hit a button marked LINK, activating the powerful magnets on a barrel's outermost latch.

The pull caught the demagnetized barrel and launched it across the aisle with crushing force. Though it hadn't been close to Crane, he scrambled a few steps back out of caution. His arms were at his sides. A throwing knife dangled from the hand he'd snaked into his tunic.

Omega ran toward the factory in a zigzag, alternating magnetic deactivations and activations on either side, creating more flying impediments, forcing Crane into a winding chase where he had to slow down to avoid being smashed by a barrel.

Clearing the stacks, Omega climbed onto a conveyor belt that guided more barrels onto new pallet stacks, its origin deep within the factory. Running against the belt's direction and maneuvering around barrels occupying the belt's center became more dangerous with every step. The belt angled up, and she'd misjudged how high it went. By the time she had bypassed a dozen barrels, she reached a height where a fall could kill.

Thank goodness she'd reached the threshold of the refinery. She ducked inside, glad to have walls around her and a floor beneath. She hopped off the belt and delved deeper into the inner workings of the mercury plant— well aware that Crane was coming, too.

Wrecker and Ponder made it to the roof of the mercantile shop closest to Jatil's clinic and waited for pickup. Tech put the *Marauder* into a hover while Phee lowered a cable to collect the clones. Ponder was strong enough to climb using only his arms and made it onto the loading ramp. Wrecker made it in right behind him. Phee sealed the ship, and Tech got them in the air.

Phee fell into the copilot's seat, and Wrecker helped Ponder into the navigator's chair.

"Where are the others?" Ponder asked.

"I've tried to reach Hunter," Tech began but was interrupted by incoming comms.

Hunter phased into holographic clarity, his projection bouncing with his gait as he ran. "We lost a fight, now Crane is after Omega and the baby."

Ponder lurched toward the image. "Where's Sohi?"

The hologram swept to her, also in motion. "I'm here."

Her voice was wheezy. Her face was soaked in sweat. Something was very wrong with her. Ponder didn't get to ask, because Hunter said,

"Look at the toppled barrels on this row. Omega did this. They're going that way."

Sohi told the cockpit, "Refinery docks . . . closest to . . . spaceport. Come get them."

The hologram vanished.

Tech set a course with no discussion.

Ponder wondered if anyone else caught Sohi's orders. Come get *them*. Not come get *us*.

"As fast as you can!" Ponder said, then hopped on one leg to the back of the ship, needing to act, to do something. Despite fearing it was already too late.

CHAPTER FORTY-FOUR

MERCURY REFINERY, FELLIAN OUTPOST, TRYTH

There was less danger of a fall inside the refinery, but other peril presented itself in the automated, ever-moving shipping lanes. Mechanized arms arranged, adjusted, and marked an endless row of conveyor-driven barrels; the magnetic latches glowed red in their deactivated state. Omega crossed belts and weaved between barrels, sure to steer clear of thousands of clanking gears that kept the facility in motion.

"Omega," Crane called somewhere behind her, "you'll hurt the baby if you keep this up. You don't want that on your conscience, do you?"

She ignored him. None of the lies he told mattered. *Coru* mattered.

The baby had stopped crying; perhaps intuiting quiet served them best now. She sucked a thumb for comfort.

Omega crossed another belt—there was just one more ahead—and then another section of the refinery, a storage area based on the shelving she saw through the gaps between barrels. Whatever was over there wasn't moving; there might be a safe path to an exit.

She prepared to make the next and final belt crossing when a crackling bolt of electricity arced between the barrels that bordered her path, forcing her to stumble backward—toward another electrical trap that made her stay centered between belts. The electric deterrent continued between several barrels, keeping her boxed in. Somehow, Crane had moved farther along the belt and affixed his jolt disks to barrels, bringing the trap to Omega. She looked for a sign of the initial disks shorting out, their charge spent, when Crane leaped over a barrel, diving for her and Coru with his fingers hooked into claws. "Give her to me!"

Omega backpedaled, turned, and raced down the belt. The jolt disks were failing, and she hopped between barrels where a shock was no longer a risk. She tried to use the temporary cover to think.

The stress was tremendous and too much for the baby. Coru shrieked.

"No, no, no," Omega cooed, trying to convey more calm than she felt.

Crane moved parallel to Omega, cutting off her route into the storage area. She reversed direction, sprinting against the flow of the barrels, and ran the path into the louder, hotter, indeed more dangerous part of the refinery where those barrels got filled. The whole time she ran, clutching Coru, she used her free hand to pluck strands of hair from her scalp and drop them on the floor below. A subtle trail.

"Help's coming," she said, assuring herself more than the baby who didn't know actual words yet. "I know it."

Omega and Coru left the system of belts to move along durasteel catwalks, factory vats hissing and steaming around them.

Tech banked the *Marauder,* putting them on the rooftop closest to the location Hunter indicated. As he did, Ponder rummaged and tossed aside crates in Clone Force 99's armory with reckless abandon.

Wrecker said, "What are you doing?"

"I went through your gear before things got buggy on Dallow, and— here it is!" He popped a latch on a box holding a 773 Firepuncher rifle, one of Crosshair's old backups. Ponder tugged it from its foam padding, inspected it, and attached desired accessories from the case.

Wrecker, confused, said, "You plan on covering us once we're out of that factory?"

Ponder was shaking his head before Wrecker finished. "I'm going in."

"How? In case you've forgotten, you're down a leg. I can't carry you in there."

Ponder looked slightly annoyed as he swapped the Firepuncher's shorter, standard barrel for a long barrel topped by a bulky suppressor. With the rifle converted to its extended mode, Ponder wedged the butt into his armpit and leaned until the barrel touched the floor, turning the weapon into a makeshift crutch. "I'll manage," he said, rushing past Wrecker for the back ramp.

Tech settled them into hover mode over the rooftop. Wrecker dropped descender cables. On the comms, Wrecker said, "Stay close."

Tech confirmed. "We're not going anywhere."

"Go get our girls," Phee said.

Ponder grabbed his cable and zipped down to the roof. Wrecker followed.

"We're coming," Ponder said to no one in particular. "We're coming."

⬯

"We're inside," Hunter broadcasted to all.

He and Sohi faced a series of fast-moving conveyor belts zipping mercury along like dense traffic on a skyway. They hopped onto the nearest belt for a higher vantage point, hoping to spot some sign of Omega or the baby.

Or Crane, Hunter thought, having already abandoned the stun setting on his blaster.

They skipped over to the next conveyor belt, then the next. Hunter concentrated on keeping his balance as the stimulant Sohi injected him with created sporadic tingling sensations in his limbs. He could handle it, but if one dose did that to him, what was a third dose of the stuff doing to Sohi? He craned his neck and noticed her lagging.

"Are you—"

"Fine!" she shouted, dripping sweat. "I'm fine. Keep going."

He tried to, but she stumbled between belts and sprawled to her knees. He went back for her.

"I said I'm fine!" She pushed herself upright, refusing his assistance. While he waited, he noticed a familiar scorch mark on the factory floor—the remnants of an intense electrical burst.

Hunter turned, saw more of the scorch marks, and followed the trail until he came across what he'd been looking for. Omega. Or, rather, tufts of her hair.

"Smart, kid," he muttered. Then he said to Sohi, "This way!"

Though she struggled, Sohi kept up.

But for how long?

"Hey, kid! You can't be in here!" a refinery worker, dressed head to toe in the kind of protective gear one *should* be wearing in such a harsh environment, yelled through a safety visor. A droid working levers and dials beside him squawked its agreement. Yet Omega skirted past them deeper into the bowels of the place.

The heat was stifling and getting close to unbearable. The fumes stung her nose. Coru squirmed nonstop, and who could blame her? As much as Omega tried to soothe the baby, there was no comfort in this place.

The catwalks ran between heavy machinery and above big-bellied vats of mercury that sputtered and bubbled like silver stew. Omega only noted the dangerous liquid beneath in her peripheral vision, attempting to focus on the path ahead and pushing away any thoughts of what boiling hot mercury could do to flesh.

She recalled the day they'd arrived in Fellian Outpost and the cabby who'd made the not-so-funny joke about workers falling into the vats. It was even less funny now.

Taking a right at a catwalk intersection, Omega intended to follow the path until she could make another right and take an alternate route back the way they'd come. But she spotted the dead end fifty meters in and attempted to reverse course.

Crane blocked her way.

He raised the hand not holding a dagger and said, "Let me help you."

A factory-wide alarm sounded. Most likely triggered by the workers who'd spotted a child and baby in restricted areas, but the intensity of Omega's panic might have been strong enough to trigger alarms on its own.

Crane came forward slowly, raising his knife hand as he closed the distance. "Omega, I think it's best you let me hold the baby."

"Crane!" Sohi yelled, rushing him. "I disagree."

She sprinted at Crane with a rifle, but she held it by the barrel in a two-hand grip as if wielding a club and swung the butt at Crane's head like she intended to knock it off.

Omega understood, of course. Crane was between Sohi and Coru. Sohi couldn't risk a rifle bolt going astray and possibly hitting the baby or Omega. So, no shooting. It was the same with Hunter, who'd holstered his blaster and drawn his vibroknife, trailing a vicious Sohi by a few meters.

The three fighters clashed at the center of the catwalk—a deadly dance of bone-cracking blunt force and gutting slices. Omega knew plenty about Hunter's hand-to-hand skills, but she was awed by Sohi's. She was an adept fighter, attacking and parrying in time with Hunter's attacks in a manner that made one believe they'd been double-teaming opponents for years. An observation that spoke terrifying volumes about Crane's combat prowess because he was holding his own nearly effortlessly.

Sohi lunged backward, dodging a swipe from Crane's dagger. She managed to trap his wrist and send the blade flying over the catwalk's rail. Hunter attempted to ram his vibroknife into Crane's ribs. Still, the investigator pivoted and countered with a kick that knocked Hunter's lead leg askew, allowing Crane to yank Hunter into Sohi and bring all three of them to the catwalk floor in a writhing mound.

"Go!" Hunter yelled.

Omega tightened her grip on Coru and sprinted directly at the battling trio, ignoring Hunter's order. Crane saw her coming and dipped a hand beneath his coat for another weapon. When he revealed a long blade, Omega anticipated it. He swiped at her legs, but she leaped, kicked off the top safety rail for additional height, and sailed over Crane while Hunter slammed the investigator's forearm into the durasteel grate to keep the knife far from Omega and the baby.

But Crane snaked loose and charged after the children.

Hunter got his feet under him and chased but wasn't sure he'd reach Crane before his blade caught Omega.

The gap between Omega and Crane shortened. As Crane inhaled for a final lunge, a rifle bolt sizzled the catwalk between him and Omega, stopping him in his tracks.

A hundred meters across the refinery floor, on top of a processing machine heavy with pipes and drains, Ponder, sitting on Wrecker's shoulder for a better vantage point, cursed and adjusted the rifle's scope.

"Did you hit him?" Wrecker said.

"No. Sight's off. Hold still." He fired again.

That time, the bolt missed Crane by a wider margin.

"Truly a team effort," Crane mused. He did not take a step closer to the children, though.

Hunter squared up to engage Crane again, but Sohi, slowly rising, clapped a hand on his shoulder. "Go," she said. "Make sure the children are taken care of."

"No," Hunter said.

Sohi ignored him and called Crane. "You want me. You know you do. Let them go, and we can settle it right now."

Crane faced her. "I'm not going to kill you or your baby, Gayla. You know that, don't you?"

"I don't plan to extend that courtesy to you. I'm done running and being a pet that you pretend is your blood."

"We've been apart too long. You're confused. I'll help you sort things out."

"I don't think so."

"Look, you can barely stand."

He wasn't wrong about that. Hunter could feel the bulk of her weight propped against him. "I can't leave you to fight, Sohi. If you lose, he's going to take you."

"No," she whispered, "he won't. Remember what I said about that stimulant? Twenty minutes are almost up. Get my baby to Ponder and away from him."

"Sohi—"

She squeezed his shoulder. Weakly. "I can't undo what I've done to your kind, but I can take down the monster who made me. Don't rob me of that."

Hunter nodded.

Sohi said, "Let him pass, Crane. Then we'll have our alone time."

Crane stepped aside. Hunter honored Sohi's wishes and walked away, though he hoped Crane would attempt something treacherous that justified Hunter blasting him in the gut. The ISB agent allowed Hunter to pass without issue, though, so he sped up after the children and wished Sohi the best.

Crane said, "First, Gayla, I'd like to apologize for any strife I've—"

Sohi charged him, delivered punches to his face and abdomen that put him on his heels but did little damage otherwise.

He rubbed his jaw, concerned. "That's poor form. You're fading. Let's walk out of this place, find a ship. I'll patch you up. Get you back into fighting shape."

Sohi threw a kick that he dodged easily. She spun with a telegraphed backfist that he avoided with a quick backward shuffle.

A rifle bolt pinged off machinery a meter over Crane's head.

Crane ducked behind a smelting pot control console, robbing Ponder of his vantage. "Is that the love who's taken you away from me? He's not a very good shot."

Sohi lurched, gripping the catwalk railing. "He's just *good*. That's enough."

"I don't want 'enough' for you. I want greatness for you. The potential is there. It'll take time, but I can make you want it, too."

She dived onto Crane, grappling with him, calling upon every bit of strength left in her body.

"You want an unquestioning follower, Crane. Me, I love having a partner." She twisted him around, blocked his attempted elbow strike, and threw a mighty kick into his midsection, forcing him to stumble backward. Clear of her.

Before he could launch a fresh attack, a rifle bolt burrowed a magma-rimmed tunnel through his chest. Crane collapsed to his knees.

From atop Wrecker's shoulder, Ponder said, "A little lower than I wanted, but it'll do."

Gayla stood over Crane and repeated something he'd spoken to her so many times. "We'll all end, so end well."

Crane seemed . . . impressed. He grinned and managed his final, raspy words. "You always were my best."

Crane's life faded fast, but he wasn't angry with Gayla—*Sohi*. He was proud of the flawless weapon he'd honed. She didn't have to give him credit for him to take his certainty into the afterlife—if there was such a thing.

His only regret . . . Cellia Moten. He would not get to watch the light fade from her eyes.

Given her penchant for malice and the enemies she'd surely acquire on her brutal and greedy ascent, perhaps someone else, someone worthy, would do the job for him.

Those thoughts flitted from his mind when Sohi hoisted him up and over the catwalk railing. He tumbled screaming into the mercury. A splash of silver heat became all he knew and all he'd ever know again.

Sohi watched the mercury take Crane. She needed to see it. She needed to know he was gone forever.

When the mercury consumed him whole, the near-supernatural reserves of strength she'd seized to take on Crane whirled from her like water from a drain.

She pressed a fist into her chest, hard, as if to slow her dangerously increased pulse.

"For you, Coru," she whispered with the bit of breath she could manage.

Sohi collapsed.

"No!" Ponder shouted, lowering the scope after watching his love slump on the catwalk.

He dropped off Wrecker's shoulders, using the rifle as a crutch once again. As he sought the most direct path to Sohi, Hunter arrived, ushering Omega, who still held Coru in her arms. Ponder only hesitated long enough to ensure she wasn't a mirage before resting a hand on his baby, and then he told Hunter and Wrecker, "Keep them safe!"

Before either of the 99s could object, Ponder was away, stepping as quickly as the rifle crutch allowed.

The factory alarms hadn't stopped, and Tech spoke through comms. "Authorities are closing in."

Hunter asked Omega, "Are you all right?"

"I'm fine."

"Wrecker," Hunter said, "get them on board."

"What are you about to do?" Wrecker asked.

"Chaperone the happy couple. Now go."

Hunter reversed course and chased Ponder.

<hr />

Hunter caught Ponder well before he got to the catwalk. He wasn't moving fast on that rifle crutch.

"Her best chance is going to be on the *Marauder*." Hunter passed Ponder. "I'll get her."

Ponder couldn't argue with that.

Hunter rushed down the catwalk and crouched beside the prone Sohi. One arm dangled over the edge, and her breathing was too quick, too shallow.

Hunter cradled her, then returned to her husband, moving at a pace Ponder could match until they reached the ladder and chute leading to the roof. Hunter went first, Sohi slung over his shoulder, and Ponder trailed as local security forces began spilling into the refinery.

On the roof, the *Marauder* remained in a low hover while Wrecker and Omega beckoned. With their aid, Hunter got Sohi on the deck and ushered Ponder on board before climbing the ramp, shouting, "We're in. Dust off!"

Tech did as ordered, rocketing them high above the strobing lights and sirens of incoming emergency vehicles. With clear skies and an unguarded orbit, Tech punched it. And as soon as they were clear of Tryth's gravitational pull, he activated the hyperdrive and took them away.

With the ship safely in hyperspace, Omega and Wrecker went to work, preparing a space to lay Sohi and aid her in any way possible. Omega hurried to clear out a space in the back of the ship to lay her flat, while Wrecker gathered all the dirty laundry they had lying around, haphazardly tied it together, and hung it up as a makeshift curtain. The new family needed their privacy. Omega injected a sedative from the trauma kit to try to reduce Sohi's alarming heart rate while Wrecker fitted a portable respirator to her face to aid her labored breathing. The *Marauder* wasn't a medical ship. There was no advanced equipment.

Omega's medical skills went only so far under those conditions. She said, "We can only keep her comfortable and wait. It's up to her."

Ponder was stoic. He leaned on his makeshift crutch with a sleeping Coru pressed to his chest. He made his way to the unconscious Sohi and took a seat next to her. He touched her hand. "If it's truly up to her, she'll make it." He kissed the baby's head. "She has a lot to live for."

Hunter grasped Omega's shoulder and thought, *Indeed, she does.*

CHAPTER FORTY-FIVE

THE *MARAUDER*, HYPERSPACE

Tech had the navicomputer pick a random hyperspace lane to confound any potential pursuers. They cruised in the tunnel. Phee occupied the copilot's seat, and they stayed mum when Hunter entered with an update.

He said, "She's tough. She's fighting. But she's been through a lot the last few days."

"More than any of us ever have," Tech admitted.

"Ponder and the baby?" Phee asked.

"Inseparable. He hasn't let her go since we took off."

Tech said, "As it should be."

Hunter flopped into the navigator's seat, exhausted. He closed his eyes, but Tech knew he wasn't going to sleep anytime soon. None of them ever did right after a fight. If he couldn't give his brother rest, he could give him a boost. "We have good news."

Hunter didn't open his eyes. "Don't keep me in suspense."

Tech motioned for Phee to tell it. She deserved the chance to make up for two extremely bad jobs. "Brown Eyes fixed the siphon code."

Hunter's eyes popped open. "You're not suggesting we try it again, are you?"

"Oh no," Phee assured. "We found an alternate use. Before we hopped off Cellia Moten's yacht and snagged the *Marauder*, I had Brown Eyes upload that code to Cellia's personal systems. The ones connected to her various funds—legal or not—throughout the galaxy."

Hunter leaned in. "Wait. You're not saying what I think you're saying."

Tech said, "Yes, brother. We are currently siphoning credits from various *exorbitant* accounts. Cellia's worth close to a trillion credits, and we are steadily draining her."

"How much did we get?"

Phee checked the monitor. "Enough to rebuild Pabu from the ground up."

"Twice," Tech added.

Hunter couldn't seem to keep still in his seat. His body wasn't used to such good fortune. "Can she find a way to take it back?"

Tech shook his head. "As I said, I fixed the code. The funds are being moved through multiple untraceable accounts. The only thing Cellia will be able to do is notice the drain, employ the best slicers she can find, and eventually they'll purge the code and stop the bleeding. I don't imagine she'll let this go on for long."

Phee said, "Unless we get lucky and she falls down some stairs before she notices."

Hunter scoffed. "When have we ever been that lucky?"

MOTEN YACHT, TRYTH

Parlin had rarely seen Mistress Moten in such distress. She sneered, cursed, threw things. She was *dirty*!

She shrieked at him, her usually careful speech and strained double entendres abandoned. "I want them dead. I want to do it myself. Phee Genoa! That blasted clone! I'll tear them apart and water my plants with their blood!"

To their credit, the pilots never took their eyes off the ship's controls. They had bigger concerns. The yacht had accelerated fine upon initial liftoff. It maintained steady momentum through the upper atmosphere of Tryth, but now that they'd surpassed the planet's gravitational pull, the beating it'd taken when in the hands of the pirate and the clone became apparent. The engines sputtered and jerked, then quit altogether. They sat stalled in shadow and orange emergency lighting.

"What's happening?" Cellia screamed, turning her ire to the flight crew. "Why aren't we in hyperspace yet?"

"I'm sorry, mistress," the captain said. "The engines are damaged, and we've switched to auxiliary power."

"Fix. It."

"Mistress," the captain said cautiously, "we don't have an astromech on board, so there's no way to do external repairs in the space vacuum. We'll need to make a distress call."

"I pay you to maintain my vessels! Go out there and fix the engine!"

The captain got stern. "You pay me to *pilot* your vessels safely. There's no way to do that now, so I will seek help."

"How long will that take?"

The copilot tensed over readings on his monitor. "Perhaps not as long as we thought. We've got movement out of hyperspace."

Before he finished the sentence, a vessel winked into the orbit. A huge vessel. An Imperial Star Destroyer.

Oh, wonderful, Cellia thought, *late to the battle.*

It hailed Cellia's yacht.

The yacht captain answered the call, and the holographic image of the destroyer's captain hovered over the control console in hazy blue. "This is Captain Torsal of the *Thrantha*. Report your operational status."

The yacht captain complied, detailing the engine damage and requesting assistance from the destroyer's engineers.

"We're here to take care of you," Captain Torsal said. "How many are on board?"

"Seven. Three flight crew and four passengers."

"Is Cellia Moten present?"

Cellia leaned toward the captain so she might be seen. "I am. Please contact Sheev Palpatine posthaste and inform him of the situation so that these repairs can be expedited."

Captain Torsal said, "*Emperor* Palpatine is aware of your situation. That's why we're here. Please initiate a docking sequence. One of his emissaries will be boarding momentarily."

The yacht captain's head tilted. Confused. "An emissary? What about our engines?"

The destroyer captain's expression was flat. "Goodbye."

The hologram blinked away.

Cellia frowned. "What's going on? I will not stand for a lengthy delay. I won't!"

The captain didn't respond. His attention was on the vessel that drifted from the destroyer's bay and accelerated toward them. He squinted to identify it and became more confused once he did.

"That's a *Nu*-class attack shuttle."

The copilot shrugged. "As long as they've got tools and a space suit on board."

The captain sighed. "Initiating docking sequence."

Cellia lowered her face into her palm, frustrated. "Parlin, go meet this emissary. I need to collect myself, or I'm likely to take their head off."

"Very well, mistress." Parlin motioned to the battle droid and the still stinky Shistavanen. They moved aft to greet the visitor.

Parlin positioned his greeting party around the air lock and confirmed the command from the bridge, so all was good on their end. The shuttle began its part of the sequence, coupling with the exterior port and venting the midpoint vacuum until a good seal was established. Parlin watched the life support indicator in the air lock transition from red to yellow to green. The portal between ships opened.

The battle droid, who displayed a sociable side that made Parlin wonder if he had protocol-droid parts in him, stepped forward at the sight of a *large* silhouette obscured by the auxiliary lighting. The emissary strode closer.

"Welcome aboard, esteemed emissary of Emperor—" The droid's vocal projections ended abruptly as his frame crunched inward with alarming speed and brutality. His chest flattened, erupting sparks from tears in his metal. His joints bent at wrong angles and then folded up off the floor because his entire body was levitating—*levitating!*—while crumpling like a tin can. His head rammed down into his chest plate before the entire destroyed body, compacted to a quarter of the droid's original size, was yanked into the wall by an invisible tow chain with such *force* the remains simply wedged into the wall itself, a full meter off the floor.

The Shistavanen reacted quicker than Parlin, aiming his rifle into the air lock. As quick as he was, there was a quicker motion ahead of them. A barely noticeable twitch, a weapon in hand, the *whoosh-hum* ignition of crimson terror. A lightsaber. A Jedi weapon.

Ambient light from the blade illuminated the air lock, revealing the emissary's hulking form.

With certainty, Parlin thought, *That's no Jedi.*

The Shistavanen fired three quick shots at the emissary, center of mass.

The red blade stuttered in time—*vwoom-vwoom-vwoom*—and those blaster bolts returned. One struck the rifle, destroying it and mangling the Shistavanen's paws in the process. One continued down the corridor, striking a doorjamb, and the last ricocheted off the floor and continued through Parlin's thigh, dropping him to one knee screaming.

The Shistavanen screamed, too. Though not for long.

The emissary emerged fully from the air lock, his heavy black boots clopping on the deck, and as he closed the distance between him and the howling beast, he raised the hand that wasn't wielding the lightsaber. His fingers curled inward, and the Shistavanen was snatched toward him by something unseen. The emissary extended his lightsaber like a spear and impaled the Shistavanen. He died instantly, and the emissary swiped upward with his saber, freeing his blade by splitting the creature in half.

He maintained a steady stride toward Parlin, and the guard saw his own terrified face doubled and growing large in the red-tinted lenses of the emissary's polished black helmet.

"Wait," Parlin begged.

The lightsaber slashed horizontally, and Parlin thought maybe, somehow, the monster had shown mercy. Then the entire galaxy tilted, turned upside down, then backward. Rolling, rolling, rolling to a stop. The lightsaber had been so clean and swift that Parlin maintained horrifying seconds of consciousness where he realized his head was no longer attached to his neck. His new view was sideways, staring down the length of the corridor as the emissary continued without a look back at those he'd slaughtered.

The emissary's black cape swished. The edges of Parlin's vision became a fuzzy black haze. Everything went dark.

Forever.

Cellia sat, drumming her fingers on the armrest of her chair. The yacht attendant lowered a tray with a single glass of warm milk, supposedly a remedy for frazzled nerves, within Cellia's reach. She snatched it and dismissed the attendant with a flicking gesture.

"What's taking them so long?" she wondered aloud, then sipped, wincing at the taste. "This is disgusting. Can't you do anything right?"

The attendant shuffled with her eyes low to retrieve the glass. "Apologies, Mistress Moten. I'll prepare another."

Scurrying away, the attendant opened the bridge door to find the way blocked. A quick red slash, and she collapsed, the tray and glass crashing to the floor. Cellia, the captain, and the copilot twisted toward the commotion, but only Cellia had time to process what she saw, and what she saw was surreal.

A giant occupied the threshold. Humanoid in shape but clad head to toe in black garb affixed with a lighted chest console of indeterminate purpose. Was this being man or machine? Whatever he was, he flung his arm to the side, releasing the blazing red lightsaber so it went spinning in a hurricane motion around the perimeter of the bridge, slicing through the captain and copilot so that their split bodies slid into neatly cauterized halves before the weapon returned to his outstretched palm. The blade extinguished with a *snap-hiss* as the being stepped onto the bridge, closing the gap between himself and Cellia.

He said, "The Emperor sends his regards."

His voice was deep as a pit, an echo in a coffin.

She scrambled from her chair and backed into a wall. "Who are you?"

"I am what your curiosity has wrought." Somewhere within the wall of black armor, a respirator *rasped* and *hissed* out of sync with his speech. "You believe the Emperor is building something. Who else have you spoken to of your theories?"

Cellia sputtered. "I—I don't know what you mean. I would never discuss Sheev's business with anyone."

He raised his hand, revealing a mini holoprojector on the massive gloved palm. It activated, splaying a hazy blue image in a cone of light. It was the Galactic News Network. An Arkanian reporter read copy that paired with unsettling images.

"Terrorist attacks on several manufacturing facilities throughout the galaxy have left many dead and clamoring for swift action on the part of the ISB and Imperial military to maintain safety and order—"

Cellia couldn't follow all the reporter said. She was too focused on the sites in the recording. Once factories, material depots, or office towers . . . now smoking craters. The Konsmata headquarters, the Incostar Systems plant, and others. All companies where sources she'd embedded fed her information used to deduce the existence, if not the details, of Sheev's massive project. All were destroyed because he didn't want her—or anyone—to know about the scheme. How important it must be.

The emissary twitched his fingers, and the hologram shifted from the news broadcast to a recording that was too familiar. Cellia's estate on Dallow. Nothing unusual about the view until orbital missiles slithered into frame, smoking contrails tracing their path from the destroyer that fired them to where they struck her home like stingers, collapsing the structure into dusty debris pits.

Cellia whimpered, and the emissary closed his palm, ending the show.

"Listen," she said, "there's been a misunderstanding. If you allow me to contact Shee—"

She couldn't finish. The emissary's hand was raised to eye level, his thumb and forefinger positioned as if pinching the air. He was not touching her, yet she felt his will wrapped around her neck like a noose. She gagged, and her vision dimmed.

The emissary relaxed his hand slightly, allowing a rush of precious air into her lungs.

He said, "Your meddling has created a great inconvenience. The Emperor needs to determine how great. Who else knows?"

"I'll . . . tell you . . . everything."

"Yes." His lightsaber reignited, washing her in red. "You will."

Cellia Moten still believed herself a god, but now she knew she was a minor deity. Not omnipotent, indestructible, or as powerful as the devil before her.

She never learned Darth Vader's name.

CHAPTER FORTY-SIX

THE *MARAUDER*, HYPERSPACE

With the ship on autopilot, Tech made his way to the closetlike galley where Phee, Omega, and Wrecker congregated in an animated discussion over the thrum of engine noise. They ceased chatting when Tech drew near.

"Is something wrong?" Tech asked.

"Nothing Hunter can't fix," Omega said.

Phee said, "Can you go get him, Brown Eyes?"

Tech noticed the provisions strewn across the galley's counter and thought he understood the issue. Yes, this was a job for Hunter. A much-needed one.

Since he'd heard the good news about Cellia Moten financing Pabu's repair, a sullen cloud had fallen over Hunter. He hadn't said much—as was his nature—and he didn't have to. Between Omega, Tech, and Wrecker, they could read one another's moods with little effort, but there was nothing complex to decipher in what had overtaken him. How many times had Hunter found a reason to pass by Sohi and Ponder's quarters, pausing for just a beat to listen for something encouraging?

As much as any of us, Tech thought.

They were all hoping for the best and bracing for the worst regarding Sohi's recovery. Even with Omega's frequent check-ins, the prognosis remained unchanged. Sohi's survival was up to Sohi at this point. Yet somehow, Hunter seemed to be taking it harder than anyone expected.

If Hunter considered you an enemy, beware. If he considered you a friend, there was no better ally in the galaxy. It seemed Sohi had slipped into a yet-unexplored crevasse between the two states. What a complex development that was proving to be.

There was nothing more that any of them could do for Sohi, though. Except for her family—they could, and would, keep loving her with every bit of strength they had.

That left Phee and Clone Force 99 without much to do but pass time. It was a long trip back to Pabu, and Tech wasn't willing to set a course until the Sohi matter was settled. Omega didn't know how it would play out, but she'd indicated it would likely take no more than a day before Sohi let them know. One way or another.

In the meantime, there was work to do . . .

"Hunter," Tech said, waiting patiently outside of his quarters.

"Come in."

Tech triggered the door release. It slid aside revealing Hunter flat on his back in his bunk, balancing a simple utility knife by its tip on his forefinger. When Tech stepped inside, Hunter made an almost imperceptible motion that flipped the blade end over end into the air. It fell in a dangerous direction, blade first toward Hunter's sternum, but he caught it by the handle with centimeters to spare. Grimly, he said, "You got news?"

"No. A task. Just for you."

Hunter swung his feet to the deck. "Trouble?"

"Of a sort. Come."

Tech turned and quickstepped to the galley with Hunter in pursuit.

"What is it?" Hunter asked. "Who's after us now?"

Tech joined the others, with Wrecker holding the most troublesome object before him. "Phee picked some of these up during a provisions run in Fellian Outpost. Thought you might know the best way to handle it."

In Wrecker's massive palm rested a plump, purple jogan fruit.

Phee said, "I told them we couldn't eat it without creating a proper garnish from its peel. We're not a wasteful crew. Ain't that right, Brown Eyes?"

"Agreed. With the proper width of a jogan fruit garnish being no greater than 4.5 millimeters it occurred to us—"

Omega jumped in. "There is only one person on board who could successfully complete the mission."

Hunter stared. Stone-faced. Would he explode and curse them all for their jest? Maybe this was a bad idea.

"What blade do you want me to use?" Hunter asked. "All of mine are stained with the blood of our enemies."

Phee said, "Please tell me we have other knives on board."

"We do," said Omega, slipping around Wrecker's hip for the sparse utensils they kept on the *Marauder*.

"Move," Hunter said, angling for the broadest chopping surface in the galley. "Expertise is required here."

Wrecker stepped aside. "So you're making dinner, then? As much as I like jogan fruit, it ain't very filling."

"*We're* making dinner. You're wanted in the kitchen."

Phee backed up Hunter. "Because that's where the food is."

Tech nodded and began to back away from what would surely amount to more tasks being doled out. "Well, I will be in the cockpit. Notify me when the meal is ready."

"No way," Omega said, grabbing his hand, then Phee's, and directing them midship. "This place is a mess. Let's get it sorted so we don't have to eat standing up."

Sure enough, there was all sorts of detritus strewn about the benches and tables in the *Marauder*'s midsection. Even Tech had to admit they'd gotten slack on cleaning duties. Clone Force 99 could be dubbed "Clutter" Force 99 at times like this. He scooped up Wrecker's helmet, a spare rifle scope, and a capacitor from a damaged comms rig. Phee started in on her own pile. Omega yelled to the front, "Mel, get in here! You're helping, too."

The droid trudged to them slowly and *blurped*.

"I love you," Phee said, "but you've got to be the laziest droid I know."

MEL-222 lifted momentarily on her treads, the droid equivalent to an "I don't care what you think" shrug. But then she got to work.

Phee said, "Look at us, Brown Eyes. Keeping house."

"It's a ship," Tech said, in that plain, agreeable way of his.

"It's more than that," Omega said. She didn't need to elaborate. They all understood.

Hunter and Wrecker made a fine meal with a proper jogan fruit garnish.

They sat. They ate. They laughed. And despite the cramped quarters that the six of them occupied, they left space for more. As always.

It wasn't anything they ever talked about. Maybe they didn't even consciously register the gaps on the benches. Phee noticed, though.

From the first time she tagged along with Clone Force 99, their table always seemed to have room. For old members and new.

Tech was next to Phee—no space between them. They bumped elbows as they dug into their plates. Their thighs brushed. Tech said, "Are you enjoying the meal?"

"I did the meat," Wrecker said out of nowhere.

Phee plucked a salty, charred chunk off her plate. "What fine meat it is. The food's great. For galaxy-hopping fugitive mercenaries, you guys are pretty good cooks."

"We're skilled at being skilled," Hunter said, deadly serious in a way that charged the room before he cracked a smile and said, "Was that too much?"

"Save it for the next bad guy," Omega said, as encouraging as always.

MEL-222 booped, sullen.

"We know you don't eat," Tech said, "but you're good company."

The droid chirped, cheery, and nuzzled up to Tech's shoulder.

Phee never said anything about it, as if voicing the observation would somehow diminish the miracle here, but in times like this, she recognized that these grown and bred warriors were among the gentlest, most hospitable beings she'd ever encountered. Pirating was her life, and she didn't know if that would change. Should it ever, though . . .

"What was that?" Tech asked, picking up on something Phee mumbled under her breath.

"Oh nothing, Brown Eyes," she said quickly. "Pass some more of that jogan fruit!"

The next day, Omega emerged from Sohi's makeshift recovery room and met the others near the cockpit. Her expression was cautiously optimistic, and it lifted spirits immediately. "She's awake and past the worst of it, I think. She's going to need a long time to fully recover."

Hunter suspected as much. What Sohi put her body through to save her child . . . he'd have done the same without question. There were consequences, though. He imagined whatever lasting damage came from triple-dosing a powerful stimulant didn't lend itself to a speedy recovery. Especially if the injured person was planet-hopping, always looking over their shoulder.

Hunter said, "I've been thinking."

"About?" Omega asked.

He explained. When he finished, there was no dissent among them. Omega hugged him long and hard. When he finally peeled Omega off, he said, "You wanna be the one to tell them?"

They went over to where the healing parents and child were holed up. A throng crowded the doorway. All were there. Wrecker, Tech, MEL-222, Phee, Omega, and Hunter.

Pale, dark-eyed, and sunken-cheeked, Sohi said with a raspy voice, "Feels like I'm going to have to walk the plank."

Hunter chuckled, but he said nothing. This was Omega's moment. While waiting, he was amazed by how much had changed in so little time. For so much of his life, he hadn't had the opportunity to get over grudges. To forgive. He'd never known how satisfying it would feel.

Ponder said, "Seriously, what have you come to tell us?"

"Not me," Hunter said.

Omega's lightness, a quality that often eluded the others, shone at full strength for them all to bask in. "Sohi, Ponder, Coru. I want to tell you about a place. It's a good place for good families."

"Okay," Ponder said, sporting a half grin. "I'd love to hear more."

"Me, too," Sohi said.

Baby Coru pumped her little fist in the air. Probably just a newborn's twitch, but Hunter now knew babies understood more than most gave them credit for. Perhaps the infant felt what was coming, her senses attuned to the underlying vibrations of the galaxy around her. Hunter could relate.

"It's Pabu," Omega said. "I think you're going to like it there."

ACKNOWLEDGMENTS

Where to begin?

I WROTE A STAR WAR, Y'ALL!

Now that that's out of the way, I want to thank the folks who made this possible. First, eternal gratitude to Gabriella Muñoz and Tom Hoeler for inviting me back to the galaxy and to Lucasfilm Animation for making the incredible show that inspired this story. Big thanks to my *Star Wars* friends E. K. Johnston, Daniel José Older, Zoraida Córdova, Justina Ireland, and Tessa Gratton for always encouraging me to pursue such far, far away opportunities. My agent, Jamie Weiss Chilton, and the Andrea Brown Literary Agency continue to be my stellar publishing family and have seen me through the greatest professional moments of my life. And always, always, *always* big love to my rebels at home, Adrienne and Melanie.

Now cue the music and the crawl . . .

ABOUT THE AUTHOR

LAMAR GILES is the acclaimed author of the novels *Ruin Road, The Getaway, The Last Last-Day-of-Summer, Not So Pure and Simple, Spin,* and *Fake ID*. He is a three-time Mystery Writers of America Edgar Award nominee, a recipient of the Black Caucus of the American Library Association's Youth Literary Award, and a founding member of the non-profit We Need Diverse Books. He resides in Virginia with his family.

ABOUT THE TYPE

This book was set in Minion, a 1990 Adobe Originals type-face by Robert Slimbach (b. 1956). Minion is inspired by classical, old-style typefaces of the late Renaissance, a period of elegant, beautiful, and highly readable type designs. Created primarily for text setting, Minion combines the aesthetic and functional qualities that make text type highly readable with the versatility of digital technology.

A long time ago in a galaxy far, far away. . . .

STAR WARS

Join up! Subscribe to our newsletter
at ReadStarWars.com or find us on social.

𝕏 **@StarWarsByRHW**

◎ **@StarWarsByRHW**

f **StarWarsByRHW**